About the Author

Joshua Hood graduated from the University of
Memphis before joining the military and spending
five years in the 82nd Airborne Division. He was
a team leader in the 3-504 Parachute Infantry
Regiment in Iraq from 2005 to 2006. From
2007 to 2008, Hood served as a squad leader
with the 1-508th Parachute Infantry Regiment
in Afghanistan for which he was decorated for
valor in Operation Furious Pursuit. On his return
to civilian life he became a sniper team leader on
a full time SWAT team in Memphis, where he
was awarded the lifesaving medal. Currently he
works as the Director of Veteran Outreach for the
American Warrior Initiative.

Robert Ludlum was the author of twenty-
seven novels, each one a *New York Times*
bestseller. There are more than 225 million of his
books in print, and they have been translated into
thirty-two languages. He is the author of the Jason
Bourne series: *The Bourne Identity, The Bourne
Supremacy,* and *The Bourne Ultimatum* – among
other novels. Mr Ludlum passed away
in March 2001.

THE BOURNE SERIES

Robert Ludlum's The Bourne Initiative (by Eric Van Lustbader)
Robert Ludlum's The Bourne Enigma (by Eric Van Lustbader)
Robert Ludlum's The Bourne Ascendancy (by Eric Van Lustbader)
Robert Ludlum's The Bourne Retribution (by Eric Van Lustbader)
Robert Ludlum's The Bourne Imperative (by Eric Van Lustbader)
Robert Ludlum's The Bourne Dominion (by Eric Van Lustbader)
Robert Ludlum's The Bourne Objective (by Eric Van Lustbader)
Robert Ludlum's The Bourne Deception (by Eric Van Lustbader)
Robert Ludlum's The Bourne Sanction (by Eric Van Lustbader)
Robert Ludlum's The Bourne Betrayal (by Eric Van Lustbader)
Robert Ludlum's The Bourne Legacy (by Eric Van Lustbader)
The Bourne Ultimatum
The Bourne Supremacy
The Bourne Identity

THE COVERT-ONE SERIES

Robert Ludlum's The Patriot Attack (by Kyle Mills)
Robert Ludlum's The Geneva Strategy (by Jamie Freveletti)
Robert Ludlum's The Utopia Experiment (by Kyle Mills)
Robert Ludlum's The Janus Reprisal (by Jamie Freveletti)
Robert Ludlum's The Ares Decision (by Kyle Mills)
Robert Ludlum's The Arctic Event (by James H. Cobb)
Robert Ludlum's The Moscow Vector (with Patrick Larkin)
Robert Ludlum's The Lazarus Vendetta (with Patrick Larkin)
Robert Ludlum's The Altman Code (with Gayle Lynds)
Robert Ludlum's The Paris Option (with Gayle Lynds)
Robert Ludlum's The Cassandra Compact (with Phillip Shelby)
Robert Ludlum's The Hades Factor (with Gayle Lynds)

Published by arrangement with G.P. Putnam's Sons, an imprint of
Penguin Publishing Group, a division of Penguin Random House LLC

First published in the UK in 2020 by Head of Zeus Ltd
This paperback edition first published in the UK in 2020
by Head of Zeus Ltd

9 7 5 3 1 2 4 6 8

A catalogue record for this book is available from
the British Library.

ISBN (B format): 9781789546460
ISBN (A format): 9781800240414
ISBN (E): 9781789546484

Typeset by Divaddict Publishing Solutions Ltd.

Printed and bound in Great Britain by
CPI Group (UK) Ltd, Croydon CR0 4YY

Book design by Tiffany Estreicher

Head of Zeus Ltd
5–8 Hardwick Street
London EC1R 4RG
WWW.HEADOFZEUS.COM

ROBERT LUDLUM'S™

THE TREADSTONE RESURRECTION

JOSHUA HOOD

PROLOGUE

BUENA VISTA, VENEZUELA

Nick Ford sat in the back of the filthy pickup, his body racked with fever, pain radiating from the bullet hole in his leg. He was exhausted, and his body screamed for sleep. But every time he closed his eyes, he found himself back in the jungle.

Caught in the kill zone. Machine guns chattering from the shadows, the caustic fog of fresh gunpowder, and the screams of his dying teammates.

Dead. All of them.

Ford still couldn't wrap his mind around what had happened. How he'd managed to lose an entire team on what was supposed to be an easy recon. There was only one answer that made any sense.

We were betrayed.

The truck rattled to a halt and Ford pulled himself to his feet and climbed down to the muddy street. He limped to the driver's-side window, tugged a sweaty wad of bills from his pocket, and passed them to the man behind the wheel.

"No, no, *señor*," the man protested, "I can't take that, not after—"

Ford was quick to cut him off. "José, you take *this*," he said, shoving the cash into the man's callused hand. "You take this and get your family the hell out of here."

"*Gracias*, Señor Ford. I wish—"

"José, you need to go, before it's too late."

"*Vaya con dios*." He nodded before shoving the truck into gear and pulling away in a cloud of exhaust.

Ford stood on the street and considered his options. He knew SEBIN—the dreaded Bolivarian National Intelligence Service—was looking for him, and he knew what they would do when they found him. There was a part of Ford that wished they'd hurry up and find him. Put a bullet in his head and get it over with.

There will be time for that later, he told himself. *Right now, you have a job to do.*

Ford hobbled across the street. The pain was unbearable. Each step more painful than the last, but he forced himself to keep moving. *March or die,* he ordered himself. *Just put one foot in front of the other.*

By the time he made it to the alley that smelled of piss and rotted garbage his shirt was soaked with sweat. He fell against the stone wall. Dug the bottle of Percocet from the pocket of the jeans José had gotten for him and thumbed the cap free.

The bottle had been full on Monday; now there were only two pills remaining. Enough to get him through the night. After that, Ford knew it wouldn't matter.

This had always been a one-way trip.

He shook the Percs into his mouth and dry-swallowed. The pills left a bitter taste in the back of his throat, and then he was moving again. Down the alley, heading north, toward the faded white sign perched atop the Hotel Bolívar.

The Bolívar was an ugly pillbox of a building, with pallid stucco walls and sagging razor wire. It was not the kind of hotel you found on TripAdvisor, but Ford trusted the owner, which made it the safest place in the city.

By the time he staggered into the dingy lobby, the pills had kicked in and muted the pain in his leg to a dull roar.

"Señor Ford," Miguel greeted him in broken English. The smile on his face crumbled when he saw Ford's condition, and he came around the desk. "You look like the shit. Should I call for the doctor?"

"No." Ford winced. "Just a room—and a bottle." He leaned against the counter and dug the last of his cash from his pocket, slapping it on the scarred surface. The effort left him out of breath.

"Of course." Miguel nodded.

He retrieved a bottle of Santa Teresa rum from the shelf and a key from the wallboard, and placed them both on the counter.

"Thank you, my friend," Ford said.

He took the stairs to the second floor, unlocked the door, and stepped inside.

The room reminded him of the shitty double-wide where he'd grown up: same cigarette-scarred table, yellowed blinds, and musty beer-cooler smell. Ford closed the door behind him and set his assault pack on a chair.

He cracked the rum and took a deep pull from the bottle. The liquor burned the back of his throat and settled hot into his gut. Properly fortified for the job ahead, he unzipped the pack and spread its contents on the table: a laptop, two shim cameras, a dirt-encrusted camera, and an M18 Claymore mine.

The rumble in his stomach reminded him that he hadn't eaten in nine hours, and he retrieved a can of pineapple that he'd picked up in a market outside of El Nula. He popped the ring and carefully peeled the lid free.

Three years ago when he first came to Venezuela the fruit would have cost him four dollars. But with the economy in free fall and the country gripped in hyperinflation, it cost three times that amount in Caracas.

Money. That's what all of this was about, he thought,

4

spearing the fruit with his knife and placing it in his mouth before picking up the shim cams and stepping out into the hall.

The shim cams were a holdover from his time in Special Forces. Each camera was the size of a tube of ChapStick, with a lens on one end and a flat tail on the other. They were old tech—massive compared to the micro–surveillance cameras on the market today. But Ford trusted them, and like the name implied, they could be emplaced anywhere.

He wedged the first camera into a crack at the end of the hall and angled the lens so it covered the stairwell leading up from the lobby. He used a strip of tape to stick the second camera to the top of the flickering Coke machine and pointed the lens at his door.

Back inside the room, he tried to pull the bed against the door, but when he tugged on the box spring, the bed refused to move. He pulled harder, and when it still didn't budge, Ford dropped to his knees.

When did Miguel start bolting the beds to the floor?

Ford knew it didn't matter and got to his feet. He retrieved a plastic wedge from his assault pack, remembering the words of the man who'd trained him: "Ford, always remember, one is none, and two is one."

Hayes, still saving my sorry ass, he thought, kicking the wedge under the frame and returning to the assault pack for a roll of hundred-mile-an-hour tape, the military's version of duct tape, and the Claymore.

He used the tape to secure the Claymore mine to the headrest of the chair, and once he was sure that it would hold, he dragged the chair across the room and checked the angle. When he was sure that it was out of the door's path, Ford screwed the blasting cap into the mine, plugged the free end of the firing wire into the detonator, and carried it into the bathroom.

Ford set the detonator on the toilet and turned on the faucet.

He splashed water over his face, his mind turning to the café outside of Bogotá and the last time he saw Hayes.

"Nick, I'm leaving."

"Leaving?" Ford laughed. *"Where the hell you going?"*

"No, I'm leaving Treadstone. I'm done."

"Done?" Ford frowned. *"What do you mean, 'done'?"*

"I'm out. Finished."

"Can you do that? I mean, are they going to let you . . . ?"

The change in the man's expression was instantaneous. His face went flat, eyes hard and pregnant with the threat of violence.

It was a look Ford had seen many times before—one

that usually ended with someone bleeding out on the floor—and despite himself, Ford took an involuntary step back.

The two men had first met in Special Forces and had forged a tight bond during multiple deployments. They were on the same team in Afghanistan when the CIA plucked them from their firebase and sent them to Treadstone.

But it was the fact that they remained close after the government-sanctioned mind job that was supposed to have ripped them down to the studs—robbed them of the ability to maintain any relationships outside of the missions assigned to them—that surprised the docs at Treadstone. The whole point of the program was to create unstoppable independent operatives.

"No one is letting me do shit," Hayes snapped, his legendary temper on full display.

"Easy, brother, I didn't mean any harm," Ford said, holding up his hands.

Hayes's face softened and a hint of a smile appeared at the corner of his lips.

"This isn't about you, bro. This is for me."

Something had happened to Hayes on his last mission, and while Ford didn't know the details, he knew that it had changed him.

"But I think you should do the same."

"Man, I don't know how to do anything else," Ford said.

"If you ever need anything, all you have to do is ask," Hayes said, and then he was gone.

Ford turned the water off and reached for a towel, catching his reflection in the mirror. He was shocked by what he saw.

The three months he'd spent in the Orinoco Delta had taken their toll, and the man looking back at him was thirty-seven going on sixty. Lean and hard, with don't-fuck-with-me eyes and the half-moon scar that covered half of his neck before disappearing into his shirt.

I should have listened to him.

Back at the table he turned on the monitor connected to the cameras and booted up the computer. He logged on and connected the mobile WiFi to the laptop. Accessed the IP anonymizer and adjusted the settings so it would bounce the laptop's Internet protocol address to a different server every ninety seconds.

He pulled out the camera that he was using for the recon before the ambush, plugged it into the computer, and, while he waited for the pictures to upload, opened an email and typed the subject.

By the time you get this I'll be dead

He saw the first photo pop up on the screen and decided they would speak for themselves. Ford was just dragging the images into the body of the email when the computer monitor flashed to life.

"Oh, shit."

He grabbed the computer and the Glock 19 and rushed into the bathroom. Slamming the door behind him, Ford set the computer on the sink and picked up the detonator. His eyes never left the spinning progress wheel.

C'mon, c'mon, he begged, willing the files to upload faster.

Ten miles to the north, a pair of eighteen-wheelers turned off the road. The lead Peterbilt slowed with a hiss of its air brakes and made a wide turn onto a cracked asphalt road.

Felix Black climbed down from the cab, a loaded H& K 416 slung against his chest. He marched to the rear trailer through the dust kicked up from the gravel lining the abandoned airfield and popped the access door.

The inside of the trailer was packed with blinking monitors, a bank of processors, and a satellite uplink— the price of each setup was more than twice the cost of the Peterbilt and trailer combined.

"Who has the lock?" Black asked, stepping inside.

A pimple-faced kid with stringy brown hair and a dingy floral-print button-up raised his hand.

"I-I do, sir."

Felix glanced at the monitor, stroking his goatee, the satphone in his cargo pocket vibrating against his leg.

Black knew the only person who had this number was his boss, Jefferson Gray, and he wanted to be sure they had their prey before answering.

"You sure *this* time?"

"Y-yes, sir."

"You better be fucking right," Black said, turning to the door.

Outside the trailer, his team leader, Murph, leaned patiently against the cab of the truck.

"What's the word?"

"Tell the boys to jock up," Black said, pulling the satphone from his pocket and answering the call.

"Yes, sir?"

"Tell me you found him," Gray demanded.

"We got him," Black said.

The clatter of the ramp hitting the ground behind him drew Black's attention to the lead trailer, where the aviation crew rolled an egg-shaped machine off the truck. He glanced at the illuminated face of the Sangin Atlas on his wrist and did the math in his head.

"We can be on target in ten minutes."

"Kill him," Gray ordered.

"Roger that."

He stowed the satphone in his cargo pocket and hustled to the pair of Little Birds, where the kill team was already strapped to the benches mounted on the outside of the helos, the green glow of their night-vision goggles pooling over their eyes.

Black ducked under the blades of the lead helo, the heat from the turbines scalding his neck. He lifted the scarred bump helmet from the bench, jammed it over his head, and rotated the noise-canceling MSA Sordin headset over his ears.

After snapping his safety lanyard into the D ring, Black pressed the push-to-talk attached to the Thales MBITR on his chest and checked in with the pilot.

"Raven One-One, Alpha Six, radio check."

"Alpha Six, read you lima charlie—*loud and clear*."

"Roger, Alpha Six, let's roll," Black said.

He rotated the PVS-15s mounted to the front of the bump helmet over his eyes. The light amplified by the night vision cast the world in an emerald-green hue.

The pilot advanced the throttles, and Black felt the increase in RPMs vibrate up his spine.

Overhead, the blades bit into the air, picking up a static charge that turned the tips yellow under night vision. The Little Bird squatted on its skids and then they were airborne.

The pilot twisted the helo south, skimmed over the trees, and shoved the nose toward the river.

"Feet wet," the pilot said.

Even with night vision it was hard to pick out any landmarks, and Black had to use the GPS monitor on his wrist to navigate. When they were five miles out, he gave the "one-minute" warning over the radio, his left hand closing around the carabiner that secured him to the bird.

"Feet dry," the pilot announced, banking the Little Bird toward the city.

Black checked his GPS and saw the target building was coming up. He leaned out into the slipstream, the wind making his eyes water behind his NOD, and when he saw the Hotel Bolívar, he used his infrared laser to mark the target for the pilot.

The Little Bird was nimble as a hummingbird and the pilot deftly bounced over a set of power lines, the maneuver causing Black's stomach to leap into his throat.

Fucking cowboys.

The pilot dropped the helo to ten feet above the road, the skids barely missing the tops of the cars parked on the street, and followed the laser like a wire-guided missile.

"Thirty seconds," Black announced.

A moment later the pilot flared the Little Bird ten feet short of the front gate. Before the skids were even on the ground, Black had unclipped from the bench and hopped free of the bird.

"On me," he said, moving across the courtyard.

The second helo touched down on the roof and the assaulters hopped from the bench, preparing to work the target from the top down. By the time Black reached the lobby door, the Little Birds had lifted off and silence returned to the street.

"Breacher up," Black whispered.

He jerked the door open and charged into the room. He dug his hard corner, the echo of the roof team's breaching charge rolling down the walls. He pivoted back to the center of the room and was about to call "clear" when he saw a man duck behind the counter.

Black had been deployed to enough shitholes to recognize when someone was going for a gun and when they were taking cover. His instincts told him the man was going to come up blasting.

He raised the H&K 416 to his eyes, thumbed the selector to fire, and activated the infrared laser. The moment his target's head eclipsed the invisible beam, Black fired.

Thwap.

The bullet hit the man below the eyes, the 5.56 hollow-point emptying his brains onto the far wall. He was dead before he hit the ground, the shotgun in his hand clattering off the tile.

Dumbass.

The rest of his chalk was already flowing up the stairs, and Black turned to follow.

"Target is in room number four," the tech's voice echoed over the internal net.

"Roger that," Murph said, "stand by for breach."

Black caught up with his team at the top of the stairs

and knew from the fact that they were standing there that Murph's chalk was already prepping the room.

No need to put more meat in the hall.

Boom.

Black leaned out to get a look at the breach and watched the first two assaulters enter the room. A third was about to follow when the room exploded.

"Man down!" Murph screamed.

Black was already moving.

He stepped into the room, saw the two men splayed out on the floor, their blood black through the night vision. *They are fucking done.*

"Get them up," he ordered, masking for the evac team.

The words weren't out of his mouth when he heard the *pop, pop, pop* of a handgun and saw the spray of plaster from the bullets punching through the wall.

"Bathroom!" he yelled as a round snapped over his head.

An assaulter booted the door and fired inside.

Thwap, thwap, thwap!

"Tango down," the shooter said over the radio.

Black lowered his rifle and checked himself for holes.

"Control, this is Alpha Six, we have two Eagles down, need immediate medevac, at grid—"

"Break, break, break," Gray broke in. "Alpha Six, this is Control, are you jackpot?"

That motherfucker, he swore under his breath.

Knowing the man cared more about the target than his men. "Stand by, Control."

Black moved to the bathroom, saw Nick Ford splayed out in the tub, his brains splattered on the tile. "Are we good?" he asked.

The assaulter spat a line of tobacco juice onto the body before answering with a "Roger that, boss."

Black flipped up his night vision before pressing the push-to-talk button on his chest.

"Control, this is Alpha Six, we are jackpot."

"Control copies."

"How 'bout that medevac?"

Silence.

Fuck. "Murph, get your boys downstairs, we will bag this shit up—"

"They're gone," Murph said.

Black lowered his head and was turning to the door when a voice stopped him in his tracks.

"Boss, we've got a problem," the assaulter said, stepping out of the bathroom.

Black turned and saw the laptop in his hand. "What the *fuck* is that?" he demanded.

"He had it on him. I checked the sent folder and the asshole got an email off before I tagged him."

Black wiped the blood and bits of pink brain from the screen with his glove and read the name in the address bar.

Adam Hayes.

1

LA CONNER, WASHINGTON

Adam Hayes was lying in the center of the bed when the nightmare came. The tremor started at the edge of his lips, a ripple that twisted into a feral snarl. He started to sweat, hands tearing at the sheets, eyes pinballing behind closed lids, mind trapped in the horrors of the past.

He waited in the shadows, eyes closed, ears straining for the sound of his approaching prey. Kill them all—that was the order. He was just the instrument—a man conditioned to kill without hesitation. His hand closed around the hilt of the knife at the small of his back. The metal hilt felt cold through the latex gloves. The blade came free with the hiss of steel on leather and Hayes opened his eyes; the sentry's face was green in the night vision.

Now, *the voice told him, and he struck.*

Hayes's hand snaked under the pillow and his fingers closed around the reassuring steel of the Springfield 9-millimeter EMP. He rolled off the bed and dropped into a crouch, the hardwood cold as a corpse on his bare knees. Muscle memory had taken over, and his hands worked independently of thought. The snap of the pistol onto the target and the flick of the thumb disengaging the safety came unbidden.

It was only when his index finger curled around the trigger, compressing the spring until all it would take was a whisper of pressure for the gun to fire, that Hayes became conscious of the moment.

Then the nightmare evaporated.

Hayes blinked the world back into focus, his eyes falling to the outstretched pistol, sights centered on the shirt hanging on the back of the door. *Jesus Christ.*

He let go of the trigger and snicked the safety into place. The realization that he'd come within a hairsbreadth of sending a 9-millimeter hollow-point through the door made him sick to his stomach.

It was 5:05 in the morning and the nightmares were getting worse.

When he trusted his legs to hold him, Hayes grunted to his feet, placed the pistol on the bedside table, and padded across the hardwood to the bathroom. He palmed the wall switch and the overhead lights flashed to life, revealing the mass of scars that crisscrossed his bare torso like lines on a topographic map.

He stopped at the sink, plucked the orange pill bottle from the open medicine cabinet, and twisted the cap free. He shook a dose into his hand. The oblong pill in his callused palm reminded him of the last appointment with the shrink in Tacoma.

"What about the nightmares?" she asked, over the scratch of her pen across the paper.

"Haven't had one in months."

"Adam, you are making wonderful progress," she said, tearing the sheet from the prescription pad, "*but.*"

There's always a but.

"But there *will* be setbacks."

Setbacks.

He felt the anger stir in his gut, like a wolf waking in its den. Three nightmares in one week wasn't a setback; it was a fucking meltdown. He was pissed. Mad that he'd listened to her—let himself believe that he'd made progress.

That he could be *normal*.

"No," he said aloud. "That's not who I am anymore."

He took a breath, placed the pill in his mouth, and gently closed the door. He took a drink of water from the sink, and when Hayes looked up, his eyes alighted on the sheet of construction paper taped to the glass. The stick-figure family holding hands beneath a lemon-yellow sun.

Hayes brushed his finger over the "I love my Daddy" scrawled in crayon, a sad smile stretching across his face.

In the shower, he twisted the cold-water knob all the way to the left and ducked under the showerhead. The water came out of the pipe ice-cold and hit his flesh with the sting of a bullwhip. His mind recoiled, muscles tensed like hawsers beneath his skin, forcing the air from his lungs, but Hayes stood fast and waited for the question that had greeted him every morning for the past eighteen months.

How did I get here?

The first time Hayes heard about Treadstone, he was in Afghanistan. Three months into a six-month tour and he'd already lost two men. That's when things started to go sideways. Lines that had been black and white started looking gray. Hayes wasn't sleeping, but he had it under control—or that's what he told himself.

Then he was called to Colonel Patten's hooch. Hayes found his boss sitting at his plywood desk, his skin an ashen gray, eyes red from the Afghani sand that seeped into every crack.

"Have a seat, Captain Hayes."

He lowered himself into the chair and listened to the echo of the helicopters coming up the valley. It was his third tour to the 'Stan and Hayes could recognize the helos by the sound. This was a Chinook; he could tell by the *thump thump* of the rotors.

Can't be resupply, they were just here, he thought. *It's too dangerous to send random helicopters into the valley.*

"I'm sending you to Bagram," Patten said, guessing his thoughts.

"For what reason, sir?"

The colonel spit a line of tobacco into the stained foam cup on his desk and leaned back in his chair. "The men are starting to talk."

"That's what soldiers do."

"The boss is worried, Adam. We all are. They are sending someone from the States, some kind of doctor who is going to check you out."

"A psych eval, are you serious?"

"Look, I don't like this any more than you do, but this came from the top. Just get on the bird and go answer the man's questions. Think of it like a break. This guy will get you squared away and you'll be back on the wall tomorrow."

It was a lie, but Hayes didn't know it at the time.

After the shower, he toweled off and dressed in a pair of worn Carhartts and a fleece button-down over a black T-shirt. He stomped his feet into a pair of worn

Ariat Ropers, tucked the holstered Springfield into his pants, and walked to the kitchen.

Breakfast was a pair of fried eggs, two pieces of wheat toast, and what was left of the steak he'd grilled for dinner last night. By the time he finished eating and carried his coffee out to the deck, most of the fishing boats were out on the water and first light was spreading across the horizon like a fresh bruise.

Treadstone was a double-edged sword, one he *thought* would allow him to make a difference. He didn't mind the pain that came with the behavior modification and the genetic reprogramming. Hayes could handle that—he could handle anything they threw at him.

It was what happened after that he couldn't handle. Which was why he was in Washington, and his wife, Annabelle, and their two-year-old son, Jack, were living halfway across the country.

Adam . . . promise you won't try to find us.

The sound of the shop phone snapped him from the memory, and Hayes tossed the dregs of his coffee off the side of the deck and followed the sound to the red barn at the rear of the cabin.

Who the hell is calling this early? he wondered, punching his code into the lock. By the time he got the door open and flipped on the lights, the machine had picked up.

"You've reached Sterling Construction, please leave your message at the beep."

"Adam, it's Sally Colvin, I need you to call me—"

Hayes snatched the phone off the cradle and killed the recording with a jab of his finger.

"Sally, I'm here," he said.

"Adam, hey, I . . ."

Sally Colvin was the realtor he'd hired to sell the Smith house, the project that had kept Hayes sane during his eighteen-month self-imposed exile.

It was also his nest egg. His last chance to show Annabelle that he could build just as well as he could destroy. And the money from the sale was going to allow him to stop fixing other people's houses and work on repairing his broken marriage.

There was something in her voice that struck a chord. *What is it?* Hayes wondered before asking aloud, "Sally, is everything okay?"

"Yeah, uh . . . I . . . I've got a motivated buyer who is interested in the house."

Again, the hesitation in her voice.

"That's great, right?"

"Well, I told him it was move-in ready," she said.

"I don't see why that's a problem," Hayes said, not understanding the panic in her voice. "All we have left to do is the flooring in the kitchen."

"Because he just called from the air. He is flying in *today* at noon."

Great, he thought, eyes dropping to his suitcase on the floor, the ticket to Florida peeking out of the side pocket.

Annabelle had agreed to let him see Jack this weekend. It was all supervised, of course, since she still didn't trust him alone with his son, but Hayes would take what he could get.

"Sally, I can't. I'm flying out at—"

"Adam, this is everything you have been working for," she said, the sudden passion in her voice catching him off guard. "My hardwood guys promise that they will be there at ten-fifteen. All I need you to do is lay the subfloor."

Hayes cast a longing look at the bag, then to the clock on the wall. It was a quarter to six. If he left now and worked fast, he could still make the flight.

"I can make it work," he said.

Hayes loaded the compressor and the rest of his tools in the back of the '66 Chevy Suburban, punched the garage door opener, and eased the truck down the gravel drive.

He turned onto the coastal road, followed it down the hill and over the suspension bridge that connected the mainland with Cliffside Island. At the end of the street, bookended between two massive pines, lay Cliffside Manor.

The manor was the brainchild of Amy Harris, a local heiress who'd taken the lonely island and turned it into an enclave for the nouveau riche. The only reason Hayes was allowed on the property was that he'd bought the Smith house in a short sale.

Hayes slowed at the gate. The squeal of the Suburban's brakes and the amused smile of the guard who stepped out of the shack reminded him that he didn't belong.

"Thought you were off today," the man said, looking down at the clipboard.

"Sally called, said she had a buyer flying down to look at the Smith house."

"No one told me."

"What do you want me to do?"

"Go on up, I'll get this sorted out," the guard said.

Hayes nodded and rolled through the gate, taking his first left onto Eyrie Drive. The stately homes with their emerald-green lawns and dazzling white picket fences reminded him of a scene from a John Hughes film. Even the pair of Jehovah's Witnesses talking to the couple outside of the tennis courts seemed right.

He followed the road around the corner, and there, perched atop the cliff at the end of the street, was the Smith house.

The first time he saw the two-story Cape Cod, it was on the verge of being condemned. The roof leaked, the eaves sagged, and all of the exterior wood was rotten. And that was just the view from outside. When he'd met the realtor selling the property, she had looked at him like he was crazy. "Full disclosure, there isn't another contractor in the area who would take this project. You sure about this?"

He'd never taken on an entire house and knew it was

a daunting task. But there was something about it that wouldn't let him go.

"Absolutely," he'd told her.

Hayes backed the Suburban up the drive and parked next to the pallet of plywood and rolls of plastic. He grabbed his tools from the back, bumped the cottage gate open with his hip, and followed the brick path to the sliding glass door at the rear of the house.

The door rolled open with a screech and Hayes stepped inside. *Need to oil that,* he thought, setting his tools on the bare concrete pad before heading back out for the plastic sheeting and tar paper.

Hayes set the Springfield on the counter next to the sink, plugged in the radio, and got to work stapling the plastic across the doorways so he wouldn't dirty the rest of the house. He covered the floor with a layer of Visqueen and tar paper and turned on the air compressor before going outside for the plywood.

He carried the first sheet of plywood to the corner, made sure that it was flush with the wall, and used concrete nails to secure it to the slab. There was something therapeutic about working with his hands. Something about hard work and attention to detail that let him shut off his mind. Forget about his problems.

Hayes settled into a routine and had half of the subfloor laid down when there was a knock at the front door. He left the air hammer on the ground, hoping it was the flooring crew here early.

"Hold on," he said, getting to his feet.

Thump, thump, thump.

He brushed his hands on his pants and peeled back the corner of the plastic sheeting. It was a straight shot from the kitchen to the front door, but instead of the flooring crew, Hayes saw one of the Jehovah's Witnesses from the street standing at the door. The man offered him a smile and a wave.

"Let me turn off the radio," he said, ducking back into the kitchen, missing the second missionary sneak past the kitchen window, a suppressed H&K MP7 held at the high ready.

Thump, thump, thump.

"Damn, dude, isn't patience one of y'all's virtues?" Hayes grumbled.

He had just stepped out of the kitchen when the squeal of the back door being pulled open triggered the instinctual part of his brain.

Get down, the voice in his head ordered.

Hayes dropped to the floor a heartbeat before the suppressed *thwaaaaaaaaap* of a submachine gun on full auto opened up behind him.

2

LA CONNER, WASHINGTON

The bullets tore through the plastic sheeting and hit the wall, spraying Hayes with chunks of drywall and masonry dust. He was caught in the open and crawling toward the living room when the second Jehovah's Witness booted the front door.

Hayes ducked into the living room and reached for the pistol on his hip. But instead of the reassuring steel of the 9-millimeter Springfield, his hand closed around thin air.

The counter.

"Bang out," the man yelled in Spanish.

As Hayes scrambled into the center of the room, the dark canister that ricocheted off the dining room wall robbed him of any chance of pursuing the thought. He dove to the floor. A split second later, the flashbang hit the ground in front of him. Hayes had just enough time before the canister exploded in a blinding flash of magnesium to close his eyes and open his mouth, so the overpressure wouldn't blow out his eardrums.

The concussion hit him like a freight train, the heat scalding his skin, filling the room with the gagging stench of burnt hair. He tried to get to his feet, but the blast had wrecked his equilibrium and he stumbled like a drunk sailor with a weekend pass.

Stretching his arms out in front of him, Hayes found the wall and managed to get out of the room. Bullets buzzed over his head like angry hornets. He staggered into the den, cracked his shins on the coffee table the decorator had staged in the middle of the floor, and went down.

His sight was the first to return, and then his hearing. The dull roar in his ears was replaced by a high-pitched whine. Hayes smelled smoke, and a glance at his shirt showed that he was on fire. He dropped to the floor and was rolling the fire out when a bullet shattered the mirror above his head.

Find a weapon. Anything.

"I am disappointed, Adam Hayes," the shooter taunted him from the kitchen. "I was told that you were a real body snatcher."

How does he know me?

But the sight of the shooter's green, aiming laser, made visible by the smoke, told him this was not the time to try to answer questions.

The laser hit the far wall, as the shooter worked it into a circle. Hayes knew the man was signaling his teammate. Letting him know that he'd pinned their quarry to the right side of the room.

Usually this was done with infrared, but the fact that he was using the green laser was telling. *He's overconfident, thinks I'm already dead.*

"He is just another *pendejo*, like Ford," the second shooter said.

Ford?

The mention of his friend's name hit him like a slap to the face, but before he could get his mind around it, the second shooter yelled, "I'm reloading."

Hayes knew he had to focus if he wanted to end this day with the same number of holes that he'd started with. *Get in the game.*

The fact that the two shooters had conducted a simultaneous breach, taken the house, and managed to pin him down in the den in less than sixty seconds told him all he needed to know. They were pros.

Tier 1 pipe hitters, and Hayes knew from experience that men like that weren't cheap.

Whoever wanted him dead had the means and connections to make sure it was done right.

But instead of finishing the job, they had decided to

toy with him, and Hayes was determined to make them pay for it.

He scooped a sliver of glass from the floor and snagged the metal accent bowl sitting atop the coffee table. Pressing himself against the wall, he angled the mirror into the laser's path, bouncing it to the opposite wall.

The second shooter acknowledged the laser with a double tap of his own. "Moving," he said in Spanish.

In the den, Hayes angled the mirror and the laser to the floor, but the hopelessness of the situation blossomed in his mind. He was half deaf from the flashbang and going up against a professional killer with nothing but a ten-dollar bowl he'd picked up at Pier 1.

This is a terrible idea.

Hayes offered a quick prayer to St. Jude, the patron saint of lost causes, and then he waited—the thousand things that could go wrong at the forefront of his mind.

The shooter entered the room with the confidence born from thousands of hours of real-world experience. Trusting that his teammate had the right side locked down, the man hooked left, eyes and muzzle finding nothing but thin air.

Hayes was on him in a flash.

He slammed the bowl against the back of the man's head. The blow would have knocked him out if the cheap bowl hadn't crumpled against his skull. The shooter stumbled forward, dazed, but not out.

He tried to turn, but Hayes grabbed a handful of hair and slammed his forehead through the drywall.

"Emilio, you good?" the voice from the other room demanded.

Hayes stomped down on the man's knee, heard the bone snap as his hand clamped around the man's mouth, muffling the scream.

He was reaching around for the man's MP7 when the second shooter appeared in the doorway.

The shooter didn't hesitate, and Hayes barely had time to twist the man in front of him, using him as a human shield before his partner opened fire.

Thwaaaaap.

"Fuck!" the man screamed as the six-round burst stitched him across the chest.

Hayes heard the clatter of his submachine gun hit the ground. He knew there was no chance he was getting the weapon now. His only hope was to close the distance. Get his hands on the second man.

Hayes rushed the shooter, muscles screaming against the deadweight of the man's partner as he pushed him into the kitchen. When he was a foot from his target, he tripped over the dead man's legs and felt himself falling. Hayes managed to shove the body forward, but the shooter sidestepped his dead teammate and attacked.

The shooter came in fast and hard. He was too close to Hayes to bring the MP7 to bear, so he used it to club the side of Hayes's head, dropping him to his knees.

Hayes was still shaking the sparks from his eyes when the shooter tried to punt him in the face.

Hayes saw the kick coming, but all he had time to do was twist his head out of the way. The force of the blow bowled him back into the island.

Now on the defensive, he fired a short kick at the man's groin, felt it make contact, but the shooter didn't even flinch. Hayes scrambled to his feet, ducked a sweeping haymaker, and stepped inside the man's guard.

The fight was up close and personal, all elbows and knees. Hayes knew he had to gain control of the MP7 and grabbed it by the suppressor. The hot metal scalded his fingers and filled the room with the bacon smell of burnt flesh.

Take the pain.

Hayes pushed the submachine gun toward the floor, stepped in, and drove his forehead into the man's nose. The cartilage exploded with the snap of wet celery, his blood splashing hot on Hayes's face.

But the man kept coming; the only sign that he'd been hit was the angry grunt in the back of his throat.

If you don't end this fast, he is going to destroy you.

On cue, the man lowered his shoulder and, using the MP7 like a ram, bulldozed Hayes over the island. Hayes landed on all fours, saw the fire extinguisher in front of him, and ripped it from the mount.

Hayes tugged the pin free and got to his feet. He stuck the nozzle right in the man's face and squeezed the handle, emptying the extinguisher in a *whoosh* of white retardant.

The shooter stumbled and Hayes vaulted the stove. He drove the extinguisher into the man's gut, folding him over.

Ummmmph.

The smoke alarm screamed to life and the shooter managed to rotate the barrel up and fire before Hayes could club the MP7 from his hands. He winced against the burn of the bullet and heard the submachine gun clatter to the ground.

Hayes dropped the fire extinguisher and bent to scoop the MP7 from the ground. But before his fingers closed around the grip, the shooter stripped a knife from his belt and slashed at his face. Hayes saw the blade glint in the overhead light, sucked in his stomach, and jerked his body to the rear a moment before the cold steel sliced across the front of his chest.

Hayes hit him with an elbow to the face and heard the grate of broken teeth when it landed. He grabbed the man's wrist and was trying to twist the knife away when the shooter kicked him in the side of the leg.

The blow landed with the snap of an ax, tripping the femoral nerve, and buckled his leg. The shooter landed a crushing backhand and Hayes's head whipped to the right. Blood splattered across the freshly painted wall.

The shooter drove Hayes to the floor, the blade inches from his neck. Summoning the last of his strength, he pushed back with everything he had, but the blade continued its march toward his jugular.

Above him, the veins in the shooter's neck bulged through the white mask of retardant.

Hayes knew in that instant that neither the promises he'd made in the past nor the plans he had for the future mattered if he was dead.

There was only one way he was ever going to see his family again.

Kill him.

He turned his head, saw the air hammer on the floor to his right, and bucked with his hips. He managed to get a knee between himself and the shooter. Just enough space to buy him another second.

The man smiled down at him.

"Die, motherfucker." He leered.

Hayes grabbed the air hammer and pressed it against the side of the man's head.

"You first," he said, pulling the trigger.

3

LAS MANGAS, VENEZUELA

Jefferson Gray stood outside the dusty Chevy Suburban and idly worked the toothpick to the corner of his thin lips. It was hot atop the low, flat hill, and the back of his shirt, like the sweatband of his straw cowboy hat, was already soaked through with sweat.

He wiped the back of his arm across his face to clear the sweat, lifted the binos to his eyes, and scanned the landscape. To the east a breeze blew across the *llanos*— the grassy plains that covered southwest Venezuela reminded him of his home in West Texas and how far he'd come since joining the CIA ten years before.

Before joining the Agency, the only thing Gray knew about the CIA was what he saw on TV or read in a spy novel. It wasn't until after he'd become a case officer that Gray learned the truth: The CIA was actually a risk-averse bureaucracy, which is why his rise from a fresh-faced recruit to the head of the Critical Actions Program was nothing short of meteoric.

But none of that mattered right now. His mind turned to the blood-spattered computer Black brought back with the bodies of his men.

"Here," he said, tossing it onto Gray's desk, jaw muscles rippling beneath his skin.

Gray opened the laptop and frowned at the dry rust-brown smear across the screen. "Couldn't have cleaned it up?" he asked, tugging a Kleenex from the box on his desk.

"I was a little busy bagging up Marty and K.P."

"Hmm," Gray said, scrubbing at the screen. "Any idea what he sent?"

"Did you hear what I said?" Black demanded.

"Yes, I heard you," Gray answered, looking up at the angry contractor standing in front of him. "They're dead, which is why I'm asking you the question and not them."

Gray watched the anger blossom in Black's eyes, his hand curl into a fist.

"He deleted the files," the man said through gritted teeth.

Gray had worked enough sensitive site exploitation

to *know that unless a target physically destroyed the drive, the data was still on the computer. All he had to do was find it.*

It took an hour, but he managed to locate the images Ford had sent. Four files.

The first three pictures were grainy and innocuous: a wide-angle shot of a dirt airstrip framed by a rusted hangar and an old DC-3, followed by one that showed men transferring pallets from the plane to the back of a truck. The third picture was barely in focus and it took Gray a moment to even realize that he was looking at the same truck as before, but this time the men were unloading the pallets.

So far there was nothing to worry about. The pictures could have been taken anywhere, and there was nothing in the photos that could be traced back to Gray.

But the moment the fourth and final picture flashed on the screen, he knew there was a problem. Oh, fuck.

Ford had taken his time with the last shot; the lighting and the focus were perfect and there was no mistaking the two men in the center of the frame.

It was Gray and Colonel Vega, the head of Venezuela's national intelligence service, and the one man his boss had ordered *him to avoid.*

"Fuck!" he shouted, slamming his fist on the desk. *Three years of work threatened by a fucking email.*

A crackle of static from the radio in the center console tugged Gray back to the problem at hand. "I've got eyes on," Murph advised from the distant collection of rocks where the sniper had set up his hide site. "Helo, coming in from the west."

"'Bout damn time," one of the men in the back said, gently stroking the assault rifle balanced between his legs.

Gray lifted the binoculars to his eyes and panned to his left, squinting against the road-flare red of the setting sun. He thumbed the focus knob until he saw the small green dot on the horizon. A few moments later it grew into a Huey with Venezuelan markings.

"Got a door gunner on the right side," Murph alerted them.

"If this shit goes sideways," Black answered, "you use that Barrett to turn Vega into pink mist."

Gray lowered the binos and glanced inside the truck to see Black staring at him from behind his dark glasses. The was no mistaking the challenge in the man's voice. He was trying to force Gray to state his allegiance in front of the whole team. Demanding to know whose side Gray was on—the team's or Vega's.

But this wasn't Gray's first rodeo and he wasn't here to play games, so instead of the confrontation that Black wanted, he sidestepped the issue.

"This is going to go nice and smooth," he said, as the

pilot brought the helo directly over the Suburban, then pulled it into a tight arc.

"We'll see about *that*," Black said, turning his attention to the men in the back. "You three keep the safeties off until we get a handle on the situation," Black told the three hard-looking bearded men who wore dusty plate carriers festooned with the tools of their trade: extra magazines for the H&K 416s around their necks, tourniquets, and M67 fragmentation grenades.

"Copy that."

After a second pass, the pilot pulled the helo skyward and settled into a lazy orbit.

"Convoy coming in," Murph announced.

Gray stepped away from the door and watched the cloud of dust that marked Vega's approach. The first truck, a green F-150, rolled into sight, the bed packed with gunmen.

"You want your vest?" Black asked.

"Not my style," Gray replied, lifting the cowboy hat off his head and running his fingers through his blond hair.

The vest brought up memories of his classmate Mike Vickers. They had gone through the Farm together. Mike was looking for a high-value target in Iraq when their convoy hit an IED. When Gray visited him at Walter Reed hospital, he almost lost it. Something about seeing Mike lying there hooked up to all those machines. His daughter crying over what was left of her dad.

Fuck all that. When it was his time, Gray wanted a clean death.

The F-150 shot up the gentle incline in a cloud of brown dirt, the faces of the soldiers in the bed covered in black balaclavas. The truck made a quick lap around the top of the hill, kicking up a wall of dust before skidding to a halt.

When the dust settled, the armed men in the back of the truck had climbed down and stood eyeing Gray's perimeter.

Nice and smooth, he thought, returning his attention to the black Mercedes SUV waiting at the bottom of the hill.

One of Vega's men raised a radio to his lips, and after giving the all-clear, the SUV started up the hill. The driver brought it to a halt in front of Gray and a slender man in an immaculate uniform and pencil-thin mustache stepped out.

"*Buenas noches,*" Colonel Vega said, dropping a bag at Gray's feet.

The impact knocked the flap wide open enough for Gray to see the stacks of banded cash that filled the interior.

"For the job at the Bolívar," Vega said.

Gray nodded for Black to retrieve the bag of cash and the two men walked to the edge of the hill, where they could not be overheard.

"I understand *we* have a problem," Vega began,

the earlier smile fading as fast as it had appeared. "Something about an email and some photos."

Shit, how does he know about that?

Vega seemed to read his mind. "Come, Mr. Gray, I would not be very good at my job if I didn't know everything that was going on in my country, now, would I?" he said.

"It is being handled."

"And you are sure you will have this situation resolved before the shipment is ready in three days?" Vega demanded, his eyes as cold as a rattlesnake's before it struck.

"I told you—" Gray snapped, momentarily losing his cool.

"My friend"—Vega held up his hands, the warmth returning to his eyes as fast as it had vanished—"there is no need to get angry. In three days you will be a very rich man with enough money to leave this life forever," he said with a sweep of his arm that encompassed the entire hill. "*But* if your CIA was to learn—"

"Be careful, Colonel," Gray hissed, cutting him off. "I don't take well to threats."

"Very well, just make sure you take care of this Adam Hayes, and soon."

4

LA CONNER, WASHINGTON

The two-inch concrete nail punched through the shooter's skull and hit the cranial vault, immediately severing all motor functions.

Death was instantaneous.

Hayes shoved the dead man off his chest. The fight hadn't lasted five minutes, but Hayes was gassed. His breath came in short, ragged gasps and his heart hammered like an AK on full auto.

Part of him wanted to stay there on the floor, catch his breath and figure out what in the hell had just happened, but he couldn't think with the smoke alarm screaming at him from the wall. Hayes rolled to his feet, twisted the smoke alarm from its mount, and fastballed it across the room.

The silence that followed was deafening.

Get up, the voice ordered.

Being a spectator in your own body was one of the aspects of the Treadstone protocol that Hayes had never gotten used to. The genetic therapy the docs had used to make his muscles stronger and faster was something that he could use—turn on and off when he needed them.

But the behavior modification was a totally different animal. According to the Treadstone doc, the science was simple.

"Your body has natural responses to certain situations. When your body needs fuel, it tells you that you are hungry. When you are tired, you feel sleepy. The hardware is all there, we just rewire it."

"Rewire it?" Hayes asked.

"Think of it this way: a car has a gas and a brake pedal, right?"

Hayes nodded.

"Now you have two gas pedals."

Someone would have heard the shooting. Cops will be here soon. Make it quick. Check the body.

He watched himself get to his feet, kneel over the dead man, and rifle through his pockets. All while a voice in his head cataloged what he found.

Cellphone. A burner. He snapped a picture of the man's face and then rolled the man over. Looked for a wallet, and when he didn't find one, glanced at his watch.

Time check. *Thirty seconds. Gotta move.*

Hayes got to his feet and was about to turn to the second shooter when something on the man's shirt grabbed his attention.

What is it? Think, damn it.

The pills . . .

The pills were the shrink's idea, one he'd fought for as long as he could.

"This drug is new, but doctors in Europe are having success using it to treat the symptoms of PTSD."

"I'm not a big fan of pills," Hayes said.

She ripped the prescription from the pad and held it between her fingers. "What about nightmares, are you a fan of those?"

Good point, *he thought, taking the paper.*

"Adam, these pills are a temporary fix. They will treat the symptoms, but they won't fix you."

The headache started at the back of his head, a blinding lightning bolt of pain that sent his blood pressure skyrocketing.

His hands were shaking, the first sign of the panic attack that started in his guts. Hayes tried to get ahead of it, but it was too late. His blood pounded so hard against the ocular nerve that the room throbbed in and out of focus.

Hayes buried his head in his hands, remembering the grounding exercise his shrink had taught him. *Picture someplace safe. A place where you are in control.* He closed his eyes and tried to picture the safe space, but the bodies of the two shooters lying five feet away made it impossible.

Eighteen months of work, gone in the blink of an eye.

The pain came back, and the image began to distort. Twisted and frayed at the edges, and Hayes's mouth stretched wide. "Not *now!*" he screamed, palms pressed hard against the sides of his skull.

He dropped to his knees, the concrete cold through his pants. *I am in control.*

It was a lie. One confirmed by the gunpowder in the air and the dead bodies on the floor. And then there was the thirst. The implacable burning that reminded Hayes he wasn't in control of shit.

Treadstone hadn't said anything about side effects when he'd signed up. They had told him it was just a job—another way he could serve. It wasn't until after his first mission, during the debrief in the room with the off-white tiles and institution-gray walls, that Hayes started to realize what he'd *really* signed up for.

★ ★ ★

The memories came rushing back. So real and visceral that Hayes could almost feel the cold metal of the stainless-steel chair against his bare skin, see the bottle of water sitting on the table in front of him. Condensation running down the plastic like fat tears. He'd never been so thirsty in his life and every fiber in his being screamed for him to snatch the bottle from the table, tear the cap off, and down it in one long gulp.

Instead he focused on the reflection in the two-way glass mirror mounted on the far wall. The face staring back at him a honed caricature of his own. Sharp cheekbones, on the verge of cutting through the tanned skin. Short cropped brown hair with flecks of gray that hadn't been there before. But it was the eyes that grabbed his attention. They were blue and cold as glacial ice.

What the hell did they do to me?

The door clicked open and the man in the lab coat and a nurse stepped in. He walked to the table and started recording Hayes's vitals in a cornflower-blue folder.

"Heart rate?"

"Eighty-nine beats per minute."

"Blood pressure?"

"One-twenty over eighty."

Hayes studied the doctor, the way a predator sizes up potential prey. He estimated the doctor to be in his late forties, with clear blue eyes, bushy brows, and jet-black hair that was way out of regulations. Even for an officer.

"Almost done, Doctor," the nurse said, pulling out the needle and replacing it with a cotton ball. "Keep pressure on it until the bleeding stops," she said, capping the needle, grabbing the three vials of blood, and walking out.

"Cigarette?" the man asked, offering the pack of Winstons he'd taken from his lab coat.

"Don't smoke," he said, watching the blood stain the cotton ball.

The doctor scraped a match across the striker and the sulfur smell took Hayes back to the mission. The smell of the pistol after it fired.

"Mr. Hayes, this is a routine debriefing," the man began. "I am going to ask you a series of questions and I want you to answer them truthfully. Do you understand the instructions?"

"Yes."

"Any attempt at deception will be noted on the machine," he said, hooking his cigarette at the monitor in the corner. "Do you understand?"

"Yes."

"Good. Roll tape," the man said, setting his cigarette into the ashtray and looking down at the paper.

Hayes looked toward the mirror on the far side of the room and saw the red light come on. He knew they recorded these interviews but had always wondered who was behind the glass watching him.

"We are going to start with the baseline. What day is it?"

"Monday."

The man looked up at the monitor, didn't see a spike, and turned back to the paper.

"What country are you in?"

"The United States."

"And the city?"

"Alexandria."

Testing. They loved to test you here.

The baseline questions were there to establish how Hayes reacted to telling the truth, and with that out of the way, it was time to begin.

"Where were you last Tuesday?" *the man asked.*

"Seattle," *Hayes lied.*

The man glanced at the monitor, an apostrophe of a frown at the edge of his lips.

"Is Adam Hayes your real name?"

"Yes."

Another lie that wasn't picked up. The frown began to spread.

"What is Treadstone?"

"Never heard of it."

The door opened and a tech slid into the room. He

walked over to the machine, looked down at the knobs and then over at the man in the white coat.

"It's maxed out," he said and shrugged.

"Problem?" Hayes asked innocently.

"No. Walk me through the mission."

"The kill order came in the usual way. A name and an address. Target's name was John Li. The workup said he was a bagman who ran numbers at the Golden Buddha. It was bullshit."

"Excuse me?" the doctor asked.

"The intel," Hayes said, looking at the mirror, "was bullshit. Li was MSS—Chinese national intelligence. Guards at the back door were carrying Norinco 9-millimeter pistols when I killed them."

"I'll put that in my notes," the doctor said.

"Li went down easy."

"Did he say anything?"

"Begged for his life. Offered me money, usual stuff." *Hayes shrugged.*

"What did you do?"

"Put a .22 subsonic in his eye."

"And what did you feel when you killed him?"

"Feel?" Hayes asked, not really understanding the question.

"Yeah."

"Recoil," Hayes answered honestly.

"Recoil?" The man smiled.

"Yeah, you know." Hayes made a pistol out of his

hand. "Boom." *He pantomimed pulling the trigger and the rise of the muzzle after he fired.*

"Any side effects? Headaches, trouble sleeping—?"

"The thirst."

"Perfectly normal," *the man said, scratching the response in the file before tossing him the bottle of water.*

Back in the kitchen, the pain subsided as fast as it had started and Hayes got to his feet. His mouth was dry as sandpaper and his legs shook as he tottered to the sink. He turned on the faucet, opened his mouth wide under the tap, and drank until he ran out of air.

Hayes caught his breath and was about to go back for a second drink when he heard the sirens and knew it was time to go.

5

LA CONNER, WASHINGTON

Hayes stuffed the 9-millimeter into his pants, crossed to the threshold, and yanked the door open. He cast a final glance over his shoulder, and when he turned to step outside found himself looking down the barrel of a Glock 17.

"*Get the fuck on the ground!*" the deputy behind the pistol ordered.

Hayes had lost count of how many guns had been shoved in his face, and even now the Glock didn't impress him.

But the deputy's shaky finger on the trigger was a different story.

He guessed the deputy was in his early thirties, but it was hard to tell with the sweat beading up on his shaved head. One thing that was certain—he was amped up. Jaw muscles flexing like gills, pupils blown out like he'd just snorted an eight-ball of coke.

Kill him, the voice urged.

"I don't kill innocent people."

"Wh-what?" the deputy stuttered, pistol shaking in his hand.

Damn it.

"Deputy Powell," Hayes began, reading the deputy's name off the brass plate on his shirt.

"Get on the ground, *now*," Powell ordered, closing the gap, "or I will blow your head off."

Hayes kept his attention on the Glock pointed at his face. The shine of the packing grease on the slide told him everything he needed to know. The pistol was brand-new, just like the deputy.

"I said on the ground, asshole."

"Easy," Hayes said, lowering himself to his knees.

A second deputy pulled up, his car's blue lights strobing. He hopped out, his pistol clearing the holster.

"Baker 210 on the scene," he said over his radio.

"Keep your face down," Powell commanded, pressing the pistol into the top of Hayes's head.

The kiss of the muzzle against his skull sent a spark coursing through Hayes's body. His muscles went tense, the voice in his head screaming for him to *kill the man.* But he had a rule. A code that he'd followed for as long as he could remember: he didn't kill cops.

I don't kill cops.

"I'm going to check the interior," the second deputy said, stepping inside the house, his pistol at the ready. His entry was marked a moment later by a curse followed by the sound of the deputy gagging.

Sounds like he found the bodies.

"You stay right where you are," Powell said, stepping to his left and peering through the doorway. "Ronny . . . you good?"

Hayes turned his head to the side, knowing he needed to get control of the situation but unsure of how to go about it, when a third vehicle pulled up on the scene. The lack of lights on the top of the Ford Crown Vic telling him that it was a supervisor's vehicle.

When he saw the man step out of the vehicle and tug the faded Stetson over his bushy blond hair before walking up the drive, Hayes let out a sigh of relief.

Lieutenant Sidney Blair was every inch the lawman: tall and rangy, with eyes that never stopped moving. He was one of the first men Hayes met when he moved to Skagit County, Washington, and his arrival on the scene was as welcome as a cool breeze on a hot day.

"Powell, how many times do I have to tell you about trigger discipline," Blair demanded, his Texas drawl on full display.

"S-sorry, sir," the deputy responded.

Hayes heard the second deputy stumble out the door, followed by the crack of bushes and the smell of vomit.

"Je-sus, Mary, and Joseph, Ronny, this is a crime scene . . ."

"Sorry, Lieutenant, but—"

"Go clean yourself up," he said before turning to Powell, "and you get some crime scene tape up. Act like one of you has some damn sense." Once his deputies were out of earshot, Blair flashed a toothy grin to Hayes. "Get your ass up." He offered his hand.

The smile disappeared and Hayes knew the reason when he saw his reflection in Blair's mirrored sunglasses. His face was red and swollen from the fight, but Hayes knew it was the threat of violence dancing in his eyes that had given Blair pause.

"Hey, now," Blair said, placing his hand lightly on Hayes's shoulder and guiding him inside the house, "Powell didn't mean any harm. You know that, right?"

"It is the only reason he's still breathing," Hayes said.

If Blair was taken aback by the statement, he didn't show it. In fact, for a moment neither man said anything.

Hayes had recognized something in the man the first time they met and knew the feeling was mutual. They both shared common values and respected the natural silence. Avoiding the need to talk just to fill the void that naturally occurred in conversation.

Both men followed the old code of the West, the rule that said a man's past was his own affair—until it *wasn't*. Hayes had never asked Blair how a Texas boy had ended up on the West Coast and the lieutenant had returned the favor.

But Hayes knew that was about to change.

Blair turned his attention to the shooter on the floor, let out a long whistle, and pushed the Stetson back on his head. "You fucked 'em up. That's for damn sure."

Hayes watched him pull a pen from his pocket and move to the dead man lying on the floor. Using the pen, Blair turned the man's head and got a better look at the hole and then looked over at the air hammer.

"First time for everything," he said, already moving to the second body.

"They didn't give me a choice," Hayes replied.

"What a mess," Blair said.

"What about me?"

"Self-defense, but I'm going to need you to go with Powell to the station and give a statement."

"The guy who almost blew my face off?"

"Hey, it's a small department," Blair said with a shrug.

Hayes wasn't thinking about the size of the department. He was thinking about who had sent the men to kill him and why.

6

Levi Shaw was unremarkable in every way. It was a skill that he'd cultivated over three decades in the intelligence field. One that had allowed him to slip unnoticed into some of the darkest corners of the globe, conduct his government business, and vanish without a trace.

Shaw stepped off the Metro at Pentagon station and disappeared into the scrum of flag-grades in their ribboned Class A's.

He rode the escalator to the landing, pulled his badge from around his neck, and nodded to the man at the security checkpoint.

"Morning, Johnny," he said, as he swiped his badge over the reader, laid his attaché case on the belt, and

57

dumped the contents of his pockets into the white basket between the metal detectors.

"Good morning, Mr. Shaw," the man said, and smiled.

"Your Nats looked good last night," Levi said, stepping through the metal detector.

"Wish I could say the same for your Mets." The guard grinned.

"Don't start," Levi said, shaking his head.

He filled his pockets, retrieved his attaché case, and followed the hall to the left.

Shaw first came to the Pentagon in the mid-nineties as a GS-13. A grade that gave him the equivalent rank of a major. The first lesson he learned was that at the Pentagon, just like in the military, everything from parking spots to office space was based on rank. Which was why Shaw was not surprised when he was assigned a windowless office in the basement of the innermost ring.

"Look at it this way," the custodian said when he handed him the keys, "you can only go up from here."

"Why is that?" Shaw asked.

"Because you're at the bottom of the building. Ain't nothing below this floor but the foundation." He smiled.

It would take almost thirty years for Shaw to learn that the man was full of shit.

There was in fact an area below the basement, and the reason it wasn't listed on any blueprint or map was because it was a Black Site. An off-the-books area funded by the National Intelligence Program's Black Budget and known simply as the Boneyard.

Located deep in the Pentagon's purgatorial bowels, the Boneyard was where nonessential Black programs were sent to die. To linger in limbo until their source funding ran out.

At the bottom of the stairs, Shaw swiped his card over the reader and waited for the magnetic lock to disengage before pulling the door open.

While the rest of the Pentagon had been modernized in 2011, the Boneyard looked exactly the way it had back in 1943, the year the building was completed. Shaw followed the exposed pipes and bundles of wire that crisscrossed the ceiling, his footsteps echoing off the dingy gray walls that still bore the original coat of Federal Standard No. 50 paint, and turned the corner.

He was almost to his office when a door to his left opened and the hall was filled with the roar of the sump pump installed to hold back the constant seep of the water table.

A facility worker stepped out, the badge on his blue jumpsuit marked with the red chevrons that gave him access to even the most secured offices in the Pentagon. The man shut the door behind him, and silence returned to the hall.

Shaw watched the man tug the red earmuffs from his head and then jump when he heard the footsteps coming toward him.

"Whoa, buddy, how'd you get down here?" the man demanded.

Shaw held up his keys and gave them a jingle.

"You got keys, good for you. Still doesn't answer my question."

"That's classified." Shaw smiled, stopping in front of the door with SB1-T-71 inscribed on the nameplate.

He opened the door and flipped on the lights. The fluorescent bulbs buzzed in their ancient baffles and slowly blinked to life, revealing a broom closet of an office with three desks, a row of scarred filing cabinets, and a water cooler that gurgled when Shaw walked in.

He was just closing the door when he heard the man's voice through the crack in the door. "Holy shit, you *work* down here? Who the hell did you piss off?"

How much time you got? he thought, gently closing the door.

Shaw hung his hat and coat on the rack by the door, his eyes on the calendar tacked to the wall. *Three more days and then Treadstone is done,* he thought.

Shaw wasn't a sentimental man. Three decades in the intelligence world had cured him of that. But when he turned to survey the office, there was a part of him that still couldn't believe how far Treadstone had fallen in the past year.

Officially the reason for Treadstone 71's relegation to the Boneyard was simple: It was outdated.

This was the digital age, and no matter how much the Treadstone doctors boosted their operatives' capabilities, they could never compete with drones, satellites, or computers. *The powers that be are always looking for a high-tech solution to a low-tech problem. They will never learn,* Shaw thought, carrying his attaché case to his office in the back of the tiny room.

He sat down heavily at his desk and typed his password into the computer. When the mainframe loaded, he typed the commands directly into the prompt.

```
>>>>CIA Remote Portal
Login: Shaw, L.
_Access Granted
>>>>Connection Established_

Status: Online
```

A moment later a satellite map popped up on the screen that brought him back to April of 2002 and his first week as Treadstone director.

He was on a guided tour of the Tactical Operations Center located in one of the offsite facilities, trying to get a handle on the scope of the operation he'd inherited. The TOC was smaller than the ones at the National Counterterrorism Center, but just as modern, with a floor-to-ceiling LCD screen and the floor of intel specialists sitting at their workstations, faces backlit by the blue glow of their computer screens.

"This is where we track the missions," the officer in charge of the TOC said. "Not as impressive as the lab, but it is all state of the art."

"How many operatives do we have in the field right now?" Shaw asked.

The man squinted up at the board. "We have three on the ground in Afghanistan and one in Iraq," he answered.

"What about the rest?"

"Well, sir, we have fifteen Gen 3's—those are the operatives put in service following the September 11 attacks—and seven Gen—"

"I know how many we have; I want to know where they are."

"Sorry, sir, but I'm not following—"

"Son, what exactly do you do here?" Shaw asked.

"My job is to track the operatives that are on mission or assigned to mission status."

"How do you track them if you don't know where they are?"

"They radio in their locations—"

"Got it, thank you," Shaw said.

Later that afternoon, he called every department head into his office.

"I'm not big on micromanaging, and usually when

I take over a program I like to sit back and watch how things run for a few months before making any adjustments," he began, looking at the men and women arrayed around the conference table. "However, I believe we have a serious security risk."

"Security risk, sir?" Don Jacobs, the bald-headed chief of operations, asked. "I'm not sure I'm following."

"Okay, let's open this up to the table," Shaw said. "How do we select applicants for Treadstone?"

"Since the majority of our operatives are former military, we mine the DoD's psychological evaluations, looking for patterns that match our criteria," a dark-haired woman with horn-rimmed glasses answered.

"And what criteria are we looking for?"

"Certain behavioral traits, such as the candidate's ability to withstand stress, extreme competitiveness, self-reliance, lack of empathy and remorse . . ."

"And then we send those people over to the doctors and they run them through behavior modification and genetic reprogramming to get rid of basic morality and turn them into killers, right?"

"Clinically speaking, what we—" a second doctor began.

"Obviously, this is a generalization. The point is we turn these men and women into apex predators and then we just let them roam free until we need them. Does anyone else think we might want to know where these guys are when they aren't on mission?"

Immediately after that meeting, every operative was unknowingly implanted with a subdermal tracking chip.

Back in his office, Shaw typed `location ping` into the task bar, and a moment later the surface of the map was covered in a handful of blinking blue dots that marked the locations of the remaining Gen 3's.

Shaw had begun to scan the map, conducting a quick roll call in his head, when the screen went black and a box popped up on the screen. `SIGNAL LOST—PLEASE CONTACT PROVIDER.`

"You have got to be shitting me."

LA CONNER, WASHINGTON

Deputy Powell was the picture of professionalism when Blair informed him that he would be transporting Hayes to the station.

"What about my truck?" Hayes asked Blair.

"I'll have someone bring it to the station."

Hayes didn't like it, but it was obvious that he didn't have a choice.

"Fine," he said, tossing the keys to the lieutenant.

"Now, you two play nice."

"Roger that, boss," Powell said, opening the rear hatch and typing his code into the vault in the back. When the lock disengaged, the deputy turned to Hayes.

"What are you looking at?" Hayes demanded.

"Your weapon," Powell said, holding out his hand.

Hayes looked at Blair. "Are you serious?"

"It's department policy," the lieutenant said.

This is bullshit.

He pulled the Springfield from his holster, dropped the mag, and ejected the round from the chamber before handing them over.

"You will get them back," Powell said, locking the vault and shutting the hatch. "No hard feelings, right?" he asked, after they had climbed into the front seat of the Explorer.

Hayes grit his teeth so hard he was afraid they were going to crack but managed a curt nod.

"We're good."

Powell started the engine, pulled a U-turn in the street, and went back the way Hayes had come in. After crossing the bridge, the deputy turned right, heading for Highway 20.

"The Army?" Annabelle had asked.

They'd met in his freshman year at college and both of them knew it was special. By the end of the semester they shared a dorm room. They never talked about marriage; they didn't have to. It was almost understood that they would spend the rest of their lives together.

Then graduation came, and instead of the finance jobs Hayes had been offered, he decided to join the military.

"Why?" she asked.

Hayes tried to explain but realized he had only pieces of the answer.

"There's a war on."

"So?"

A few months ago, he would have said the same thing, but that was before he went back to visit his parents in Tennessee, where he learned that two of the boys from the old neighborhood had been killed in Iraq and two more in Afghanistan.

Hayes had been nineteen years old on September 11, too young and too distant to know anyone who died in the attacks. He saw the names of the dead on television, read about the casualties in the papers, but they were just names. It wasn't until he went out to the veterans' cemetery and saw his friends' names carved into the white stones that the scales fell from his eyes.

"Doesn't it bother you?" he asked.

"Is this about your friends?"

Hayes didn't have an answer, but he instinctively knew that if he didn't do his part, he would forever regret it. So he joined up and spent his summer at the Infantry Basic Officer Leader Course in Fort Benning, Georgia.

They drove in silence, Powell behind the wheel grinning like a cat with a mouse and Hayes checking the mirrors, his attention bouncing between the fact that someone had just tried to kill him and the realization that his nest egg was now a crime scene.

"Full disclosure," he said aloud.

"What was that?" Powell asked.

"It's a law that says I have to provide a potential buyer with all information needed to properly negotiate a price."

"You know, I was thinking about buying a house last year," Powell began. "Figured I've been living with my folks long enough."

"You live with your parents?" Hayes asked.

"Since I was born." Powell smiled.

"And how old *are* you?"

"Thirty-two, but you wouldn't know it by the way my mom acts when I bring a girl home," Powell said, his face turning serious. "Did you know that I can't have a lady friend stay past eleven-thirty?"

"I did *not* know that, Powell."

"Yep, so I figured it was time to spread my wings, get out on my own. Now, I can't afford anything like what they've got at Cliffside, but I found a nice place over on Whidbey. Almost made an offer, too."

Despite himself, Hayes realized he was intrigued. "What happened?" he asked.

"Same thing you were talking about with the full disclosure."

"Someone was killed in the house?"

"Worse."

"What's worse than a homicide?"

Powell paused and looked over at Hayes as if he were gauging the man's trustworthiness, and when he finally spoke his voice was hushed, almost a whisper. "Realtor said the previous owner conducted animal sacrifices in the basement."

"Are you fucking with me?" Hayes demanded.

"Hand to Jesus," Powell said. "I told that lady I didn't want anything to do with a witchcraft house."

Hayes turned his head back to the mirror, barely able to contain his laughter.

"I don't think your mama would have liked that too much," he managed to say.

"Why, hell, no, she wouldn't, being a Methodist and all."

Hayes was about to respond when he noticed a black Suburban tuck in behind a minivan two cars to the rear of the Explorer. He was still watching the truck when Powell hit the blinker and angled for the exit ramp.

"Where are you going?" Hayes asked.

"The ferry; it's the fastest way to the office."

Hayes was about to protest, but when the Suburban didn't follow them down the ramp he settled back and decided to enjoy the ride.

It was a five-minute drive to the ferry station, and by the time they arrived the weather was starting to change. The clear blue sky that had greeted the day was gone. Replaced by charcoal-gray clouds and choppy, white-tipped waves that buffeted the gunwales of the ferry moored at the dock. Drenching the yellow-slickered Washington Department of Transportation employee standing on the deck.

Powell pulled behind a truck at the ticket booth and checked his hair in the mirror. Satisfied that he looked presentable, he rolled down his window and let off the brake.

Hayes guessed the blond-haired woman in the booth to be in her late thirties, and he noticed her pop the top button on her blouse when she saw Powell pull up.

"Hey, Rhonda," Powell said and grinned.

"Deputy Powell," she said, a conspiratorial smile spreading across her face. "How are you this morning?"

"Just out enforcing the law," Powell puffed. "It's boring, but it is part of my life."

"Is he your prisoner?" she gushed.

"Naw, just a witness."

"Well, you be careful, you hear," Rhonda said, hitting the plunger that activated the traffic arm. "And I'll see you later tonight."

Powell eased the Explorer down the gangplank and over the metal ramp. At the bottom he followed the soaking-wet man in the yellow slicker waving them into the center lane.

The M/V *Suquamish* was a 362-foot Olympic-class auto/vehicle ferry capable of transporting one hundred and forty-four vehicles. It was one of the newer vessels, and inside the hold the white-painted walls and yellow lines separating the three parking lanes had yet to fade.

"Does your mama know about Rhonda?" Hayes asked over the flat-handed smack of the waves against gunwales.

A deep crimson blush spread across Powell's face and he jammed the transmission into park.

Outside the ferry, an employee shouted an order that was answered by the ring of a buzzer that signaled the end of boarding. The gangplank motor rumbled to life and Hayes turned to see the ramp lift into the air. He held the view for a few moments, watching for the flash of headlights that would warn him of any latecomers. When he didn't see any, Hayes turned around and heard Powell mutter, "She's a nice girl."

"I was just messing with you, Powell," he said, turning his attention to the deputy and missing the blacked-out Suburban creep down the ramp behind him.

8

LA CONNER, WASHINGTON

Felix Black sat in the back of the Suburban, rubbing his hand over his goatee and watching the Sheriff's Department Explorer park ahead of him. He was used to rush jobs, but there was something about the hit on Adam Hayes that had felt off from the beginning.

"Who the fuck *is* this guy?" Murph asked from the front seat.

It was the same question Black had been asking himself since watching Adam Hayes kill two of his men.

They had the drop on him. How in the hell did this even happen?

Black looked down at the picture he'd taken of Hayes when he pulled up. The man might be able to hide his identity, make it look like he was a nobody on paper, but there was one thing Hayes couldn't hide: his eyes. Light blue and cold as a pimp's heart.

A killer's eyes.

The tech had already run Hayes through the DoD and DoJ database. Each query went back twenty years, but the only result he got was a Washington State driver's license issued in 2016 and a State of Washington contractor's license.

"Nothing," the tech said. "Not a damn thing besides what we already have."

"So, according to the United States government, Adam Hayes didn't exist before 2016. Is that what you are telling me?"

The tech shrugged.

Bullshit.

The satphone in his hand rang.

"What's the status?" Gray asked.

"Who the fuck is this guy?"

"He's a target. Nothing more," Gray replied.

"Bullshit," Black said, looking up at the Explorer. "This guy is a spook."

"We don't know that."

"Gray, he terminated two of my assets."

"What is our visibility?"

"It's a shit show. Cops are all over the scene. Hayes is in custody."

"And the bodies?" Gray asked.

"I'll take care of Hayes—" he began.

"*No*, Black, you won't," Gray snapped.

Black's fingers curled around the phone, the anger rising to his face. His mind returned to the Hotel Bolívar and the two men he lost there. *He is going to pull me off the op.*

"Look, you are the guy on the ground, and I respect that, but this operation is blown . . ."

"I can make this work," Black pleaded.

"There is too much on the line, and right now we can't afford any more mistakes. I want you to wave off."

Black looked up at the Explorer twenty feet away and Hayes's silhouette in the front seat. *He's right there.*

"Did you hear what I said?" Gray asked.

Silence.

"Black, I can hear you breathing. Did you *hear* what I just said?"

"Yeah . . ." Black answered. "I heard you."

"Good. I'll see you back in Venezuela," Gray responded.

Black ended the call and set the phone on the seat beside him. He agitatedly rubbed his goatee.

"What did that asshat say?" Murph asked from the front seat.

Black ignored him. If Gray had just let him handle the takedown the way he wanted, none of this would have happened. But because of *him*, Black had lost four men in twenty-four hours.

Fuck Gray. This ends today.

"Boss?" Murph asked.

"He told us to handle it," Black said, grabbing his rifle and reaching for the door.

9

Hayes was watching Powell fiddle with the radio, the sound of the ocean reminding him of the beach in Florida.

He was on vacation in Florida when the kill order came.

"Adam, you are on vacation, put your phone away and pay attention to your son," Annabelle said.

"Sorry," he said, shoving the phone into his pocket and squatting down beside his son.

"Whatcha working on, bud?"

"A drawing," Jack said, adding a final swirl of blue

to the ocean before holding the picture up for Hayes to inspect.

"Is that the beach?"

"Yep, I drew the crabs and the tree and Mommy . . ." Jack said, pointing at the woman with the lemon-yellow hair.

But it was the frowning figure at the end who grabbed Hayes's attention.

"Why is everyone smiling but me?"

"Because you never smile, Daddy," Jack said, grinning.

"What are you laughing at?" he snapped, the anger flowing out of him before he could check it. Across the room, his wife's smile evaporated, and she got to her feet with a sob.

"Belle, I'm sorry," he said to her back.

"Why do you always make Mommy cry," Jack demanded, throwing his crayon on the ground before following his mother into the other room.

The memory passed in the blink of an eye, but it was enough to remind Hayes about his flight to Florida.

"Son of a bitch," he spat, the anger in his voice making Powell jump.

"You scared the crap out of me. What the hell is wrong with you?"

"Nothing . . . I just remembered something I was supposed to do."

She is never going to understand. Never going to believe me, he thought, looking out the window and at the cloudy bay beyond.

His eyes dropped to the side mirror, and when he saw the Suburban a forgotten tingle ran up his spine. The shot of adrenaline sparked through his synapses, and Hayes was immediately on guard.

"Turn the radio off," he ordered.

"What?" Powell asked.

Hayes reached over and hit the power button with his left hand, his right hand finding the window control. He pushed down, cracking the window.

A rush of salt air blew into the SUV, but other than the rumble of the engines and the distant caw of the seagulls, the hold was silent.

"What's going on?" Powell asked.

Hayes wasn't even aware that his hand had dropped to the center console until he felt the switch beneath his fingers. Without knowing why, he pushed it and heard the click from the mount securing the Remington 870 shotgun to the roof of the Explorer.

"Hey, you can't do that," Powell said. Hayes ignored him and pulled the shotgun free of its mount, racking a shell into the chamber. "Get your pistol out," he commanded, his right leg already out of the SUV.

"I don't—"

"Listen to me—that truck has been following us since we left Cliffside," Hayes said, stepping out of the SUV and moving around the front to the driver's side. He pulled Powell's door open and grabbed him by the shoulder, eyes never leaving the Suburban.

"The men inside that truck, they don't give a fuck about you *or* your badge," he warned, pulling Powell out of his seat.

"Get off of me," the man said, twisting out of his grip. "You don't make the rules here, I do, got it?" Powell told him, his hand dropping to the Glock.

"Then you're on your own," Hayes said, but before he could turn away, the doors of the Suburban swung open and four men in dark jackets and body armor stepped out of the truck.

"Who are these—" Powell said, trying to tug his pistol from its holster.

Before the words were out of his mouth, the passenger laid his rifle across the doorjamb and opened fire.

Braaaap, braaaap, braaap.

Hayes rushed the shotgun into action. He pulled the butt pad into the hollow of his shoulder and centered the bead on the man's chest and then remembered his target was wearing body armor. Hayes readjusted his point of aim to the man's throat, knowing that the momentary adjustment had probably just cost Powell his life.

His finger curled around the trigger and Hayes started to pull the slack out when the shooter fired.

In the tight confines of the hold, the H&K sounded like a hammer smacking an anvil. The first shot hit Powell in the center of the chest and the impact shoved the deputy backward. Powell slumped into the back of a van, his mouth forming a silent O.

A second later the shotgun recoiled hard against Hayes's shoulder, slinging a spread of nine .33-caliber pellets toward the shooter. The blast of double-aught buckshot hit the shooter just above his plate carrier and his throat and lower jaw disappeared in a spray of crimson.

"Murph!" a man with a goatee yelled.

Pandemonium broke out as screaming passengers abandoned their vehicles to seek shelter within the ferry's interior.

Hayes threw himself to the ground while the shooters dumped their magazines into the SUV. The bullets rocked the Explorer on its springs and the windows exploded. On the ground, Hayes covered his head against the cascade of glass and slivers of metal that rained down on him.

He looked up and saw Powell's knees buckle, watched the deputy slide to the ground, the front of his pants stained red with his own blood.

Who the hell are these people? Why are they coming after me now? he asked.

Does it matter? the voice replied.

Hayes had left Treadstone with more enemies than he could count. And it wasn't like Treadstone sent their assassins after low-level criminals. No, the targets Hayes went after were at the top of the pyramid. Cartel leaders, spies, even rival assassins. Men and women with the power, means, and opportunity to take their revenge.

It was a simple numbers game. Every time Hayes put some shithead in a box, he gained more enemies. Families and friends, brothers and sisters, who would do anything to get revenge.

Did you think they would stop because you did? Did you really think that they would forget? the voice chuckled.

Hayes needed to get Powell out of the line of fire, but he was pinned down, unable to move without exposing himself to the deadly hail of lead.

"Powell, crawl to me!" he yelled.

Leave him, the voice urged. *Or die.*

The rate of fire on the Explorer had slowed and Hayes didn't need to see the shooters to know what they were doing. Gunfighting was all about working the angles—shooting and moving. Hayes knew that while the one shooter kept him pinned down, his teammates were already maneuvering on him.

"I'll be right back," he shouted to Powell before crawling over to a Chevy pickup and out of the line of fire.

He racked the pump and hazarded a glance over the bed of the pickup.

"There!" one of the men yelled.

Hayes fired without having time to aim and ducked out of sight, trying to move to the right and flank his attackers. But the shooters were good and worked to close off the angles. Hayes racked a fresh round into the chamber and was planning his next move when he saw the mirror attached to the ceiling off to his left. In the reflection he saw Powell fumbling to get his pistol out of the holster when a man with a shaved head stepped into view and raised his rifle.

Powell abandoned his pistol and Hayes saw his mouth moving. He didn't need to be a lip reader to know the deputy was begging for his life.

The man with the goatee was a foot away from Powell when he shook his head and raised the rifle to his eyes.

"Noooo!" Hayes yelled.

But it was too late.

10

CAR DECK, M/V *SUQUAMISH*

The man with the goatee fired a single bullet into the center of Powell's forehead.

Hayes fought the rage building up, knew he had to stay in control if he was going to make it out alive.

Think, damn it.

He scanned the abandoned vehicles around him, looking for anything he could use, and was about to give up when he saw an aluminum pole with a blue handle protruding from the back of a Dodge Ram two car lengths behind him.

Hayes made his move, hooked left, and squeezed between the front bumper of a Volkswagen Beetle and the trunk of a red Miata.

One of the shooters saw him slip from cover and yelled, "Flank left!"

But Hayes was already in the next row, squeezing himself between a black panel van and the Ram's tailgate. Relief rushed over him when he saw the bed of the truck was filled with pool-cleaning supplies. Despite the fact that the van shielded him from the shooters, Hayes knew he didn't have long. He dumped the shotgun and hurriedly rifled through the plastic bins intermixed with the lengths of hose, filters, and pool skimmers that littered the bed.

The third pail contained what he was hoping for: three-inch chlorine tablets. Hayes grabbed two of the tablets and shoved them into a black trash bag before hopping down.

"Where is he?" a voice yelled.

Hurry, the voice urged.

Hayes moved to the gas tank and dropped to a knee. He stomped the chlorine tablets, using the heel of his boot to grind them into a powder. When they were small enough, Hayes shook the powder into the corner of the bag, tied it off, and ripped the plastic above the knot.

He opened the fuel door with his left hand, twisted the cap free, and stepped out into the lane, staying in the open just long enough for the shooters to see him.

"I've got him."

Hayes ducked back to cover for a moment before a

shot rang out and the bullet sparked off the left side of the Ram's bumper.

Back on the driver's side, Hayes shoved the bag full of chlorine powder into the gas tank and closed the fuel door. He wasn't sure how long it would take for the gasoline to eat through the plastic, but he knew he didn't want to be anywhere near the truck when it did.

He rushed forward and had just ducked behind a Honda Accord when the two shooters reached the back of the Ram and then the truck exploded, filling the cargo hold with acrid smoke and the screams of the burning shooters.

The fire-suppression system kicked on, filling the cargo hold with halon, sucking the air out of the fire, and Hayes knew it was time to go. Holding his breath, he sprinted from cover, angling for the far rail.

Off to his right, the burning shooter was on fire, an FBI windbreaker melted to his skin. A few feet away, his partner lay motionless on the ground.

That's three. Where's the man with the goatee?

Hayes grabbed the rail and lifted himself up. It was a fifteen-foot drop to the water, but it wasn't the height that bothered him. Hayes knew that he had to jump clear of the wake or risk being sucked under the ferry.

Hayes flexed his muscles and was about to jump when he felt a sledgehammer blow to his shoulder followed by the crack of a rifle. The bullet spun him sideways, and instead of diving from the rail, he was falling.

He hit the water hard. The impact blew the air out of his lungs.

Hayes had always been a strong swimmer, thanks to the wide shoulders and powerful frame he'd inherited from his father. But the shock of the cold over his skin caused a temporary short in his nervous system, and despite his urging, his muscles refused to respond.

One moment he was on the surface, and in the next instant an invisible hand dragged him beneath the moving boat. The shock of the water had worn off and Hayes regained control of his muscles, but he knew that no matter how great of a swimmer he was, there was no way in hell he was outrunning the ferry and its six-thousand-horsepower twin diesels.

There was only one way he was getting out of this.

Hayes swam toward the keel, and the moment his shoulder slammed into the metal, he twisted his body around so that his feet were pressed against the bottom of the boat.

While he worked to get into position, the ferry continued moving above him, and Hayes watched the twin screws chopping through the water.

Got to time this just right.

He waited until the last possible second and then pushed off, diving deep, his arms clawing at the water, muscles burning from the buildup of lactic acid.

The big diesels were above him now, the freight train roar of the screws ordering him to go deep or die.

Finally the engine sounds started to recede, and Hayes checked his descent, kicked off his boots, and scrambled for the surface.

Air. It was all Hayes could think about.

He'd been almost out of air when he pushed off the boat; now the lack of oxygen was at a critical level. It had begun as a flicker of discomfort, but now his lungs burned like someone had filled them with battery acid.

The edge of his vision was beginning to darken from the lack of oxygen, and he remembered the stories about people who'd drowned. How the primal need to breathe had gotten so bad that they had opened their mouths underwater and sucked in a lungful of salt water.

At the time it sounded like bullshit, but the closer he got to the surface, the louder the voice in his head begged for him to open his mouth and take a breath.

The moment his face cleared the surface, Hayes opened his mouth and tried to take a deep breath, only to find he didn't have the strength to keep his head above the waves.

Exhaustion had set in and his leaden muscles were useless.

Hayes felt the panic rise up from his guts, the hollow helpless feeling that he was about to die and there was nothing he could do about it.

Despite the fact that he'd spent most of his adult life sending his enemies to the afterlife, Hayes never took the time to ponder his own mortality. He'd grown up in the South and had his fair share of church, and while he had a general idea of what was *supposed* to happen, the only thought that came to his mind was *Is this it? No bright light, no tunnel? This is bullshit.*

At that moment, he remembered the water-survival course that he'd taken in the Army. Hayes took a breath of air and let himself sink. Underwater, he unbuckled his belt and stripped off his pants. He tied the pant legs together with a square knot and by sheer force of will surfaced for a second time.

Hayes arced the pants over his head, filling the legs with air before slapping them back into the water. With a final surge of strength, he slipped the knot over his head and collapsed into his makeshift float.

He lay there panting, muscles aching from the frigid water. The bullet wound to his shoulder ached like someone was hammering nails through his skin.

Hayes had been here before, wounded, alone, and on the run. Wanting to quit, but unable to, thanks to the mind job the Treadstone docs had done on him. Survival: It was the only thing that mattered.

And revenge, the voice reminded him.

11

THE PENTAGON

Deep in the bowels of the Pentagon's subbasement, Levi Shaw sat at his desk, his ear hot against the phone's receiver. He'd been on the phone, trying to get the secure Internet connection turned back on since arriving at the office, but despite being transferred to five separate departments, Shaw was no closer to fixing the problem.

He was about to hang up when a voice finally came back on the line.

"Sir, are you still there?" the IT tech asked.

"Yes, I'm here," Shaw replied, switching the phone to the other ear.

"The good news is that we have located the issue."

"Great," Shaw said, feeling a spark of hope. "Can you fix it?"

"Well, that's the bad news. The work order to terminate your connection originated outside of our system."

"Who issued the work order?"

"Hold on one second," the tech said.

Shaw closed his eyes and listened to the clatter of the tech's fingers over the keyboard. He felt a headache building and rubbed the bridge of his nose, wishing nothing more than to get off the phone.

"Looks like the issuing authority was A. Wallace."

The mention of the name was enough to tell Shaw that any additional investigation was a fool's errand. Instead, he thanked the man for his help and slammed the phone on the cradle. "Fucking Wallace," he swore, opening the middle drawer of his desk and pulling out a half empty bottle of aspirin.

Shaw popped some pills into his mouth and was heading for the water cooler when the phone rang. "Yes?" he answered, wondering who in the hell even had this number.

"Mr. Shaw?" a faraway voice asked.

"Yeah?" he asked, trying to hear over the loud whine in the background. "Who is this? I can barely hear you."

"Sir, this is Captain Jeffries. Deputy Director Carpenter sent me to pick you up."

"For what?"

"I'm not sure, but he's expecting you in twenty minutes. If you wouldn't mind coming out to the north lot, I'll pick you up."

"On my way," Shaw said, slamming the phone on the hook. *Twenty minutes. What the hell?*

He grabbed his coat and hat and rushed up the stairs. Three minutes later he stepped outside the doors and was looking around for the driver when a UH-60 Black Hawk thundered in over the trees and settled in the parking lot.

If there was *one* thing he'd learned during his twenty years in the intelligence field, it was that nothing good ever came from the deputy director of operations sending a helicopter to pick you up.

"Mr. Shaw?" the crew chief asked, as he ducked beneath the rotors.

He nodded and climbed through the troop door, took a seat on the nylon bench, and pulled the bulky headset over his ears.

His first thought was that he was being called to Langley, which meant a visit to the seventh floor, where the director had his office. But when the pilot lifted off and turned the helo east, Shaw realized where they were going.

Well, this day just keeps getting better and better.

Buried deep in the countryside of Charles County, Maryland, Naval Support Facility Indian Head was a hard place to find—even if you knew where to look.

It was a "blink-and-you-missed-it" post made up of a runway, a line of aluminum hangars, and a handful of brick buildings for service and support.

The reason for Indian Head's isolation could be traced to the interconnected web of dirt mounds that covered the rest of the 3,500-acre base, giving it the appearance of a massive prairie dog colony. Since its establishment in 1890, the base's sole purpose had been the manufacture, storage, and testing of energetics: the high-explosive powders and munitions used by the United States Navy.

It was the perfect cover to hide one of Langley's best-kept secrets: the CIA's offsite annex. A place simply referred to as Site D.

The helicopter touched down next to the hangar and Shaw grabbed his leather attaché case and waited for the crew chief to open the hatch before climbing down. He stooped under the spinning rotors and walked toward the man in a dark suit standing next to a dark blue Chevy Tahoe.

"Mr. Shaw," the man said, opening the back door.

The driver followed the asphalt past the gate guard before turning east on Bronson Road. Two miles down the road, he turned onto a gravel path, passing the sign that announced DEADLY FORCE AUTHORIZED BEYOND THIS POINT.

The road had been cut through a thick strand of pines, and the trees formed an impenetrable canyon of green that blocked out the light. In the back, Shaw found himself overcome with a sudden wave of claustrophobia. He reached for the window control. *I need some air.*

He was still fighting the urge when the road doglegged back to the north and the trees opened up. The Tahoe pulled into the clearing, and the open space alleviated the panic growing in Shaw's chest. He took a breath, feeling his heart rate return to normal as the driver slowed before the silver guard shack surrounded by a ten-foot fence topped with razor wire.

A man in olive-drab BDUs stepped out of the shack, right hand resting on the pistol grip of the H&K 416 assault rifle slung over his plate carrier, left hand motioning for the Tahoe to come to a halt.

Shaw passed his identification card to the driver, who scanned the ID while a second guard appeared with a telescoping mirror, which he used to check the Tahoe's undercarriage. The guard handed Shaw's and the driver's IDs back, and when his partner finished his sweep, said, "You're good to go."

The driver handed Shaw his identification card, but instead of pulling forward, kept the Tahoe in park. Levi's eyes drifted knowingly to the glowing red light mounted to the gate and remembered the first time he'd been called out to Site D.

★ ★ ★

It was in mid-November, the peak of the rut in Maryland, and he was running late to a last-minute meeting. Shaw was a stickler for punctuality, and as a rule arrived ten minutes early to every meeting he attended. He remembered sitting in the back of the truck, foot tapping against the floorboard, trying to bleed off some of the anxiety coursing through his body.

Why aren't we moving?

He was about to ask the driver, when the man's eyes ticked to the rearview. Sensing the question on his passenger's mind, the man pointed to the red light.

"I don't—"

Before the words were out of his mouth, an eight-point buck came crashing out of the wood line directly in front of the vehicle. Its hooves had barely touched the ground when a finger of yellow flame erupted from the opposite tree line and the buck evaporated in a crimson mist.

"Holy shit," Shaw said. "What was that?"

"Sentry guns. Radar-guided Vulcans." The driver smiled. "Fourth buck of the week," he said, grinning. "As long as that light's on, I stay right here."

Shaw had seen a GAU-17's Vulcan cannon in action once before and knew the six-barreled cannons were capable of firing 6,000 7.62x51-millimeter rounds a minute.

I don't think I mind being late this once.

★ ★ ★

Back in the now, the light switched to green and the driver shifted into gear and followed the gravel path for another two hundred yards until the road ended.

From the air, Site D was just another Indian Head magazine, a needle hidden among a stack of needles. But that façade disappeared at the bottom of the ramp. The driver eased the Tahoe into the white rectangle spray-painted on the ground, stopping short of the three metal pylons blocking the reinforced blast door.

To the left, a second set of guards sat safely ensconced inside the lead-shielded cubicle, waiting for the X-ray machine buried beneath the white rectangle to scan the vehicle and its occupants. The sign that everything checked out was the blare of the warning horn that reverberated off the concrete confines of the ramp and the rumble of the motor beneath the Tahoe, followed by the pylons retracting into the ground and the clang of the 3,000-pound blast door cracking open.

The doors yawned open and the driver eased the Tahoe into the well-lit garage and stopped next to a single stainless-steel elevator.

His driver shifted into park and Shaw was about to get out when the elevator swished open and a man wearing a shiny suit and burnished leather shoes stepped out.

"Fucking Wallace," Shaw grunted. "Any chance you can give me a lift back to the helo?"

"Wish I could," the driver said and smiled.

Great.

Shaw climbed out of the truck, adjusted his suit coat, and took his time walking over. Savoring the change in Archie's expression from bored to annoyed.

"Levi," the man said, extending his hand.

"Just washed my hands," Shaw said, stepping past him and into the elevator.

"Have it your way." Wallace glared.

Like any bureaucracy, the power at the CIA lay not with the operatives who put their lives on the line or the techs who mined the shadows for the next threat, but with the managers and bureaucrats who controlled the flow of information in and out of Langley.

Men like Archie Wallace.

Wallace had started out in the Intelligence Analytical group, where he ran a team of analysts who collected data to establish models for predicting future attacks. As a project manager, he came to the attention of Mike Carpenter, and the deputy director of operations chose him as his chief of staff.

More than anyone else at the CIA, Wallace was responsible for the shift from human intelligence to the reliance on signal intelligence. It was his view that programs like Treadstone were old tech. His favorite argument was "Why send a man when we can send a drone?"

"So how is basement life?" Wallace asked, his sneer reflected in the elevator's door.

"Keeps me away from the assholes." Shaw smiled,

his ears popping as the car descended into the bowels of the earth.

The elevator settled with a bump and Shaw stepped out into a hallway overlooking the pit—the unofficial name for the operations floor.

"You Cold Warriors are all the same," Wallace began, "a bunch of dinosaurs who refuse to understand that the days of sending a man with a gun to take out a target are over. Treadstone is done. Old tech. This," he said, looking down at the pit, "is the future."

"Whatever you say, Wallace."

"I'm serious, that Summit supercomputer," he said, pointing at the black box the size of a tractor trailer, "can crunch data at two hundred petaflops. Hooked up to the ESnet, I can stream data at one hundred gigabytes per second."

"Then why am I here?" Shaw asked.

"Fuck you, Levi," he said, turning to his right and following the hall to a large office at the end.

Deputy Director Mike Carpenter's office was large and fitting of America's chief spy, with slate-gray carpet and a pair of matching black faux-leather chairs. At the head of the room, Carpenter sat at his desk, the wall behind him covered in plaques, awards, and pictures that showed the director shaking hands with various dignitaries, including the president.

"This shit is getting out of hand," he said, nodding to the television on the far wall.

Shaw turned his attention to the screen, where a black-haired reporter stood on a balcony, addressing the camera.

"Tensions are growing as protesters in northern Caracas take to the street, demanding President Díaz resign as president of Venezuela," she began.

Shaw thought she looked tired, frazzled, despite the liberal application of makeup, and the moment the camera panned over her shoulder, down to the Calle Cotiza, he knew why.

Three stories below, the street was alive with bandana-wearing protesters hurling rocks at the soldiers knotted around the pair of armored personnel carriers blocking the road, their angry chants echoing off the walls.

What are they saying?

Muerte a Díaz. Death to Díaz.

"The violence in the capital city is reminiscent of the terror attacks that rocked Caracas in 2009. Attacks that led to the military coup which brought then-General Díaz into power."

"Here are some forensic results we got from a murder scene in Venezuela. What do you know about this?" Carpenter asked, rounding the table with a plain sheet of white paper in his hand.

Shaw scanned the heading, but it wasn't until he'd read halfway down the memo that his heart jumped into his throat.

TOP SECRET/EYES ONLY

Subject: DNA Match

Results of tissue sample taken from remains recovered in

AO Apure:

Positive Match: Database <Site R:> //SAP/Directory/

Operations: Treadstone

Name: Ford, Nicholas

Ford? What the hell were you doing down there?

"He's one of yours?" Carpenter demanded.

"Yes, but—" Shaw began.

"This is the shit I've been telling you!" Wallace exclaimed. "Levi Shaw, running black ops down in South America like it's fucking 1985 and not bothering to tell anyone what he's doing."

"Is that true?" Carpenter demanded.

"Absolutely not," Shaw said, glaring at Wallace. "Treadstone hasn't had an active mission in four years. Your lapdog has my budget so wrapped up in appropriations that I have to submit a memo to Congress just to buy a roll of toilet paper."

"Bullshit, Levi," Wallace snapped.

"Go fuck yourself, Archie."

"Enough!" Carpenter barked, rounding on Levi. "If I find out that you are lying . . ."

"You won't. Ask Senator Mendez. As the head of the Senate Actions Committee, he has to sign off on every operation."

"Just where in the hell do you think this memo came from?" Wallace hissed.

Shaw had survived in the game this long because he lived by a simple rule when faced with a situation with an unknown outcome: Lie, deny, and make counteraccusations. The only problem was, this time he was telling the truth.

He had no idea what was going on.

"This is a frame job. Someone is trying to railroad me."

"Well, you have three days to figure it out, because I just received a second memo from the senator's office. Mendez is calling an emergency meeting of the Senate Actions Committee in three days, and he is looking for a head to put on a pike, and I can promise you that it isn't going to be mine."

12

SKAGIT BAY, WASHINGTON

The current was strong and carried Hayes across the bay, toward the pine-clad shores of Whidbey Island. He was exhausted, the cold water sucking the heat from his body, leaving his extremities numb.

Think about something else, the voice in his head ordered. Hayes complied, turning his attention back to the call that had started the day.

Fear. That's what he'd heard in Sally Colvin's voice. Why she'd sounded strange on the phone.

"Adam, it's Sally Colvin . . . I need you to call me . . ."

It wasn't hard for him to imagine how the call had gone down. The shooters breaking into her house, rough hands yanking Sally out of bed, the press of the pistol to her head or the blade against her skin a warning of what would happen if she didn't sell the call.

How did they find me?

It was the first question that came to his mind. He'd done everything he could to separate himself from his past. Gone so far as to move way the hell out to Washington, hoping the change in scenery would give him a fresh perspective. Before dropping off the grid, he spent six months combing the public domain, destroying any thread that could connect Adam Hayes the private citizen to his former life as a government assassin. By the time he settled in Washington, everything that Hayes owned—the house, the phone, even the Suburban—had been bought and registered through intermediaries.

But he knew that no matter how many threads he cut or how far he moved, there would always be one set of records that he couldn't touch: his file in the Treadstone archives.

It is the only way they could have found me. But who has that kind of access?

He knew there was only one way to find out. But first he needed a car.

By the time he scrambled onto the cement-gray beach, Hayes was shivering, his extremities numb from the water. He unknotted his sodden pants and pulled them over his legs, and, after tightening his belt, crossed the beach to the public bathroom.

Hayes ducked into the women's restroom and, once

he was sure that he was alone, locked the door behind him. At the sink he turned on the hot water, took off the jacket, and shrugged out of the button-up.

The fabric closest to the wound had already dried, and it stuck to his skin. He knew better than to rip the scab, and while waiting for the water to heat up, he took out his knife and pried the face off the sanitary pad dispenser mounted to the wall.

Steam rolled up from the sink, and he splashed the hot water over his shirt until he was able to peel the fabric free.

The bullet had caught the top of his shoulder and the wound looked nasty, pale and wrinkled from the water. Hayes knew he had gotten lucky. If he'd been hit an inch lower, he would have been in serious trouble.

Using hand soap and paper towels, he cleaned the wound as best he could and made sure it was dry before sticking the pad to the wound.

It wasn't his best work, but he knew the field-expedient patch job would hold until he could stitch it up later.

Hayes wiped down the sink and buried the bloody paper towels in the bottom of the garbage before gingerly pulling on the wet jacket and walking to the road. He needed a car, but with a dead deputy plus the other bodies on the ferry, Hayes knew that by now his face would be all over the news. Which meant renting one was out of the question.

Going to have to steal one, he thought, slipping across the road and ducking into the woods that separated the neighborhood from the road.

Thanks to the additional Naval Air squadrons that had come to Whidbey, the island was in the midst of a growth spurt and builders were putting up new houses just as fast as their crews could work.

Hayes hadn't boosted a car in years and needed a vehicle with minimal security features. He remembered an article that listed the Honda Accord and Toyota Camry as the two most stolen vehicles in the U.S. According to the report, you could steal one with a tool as simple as a pair of scissors.

In the end he settled on a late-model Toyota pickup with a faded silver toolbox parked in front of a house at the end of the block.

Hayes stayed in the trees and managed to get within twenty feet of his target. The street was still and quiet, the interior of the house dark, when he bounded into the open, wet socks squishing across the pavement.

The toolbox was unlocked, and Hayes lifted the lid, wincing at the squeak of the hinges that sounded impossibly loud in the still morning air. He rifled through the contents, fully expecting to hear a nosy neighbor threatening to call the police, but his luck held and not only was he *not* discovered, he also found a flat-head screwdriver among the tools inside the box.

With the screwdriver in hand, he moved to the door,

stripped the drawstring from the hood of his jacket, and tied a slipknot in the end. Holding the string in his left hand, Hayes jammed the screwdriver through the weather stripping at the top of the door, working the tool back and forth until he'd forced a gap.

Hayes fed the makeshift lasso through the gap and settled the loop over the lock. A gentle tug was all it took to close the loop, and when he was confident the knot wouldn't slip free, he gave the drawstring a hard jerk and the lock popped open.

Now comes the fun part, he thought, sliding behind the wheel.

Hayes stuck the screwdriver into the ignition and twisted until the lock snapped free and the ignition rotated to the "on" position. The final step was to pop the hood, locate the starter solenoid, and use his trusty screwdriver to close the circuit between the starter post and the terminal.

The engine roared to life, and thirty seconds later he was turning out of the subdivision, the heater cranked all the way up.

13

SAN CRISTÓBAL, VENEZUELA

Jefferson Gray stood at the window of the apartment he'd rented in San Cristóbal, watching the fog clear from the jagged spires of the Cordillera de Mérida mountain range. It was a beautiful view, one that usually helped calm his mind, but today all Gray could think about was that Black still hadn't reported in.

He moved back inside, remembering the saying the analysts at Langley liked to throw around: No news is good news. But then his eyes dropped to the satphone sitting silent on the table.

It was a routine hit; just let it play out.

It was a good thought, but every time Gray tried, his mind went back to the meeting with Vega and the way Black had challenged him in front of the men.

No. He's been radio silent for too long. Something is wrong.

Gray turned on the television and flipped it to CNN before pulling his laptop over and logging in to the Homeland Security database. He started a Washington State query, checking the box to include police, fire, news outlets, and social media, and was about to hit enter when a banner with BREAKING NEWS flashed on the bottom of the screen and the camera zoomed in on the black-haired anchor behind the desk.

"Breaking news out of Washington State, where we have learned of a possible terrorist attack aboard the M/V *Suquamish*, a Washington State Department of Transportation ferry." As the man spoke, a second window appeared on the screen, showing a live feed of a smoking ferry surrounded by rescue boats.

"According to local police, passengers called nine-one-one after hearing automatic rifle fire in the hold of the *Suquamish*, followed by a massive explosion, as you can see . . ."

"Fucking Black," Gray shouted, jumping to his feet. The anger was short-lived, replaced all too fast with fear. *How exposed am I? Can this be traced back to me?*

Gray found himself pacing the room, thinking back to the man who'd sent him to Venezuela in the first place: Senator Patrick Mendez.

★ ★ ★

After graduating at the top of his class from the Farm, Gray was sure he was going to be sent to the Directorate of Operations, or DO, as it was known in the CIA. Getting into the action was all he cared about. The region didn't matter. The CIA could send him to Afghanistan, Iraq, Yemen—Gray didn't care, as long as it was still bleeding.

When he finally got his assignment, he couldn't believe it.

"The NR, are you sure this is right?" he asked the personnel manager. The National Resource Division, or NR, was the domestic branch of the CIA. It was where the Agency sent their burnouts and fuckups.

"Yep, the CIA doesn't make mistakes."

Gray rented a small apartment in Falls Church and had to drag himself out of bed every morning. He spent his days at the office, debriefing government workers about the dangers of traveling abroad. When he wasn't doing that, he was expected to troll the local colleges, looking for foreign nationals he could recruit to spy for the U.S.

Gray wasn't cut out for an office job and was considering resigning from the CIA when he was invited to attend a diplomatic meet-and-greet in Georgetown.

It was an invitation that would change his life.

A diplomatic ball was a great place to collect intelligence, and Gray was expected to attend. He was also warned about getting too close to politicians.

"*You are going to be rubbing elbows with some powerful people; try to keep your wits about you,*" his boss had advised.

Gray was following that advice, having a drink, when a tall dark-haired man in an immaculate Hugo Boss suit drifted into the bar, flashing a thousand-watt smile to a few well-wishers before locking eyes with Gray and angling over.

He sidled up next to Gray and ordered a scotch neat from the man behind the bar.

"Patrick Mendez," he said, extending his hand.

Gray knew who he was the moment he'd walked into the room. Everyone in the CIA knew Senator Patrick Mendez, the chairman of the Senate Actions Committee.

"Pleasure to meet you, sir," Gray said, taking his hand. "I'm—"

"Jefferson Gray, the new man at the NR."

"Yes, sir, how did you know?"

The barman appeared with the senator's drink and set a napkin in front of him, followed by the scotch.

"How did I know your name?" He smiled as he raised the glass and took a sip. "A man in my position is always looking for new friends."

Gray was intrigued. Why would an influential senator be interested in him?

"If you don't mind me asking, how did someone who graduated cum laude from Yale and then top of your class at Langley end up at the NR?"

"I've asked myself that same question more times than I care to remember."

"I'm sure it has its perks." Mendez tipped his glass toward the pair of gorgeous socialites gliding into the bar.

What is it he wants?

"But on the other hand, it can't be easy for a guy like you to be riding the bench when all of your classmates are in the game."

Then it hit him. The senator was working him.

The CIA called it developing an asset, and it was the third phase of the recruiting process. Gray wasn't sure what he was after, but he was smart enough to know when to talk and when to listen.

"Tell you what," Mendez said, pulling a card from his pocket and handing it over. "When you get tired of riding the bench, why don't you give me a call."

While Gray looked at the card, the senator pulled a wad of cash from his pocket, snapped a hundred-dollar bill off the top, and placed it on the bar next to his half-finished scotch.

"Maybe we can help each other out."

And then he was gone.

Gray waited a week before calling him. The senator told him to meet him back at the same bar.

"What do you know about Venezuela?" he said once they were seated.

Gray knew plenty about Venezuela and none of it was good.

"I know it's a shit assignment. A fucking backwater post," he said honestly.

"My colleagues and I have spent the last three years working tirelessly with President Diego Mateo. We have done everything in our power to shore up his regime, and what does he do?"

"Well, I know he started his own cartel, used American assistance money to help recruit high-ranking members of the Venezuelan Army to protect his dope, and then invited Hezbollah, the Iranian-backed terror group, to help transport it. Then he allowed Russia to—"

"It was a rhetorical question," Mendez grunted. "The point is, we had an agreement, and now that he is making millions of dollars a month in profits, he pretends he doesn't know us."

"So what do you want me to do about it?"

"You are going to go down there and get my money," Mendez ordered.

"And how am I going to do that?"

"I don't care how you do it, just get it done."

Gray had spent six months working on President Mateo. He'd begged, cajoled, and threatened the man, but he wouldn't come around. His last hope came at the tail end of a state dinner when Gray was able to get five minutes of face time with Mateo.

"Sir, Senator Mendez is not happy about the current situation."

"You mean he is not happy that I've decided to stop cutting him in on every oil deal I sign?" Mateo asked.

"He considers this a breach of your agreement."

"I want you to take a message to Senator Mendez, can you do that?" Mateo asked.

"Yes, sir." Gray nodded.

"Tell him that Venezuela will always be appreciative of his support, but it will be a cold day in hell before he gets another cent from me." He glared before turning and leaving the room.

That night Mendez called for an update. "How did it go?"

"It doesn't appear that President Mateo intends to honor your deal."

"Is that a fact?" Mendez asked, the anger in his voice clear beneath his Southern drawl. "Just what did he say?"

"He said that he appreciates all of your support, but . . ." Gray trailed off, trying to think of a way to soften the president's words.

"Spit it out, Jefferson."

"He said it would be a cold day in hell before you got another cent out of him."

There was silence on the other end of the line, and

Gray knew the senator was considering his options. Mendez and his cronies on the Senate Actions Committee had a sweet deal in Venezuela and had made enough money off of President Mateo to ensure their children's children didn't have to worry about a job. But Gray wasn't dumb enough to think this was all about money.

This was about power, and Gray knew that his boss would eat a bullet before he went back to his peers and told them that a Third World president had just told him to fuck off.

"Well, that dog's not going to hunt, Jefferson," the man finally said.

"What do you want me to do?"

"Seems to me that if President Mateo doesn't want to honor our deal, you need to find someone who will."

"You are talking about regime change," Gray said.

"Call it what you want, just get it done," Mendez said before hanging up.

Gray had used every dirty trick in the book—falsified documents, faked assets, and massaged intel—all to make it look as though Mateo was working with the Russians. Once he had the material set, he kicked it up the chain.

He didn't know exactly where Mendez would send the information, but he knew the outcome, which was why Gray was the only man in Venezuela *not* surprised when the word got out that President Diego Mateo had been assassinated.

He'd overthrown a government, brought General Díaz to power—and all he got was a bullshit title and a ten percent bump in pay.

Now you are about to lose it all.

Gray was still considering what to do when the satphone rang.

"Black, where the *fuck* have you been?" he demanded.

14

Like everyone else in Treadstone, Hayes had heard about the operative who'd taken a bullet to the head and lost his memory. The problem for Hayes was that two years after his last operation, *his* memories were getting clearer by the day. A fact that made him wonder if not being able to *remember* made life easier than not being able to *forget*.

All the fights, and the lies. The countless apologies and unsaid words that filled up the space between them with everything he *cannot* say.

It seemed that when he was gone Hayes was dreaming of home, only to realize, when he got there, that he was a stranger in his own house.

That was what Treadstone did to a man. Kept him

running from one shithole country to the next. Always looking over your shoulder, never knowing if you were blown. If the man standing on the corner with the phone in his hand was a lookout or just talking to his wife.

It wasn't long before Hayes was seeing enemies everywhere, even at home. He found himself running surveillance-detection routes on the way to the grocery store.

Hayes did his best to hide what he was doing from Annabelle, but trying to run countersurveillance and pay attention while she told him why she'd bought the red flats instead of the blue ones at Bloomingdale's proved harder than he imagined.

Always have an out. It was the first thing they'd taught him at Treadstone, and the words echoed in his head as Hayes drove north toward Oak Harbor.

He had gone into every operation thinking that he was already burned. That the enemy knew he was coming, already had his safe house, his commo, resupply, and face. He carried his operational security over to his personal life, so much so that Annabelle used to joke that she'd married the most cautious man in the world. That caution turned into downright paranoia when his son, Jack, was born.

There was something about holding his son in his arms—seeing how defenseless he was—that fired up the protector in Hayes. *Jack. The flight. Damn it.*

He parked the truck behind the storage lot and

walked the chain-link until he found a hole behind a bush. Hayes ducked through, followed the runoff ditch that ran under the overpass. The sounds of the cars drifted down to the concrete with the rush of wind through a canyon.

People going on with their lives with no idea what was happening in the world. *It's the American way,* his old team sergeant had said after they rotated home from Afghanistan. "World War Two affected everyone; this shit has been going on so long that they just pretend it doesn't exist."

The sight of the rusted orange Conex box nestled behind the pylons brought his attention back to the task at hand. He'd found the box when the city was working on the drainage, before they put up the fence. It was the perfect location—invisible from the road but close enough to a junction box that Hayes had been able to pigtail into the power grid.

He lowered himself into a crouch and checked to see if the folded section of 3x5 card was still stuffed in the crack of the door. Then he checked the lock. They were simple anti-intrusion devices. The fact that it was still there, combined with the dab of wax he'd melted over the keyhole, told him that no one had disturbed the box.

He pushed the key through the wax, stepped inside, and tugged the brass chain connected to the bare bulb hanging from the ceiling. Yellow light filled the interior of the box and glinted off the windshield of a late-model Volvo station wagon.

The first order of business was to get dry. He stripped out of his wet clothes and shoved them into a black contractor's bag with his wallet and identification. Hayes checked the patch job and saw that the wound had stopped bleeding, but the fact that the exposed skin was hot to the touch had him worried about infection.

He knew that he had to have the gunshot wound looked at, but before venturing out into public he had to do something about the way he looked.

Hayes went to the safe and spun his combination into the dial and opened the door. The interior was neatly divided and contained everything Hayes needed to slip back into his old life. The left side was sectioned off for rifles and pistols, the shelves filled with ammo, suppressors, and extra magazines.

Hayes ignored the weapons and pulled a deck of passports from the shelf on the right. He chose a Canadian passport, took the corresponding driver's license and credit card clipped to the cover, and flipped to the picture at the front of the passport.

"Peter Kane," he said, reading the name printed below the black-haired version of himself. Still holding the passport, Hayes bent to the bottom shelf and retrieved the Arc'teryx duffel and carried it to the worktable. The duffel was his "go bag," and besides the papers, it contained everything Hayes needed to sustain him for seventy-two hours. He dressed quickly in fresh boxers, wool socks, jeans, and a pair of Asolo hiking boots. Instead of a shirt, Hayes grabbed the faded waxed canvas toiletry bag, undid the clasp, and laid the contents on the table.

Changing your identity was one of the foundations of tradecraft, which was why Treadstone operatives received extensive training in special-effects makeup.

In the field, you had to use what you had, and while the techniques weren't particularly high-tech, the change was still effective. The first thing Hayes had to do was change his hair. He plugged in the electric hair clipper, chose a low guard, and bent his head over the contractor's bag.

The devil was in the details, and Hayes needed his hair short enough to match the passport photo, but not so short that it drew attention to his white scalp. He took his time, and when he was satisfied with the results, he shaved off his beard.

Using concealer, Hayes masked the bruises that covered his face and then added a bronzer to darken his skin. Finally he pulled on a pair of latex gloves, opened a bottle of hair dye, and worked the product in with his fingers.

According to the instructions on the box, he had to wait ten minutes for the dye to dry. *Might as well get this over with,* he thought, taking a laptop box from the safe.

The computer was air-gapped, which meant that it had never been connected to the Internet and was therefore impossible to trace back to Hayes. He plugged it into the wall, and while it booted up, Hayes wondered what in the hell he was going to say to Annabelle.

Pretty sure "I was doing fine until someone tried to kill me" ain't going to work.

When it was ready, he double-clicked the Internet Explorer icon and logged in to his Gmail account. He was still trying to think of the right words when he saw the bolded, unread message in his inbox.

His first thought was that Annabelle had beaten him to the punch. *I bet this is going to be a sweet little note,* he thought, trying to laugh off the knot of dread cinching his stomach.

But he forgot all about the nerves when he saw the sender of the email.

Nick Ford?

The name took him back to the shooter who'd attacked him at the Smith house. *Just another* pendejo, *like Ford.*

When he looked at the subject line, his heart stopped.

He opened the email, but there was just a hyperlink to an encrypted email server, and Hayes couldn't see the message without the encryption key. In a normal situation, he and Ford would have shared a key with each other so they could send and receive encrypted emails, but Ford had clearly sent this out of desperation, or didn't have time or a way to get Hayes the key. Staring at the hyperlink, Hayes felt like it was taunting him; he had to find a way to decrypt it, because he knew that what it contained was a life-or-death matter.

Hayes took a deep breath; the subject line had regained his full attention.

By the time you get this I'll be dead

15

PUGET SOUND, WASHINGTON

"What do you mean, gone?" Black asked the tech seated in front of the Toughbook. "Half the fucking county is out there on the water," he said, pointing to the bay, where a tugboat shepherded the wounded ferry back to the dock.

"I've accessed every street camera, cellphone, and security feed from here to Seattle," the tech said, pointing at the screen. "I don't know what else you want me to do."

"I want you to find this asshole," Black shouted, slamming his hand on the table.

"Well, if that is the case, we need a better setup than this," the tech replied.

Black had to admit the converted fishing trawler they

were using as a safe house was not ideal, but after what happened on the ferry, what was left of his team had to stay mobile.

"Why don't you call the boss—tell him what we need?"

"You worry about finding Hayes, let me worry about the rest, got it?" Black said. "I'm going to get some air; you better have something when I come back."

He went out on the deck, his mood as dark as the thunderheads rolling in from the north. Black stared out to sea, his thoughts turning back to the gunfight on the ferry.

His time on the SEAL teams had taught him the value of the after-action reviews, or AAR. The ability to build on what had worked and fix what *had not* was one of the main reasons Special Ops continued to have such a high rate of success in places like Iraq, Afghanistan, and the handful of other shitholes that CNN didn't bother to cover.

An AAR was the one place on a team where rank didn't matter. It didn't matter if it was a training event or the real world, if you fucked up, you were going to hear about it. Black ran it the same way he would if his team had been alive, not flinching from his share of the blame.

Murph was keyed up when he got out. He jumped the gun, made contact with Hayes before the rest of the team had a chance to set up a base of fire . . .

Black's thoughts trailed off, turning to Hayes.

He'd never seen a man react like that. *Even if Murph hadn't jumped the gun, it was like he knew we were there. How is that possible?*

Black had lost men before, and that wasn't what was bothering him. It was the fact that without any intel on Hayes, he had no idea who he was up against. Black glanced down at the satphone, the screen alerting him to five missed calls.

Can't duck him forever, he thought, picking up the phone.

"Black, where the fuck have you been?" Gray demanded.

"I'm sure you've seen the news," Black growled, making no effort to hide the annoyance in his voice.

He'd worked for men like Gray before, men who didn't know the first fucking thing about leading soldiers in combat. They were sycophants. Peacocks in starched cammies and polished boots, whose only job was to make life miserable for the real warriors.

"Was I in *any way* unclear when I told you *not* to go after Hayes?"

"*Enough!*" Black shouted, finally losing his temper. "Don't talk to me like I'm one of your buddies at the Agency, *Gray*. Since this bullshit started in Venezuela, I've done your dirty work and never said a word, but I'm done with that shit. Now, do you want this guy or not?"

There was silence, and when Gray finally spoke his voice was ice cold.

"Yeah, Black, I want him. But the real question is, can you get him?"

Black moved to the rail and gazed out over the sea. The endless white-tipped blue of the water quenched his anger, leaving him feeling tired and old. How the fuck did this happen?

Black remembered the first time Gray had brought up the plan in the bar outside of Caracas.

"What if I told you that in two years, I can make you rich?"

At first, Black thought it was the booze talking; he glanced at the empty bottles that lined the table.

"Rich, huh?" Black said, rolling his eyes.

"I'm serious." Gray leaned in.

"Let me tell you something," Black said, taking a pull from the bottle of La Polar and setting it on the table. "I'm on my tenth deployment, been all over the world. You know what they all have in common?"

"You mean besides the bad food and killing scumbags?" Gray asked.

"Yep."

"No idea." Gray leaned back in his chair. "Why don't you enlighten me."

"There is always one asshole with a get-rich scheme

and it never works out." Black shook his empty bottle at the waiter, who promptly ignored him.

And these sons of bitches wonder why they are so damn poor.

"Tell you what," Gray said, pulling a rectangular bundle wrapped in a white cloth from his assault pack. "How about I go get us a couple more drinks, and while I'm gone, you take a look at this." He got to his feet and placed the bundle in the center of the table.

"It's your nickel," he said.

If anyone else had made the proposition, Black would have left the bundle in the center of the table, taken the free drink, and gone about his day.

But it wasn't.

Just like everyone else at the CIA, he was aware of Gray's reputation and knew the man hadn't shot through the ranks because he was full of shit. There was a reason nine years after leaving the Farm, Gray had his own special access program while his classmates were still zapping camel jockeys with Hellfires: the man got results.

Which is why Black scooped the bundle from the table, placed it in his lap, and pulled back the cloth.

"Holy shit!"

"Still think I'm full of shit?" Gray asked, returning with the drinks.

"Are you serious?" Black demanded.

"*As a fucking heart attack.*" *Gray's expression was grim.* "*So yes or no, are you in?*"

"Black, are you there?" Gray demanded.

"Yeah," he said, feeling his anger ebb. "I'm here."

"Can you get him?"

"If you get the intel I need," Black replied, suddenly feeling exhausted.

"What intel?" Gray demanded. "You have the same security clearance that I do, which means you have access to every database there is."

"How do you know that?" Black asked, not sure where the question came from, but feeling their worth the moment the words tumbled from his lips.

"Here we go with this—"

"No, hear me out," Black said, trying to chase the idea to its logical conclusion. "When I first became a SEAL, we all had to get secret clearances just because of the encryption our radios had. It wasn't until I went to Team 6 and got a top secret that I got my first peek behind the curtain."

"What's your point?" Gray huffed.

"My point is that I didn't even know what the fuck a special access program was until after I left the Navy, and I was on the team that took down bin Laden."

"Well, that's kinda the point of a 'need-to-know basis,' don't you think?" Gray quipped.

"Exactly, and right now, all we know is what your buddy Senator Mendez is telling us."

There was silence on the other end of the line, and Black knew he had him.

"Forget everything you think that you know about Hayes for a second," he said. "This guy has a skill set that I've never seen before, and I've been in this game a long time."

"He's good, so what—" Gray interjected.

"No, I'm good," Black said, "Hayes . . . is . . ."

"He's what?"

"Look, I don't know what the hell he is, but I can promise you one thing, guys like that aren't born, they're made, which means he is in a database somewhere. A database we don't have access to."

"So what do you want me to do about it?"

"Well, that's up to you, but if it were me, I'd walk into Mendez's office, put a 9-millimeter to his head, and tell him to give me the access I needed, or I'd empty his brain on that five-thousand-dollar desk of his."

"You'll have it by the end of the day," Gray said before hanging up.

16

WHIDBEY ISLAND, WASHINGTON

Hayes pulled a jacket on, shoved his papers into his back pocket and the "go bag" into the truck. He grabbed a Smith & Wesson .38 in an ankle holster from the safe and strapped it above the hiking boot. After making sure the retention band held the pistol tightly in place, he grabbed a Glock 19 from the shelf, racked a round into the chamber, and then threw the Conex doors wide.

Five minutes later he exited the gravel service drive and turned onto State Highway 525. He drove north for an hour, turned east on Quarry Road, and followed the hardpan until he came to a gravel drive that wound through the pines. Hayes cut the engine and eased the door shut before making his way to a rusted fence with a FORGET DOG—BEWARE OF OWNER sign attached to the chain-link.

Good ol' Deano, he thought.

This sign was a joke. A gag gift he'd given Deano after the five-thousand-dollar Doberman he'd bought to guard the house turned out to be scared of its own shadow.

Hayes threw his leg over the top of the fence and dropped lightly into the yard. Once on the other side, he offered a light whistle and called to the timid guard dog.

"Scout, come here, girl."

Nothing. *Must be inside.*

He moved through the trees and into an open area where a wood-framed cabin sat behind a low stone wall. Hayes was five feet from the porch when he heard the light press of paws against the pine needles behind him.

"There you are."

Hayes turned with a smile, but instead of the cowardly Doberman, he was greeted by the low growl of a Malinois.

"You're not Scout," he said, taking a step back—wondering if he could make it to the porch. The Malinois flinched at the movement, and its growl deepened from ominous to downright threatening.

According to the training manuals, the best way to thwart a dog attack was to make yourself look large and threatening. Hayes raised his arms over his head, stood up on his tiptoes, and let out a growl of his own.

He saw laughter in the dog's eyes followed by a flash of teeth and the quiver of muscles.

Shoot the dog.

"Deano!" he yelled over his shoulder. "Deano, come get your damn dog!"

There was no response.

Hayes had seen the Malinois in action in both Iraq and Afghanistan and knew he didn't have a chance in hell of outrunning the dog. "*Deano!*" he yelled again, the plaintive tone in his voice echoing off the trees.

He didn't want to shoot the dog, but at the same time a trip to the ER for a dog bite wasn't on his agenda, either, and Hayes eased his hand toward the pistol at his waist when he heard the squeak of hinges followed by the rack of a shotgun.

"Mister, you picked the wrong house."

"Deano, thank God, now call off your dog."

"Hayes . . . is that you?"

"Yeah, it's me. But seriously, call off this fur missile before it rips out my throat."

"Ajax, *plaats*," Deano ordered in Dutch.

The Malinois gave Hayes a parting snarl before bounding past, and he gave it another second before turning to the porch.

"What the hell happened to you?"

"Someone tried to kill me."

Deano nodded like it was a perfectly acceptable answer and stepped closer. "Well, let's get you patched up," he said, opening the door. "Martha, get the gunshot kit."

A middle-aged woman with kind eyes and long gray hair appeared from the kitchen, wiping her hands on the front of her floral apron.

"Adam, is there something wrong with our front door?" she asked.

"No, ma'am," he said, and grunted.

"Well, c'mon in." Martha waved.

Hayes managed to make it over the threshold before reaching the end of his strength, forcing him to lean against Deano, who helped support him on the way to the bathroom.

"Let's get that shirt off and see what all this fuss is about," Martha ordered, and poured alcohol over her hands before donning a pair of latex gloves.

Hayes shrugged out of his jacket and pulled his shirt over his head as Deano edged toward the door.

"Where are you going?" he asked.

"Man, when she gets into nurse mode, it's best if I—"

"Well, if you're going to go, then go," Martha said.

"On second thought, maybe this wound isn't as bad as I thought," Hayes said, trying to get to his feet.

"Oh, no, you sit your butt down," Martha replied, opening a bottle of pills.

"What are those?"

"Percocet, for the pain."

"No."

"Adam, honey, this is going to hurt . . . a lot."

"I don't care. No drugs."

"Hardheaded ass," she muttered. "Well, suit yourself. I've got a little lidocaine left over."

She took a syringe from the medical bag, cracked an ampule of lidocaine, drew up the dose, and pushed the plunger forward to eject the air bubbles.

In the other room Hayes heard the sound of Deano roughhousing with Ajax.

"That man," she said. "How are Annabelle and little Jack?"

"She left me," Adam said, trying to hold her gaze and failing.

"Girl had more sense than I gave her credit for," she said, injecting the anesthetic into the skin around the wound.

"Martha, leave it," Deano said from the other room.

"No, she's right," Hayes said, watching as Martha irrigated the wound with a saline-and-iodine solution.

"Looks like the bullet went all the way through," she said to herself.

"What was it, 5.56?" Deano asked from the doorway.

"H&K 416," Hayes replied. "Tricked out with all the bells and whistles, and the man behind the trigger knew what he was doing. When I rabbited on them, he let the rest of his team pursue, waited to see how it would shake out."

"Anything about him stand out?" Deano asked.

"He was older than the rest of the guys," Hayes said, remembering the salt-and-pepper goatee. "I'd guess mid-forties, definitely ex-military, with eyes as dark as two pissholes in the snow."

"Adam, please," Martha said, digging into the wound.

The lidocaine had numbed the nerve endings, but the grate of the metal tweezers against bone made him cringe, and Hayes felt himself flinch.

"Will you sit still?" Martha chided him.

"I thought you said it was a pass-through," he said, glaring.

"It is," she replied, eyes narrowed in concentration. "But it looks like there is a piece of bullet fragment lodged against the bone. If I don't get it out, the wound could get infected."

Hayes closed his eyes and retreated into himself, just as he'd been taught. *There is no pain,* he told himself, focusing on his breathing and wishing the exercise worked as well as it had back in Treadstone.

"Almost . . . got it . . . There," Martha said triumphantly.

"Damn," Hayes protested. "Didn't you nurses take an oath about *not* doing harm?" he asked, as the tweezers came out of the cavity with the wet suck of blood and tissue.

"You men are such babies," Martha said, holding up the tweezers.

Hayes forgot all about the pain when he saw the object held in the tweezers.

"What in the hell is that?" he asked aloud.

17

DECEPTION PASS, WASHINGTON

Hayes held up his hand and nodded for Martha to drop the grain of the rice-sized object into his palm.

"Is *that* what you were squalling about?" Deano asked incredulously. "*That* tiny little bit of frag?"

When Hayes first came to Treadstone, the only time you really had to worry about finding fragmented bits of copper or lead inside a wound channel was when you were hit by a pistol round. But that all changed with the bin Laden raid.

According to the 1899 Hague Peace Conference, the basis for the U.S. military's current law of war, it was illegal for any army to use bullets that flattened or expanded. Which is why soldiers deployed to Iraq and Afghanistan were still carrying ball ammunition—bullets with a soft lead core encased in a harder metal jacket. Because of ball ammo's aerodynamic design, a bullet was able to maintain higher velocities, which was great for long-distance target shooting, where higher velocity equaled greater distance.

But like many soldiers, Hayes knew high-velocity bullets were worthless against flesh. Which is why the SEALs who went after bin Laden were carrying Black Hills 77-grain hollow points. Once word leaked that SEAL Team 6 had used a hollow point to kill the world's most-wanted man, every ammunition manufacturer in the country started working on "tactical rifle rounds"— bullets that created devastating wound channels on impact.

With the prevalence of expandable bullets, hollow points that expanded on impact, and frangibles that literally disintegrated on contact with tissue, it was common to find bits of copper or chunks of lead in a wound channel.

"This isn't from a bullet, at least not one I've ever seen," Hayes said, rolling the object around in his hand.

"I don't see how you can tell what it is with all that blood on it," Deano said, taking the tweezers from his wife. "Let me clean it off for you."

Before Hayes had a chance to offer a protest, Deano had plucked the object from his palm and turned to the sink.

"You better put your readers on first," Martha chided.

"Woman, please," he said, turning on the water.

Hayes tracked his progress in the mirror, watching Deano place the tweezers under the water long enough to wash the object clean and then hold it up to the light.

"Looks like some kind of polymer," he said. "you know, I *heard* the Agency was working on a polymer bullet . . ."

Hayes watched Deano's face crumble and his eyes drop to the sink, knowing what had happened the moment he heard the gentle *tick* of the sliver hitting the bowl.

"Shit," Dean cursed, his left hand shooting toward the drain.

"You dropped it, didn't you?" Martha demanded. "Didn't I tell you to put on your damn glasses?"

"Whatever it *was*, let's hope it wasn't important," Hayes moaned.

"Don't make such a fuss, it's still in the P-trap," Deano said, dropping to a knee and opening the cabinet beneath the sink.

"Why don't you do something useful, like taking your butt in the kitchen and putting that meat loaf in the oven." Martha frowned.

"But—"

"Unless you want to sew Adam up."

"No, thank you. I've seen *his* stitch jobs," Hayes said.

"That man, I tell you what," Martha said under her

breath once Deano was gone. "He means well, but sometimes . . ."

Five minutes later, she tied off the final suture and pressed a 4x4 bandage over the wound. "Good as new," Martha said, stripping off her gloves. "Now, how about some dinner?"

After dinner Hayes followed Deano across the yard to a small outbuilding with light brown vinyl siding. "This is my man cave. The building came with the house, but I made a few modifications," he said, thunking the steel handle down and tugging the heavy door open.

Hayes paused to let Ajax pad into the room and examined the four-inch-thick door. "You put a blast door on your man cave?"

"Well, I made a *few* modifications," Deano said and shrugged.

Most residential doorframes were four inches wide, but due to the weight of the blast door, its frame was twice as thick. Since the front of the door was flush with the exterior wall, Hayes expected to see some overlap when he stepped inside, but the interior wall was flush with the frame.

"Put in a layer of cinder blocks," Deano said, pulling the door closed behind them. "Never can be too careful."

"This isn't a man cave, Deano, it's a bunker."

The interior was tidy, and the cast of the overhead light off the pine floor and the sand-yellow paint on the walls gave the room a warm, open feel.

"Bunkers don't have sitting rooms," Deano said, nodding toward the couch in front of the coffee table made from an old pallet. "Or an office."

"I didn't know you could read," Hayes said, taking in the floor-to-ceiling bookshelves flanking the sawhorse desk on the other side of the room.

"Came with the house, smartass," Deano said, stepping into the short hallway to his front. "Latrine is in there." He nodded to the door on his right.

"And what is behind door number three?" he asked, while Deano punched a code into the keypad mounted in the center of the metal door.

"My arts-and-crafts room," Deano said and winked.

The locking bars disengaged with a *thunk* and the door swung open on well-oiled hinges.

Between his time in Special Forces and Treadstone, Hayes had seen his share of arms rooms. But nothing prepared him for what lay beyond the door. It was a gun owner's wet dream, and despite himself, Hayes felt his jaw drop.

"Okay, now I'm impressed." Hayes nodded as he walked over to the fully stocked armorer's bench in the near corner.

"You haven't even seen the best part," Deano replied. He flipped a second switch and the ceiling lights blinked to life, illuminating a row of climate-controlled display cases on the far wall.

"Impressed *and* maybe even a bit jealous." Hayes examined the first case and tugged a Springfield SOCOM 16 with a thermal scope from the rack.

The SOCOM was a modern version of the classic M14—the last of America's great battle rifles. The M14 was designed to replace the legendary M1 Garand, and like its illustrious predecessor, it came to be known for its knockdown power, accuracy, and for being heavy as hell.

Springfield fixed the weight problem with the SOCOM 16 by replacing the wood stock with a lighter composite stock and cutting the barrel from twenty-two inches to sixteen. Hayes hadn't thought it possible to improve on perfection, but the feel of the rifle in his hand told him that he was wrong.

"Now, this is a man's gun," Hayes said, dropping the magazine and looking at the ballistic-tipped hollow-points inside.

"You always did have a thing for the classics," Deano said, taking a bottle of rye off the side table, pulling the stopper, and filling two mason jars.

"Call me crazy, but I like it when I shoot someone and they stay down," Hayes replied, rocking the magazine home and returning the rifle to the shelf.

"This ought to take the edge off," Deano said, passing him a drink.

"Thanks, brother." Hayes took a slow sip from the drink. "Speaking of edges, did you ever have any side effects when you were in?"

"Well, there was the fucking thirst. Back then we called it the beast. Damn near drove me crazy the first couple of times."

"I know the feeling," Hayes said. "What about the nightmares? You still dream about it?"

"Not really."

"No nightmares at all?" Hayes asked, reaching down and scratching the dog's ear.

"It was different when I went through. I was a Gen-2."

"Gen-2?"

"Yeah, Gen-2. It was the only thing written on the vials."

"I'm not following you."

"You know how Treadstone was started, right?"

"Yeah, during Vietnam."

"Yep, well, what they don't tell you is that there isn't a manual out there on how to fuck up a man's brain so you can turn him into an assassin. They were pretty much figuring it out as they went along. Back when I came through, the doctors hadn't figured out *half* the shit that they used on you guys."

"So how did they do it?"

"Drugs, mostly. Subdermal applications of God knows what. After a few rounds you didn't feel anything but rage. They told you to go kill someone and you did it; when you came back, they gave you another shot, and you'd forget all about it. Those were the easy days, but that all changed during the Cold War, when they started using us as rat catchers."

"I've never heard of a rat catcher," Hayes admitted.

"It's what British Intelligence used to call their spy hunters. Any idea what the life expectancy of an American operating in Soviet Russia was in the eighties?"

Hayes shook his head.

"Not long. Even with the chems."

"Chems?"

"CNS stimulants, old tech. We used to carry this little pill case around our necks. Green pill for go, blue for stop. The blues were supposed to help us deal with stress, but . . . shit, I haven't talked about this in years."

"Did they help?"

"Naw. Even with the blues, the stress got so bad that some of the guys started eating their guns. I'm going to be honest, I just couldn't take it. The nightmares, taking one pill to keep you up, another one to bring you down. So I just said fuck it."

"The entire time I was in, I don't think I ever heard anyone talk about the life expectancy of an operative," Hayes said.

"You were a smart kid, getting out when you did, because on a long enough timeline we all end up at zero."

It didn't feel like a win to Hayes. Treadstone had taken everything.

"The VA had this thing—memory removal trials up at U of W."

"Sounds like some heavy shit," Deano said, pausing for a moment before getting to the subject at hand. "So what happened today?"

"I got an email from Ford," Hayes began. "It's encrypted, so all I could read was the subject line."

"What did it say?"

"It said, 'By the time you get this I'll be dead.'"

18

Felix Black backed the Dodge Challenger into the parking spot outside Denny's and cut the engine. He reached into his pocket and pulled out a silver disk about the size of a can of dip. Holding the base firmly in the palm of his hand, Black twisted the top section clockwise, ignoring the red safety seal that warned users not to exceed two doses per twelve-hour period.

He was exhausted. Worn thin from the past thirty-two hours, and at forty-three, Black knew his days of running and gunning without a little help were long gone. That's where the device in his hand came into play.

The single-serving amphetamine inhalers were the latest in a long line of battlefield innovations designed and manufactured by the Defense Advanced Research Projects Agency, or DARPA. The inhalers were designed to replace the old-school go pills that had gotten Black and most of his teammates through Iraq and Afghanistan.

The instant upper had been distributed to Special Operations Command six months ago, and the reviews from downrange were glowing. Not only did the instant release get into the bloodstream faster, but it lasted longer.

However, it had already been recalled because, like Black, most hard-charging Spec Ops soldiers subscribed to the P-for-plenty philosophy of life and there had already been three reported heart attacks in Africa.

But that didn't stop Black, and as soon as the spring locked into place and the dispense button on the side of the inhaler snapped into position, he brought the inhaler to his lips and sucked the contents into his lungs.

The IR formula worked as advertised, and a moment later Black felt the worrisome offbeat flutter in his heart followed by cold sweats—two common side effects of too much speed.

Black knew what he was doing to his body wasn't healthy, but calling time-out wasn't an option, and if he failed again, he knew that he'd have eternity to rest.

You want to live forever? he asked himself, scanning the parking lot outside the diner.

It was only 1500 hours, but the lot was already

starting to fill up with seniors looking to eat an early dinner so they could be back in front of the TV before *Judge Judy* came on. Black watched a Cadillac DeVille whip into the lot, the blue hair behind the wheel steadily puffing on a Virginia Slim as she trolled for an empty spot.

From his position, Black could see plenty of open spots on the back row, but apparently the woman wasn't a fan of walking and was hellbent on fitting her Caddy in the minuscule space between a Dodge Caravan and a Buick LeSabre. She might have made it, except that the Buick had come in at an angle and the back tire was hanging over the white line.

Not going to make it, Black thought.

But the woman disagreed and cut the wheel hard to the left and inched forward until Black heard the screech of a collision. "Told ya," he said aloud, expecting the woman to realize that she'd hit the Buick and back up.

Instead, she goosed the accelerator and used the Caddy to bulldoze the Buick back over the line, centered her car in the spot, and parked like nothing had happened.

That's an impressive display of not giving a shit, he thought, tossing the expended inhaler onto the floorboard with the rest of the empties.

When he looked up, he noticed a black Audi pulling into the lot. A man in a blue shirt and glasses got out and headed inside. Black waited for him to be escorted into the dining room before getting out and heading inside.

The interior of the restaurant looked like every other Denny's Black had ever been in—the same puke-green carpet, grease-stained wallpaper, and hazy windows. The air smelled of superheated butter, day-old grease, and burnt coffee.

A girl with bleached-blond hair and too much makeup was slumped over the hostess station, red-rimmed eyes glued to the cellphone in her hand.

"Help you?" she asked without looking up.

"Restroom?" Black asked.

"Back thataways, but it's for paying customers only."

"Good to know," he said, heading in the direction she'd nodded.

He'd learned long ago to never walk into a place without knowing how to get out. It was a habit that had saved his life more than once. Black passed the emergency exit and made a note that it was wired to an alarm, before heading into the bathroom.

The floor was slick from either grease or oil, which made his shoes slip. He checked for a window, and after seeing there wasn't one, went back through the dining room, passing the hostess, who still hadn't looked up from her phone.

In the rear of the diner, David Rogers sat with his back against the wall, pretending to read the paper. In his blue button-down and gold-rimmed glasses he looked like an accountant, but Black knew better. David Rogers had been a legend at the NSA and helped design most of the signal intercept platforms the Agency used to combat the War on Terror before he got tired of his bullshit salary and entered the private sector.

"Felix," he said with a nod. "You look like shit."

"Been a shitty day," Black said, taking a seat.

"Can I get you anything?" the waitress asked.

"Just a coffee," Black said.

Neither man spoke until she returned with his coffee.

"I don't want to come across as rude, but I am kind of in a hurry," Black said, ignoring the coffee. He reached into his coat pocket, pulled out a thick yellow envelope, and laid it in the center of Rogers's open newspaper.

Rogers deftly closed the page over the envelope and pulled it into his lap. "Sugar packet holder," he said, nodding to the plastic container near Black's elbow.

He pulled it over, and nestled between the blue packets of Equal and yellow packets of Splenda was a thumb drive with a sliver of paper rubber-banded around it.

Black plucked the drive from the container and dropped it into his shirt pocket.

"Felix, if it was anyone else, I wouldn't say a word. But you and I go back, what, ten years?"

"Twelve," Black answered. "What's your point?"

"Twelve years and I've never given advice that you didn't *ask* for."

"David, cut the foreplay and just say what you got to say."

"Update your will before you take this guy on."

"Good to know," he said, getting to his feet.

Back in the Challenger, Black took the laptop off the passenger seat, stuck the drive in the USB port, and typed in the passcode printed on the sheet of paper.

```
>>>>CIA Remote Portal
_Login ID
>>>>Connection Established_
Query: Hayes, Adam

1 match-
Programs_TREADSTONE/BlackBriar
```

Well, that explains things.

He looked down at the note and typed in the words written in black ink: location ping. A moment later a satellite image popped up, the crosshairs centered on a blue dot near Deception Pass.

"Got you."

19

DECEPTION PASS, WASHINGTON

Jesus, Adam, what did Nicky get into?" Deano demanded.

"I have no idea, that's why I was hoping you could break the encryption."

"Shit," Deano said, lowering his voice, his eyes ticking toward the wall that faced the house. "If Martha found out . . . You know what she thinks about this Treadstone shit."

"Deano, I hate that I even have to ask, but whatever Ford sent is the reason they are trying to kill me."

"Damn it," Deano said, getting to his feet. "Go on and log in, I'll see what I can do."

"You sure?" Hayes asked.

"Yeah, I'm sure. Just got to find my damn readers

first. And you might want to put on a pot of coffee, 'cause I'm not as fast as I used to be."

Hayes logged in to his email and then walked over to the coffeepot in the corner of the room.

"Coffee is in the cabinet. Got a few bottles of water in that fridge over there," Deano said, frowning at the screen.

Hayes got the coffee started and sat down on the couch to wait. He didn't realize how tired he was until he sank back into the couch.

Just going to close my eyes for a second, he thought.

Hayes slithered out of the mangrove swamp and through the tall grass that lined the shore. His fatigues were torn from his time in the swamp, and stained black from the mud in the Orinoco River. The insects buzzed around his head, drawn to the sweat cutting white rivulets through the camo paint smeared across his face.

The swamp had taken its toll and Hayes was exhausted. He'd run out of food the night before, and his eyes burned from lack of sleep. But he forced himself to keep moving. At the top of the hill, Hayes paused and glanced over his shoulder. Even through the emerald-green hue of the night vision, there was no hiding that it was rough country. Desolate and unforgiving. The last place a sane man would choose to visit.

But quitting wasn't a choice. Free will wasn't exactly an attribute Treadstone cultivated in their operatives. They were in the complete-the-mission-or-die-trying business.

The mission had been fucked from the beginning. Infil routes covered, the safe house was blown like they knew he was coming.

There was a leak, but where and, more important, why?

He'd spent the last three days tracking the convoy carrying his target. Sleep was out of the question. Even in the swamps, there were patrols—men looking for the American sent to kill the colonel.

He was exhausted, and his body had taken a beating. The skin on his neck and arms was covered in mosquito bites, and the puckered half-moons marked where he'd cut the leeches from his skin.

But he was alive, and there was still a mission to complete.

Hayes shrugged out of the pack, thumbed the cover from the CamelBak's bite valve, and plugged it in the corner of his mouth. He took a long pull, the water bitter from the iodine tab he'd used to purify it.

But it was wet, and that was all he cared about.

When he'd drunk his fill, Hayes pulled the night-vision binoculars from the pack and trained them toward the road. The distant yellow of headlights alerted him that his prey had arrived. Hayes watched the line of dark green trucks bounce over the muddy road. The lead vehicle stopped at the gate and a soldier got out, an AK-47 slung low over his chest.

The soldier unlocked the gate and motioned the convoy forward. Hayes shifted his attention to the middle truck, watched it stop in front of the house with the white columns. The door swung open and his breath caught in his chest as his target stepped out of the car.

"Got you," he said to himself.

"Hey, Adam—"

Hayes felt something grab his shoulder. *A hand*, his mind told him. He grabbed it and twisted, ignoring the star cluster of pain through his head, left hand reaching for the pistol.

"Easy, little brother," Deano said. "You were having a nightmare."

Hayes checked his watch. It was midnight; he had slept for four hours, which explained the dried-out burn in the back of his throat.

"Slept longer than I expected." He coughed.

"How are you feeling?" Deano asked, limping around the desk and bending down to open the small fridge.

"Better than I hoped. Martha knows her stuff," he said, testing the range of motion in the arm.

"She should," Deano said, retrieving a bottle of water and tossing it to Hayes. "Hell, she worked in the emergency room at Ryder Trauma Center for seven years."

"The ER in Miami?" Hayes asked, twisting the cap from the bottle of water and downing half of the contents in one gulp.

Nothing had ever tasted that good.

"Yes, sir—same hospital they send the Special Forces medics to to get their training," Deano said, crossing to the printer next to the computer.

"Martha's a miracle worker," Hayes gasped when he finally came up for air.

"She's not the only one." Deano beamed, plucking three pages from the tray and holding them up for Hayes's inspection.

"Wait . . . *you* cracked it?" Hayes asked, jumping to his feet, eyes locked on the photos in Deano's hand.

"Oh, yeah, and let me tell you—"

Before Deano could finish, Ajax leapt from his bed and rushed to the door, an ominous growl emanating from deep inside his chest.

20

DECEPTION PASS, WASHINGTON

Felix Black turned off State Highway 525 and drove east, slowing to let the silver panel van carrying the Strike Team catch up. He followed the road for half a mile, cut the lights, and eased the car onto the gravel road he'd seen on the satellite map.

He grabbed the H&K 416 from the seat and hopped out of the car, motioning for the van to pull deeper into the trees. When it stopped, Black pulled open the door and climbed inside.

No one spoke in the cargo compartment. The only sounds were the metallic snaps of magazines being shoved into rifles and the thump of their bolts slamming bullets into chambers. Felix Black had already briefed the Strike Team that had flown in from Langley, told them what kind of man they were going after, but he wanted to make sure there was no confusion.

"Listen up," he hissed.

The men stopped what they were doing, and all eyes turned toward him.

"You guys are the best in the business; that's why you're here. But I want you to forget everything you *think* you know. In the past thirty-two hours, our target has killed five of my men—guys who'd been there, done that, and got the T-shirt."

He paused, let his words sink in before continuing with the brief.

"This is a straight kill mission and we are weapons-free as soon as we step out of this van. Do you understand?"

The men nodded.

"I am going to give you one piece of advice. If you see anything inside that fence *not* marked with an IR beacon, you kill it. Because if you don't, Adam Hayes will put you in a box."

Black pulled his night-vision goggles over his eyes, grabbed his H&K 416, and opened the back door. He waited for the rest of the team to form up around him, then they crept east toward the fence line, stopping short to let the breacher cut a hole in the chain-link.

"Let's get those machine-gunners on the flanks," Black ordered.

The two M240 Bravo gunners moved out to the left and to the right to set up their positions. Black took a knee next to a bush and tugged a ruggedized Android tablet from the pouch attached to his plate carrier.

"We're set," the gunners announced over the radio.

"Roger that, standby," Black replied.

He depressed the button on the corner of the device and the screen flashed to life. The startup message announced `kilswitch v-2`, followed by a satellite overlay of the target area.

When Black joined the SEALs in 1994, GPS units weighed thirty pounds. Since they were too heavy to be practical in the field, he learned to call in air strikes with a map and compass. That changed in the early 2000s, when civilians were finally allowed unrestricted access to the military satellites.

In 2001, when Black bought his first Garmin eTrex for two hundred dollars, the unit was the size of a remote control and ran on AA batteries, which made it light enough to carry in his pocket. Black took it with him to Afghanistan and it turned out to be a game changer. Not only was it light and resilient, the Garmin was capable of pinpointing a location within one meter.

Accuracy that allowed him to bomb the Taliban into submission.

At the time Black thought it was the greatest innovation in modern warfare, but the Garmin had nothing on the Kilswitch. He slid the stylus from its holder and tapped on the blue dot that marked Hayes's location in the house.

Prosecute this target?

Black opened the Persistent Close Air Support window. The onboard GPS system automatically established an uplink, and a moment later the Available Air Assets window was auto-populated with two columns: Armed and Unarmed.

Let's see if Gray came through, Black thought, as he tapped the Armed block and waited for the spinning hourglass on the screen.

```
1 Asset: General Atomics MQ-9 Reaper
Armed x2 Hellfire
Execute: Y/N
```

"You guys might want to grab some cover," he said over the radio before tapping the Y with the stylus.

It took less than a second for the signal to travel from the unit to the CIA-operated General Atomics MQ-9 Reaper loitering 10,000 feet overhead. The UAV received the targeting package, but before processing the strike the onboard security system sent an encrypted authorization request back to Langley.

In less than five seconds the drone had received a response. Strike Authorization Confirmed.

The Reaper banked to the left, its onboard navigation system guiding it into a sweeping turn that brought it online with the uploaded coordinates. Twelve miles from the target, the Reaper leveled off, and the targeting system activated the laser that would guide the AGM-114K to the target.

On the ground, Black watched the progress on the screen.

```
Laser Armed . . . Master Arm Hot . . .
Target Lock . . . READY TO ENGAGE
```

He tapped the fire button and the word RIFLE flashed on the screen, the signal that the Reaper had launched the hundred-pound Hellfire.

```
Impact In 10 . . . 9 . . . 8 . . . 7
```

The missile was on its way and Black turned his attention to the target building. *See you in hell, motherfucker.*

21

DECEPTION PASS, WASHINGTON

Ajax stood at the door of Deano's outbuilding, hackles bristling down his neck.

"Ajax, *foei*"—no.

But the dog ignored him and continued to growl at the door.

"You think something's out there, well, let's take a look," he said, fingers flashing over the keyboard. "This security system was a birthday present from Martha. State of the art. It covers both the cabin and this building."

But Hayes wasn't listening; a distant, familiar sound had caught his attention. "You hear that?" he asked, stepping closer to the door. Praying that it had just been the wind or a figment of his imagination, because the only other explanation didn't make any sense.

"Oh, shit, we got zips in the wire," Deano shouted, running toward the arms room. He reappeared a moment later with the SOCOM 16. "These sons of bitches picked the wrong *fucking* house," he said, heading for the blast door.

"Deano, wait," Hayes said, trying to cut him off, but there was murder in the man's eyes, and he shoved Hayes out of the way, threw the latch on the blast door, and stepped outside.

Hayes had regained his balance and turned to follow Deano when he heard the freight-train scream of a supersonic object cutting through the air. A sound pregnant with the promise of imminent death.

He opened his mouth in warning, but his words were lost beneath the earth-shattering rumble of the Hellfire slamming through the roof of the cabin and detonating.

Time stopped on a dime and Hayes watched in horror as the eighteen-pound thermobaric warhead detonated, the sudden change in pressure creating a vacuum inside the enclosed space. Sucking the cabin walls in on themselves. The pressure building until it reached critical mass and then *ba-boooom*.

The second detonation sent a wave of superheated gas and flame rolling outward from the point of impact. It vaporized the drywall, sheared through the pipes and the studs like a scalpel through flesh before fireballing through the exterior wall of the cabin.

"Martha!" Deano screamed, and then the shock wave punted him across the yard and threw him into the side of the outbuilding.

Hayes was lifted off his feet and slammed into the wall. The impact punched the air from his lungs, and he fell to the floor, gasping for breath—choking on the caustic black smoke that filled his lungs and scalded his eyes.

There was no doubt as to what had just happened. The evidence was in every breath—the acrid taste of burnt fuel and explosives telling him someone had called in an air strike on the house.

In an instant the fragment Martha had removed from the wound made sense. *Fuckers put a tracker in me.* But there was no time to worry about that now. The fire had spread from the cabin to this building. The crack and pop of the roof joists overhead warned that he didn't have long before the flames found the support beams and the roof caved in, trapping him in the inferno.

Move.

Hayes crawled along the floor, trying to stay below the thick blanket of smoke that was forcing the breathable air from the room. He lowered his head and moved forward, ignoring the burn of the flaming embers against his exposed flesh, following the gentle caress of the cool air wafting in through the open door.

I'm not dying here.

Hayes made it outside and tried to take a breath, but his lungs recoiled from the scorching air. He was overcome with a fit of coughing that left him with the copper taste of blood at the back of his throat. Hayes crawled to the well halfway between the smoldering cabin and the outbuilding.

His hands closed around the pump, and he primed it, putting his face underneath the spigot as he pumped. The water gushed over his face, clearing the cinders and dust from his eyes, quenching the burn on his bare skin.

God, that feels good.

Hayes finally could see what was happening around him, and he knew it was a scene he would never forget.

Everything within a twenty-foot radius of the blast zone was on fire. The pine trees burned like roman candles in the night, and the heat from the flames caused the sap in the trunks to boil. Expanded until they exploded with the crack of a high-powered rifle.

Ten feet to his right, Hayes saw Deano lying motionless against a tree, his neck bent grotesquely to one side, blood trickling from his nose, the sling of the SOCOM 16 still wrapped around his forearm.

Hayes rushed to his side, ignoring the voice in his head warning him that the fight wasn't over.

Get down, it ordered.

But the warning fell on deaf ears.

Hayes knelt beside his friend, knowing in an instant that he and Martha were dead, and that it was *his fault*.

"I never should have come here," he whispered. "I'm sorry."

He wanted to say more, but his grieving was cut short by a shout in the distance, followed by the unmistakable *brrrraaaaaaap* of a machine gun opening up.

Hayes threw himself to the ground a moment before a coil of tracers came lashing through the flaming trees. The bullets snapped overhead, cracking through the air like a bullwhip. The last time Hayes had been under machine-gun fire was in Afghanistan, in the Helmand River Valley—Taliban country.

His team was there to assist the Afghan Army in the Taliban from their opium-rich stronghold.

They were crossing a poppy field, the team sergeant on point, eyes open for any Taliban ambush, and Hayes bringing up the rear, watching their so-called Afghani allies in case any of them wanted to score a few points by killing an American.

Hayes had just turned to check their six when a Taliban fighter armed with a Soviet-made PKM opened up on the formation. He remembered the fear that came from being caught out in the open. Pinned down, the bullets chewing up the earth in front of his face, kicking dirt into his eyes.

It took a special kind of man to lie there and let someone shoot at you. To ignore the voice in the back of your head screaming at you to get up and run. At the time he'd thought self-preservation was the most powerful of all man's instincts and the desire to live for just one more minute was the most compelling force in the world.

But lying there in the dirt, eighteen months after losing everything he'd ever cared about, Hayes realized the lesson he'd learned in Afghanistan was wrong. *Vengeance was the most powerful instinct.*

22

DECEPTION PASS, WASHINGTON

Crouched safely behind a tree one hundred yards north of the target building, Felix Black was well out of the blast zone. Black was staring at the cabin when the Hellfire flashed into view. He saw it for only a second, the brief flicker of the Hellfire's rocket motor that looked yellow through his night-vision goggles.

Then the antitank missile hit the target and exploded, the flash of light flaring his night vision, leaving him temporarily blind. He rotated the goggles up and out of the way, blinked his eyes at the wall of orange and black smoke that washed over the scene. Despite the distance from the blast radius, he felt the concussion in his chest. A backhand of pressure across the front of his plate carrier.

"Keep your head down," he yelled a moment before he heard the rush of shrapnel cutting through the trees.

No one could survive that, he thought, savoring the raging inferno with his naked eye.

But the satisfied smile had no sooner creased the corner of his lips than Black heard the staccato chatter of the belt-fed machine gun on his left chug to life.

There is no fucking way.

"I've got a runner!" the gunner yelled.

Black followed the orange tracers that marked every fourth round toward their target, but all he could see was the flicker of shadows in the flames. He was about to call cease-fire when the second gunner added a long burst that echoed through the darkness like a hammer against an anvil.

He knew the men were too well trained for sympathetic fire. If they were shooting, it meant they had a target.

Black's hand closed around the hand mike strapped to his chest. "Air One, this is Alpha Six, we have a squirter on the south side of the building."

"Roger that, Alpha Six, I am en route," the pilot responded, his voice calm and distant over the radio.

"Keep his head down!" Black yelled as he got to his feet and ordered the rest of the Strike Team to get in line. He shouldered his H&K 416 and waited for them to form a skirmish line, lowered his night vision, and bounded forward.

He ducked behind a second tree three feet away and scanned for a target. "Set!" he yelled, letting the next man in the team know he was clear to move past him.

The next shooter came in from his left. He dropped behind a pile of rocks, his muzzle pointed toward the target. When Black saw the man's mouth open, he knew he was yelling that he was "set," but the word was drowned out by the whine of the AS350 Eurocopter turbines.

The helo thundered overhead, and the pilot activated the searchlight mounted beneath the tail. The high-intensity SX-16 Nightsun was well named, and with an output of 30,000 lumens, it easily cut through the smoke kicked up by helicopter rotors and turned the night into day.

If Hayes was down there, the helo would find him.

The pilot bent the helo into a tight orbit while the copilot worked the powerful light over the outbuilding.

In his peripheral vision, Black watched the third member of the Strike Team angling for position. The man was three feet short of the stump he was planning to use for cover when his head snapped back and he dropped like a stone.

"Man down!" someone yelled.

"Alpha Six, I've got eyes on the shooter."

"Take him out," Black ordered.

Instead of staying in his orbit, the pilot decided to give his shooter a more stable platform and settled into a hover. Black had warned them *not* to play around with Hayes and couldn't believe it when he saw the sniper lean out of the helo and take his time lining up the shot. "Stand by for shot . . ." the pilot said.

Black keyed his hand mike, trying to tell the pilot that he needed to keep moving, but the radio bleated in his hand. The long tone told him that someone inside the helicopter had their thumb on the transmit button.

In the military they called it hot-miking, and not only could Black not get on the radio, but he and the rest of the team could hear everything being said in the cockpit.

"C'mon, take the shot," the pilot said. "You got my ass hanging out in the breeze here."

"Hold her steady," a second voice replied.

There was a time in Special Operations when men thought that they were safe inside the helicopters that carried them into battle. That changed on October 3, 1993, in the streets of Mogadishu, Somalia.

Black joined the Navy SEALs one year after Operation Gothic Serpent, when the scars from the battle known as Black Hawk Down were still fresh in everyone's mind. The primary lesson learned during that twenty-four-hour firefight—where members from team Ranger fought to recover the bodies from the two Black Hawks that had been shot down—was that a hovering helicopter was an inviting target.

But with someone inside the Eurocopter hot-miking, all Black could do was scream "Get the hell out of there!" and watch the two muzzle flashes blink from the shadows.

The first bullet hit the sniper and he tumbled from the helicopter, still connected by the retention line snapped to the ring inside the cargo hold. In the cockpit, the pilot increased the throttle and jerked the helo out of the line of fire. He overcorrected, pulling the helicopter backward and into the trees, dragging the suspended sniper through the flaming limbs.

"Air One is hit, Air One is hit!" the copilot screamed over the radio, and Black heard the beeping of the alarm bells going off inside the cockpit.

The helo torqued left, the spotlight blinding the Strike Team on the ground. For the second time in five minutes, his night vision was useless, and he flipped the goggles out of the way. Black raised his hand to shade his eyes against the powerful glare, and when his vision returned, the flames from the burning trees fell across the glass of the cockpit, revealing a single hole in the center of the windshield.

Pumped up by adrenaline, the copilot overcorrected and yanked the stick to the rear, and Black watched the tail rotor sideswipe a limb. The helicopter shuddered, veering to the right, the fear in his voice evident over the radio.

"I'm putting her down."

"*Negative!*" Black roared into the radio. "Get that bird *back* in the fucking air and finish the job."

But the man wasn't listening.

The hell with this, Black thought, leaving his position.

"Everyone up," he yelled, grabbing the closest shooter by the backstrap of his plate carrier and yanking him to his feet. "Get a perimeter around that bird," he ordered, shoving the man toward the settling helicopter. "Let's go, let's go."

"On it," a second shooter yelled, as he rolled out of his position on the left flank and started toward the Eurocopter.

Black forced his tired legs into a sprint and ducked his head at the snap of a bullet passing close by. *That fucking Hayes.*

23

DECEPTION PASS, WASHINGTON

The voice in his head screamed for him to get down, but Hayes was no longer in control of his body. Something had broken loose and all of the rage and anger he'd stuffed deep inside of him for the past eighteen months came rushing free.

It rolled out of the depths of his soul and into his veins. A river of fire that tumbled and churned its way to his heart. Turning it into a war drum that beat with one resounding note. A single word that echoed with every beat.

Kill . . . kill . . . kill.

The rage consumed him, left him wanting to eat fire, breathe smoke. Devour the men who'd killed his friend and his wife and tried to destroy *his* life. Hayes lifted the SOCOM 16 to his shoulder and pressed his eye to the Trijicon MK II mounted to the rail. The thermal scope displayed the world in shades of black and white. Objects with ambient temperatures such as rocks and trees showed up dull gray, while the man in full kit, running toward cover, was bright white.

Hayes twisted the knob to max power and the man's face leapt into view. At that moment he ceased to be a human being. He was now a target, an object to be dispatched as efficiently and quickly as possible.

Target: one hundred meters. Wind negligible at this range. Steady sight picture, safety off. Breathe . . . wait for it . . .

Crack.

The rifle bucked against his shoulder, the recoil from the 168-grain Hornady hollow-point leaving the barrel at 2,650 feet per second, driving the muzzle skyward. Hayes shoved his shoulder into the butt stock and slammed the rifle back onto target, ready for a follow-up shot.

But there was no need.

His target was down.

Hayes rolled onto his back and pointed the rifle toward the Eurocopter hovering above him. He was about to put a bullet in the spotlight when he saw a shadow of movement at the open troop door. *Sniper.* Hayes arced the rifle onto the target—*target: twenty-five meters. No time, just put the warhead on the forehead.*

Hayes centered up on the man, fully expecting to feel the burn of a bullet at any moment. He could see the sniper's barrel pointing back at him through the glass. There was no time for fear, or thought, just the action— the one constant that separated the quick from the dead.

Crack.

The bullet dropped the sniper like a lead weight. He dropped the rifle and tumbled headfirst from the troop door. The retention line tethering him to the helo snapped taut, leaving him swinging beneath the Eurocopter like a stone on a string.

Go now, the voice ordered, trying to regain control.

But Hayes wasn't finished, and he shifted the reticle onto the cockpit, his mind working through the challenges of the shot.

If he'd been engaging the pilot in command, or PIC, of an airplane, what the military referred to as a fixed-winged aircraft, Hayes would have targeted the man in the left seat. But as a pilot himself, he knew that in a helo, the PIC sat on the right.

The reason for the change came from the fact that unlike a plane, a helicopter didn't actually fly—it beat the air into submission. To keep a helo steady, especially in hover operations, was a balancing act. One that Hayes's flight instructor at Treadstone compared to "juggling while riding a unicycle on the ice." It required constant adjustments to the *cyclic*, the stick that controlled the altitude and direction of the helicopter.

Due to the fact that a helo was inherently unstable, a good pilot was trained to keep his right hand on the stick anytime the bird was in flight.

Hayes shifted his aim to the right, the thick glass of the Eurocopter's windscreen distorting his target's heat signature. Giving it a fuzzy, spectral quality that reminded Hayes of a cartoon ghost. *Drop the magnification.* His non-firing hand twisted the knob, backing the scope's power to normal.

The sight picture cleared and he placed the reticle on the top of the target sternum. *Lower, in case the glass deflects the bullet.* The entire sequence happened in the blink of an eye, and after Hayes made the minute adjustment to his point of aim, he was ready to fire.

Crack.

The round punched through the windscreen and the glass stripped the copper jacket from the lead core. Hayes kept his eye in the scope, watched the spray of white that marked the moment the lead core slammed into the target's chest. He knew that the lead core had mushroomed on impact, expanded to twice its size, and slowed from 2,500 feet per second to a dead stop in the blink of an eye.

Before the blood had cooled in the air, all of the bullet's kinetic energy had been transferred into a bulging wave of hydrostatic pressure that tore through the pilot's internal organs like a hand grenade dropped into a pool.

Killing was the easy part.

The 240 Bravo machine gun anchoring the attackers' right flank fell silent and Hayes keyed in on the gunner's curse, knowing what had happened without having to be told. He pivoted toward the sound, and through the thermals saw the man up on his knees, trying to clear the jam.

Hayes shot him above the vest, low in the neck, the gushing spray of blood from the carotid telling him that the man had seconds left on this earth. When there were no more targets, Hayes took his eye from the scope and glanced left, toward the fence line where he'd left the Volvo.

The gunner on the left flank was still firing in short, steady bursts. He was firing high, the bullets passing harmlessly above Hayes's head, but the man still had a solid base of fire.

Hayes needed to slip the ambush but knew the moment he moved out of the low ground and made a break for the fence line, the gunner would cut him down.

Shit, where do I go?

The revving turbine of the helo drew his attention skyward, and Hayes looked up in time to see the Eurocopter's tail rotor clip a limb and veer hard to the right. He grasped the situation in an instant, knowing that the copilot had been fighting to regain control of the helo after the pilot was shot and had overcorrected.

Hayes knew the man had two options. He could increase the throttle and try to clear the obstacle or pitch the nose down and land.

But he doesn't know if he damaged the tail rotor or not.

Hayes knew there was only one way the copilot could tell.

He's going to put it down.

It was just a hunch, but right now it was all Hayes had.

24

DECEPTION PASS, WASHINGTON

Hayes burst from cover, angling for the helicopter settling to the ground ten feet in front of him. He knew the bird wouldn't be on the ground long; once the copilot regained control and checked the control surfaces, he would learn what Hayes already knew— the helo was undamaged.

He was five feet from the helicopter when the sniper, still suspended by the retention line, settled to the ground. The man pushed himself to his knees, tore the plate carrier that saved his life from his shoulders, and rubbed both of his hands over his chest.

Hayes knew that without night vision the only way that man could tell if he'd been shot was by smelling the blood on his hands.

Wrong time for a blood sweep, Hayes thought, putting a single round through the side of his head before ducking beneath the spinning rotors.

He was about to jump inside the cargo hold when three silhouettes came running out of the darkness, heading for the open door on the other side. Because of the angle, Hayes's only shot was the man on his far left.

The fact that he was running took a headshot out of the equation, and Hayes knew from the sniper that the Springfield wouldn't punch through his body armor. His only option was to aim low, try for the crease at the bottom of the body armor.

Hayes fired until the bolt locked back; he dumped the Springfield and climbed inside the helo. Without the thermal scope, he knew he'd be firing blind, so instead of engaging, Hayes slipped into the cockpit.

Despite the gunfire, the copilot sat vapor-locked behind the controls, eyes glued to the instrument panel, blood from the dead pilot's chest wound spattered across the right side of his face.

By the time he realized Hayes was inside the helicopter, it was too late. He tried to make a play for the pistol in his shoulder holster, but Hayes grabbed him by the helmet and slammed his head into the metal post, knocking him unconscious. He was trying to strip the copilot from his harness when a pair of rough hands grabbed the back of his shirt and yanked him off-balance.

There was no time to think, only to react. Hayes grabbed for the copilot's pistol and then he was jerked off his feet and slammed backward onto the deck of the cargo hold.

"I've got you now," his attacker yelled, raising his boot and aiming it at Hayes's face.

"Don't think so," he said, leveling the pistol and firing a round through the bottom of the man's boot.

Boom.

The man screamed in pain, his mouth a gaping black O, but Hayes wasn't listening. He twisted onto his side, shoved the barrel against his attacker's left knee, and fired. The bullet pulverized the man's kneecap, sending a spray of tendon and bone spewing from the exit wound.

He dropped like a stone and Hayes scrambled to his knee and ended him with a kill shot to the center of the forehead.

One left.

Hayes was already behind the eight ball when he pivoted to his left, eyes squinting against the darkness. Searching for the man he knew was there but couldn't see.

"Haaaayes!" the man screamed.

At the sound of the voice, Hayes was back on the ferry, watching Deputy Powell beg for his life, unable to stop the man with the goatee from putting a bullet in the police officer's brain.

He managed to get off one shot, knowing that he'd missed the moment the bullet left the barrel, and then the man was all over him.

"Miss me, motherfucker?" he demanded, slamming his helmet down on the bridge of Hayes's nose.

The blow sparked stars in his vision and a flash of blood across his face and into his eyes. "You," Hayes managed, before the man grabbed him by the front of the shirt and blasted the air from his lungs with a knee to the gut.

"The name's Felix Black," the man said, jerking Hayes upright, stretching him out before landing a hammer blow to the face. He caught Hayes square and sent him sprawling into the cockpit.

Hayes bounced off the control panel and fell across the dead pilot, his left arm hooking the stick backward and his hip hitting the throttle at the end of the collective, twisting it to full power.

The helo bounced into the air, but without anyone to shove the foot pedals to the left and counteract the torque of the main rotor, the helo began to spin.

That's not good.

In the back, Black lost his footing and slammed headfirst into the doorframe. He dropped to the floor.

Hayes groaned to his feet and wiped his face across his sleeve, clearing the blood out of his eyes. Outside the canopy the spotlight showed a spinning mass of green leaves and brown trunks. He held on to the stick with his left hand and unclipped the dead pilot from his harness.

Sorry, I'm not sorry, Hayes thought, dumping the pilot unceremoniously out of his seat and climbing in.

The instrument panel was a sea of red warning lights and yellow cautions intermixed with the electronic voice repeating "Altitude—pull up. Altitude—pull up."

Hayes pushed the pedals hard to the left, fighting against gravity and the nauseating spin of the helo. The seconds seemed to stretch into hours as Hayes fought to regain control. A glance at the altimeter showed they were fifty feet above the ground, which wasn't high, considering the hills that dotted the landscape outside the bird.

The rush of air spraying through the bullet holes in the glass wasn't helping, either, and when Hayes wasn't dodging trees, he was wiping the tears from his eyes. Sweat poured down his face, scalding the laceration that adorned the bridge of his nose.

He kicked the pedals to the left and then back to the right, slaloming the Eurocopter through the stand of trees, ignoring the incessant beep of the ground-collision warning that decided to add its voice to the cacophony of chimes and whistles echoing through the cockpit.

"I know, I know," Hayes shouted, catching a glimpse of an open area to his left.

He cut the stick and banked the Eurocopter onto

its side, the blades narrowly missing a stout pine as it thundered into the clearing. Hayes was maneuvering back to level flight and paused to wipe the sweat out of his eyes when the copilot came to with a shout.

"*Mother of God*, we're going to crash!" he screamed, grabbing the controls and yanking the stick in the opposite direction.

"Power lines!" Hayes yelled, catching the glint of the spotlight off the high tension wires that suddenly filled the windscreen.

"We're going to diiiiiiie!" the copilot screamed, letting go of the controls and covering his face with his hands.

"Fuck it. I'm not dying here," Hayes swore, dropping the nose and kicking the pedals to the left. "But it's going to be tiiiiiight," he said, barely inching the rotors beneath the lines.

And then, just as fast as the chaos had begun, they were out of the trees and thundering east over open water.

Hayes's shirt was soaked through with sweat and his muscles burned from the buildup of lactic acid when he settled back into the seat. He looked over at the copilot, who was just now lowering his hands from his face.

"Thanks for all the help, dickhe—" he began.

But before Hayes could finish cussing the man out, Black was at his shoulder.

"We aren't done yet," he said, launching a stiff right

hand that caught Hayes square on the jaw and sent his head smashing into the seat post.

He saw the choke coming and tried to dip his chin, but Black was quick and locked his arm around Hayes's neck and dragged him out of the chair.

"Hold it steady," Black yelled at the copilot, locking the choke in tight. "I've got some trash to throw out."

The pressure of Black's arm against his carotid artery disrupted the blood supply to his brain and his vision started to tunnel at the edges. Hayes knew he had five seconds max before he passed out.

He brought his legs up, planted his feet against the bulkhead, and pushed off as hard as he could. The move caught Black off-balance and he stutter-stepped backward but refused to relax his grip.

Hayes thrashed back and forth, stomped down on Black's feet, tried to butt him with his head, but he couldn't break free.

"You ready to fly?" Black demanded, turning him toward the open left door.

25

It was two a.m. when the black Lincoln town car pulled through the gate of the Washington Executive Airpark, the general aviation airport outside of Clinton, Maryland. In the back seat, it took every ounce of Jefferson Gray's composure to keep the smile off his face when he saw the Gulfstream GV in the hangar.

He waited for the driver to bring the car to a halt and then stepped out, a silver attaché case handcuffed to his wrist. Gray took the stairs two at a time, knowing that he wouldn't be safe until he was out of the United States. He carried the case to the rear of the plane and dropped into one of the oversized seats, loosening the tie that he'd been wearing since landing at eight that morning.

"Can I get you something to drink?" the steward asked.

"Blanton's," Gray said, "make it a double."

While he waited for the drink, his mind slipped back to Mendez's office.

The reception area was formal but warm with deep blue carpet and a pair of matching distressed leather chairs. On the wall to his right a large Texas flag hung over the secretary's mahogany desk.

"Morning, Sarah," Gray said, walking through the door like he owned the place.

"Mr. Gray, uh . . . good morning," Sarah said, her bright Southern accent unable to hide the confused frown that adorned her face. Her brown eyes dropped to the calendar on the desk and Gray knew she was looking to see if he had an appointment.

"The senator is expecting me," Gray lied, passing her desk and heading for the door on the other side.

"Mr. Gray, wait—I have to—"

But it was too late. Gray already had the door open and was stepping inside.

The senator was sprawled out on a leather couch, feet up on the table, eyes glued to the television mounted to the wall.

"Damn it, Sarah, I said that I didn't want to be

disturbed," he barked without taking his eyes from the television.

"Sorry to intrude," Gray said, savoring the confusion on the senator's face when he turned to look at him.

"Gray, wh-what the hell are you doing in D.C.?"

"We have a problem," he said, closing the door behind him.

"A problem?" Mendez quickly regained his composure and jumped to his feet. "Are you out of your fucking mind coming here?"

"Sir, you know I wouldn't break protocol if it wasn't absolutely necessary, but—"

"But what?" Mendez demanded, throwing the remote control on the couch before rounding the coffee table. "What is so urgent that you found it necessary to come to my fucking office?"

Gray knew in Venezuela that he was taking a big risk flying back to D.C. and confronting the senator on his own turf. But it was either that or lose everything he and Vega had been working on.

"It's Adam Hayes."

The name stopped Mendez in his tracks and the look on the senator's face—the flicker of fear in the man's eyes—shattered any doubt Gray had about his choice.

"What about him?"

"The hit team we sent, Hayes neutralized them."

"Christ," Mendez said, turning to the window.

"*Sir, I need to know who this man is. I need to know what you know.*"

Mendez turned from the window, sizing him up, and Gray felt a flicker of uncertainty. You have him on the ropes, but he isn't down yet, *he told himself.*

"*Sir, as you know, Colonel Vega has extensive connections in the intelligence field. It is only a matter of time before he learns that Hayes is still alive, and when that happens, he will go to President Díaz and we will be in the same position that we were before.*"

Gray watched the senator's resolve crumble, the look in the man's eyes telling him that his bluff had hit home.

"*Treadstone,*" Mendez spat out. "*Adam Hayes is from Treadstone.*"

Shit.

Like the rest of the officers who staffed the ranks of covert intelligence, Gray had heard rumors of Treadstone 71 and their modified super assassins. But he'd always believed that the program was a myth, an urban legend like the UFOs out in the Nevada desert.

Mendez must have seen the skepticism on his face because he took a step closer, and when he spoke, his voice was low and urgent.

"*Gray, I need you to listen to me. Treadstone is real. Everything that you've heard, the rumors, the crazy stories about what they do to them, it is all real.*"

"*Th-that's impossible.*"

"Did you really think SEAL Team 6 killed President Mateo and his entire family?"

It doesn't matter who trained Hayes, *Gray thought.* It doesn't even matter if Black can kill him. The only thing that matters is that he slows Hayes down long enough to do what you need to do.

"How do we find him?" Gray asked.

The Gulfstream GV raced down the runway and leapt into the sky. In the back Gray looked out the window and saw the nation's capital lit up for the night. It was a panorama he'd seen hundreds of times from the air. One that evoked the same memories.

Gray's eyes drifted to the 14th Street Bridge—the same road he'd taken the first time he visited D.C. fifteen years ago. He vividly remembered sitting on the steps of the Lincoln Memorial. Seeing the alabaster shine of the Washington Monument towering over the emerald-green grass of the National Mall. Knowing that less than a mile away the most powerful man in the world was sitting in the White House.

It was a potent moment for a wide-eyed boy from Iowa.

Now looking down on the nation's capital for the last time, Gray knew that whatever patriotism the Agency had instilled in him was long gone. His time at the CIA had given him a peek behind the curtain. Shown him that in D.C., the real power lay not with the people but with senators like Mendez. Men who used their office and their secrets not to serve but to amass money and power for themselves.

Gray had used that knowledge to push Mendez into a corner, to bend him to his will, and when push came to shove, the senator had crumbled. The senator had given him everything that he'd asked for—the Treadstone files, access to the tracking program that helped Black locate Hayes, even dispatching a strike team to the West Coast.

For a moment Gray let his thoughts shift to Black. The man had every advantage. He had Hayes's location and a highly skilled tactical team to take him down. By every account, Black should have no problem taking Hayes down. But if even half of what Mendez had said about the Treadstone operatives and their training was true, Gray wondered if it would be enough.

26

KIKET ISLAND, WASHINGTON

Wind whipped in through the open door of the chopper, buffeting Hayes and Black in their deadly embrace.

Hayes had been here before. Locked in a fight where there was no time to think and barely enough time to act. There were no time-outs or breaks, just the knowledge that the only thing separating you from death was one wrong move.

His brain was in panic mode, and the flash of neurons that carried the signals to his extremities had slowed to a crawl. The pounding buzz of his pulse in his ears and the tingle of his facial nerves signaled that he was about to pass out.

He wasn't afraid of dying, but if today *was* his day, Hayes sure as hell wasn't going alone.

By the time Hayes stripped the Glock 19 from the holster his field of view had shrunk to the size of a quarter. Lining up the front and rear sight was out of the question, and the best he could do was point the barrel at the back of the copilot's chair and pull the trigger until the lights went out.

Hayes was aware of the Glock bucking in his hand and the yellow flash of the muzzle blast, but had no idea where the bullets were going or how many times he'd fired. All he knew was that he had to keep shooting, and then the darkness enveloped him.

When he came to, the helo was on its side, the smell of leaking fuel and flash of yellow sparks telling Hayes it had crashed. He grunted to a sitting position and followed the *pat-pat* sound of dripping fluid to the crumpled cockpit.

The back of the seat was riddled with a wide group of bullet holes, and on the other side he saw the copilot's dead body hunched over the controls.

That worked out better than I imagined, he thought, crawling painfully out of the helicopter and dropping to the ground.

Hayes was searching for a landmark when the scratch of metal on stone drew his attention to a gravel path and a pair of boots sticking out of the brush.

Black was on his stomach, dragging himself toward the pistol lying in the roadway. Both of the man's legs were broken, and Hayes suspected at least one compound fracture from the blood slick that marked the man's progress.

Black glanced over his shoulder, and beneath the bloody mask that covered his face, Hayes saw fear in the man's eyes.

Black cursed and redoubled his efforts. He snatched the Sig Sauer pistol off the ground and flipped onto his back with a pained grunt.

"I've got you," Black said, the pistol shaking in his hand.

"Is that a fact?" Hayes asked.

Black grinned and pulled the trigger, the triumph evaporating when the striker snapped on an empty chamber.

"Wow," Hayes said, walking over and dropping the medical kit on the ground before easing himself into a crouch beside the man. He reached over and plucked the empty Sig from Black's hand. "You aren't very good at this, are you?" Hayes asked, tossing the pistol into the darkness.

"Fuck you," Black spat.

"I'm going to level with you," Hayes said, glancing over at the crumpled form of the Eurocopter. "If we were anywhere else in the United States, a helo crash landing in the middle of a field wouldn't go unnoticed, but out here"—he gestured at the wide-open nothing of their surroundings—"out here, though, it might take some time."

"What's your point?"

"My point is," Hayes answered, opening the medical kit and pulling out a nylon tourniquet, "time isn't a commodity you have."

He tore the tourniquet free from the clear package, unrolled the three-inch-wide nylon band, and wrapped it deftly around Black's thigh. Hayes ignored the man's screams of protest, routed the free end through the buckle, and yanked it tight.

Black bit down on the pain, cursing behind gritted teeth as Hayes spun the metal handle until the strap was tight enough to cut off the blood flow.

"Can't have you bleeding out on me," he said, plucking the second tourniquet from the front of Black's plate carrier and starting on the left leg.

"Y-you trying to save my life or something?" Black moaned, sweat pouring down his ashen face.

"Shit, no." Hayes laughed.

"Then what do you want?"

"I've got some questions," he said, tugging the .38 from his ankle holster, "and *you* are going to answer them."

"Not happening," Black grunted.

"Oh, yeah?" Hayes asked, pressing the barrel of the .38 against the exposed bone sticking out of Black's leg.

"You fuuuuucking do what you—" Black began, until the pain cut him off.

"What was that?" Hayes asked, lifting the stubby barrel away from the wound.

"Y-you . . . you do what you have to," Black said, biting down on the pain, "but I've gone through the same training as you, my friend."

"Wait, you went to SERE training?" Hayes gasped in mock astonishment.

He was referring to the survival evasion and resistance training all Special Operations soldiers went through at Fort Bragg. The school where they taught men how to resist torture.

"Yeah."

"Well, shit. Guess I should pack up my stuff and head on home."

"Like I said. Do what you've got to do."

"Man, you SEALs are tough as nails," Hayes said sarcastically.

"I—"

Hayes was on him in a flash, cutting off whatever he was about to say by backhanding him across the face with the .38.

"That man you killed was a friend of mine," he hissed, grabbing Black by the throat. "He knew the risks of the game, but his wife. His *wife* was a fucking civilian," Hayes said, dropping his knee onto the man's leg.

Black started to scream, but Hayes choked it off

at the source, closing his fingers around the man's voice box.

"Look at me," Hayes snapped, pressing the .38 beneath Black's chin and pushing it skyward, until they were face-to-face. "Look into my eyes and tell me that you *really* believe some bullshit military school that you went to back in the nineties is going to keep me from getting the answers that I want."

He let go for a moment before Black passed out, opened the cylinder on the .38, and shook the six rounds onto the ground.

"What the *hell* are you going to do with that?" he asked, eyes wary.

"It's like I said before," Hayes answered, picking one of the rounds out of the dirt. He held it up for Black to see, before sliding it back into the chamber. "I've got some questions," he said, and slapped the cylinder with the flat of his hand, letting it spin freely, "and *you* are going to answer them."

"Not happening," Black said.

"First one's a gimme. You ready?" Hayes asked, snapping the action closed with a flick of the wrist and cocking the hammer with his thumb. "Why are you trying to kill me?" He punctuated the question by jamming the barrel into Black's groin.

"Hey . . . Wh-what the hell are you doing?"

"That's not the right answer," Hayes said, pulling the trigger.

The hammer fell on the empty chamber with a metallic *snap* and Black startled like he'd actually been shot.

"Why did you try and kill me?" he asked again, thumbing the hammer into position. "Beep, time's up," he said.

Snap.

"FUCK YOU!" Black shouted.

Snap.

"That's not it. three left, though. You sure you want to keep playing games?"

Snap.

He could see the terror starting in the corner of Black's eyes; he was getting close, but Hayes knew he didn't have him yet. "Nobody is that lucky. Is this thing loaded?" Hayes asked aloud. "Maybe I got some bogus rounds?"

Hayes opened the chamber and showed it to Black. "Nope, there it is." He snapped the chamber shut, but this time he left the hammer down and took an exaggerated breath.

"Next one is hot, you ready for it?" he asked, letting it out and inching the pistol back to the man's groin.

Black was shaking now, the tremors starting in his legs, moving up his body, until it looked like he was hooked up to a car battery. Sweat poured from his body, soaking his shirt, filling the room with the dank stench of fear.

"Here we go," Hayes said, his finger closing around the trigger. He started to pull out the slack and both men watched the hammer inch back, and the cylinder start to turn, rotating the live round in line with the barrel.

"Don't . . . don't do this . . ." Black pleaded.

The hammer hovered at the end of its journey. A tiny bit more pressure and it would slam forward.

"Did my friends beg for their life?" Hayes asked, his voice cold as ice.

"I'll tell you!" Black screamed. "Jefferson Gray, he ordered the hit on you and Ford."

"Still on the clock, who the fuck is Jefferson Gray?"

"He works for the CIA, some special-mission program, that's all I know."

"How do I find him?"

"He has a satphone, keeps it on him all the time," Black said, rattling off the numbers.

"Man, that was a close one. I've got to give it to you, Black. You have balls of steel. Took that one all the way to the wire," he said, taking the pistol away. "So why did you come after me?"

"The email that Ford sent . . . I was just following orders."

Hayes gathered the bullets off the ground and got to his feet. "Just following orders, huh?" he asked, thumbing the bullets back into the revolver and cocking the hammer to the rear.

"I'm a soldier," Black pleaded, "just like you."

"No, you're not," Hayes said, centering the front sight on Black's forehead. "soldiers don't kill *innocent* people."

27

SEATTLE, WASHINGTON

It felt like an eternity before the echo of the gunshot finally faded into the night, and when Hayes lowered the pistol, Black was dead. For a moment his instincts took over, and Hayes started thinking about how he was going to tidy up the scene.

Make sure no one could connect it back to him.

But then he remembered who'd sent Black after him in the first place.

Fucking CIA, he thought, eyes drifting over to the tangle of metal that had been the helicopter. *Let them clean up their own mess.*

Hayes shoved the pistol back into the ankle holster and realized his most pressing problem was finding out where in the hell he was. He tried to remember the last few moments before the helicopter went down.

We were flying east over the water. That would put us back over Similk Bay.

Hayes knew there was only one way to find out and continued east until he came to a series of tombolos—low sandbars that connected the island to the mainland. He made his way across and found a parking lot on the other side with a sign welcoming him to the Swinomish Indian Reservation.

Now that he knew where he was, Hayes's mind turned to transportation.

The reservation was mostly unspoiled timber, a snapshot of how the area used to look before developers started scooping up land and building lakefront estates. It was quiet and rural, and Hayes followed the road leading from the parking lot for half a mile without seeing a single car.

But Hayes knew that even out here, someone had to have heard the helicopter go down—which meant it was only a matter of time before the cops showed up. His one chance was the cluster of cabins that he'd spent a week rewiring last fall. Hayes cut through the trees, praying the owners had gone through with their plans of renting the cabins out for the summer.

When he finally cleared the trees and saw the trucks parked on a gravel drive in front of the rentals, Hayes let out a sigh of relief. He picked the oldest vehicle, a Chevy pickup, and crept to the door.

It was unlocked. Hayes opened the door, wondering how he was going to boost the truck without any tools, when he saw the key was still in the ignition.

Four hours later, Hayes was twenty miles from Seattle and the lights from the oncoming cars were giving him a headache. *Light sensitivity—another side effect Treadstone had forgotten to mention.*

But the headache was the least of his problems. Hayes was having a hard time staying focused, keeping his mind on the task at hand. He knew there was a reason he was driving, but at the moment he couldn't remember where he was going *or* why.

Hayes wasn't sure if the cognition issues were from the helicopter crash or the fact that it had been thirty-two hours since his last pill. All he knew was that every time he established a clear thought, his mind popped out of gear, shifting from the present to the past, like a truck with a busted transmission.

"Think, damn it," he said, slamming his hand down on the steering wheel. "What did Black tell you?" Hayes cracked the window, hoping the air would clear his mind.

According to Black, Ford was dead and the man who'd authorized the hit was . . . *Shit, what was his name?*

One moment he was on the road and in the next

instant he was back in the shrink's office, lying on her $2,000 Corinthian leather couch, talking about the side effects of the OxyContin she had prescribed him.

"*What happens if I miss a dose?*"

"*Just one?*" *she asked.* "*Common side effects will be trouble recalling information, staying focused, restlessness, anxiety, aggression, some paranoia . . .*"

"*Sounds shitty.*"

"*Only if you forget to take them.*" *She smiled.*

Hayes hadn't wanted to take them in the first place. He hated the idea of being dependent on something. Having a little yellow pill rule his life.

"*And more than one? What happens if I don't like them and decide to stop altogether?*"

"*You ever see anyone coming off a drug addiction?*"

Hayes had. It was why he wasn't comfortable with the idea of the pills.

"*Once, after a surgery. I fractured my back when I fell off a scaffold at work,*" *Hayes said, the half-truth sliding easily from his mouth. He'd been at work, all right, but it wasn't the construction job he'd mentioned in their first meeting. It was at the Hotel des Bergues in Switzerland, and the fall wasn't from a scaffold, it was out of a fourth-floor window, his arms around the waist of Pieter Ernst, the German double agent he'd been sent to kill.*

Ernst was dead from the blade in his neck before they hit the ground, leaving Hayes to hobble down the alley with a fractured spine and a dislocated shoulder.

Up until that point his only contact with the support personnel had been the quarterly psych evaluations and blood draws to which every asset was subjected. It wasn't until after the surgery, when Hayes complained about the pain and they sent him to one of the Treadstone pain-management clinics, that he realized how many support personnel there were.

"I can't sleep, Doc, the pain, it just won't let go."

"Not a problem," the doctor replied, handing him a bottle full of white pills.

"What's this?" he asked.

"Ranger Candy," the man said and smiled.

Ranger Candy? When he was in the Army, Ranger Candy was the name given to the 800-milligram ibuprofen the medics were always handing out. "Look, Doc, I don't mean to complain, but I'm going to need something stronger than Motrin."

"No, that's just what we call it because we hand it out like it's Halloween around here. That's not ibuprofen, it's Oxy."

"Well, how many do I take?"

"As many as you need," the doctor said and shrugged. "That's a six-month supply. Let me know if you run out."

It was the first time Hayes had ever taken anything

stronger than Motrin. At first he took them only when he was in pain. He liked the way the pills made him feel. How the pills helped him sleep when you mixed them with a little booze before bed.

One pill for pain turned into four by lunch, then came the night at the restaurant, Annabelle looking at him over her menu.

"Are you okay?"

"Yeah, why?"

"You're sweating."

"It's hot in here."

"No, Adam, it's not," she said, watching his hand snake to his pocket. "You can't keep doing this shit. Taking those pills."

"Why not?"

"Because I'm pregnant. You're going to be a father."

The neon blaze of a truck stop at the top of the hill reminded him why he was on the road. *Jefferson Gray . . . Phone call . . . Shaw.*

He pulled into the gas station and circled around the back to the payphone. Leaving the truck running, Hayes dumped two quarters down the slot, dialed, and pressed his back to the booth so he could watch the street.

The line rang twice, then a recorded voice instructed him to "leave your message at the beep." The system was analog—ancient by today's standards, but it worked.

Hayes read the phone number off the faded sliver of paper mounted to the payphone's body so they would know where to reach him.

There were three distress codes a Treadstone operative could send from the field. He dialed triple 9—the code for a compromised operative—and hung up.

That ought to get someone's attention.

His hand wasn't even warm in his pocket before the phone was ringing.

Hayes picked it up but didn't say anything.

"Who is this?" Levi asked.

"Someone at the CIA sent a kill team after me. What do you know about it?" he asked.

"Hayes . . . Adam Hayes, is that you?"

"I know how long it takes to track a call, so cut the shit and answer the question, Levi."

"Washington. The ferry on the news, that was you?"

"Yeah, I'm two and zero right now when it comes to putting kill teams in the dirt."

"This is not something I feel comfortable talking about over the phone."

I bet not.

"We need to meet. Tell me where you are and I will send a plane."

28

MCLEAN, VIRGINIA

Levi Shaw pulled onto the Beltway, but instead of heading home to Alexandria to catch the end of the Mets game, he merged onto Dolley Madison Boulevard and headed west.

Traffic was light, and ten minutes later Shaw arrived at his destination. A Beltway-boring collection of concrete buildings surrounded by mismatched hedges and short-cropped grass.

Which was exactly the point.

The first sign of the building's significance came when Shaw turned onto Tysons McLean Drive and followed the asphalt to the security gate, where two men in black BDUs and with automatic rifles slung over their shoulders motioned for him to stop.

Shaw handed his ID to the first guard while the second man checked the underside of his black Lincoln Navigator with a mirror.

"You're good to go," the man said.

Shaw followed the asphalt around to the west side and parked in front of the main entrance and headed for the door.

The National Counterterrorism Center (NCTC) was built in response to the 9/11 attacks with the goal of "leading and integrating the national counterterrorism effort." It was a living reminder of how far Shaw had fallen in the intelligence world. Three years ago, his status as director of Treadstone meant that he had a satellite office on the second floor of the NCTC, complete with a full-time staff of intelligence liaisons.

But those days were gone, and this time Shaw was just grateful that his badge unlocked the door to the operations center.

Once inside, Shaw crossed to a spare office on the back wall, shut the door behind him, and logged in to the computer. *What the hell were you doing over there, Ford?* he wondered, typing the man's name into the database.

```
>>>>TREADSTONE Remote Portal
Login: Shaw, L.
_Access Granted
>>>>Connection Established_
```

```
Status: Online
Query: Ford, Nicholas—VENEZUELA
```

The connection in the NCTC made what he had in the Boneyard look like a decaf latte, and his fingers had barely cleared the enter key when the results popped up.

```
Mission Log: Ford, N
Venezuela—Operation Mongoose
Target—Mateo, Diego
```

During his time as director, Shaw had authorized thousands of operations. Due to the sheer volume of assisting with the War on Terror, he'd forgotten more than he could remember, which was the reason every Treadstone operation that ended in a kill chain was recorded.

But Shaw didn't need the video to remember Mongoose. He would go to his grave remembering that operation.

"Shit," he said, his hands finding their way to his eyes. Even with his eyes closed he could remember every detail of that night.

While he waited for further results, Shaw leaned back in the chair and glanced over the freshly painted wall and brand-new carpet. There was a small part of him that felt marginalized, almost slighted, when he compared this empty office to what he had to work with; the rest of him was just happy that he was back in the game.

Shaw was still waiting for the results when his cell alerted him to an incoming text, and when he saw the number, he forgot about everything else that had happened that day.

9-9-9.

He didn't believe in coincidences and knew there was no way someone could have accidentally made the call.

Who the hell could it be?

He knew there was only one way to find out.

Shaw dialed the number. The line connected, but all he heard was the rush of cars in the background.

"Who is this?"

"Someone at the CIA sent a kill team after me. What do you know about it?"

The voice sent a chill running up his spine, and there was no doubt who was on the other end of the line.

Hayes.

From the first moment Shaw had looked at Hayes's service record it was clear that the man was made for the job. Still, he had to be sure, which is why he hopped a flight to Afghanistan, pulled some strings, and had the man choppered back to Bagram for a session with a "psychologist"—actually Shaw himself.

"*According to your file, you spent your first tour in Ramadi with the Eighty-second Airborne,*" *Shaw said.* "*Then you went to Special Forces selection, got sent to First Special Forces Group in Washington. Six more deployments after that. Says here you've spent more time overseas than you have at home. Distinguished Service Cross presented for extraordinary heroism on July tenth, 2005, in Iraq. Silver Star, Afghanistan, 2007. A second one in 2009, this one with a Purple Heart,*" *he read, nodding his approval.* "*Sounds like you've seen the elephant a time or two.*"

"*That make me special?*" *Hayes asked.*

Shaw had been recruiting men for Treadstone long enough to recognize the hard cases, and he didn't need a psychology degree to see that the death of Hayes's teammates as well as the never-ending grind of the War on Terror had taken their toll.

Hayes's posture told him that the man was walled off, and a look into his eyes that he was checked out. Getting through to this one wasn't going to be easy.

"*Captain Hayes, you've got it all figured out, don't you?*" *Shaw began.* "*Lose a couple guys in combat and you decide to check out of the game.*"

"*You're the doctor, why don't you tell me,*" *Hayes said.*

"*Says here that on March twelfth your team was on a routine patrol when you came under fire. You lost a man that day.*"

"*There is a war going on,*" Hayes said. "*We all lost people, doesn't make me special.*"

"*Two days later, your medic was hit, Staff Sergeant Deets—*"

Hayes was on his feet at the mention of his friend's name. "*Fuck this,*" *he said, turning to the door.*

I've got him.

"*You can walk out that door if you want, but I promise you that you will be back.*"

Hayes's shoulders slumped and he turned back to his seat.

"*What the hell do you want from me?*"

"*How did it make you feel, losing your men?*"

"*Like throwing a parade,*" *Hayes deadpanned.*

"*Is that when you stepped off the reservation, or, as your battalion commander put it, 'subsequent to ambush of March twelfth, Captain Hayes displayed anger issues and put himself in harm's way unnecessarily.'*"

"*It was a hot AO, I was doing my job.*"

"*But you were angry, yes?*"

"*Yeah.*" *Hayes nodded.* "*I was pissed.*"

"*You wanted revenge on the people who killed your friend.*"

Hayes nodded again.

"*But they wouldn't let you, would they? Rules of engagement and all that.*"

"*Look, man,*" *Hayes said.* "*I don't know who the hell you work for, but we both know you aren't a doctor.*"

The only thing I do know is that we've been at war since 2001 and not a damn thing has changed. People think . . ." He paused. *"Fuck it. If you want to put me away for doing my job, then go ahead."*

"Put you away . . . you got this all wrong, son." Shaw smiled. "I'm not here to put you away."

"Then why are we here?"

"I'm here to offer you a job."

"Tell me where you are and I will send a plane," Shaw said, reaching for a pen.

29

Hayes drove west to the airfield and parked in front of the hangar with the faded AIR POTOMAC sign hanging over the door.

Air Potomac was one of a handful of shell corporations owned by the CIA. The Agency had been setting up cutouts since Vietnam and had it down to a science. They preferred countries in the Caribbean. Islands like the Caymans, where you could get a company incorporated in three days if the paperwork was in order and you knew what gears to grease.

Once the shell companies were legal, the CIA could use them to ferry assets anywhere they needed to go.

The stewardess was waiting for him on the tarmac.

"Good afternoon, sir," she greeted him. "My name is Emily. Can I take your luggage?"

"No, I'm good," Hayes said, walking up the stairs.

The pilot, a tanned, blond-haired man in a floral shirt, waited for him at the top. "Adam Hayes, holy shit, is that you?" the man asked.

"Dick Waters," Hayes said, grinning. "I thought you were done with this shit after that little dustup in El Salvador."

"That was the plan." The pilot grimaced.

"What happened?"

"Came home early from a run and found the wife fucking the pool guy."

"The pool boy? C'mon."

"Hand to God, just like a country song. She took the house, the car, and the dog."

"Damn, that's . . . Well, that's just wrong," Hayes said, not sure how to respond.

"She was a bitch anyways, but hey, the boss says we're getting the band back together."

Hayes rolled his eyes. *Fucking Levi.*

"Speaking of, where is the old man?" Hayes asked.

"If you will follow me, sir," Emily said.

He followed her through the curtains and found Levi comfortably ensconced in a leather chair. There was something in the man's eyes that sent Hayes's hand to the pistol on his waist, but the press of a muzzle against his lower back changed his mind.

"I'd advise against that," Levi Shaw said. "Emily is more than just a pretty face."

"We're going to do this nice and slow, Mr. Hayes," Emily said, nudging him forward. "I am reaching for your sidearm. Believe me when I tell you that I will shoot if you resist."

"What the hell is this?" Hayes asked, raising his hands.

Emily moved to the side, the Sig 229 steady in her hand, and was reaching for his pistol when Hayes's left hand snapped down on the slide and shoved it back a quarter of an inch, just enough so he could see the glint of brass in the chamber. Emily's first reaction was to snap the trigger to the rear, and her eyes went wide when the Sig didn't fire.

"Out of battery," Hayes hissed, right hand closing over his left. In one smooth motion he twisted the SIG from her hand, racked the slide to get it back into action, and pressed the barrel under her chin, twisting his body so the pistol was out of her reach.

"Don't kill me," Emily whispered, the fear in her eyes blossoming in Technicolor.

"I've had a really shitty day, so it's your call," he said, looking at Shaw.

"Hey, I had to make sure you still had it."

Hayes handed Emily back the pistol. "Sorry about that."

"Asshole," she said, glaring at Shaw as she shoved it back into her holster.

"Still a hit with the ladies, I see," Hayes said and grunted, dropping himself into a seat.

"We are not here to talk about me. Word on the street is that you have run into a little trouble."

"That's the understatement of the year," Hayes said, pulling his knife out of his pocket, thumbing the blade open, and scraping the dried blood off his forearm.

"You know, kid, you don't always have to be such a hard-ass." Shaw sighed.

"Well, I had a good teacher," Hayes said, looking up from the blade. "Way I remember it, I was doing just fine before you showed up in Afghanistan. Took me back to the States and let Treadstone get their hooks in me."

"You're breaking my heart," Shaw said, buckling his belt. "I don't remember having to twist your arm. We've had our differences in the past, but, hey, I'm a live-and-let-live kind of guy. Hell, I don't even remember who swung first."

"I do," Hayes said, remembering their last meeting.

"I want out."

"Out? You had a bad op, we've all been there, but getting out . . . C'mon, Hayes."

"That last mission was fucked . . ." Hayes began,

but quickly changed his mind. He didn't want to think about it, and reached into his pocket for the bottle of Oxy he'd picked up on the way to the meet.

"Is that the new bottle? I thought you kicked that stuff."

"Don't start."

"Hey, it's your life, you can leave if you want, this isn't the Mafia, but—"

"But what, Levi? If I want to leave, what are you going to do to stop me?"

"This was a mistake," Hayes said.

"It's not too late, we haven't started taxiing yet," Shaw said, tapping the window with his finger. "There is still time to do what you do best."

"And what's that?"

"Run away," Shaw snarled.

Hayes felt the rush of adrenaline that always came before a fight hit his central nervous system like a shot of ether to a cold engine. There was a moment of clarity—a split second of crystal vision that revealed every detail of the situation.

He was aware of Emily standing near the front of the plane and knew he could be up and have the blade in Shaw's throat before she even knew what happened.

No . . . he's testing you, the voice said.

"I didn't drive all the way out here to play your

games, Levi," Hayes said, "so unless you're going to tell me why the CIA sent a team after me, I've got people to kill."

"Ford's dead," Shaw said.

How could he know that already?

"Tell me something I don't know," Hayes said.

"He was working for the DEA."

30

IN FLIGHT

Ford was freelancing for the DEA," Shaw said, taking a manila folder with CONFIDENTIAL stamped across the cover and handing it over.

The folder was typical of a federal personnel file, and on the first page Hayes found a headshot of a clean-cut man with brown hair and gray eyes paper-clipped to the front cover. *Special Agent Cole Boggs*. According to the file, Boggs came over from the DEA after five years in the Marines. Spent three years working the border before being moved to the Dallas office. He was a good agent, but his personal life was a train wreck.

Two ex-wives, one child. The first marriage was in the Corps and didn't last through the first deployment. The second one would have had a shot if he'd had a

9-to-5, but once Cole went into undercover work it didn't have a chance in hell.

What about the kid?

"What does he have to do with Ford?" Hayes asked.

"Special Agent Cole Boggs worked deep-cover operations for the DEA's Cartel Exploitation Team."

"Never heard of it," Hayes admitted.

"Me either. Not much info in the database, so I ended up calling in a favor, got in contact with Boggs's handler. From what he was willing to share, CET is some secret-squirrel, black-bag caper the DEA's been running in South America."

"You said 'worked.' Did Boggs get fired?" Hayes asked.

"Not exactly. According to Cole's handler, the CET was comprised primarily of senior special agents, men who'd shown the ability to operate with a minimal amount of oversight."

"Makes sense." Hayes nodded. "Hard to keep in contact with a boss when you are undercover."

"Exactly. Sometime in the last three years, Mr. Boggs developed an unhealthy fascination with Colonel Carlos Vega—the head of Venezuelan Intelligence."

"What does SEBIN have to do with this?" Hayes asked.

"To understand the current situation in Venezuela," Shaw said, leaning back in his chair, "we have to go back to 2017 and the assassination of President Mateo."

Mateo.

It was a name Hayes hadn't heard since leaving Treadstone. One he'd buried deep into the catacombs of his mind, sworn to forget, no matter what the cost.

But the mention of the former president of Venezuela caught him off guard. It bounced off the floor of his mind and exploded like a flashbang inside a concrete room.

Shit, not now. Not again, Hayes begged. He grabbed his skull, tried to keep the flood of images from breaking free, but the damage was done, and he was caught up in the rush of memories that sent him tumbling back to Venezuela. Back to the house with the white columns.

The lights were off when he picked the lock and disabled the alarm, the interior of the house a dull green from his night vision. Hayes stepped through the door, his feet silent over the tile. He climbed the stairs, found a second guard sleeping in a chair on the landing. Hayes guessed he was in his mid-teens, not yet old enough to shave and much too young for the AK-47 propped against the wall.

Kill them all—that was the order. He was just the instrument—a man conditioned to kill without hesitation.

Hayes pressed the MK VI suppressor into the notch

below the man's ear, held his thumb against the slide to keep the .22 from cycling, and pulled the trigger.

The shot was a muted cough barely noticeable over the sound of the television playing at the end of the hall. Hayes pulled the slide to the rear, and the expended brass cartwheeled into the air.

He caught it with his left hand and shoved the brass into his pocket.

He followed a murmur of voices down the hall. A quick glance around the corner revealed a woman sitting on a couch, her back to him. The voices were coming from the telenovela that had her rapt attention.

Hayes slipped up behind her, let her feel his presence.

She held up her empty glass without turning from the TV, and he waited patiently for the shot.

"Diego, what are you—"

The woman turned her head, and Hayes put a bullet through her eye.

One more.

He moved down the hall, drawn to the closed door by the sound of the voice inside. "I don't care what you have to do, get me out of the country!" President Mateo shouted.

Mateo was sitting at his desk, his back to the door, phone at his ear.

Hayes extended the barrel toward the back of the man's head, let it hover there for a moment until the man felt his presence and turned.

"You . . ."

The pistol jumped in his hand, the bullet smacking President Mateo in the face and blasting him back into his chair.

"Adam, Adam!" Shaw shouted.

Hayes's transition from the horrors of the past to the calm of the present was marked by the full-auto rattle of his heart in his chest and the clammy feel of the sweat rolling over his skin. He blinked free of the flashback and found Shaw staring at him, the expression on his face a mix of concern and horror.

"The doctors told me it was impossible to kick the behavior meds," he began. "It was part of the safeguard protocol in case any of you went rogue."

"You mean in case any of your science experiments ever got out of the lab?" Hayes asked.

"They said kicking it cold turkey would break a man's mind."

"I don't know about all that, but I can tell you I don't recommend it."

"So just how fucked-up are you?" Shaw asked.

"Well, you made me," Hayes said and shrugged.

"Like I was saying, smartass, it would appear that Colonel Vega has friends in high places and Boggs's handler received a notification from a joint DoD–CIA task force to leave Vega alone."

"CIA has a lot of balls trying to pull rank on the DEA in their own sandbox. What were they basing the warning on?"

"Counterterror operations have priority with both the White House and the State Department. So JSOC and the CIA told the DEA to get fucked," Shaw answered. "They claim that they have positive intel of a terror cell in the area, and since it's no secret that Hezbollah was operating in South America, selling drugs to fund their war on the west, everyone just lets them be."

"Is this where you get to the point and tell me what any of this has to do with Ford?"

"Boggs contracted Ford to set up a team to grab Vega. Didn't work out for him."

The pictures.

"The email Ford sent had these attached," Hayes said, pulling the printouts of the images from his back pocket and handing them over. "The last photo, the two men in the hangar."

"Vega," Shaw said, pointing to the man in uniform.

"And the other guy?"

"Never seen him before," Shaw said.

"Levi, look again," Hayes said, pointing at the photo. "You've never seen this guy before. You're sure?"

"Yes, Adam," Shaw replied, "I'm sure."

"Well, shit, I was hoping you could ID him."

"Sorry to disappoint."

"What about this Boggs character, can you at least put me in contact with him?" Hayes asked.

"His handler says Boggs became eccentric after the CIA warning."

"Eccentric?" Hayes said, throwing his arms in the air. "Jesus, Levi, I don't want to date him, I just want to talk to him. Can you put me in contact with him or not?"

"He has gone dark, and since this is a time-sensitive operation, I think your time would be better spent—"

"Wait, time-sensitive," Hayes broke in. "Do you have somewhere you need to be?"

"No, it's just that . . ."

"Spit it out, Levi."

"Well, Treadstone has funding till the end of the month," Shaw answered.

"What happens then?"

"They are closing it down."

Hayes glanced at the Submariner on his wrist, the date window telling him it was the thirtieth, and then threw his head back in laughter. "Levi . . . you're kidding, right?"

"No, Adam, I am *not* kidding."

"If we're going to do this, we do it my way," Hayes said.

"Well, what do you need?"

"I need a team, a briefcase of cash, and guns. Lots of guns."

31

CÚCUTA, COLOMBIA

It was raining in Cúcuta and Cole Boggs sat in bed, watching the white flash of lightning illuminate the half-empty bottle of Wild Turkey that sat on a shelf across the room. Just the sight of the bottle and the hope that its amber contents would calm his mind were enough to send his legs swinging to the floor.

He padded across the room, the tile warm on his bare feet, and grabbed the bottle by the neck. Boggs eased back into bed, trying not to disturb the sleeping figure beside him, but the squeak of the bedsprings betrayed his plans.

"Can't you sleep?" she mumbled through half-open lids.

"Go back to sleep, girl," Boggs answered in Spanish,

switching the bottle to his left hand so he could rub her back with his right.

The woman purred and settled her head into the pillow, leaving Boggs to nurse the bottle in silence.

A breeze billowed through the curtains on either side of the French doors and waltzed into the room, laden with the wet-dirt smell of rain that reminded him of growing up in Iberia Parish, Louisiana. The thought of home made him want a cigarette. He set the bottle down on the nightstand, exchanging the whiskey for a soft pack of Camels. Boggs shook a cigarette into the corner of his mouth and fired it with the blue lighter and blew the smoke toward the ceiling.

We a looong way from there, aren't we, boy?

A second bolt of lightning followed the first and Boggs found himself counting in his head, the way his mama had taught him when he was a boy. *One Mississippi, two Mississippi, three Mississippi . . .* Before Boggs got to four, he heard the distant growl of thunder that told him the storm was three and a half miles out.

Never should have asked for those pictures, he cursed himself.

Boggs had been with the DEA for ten years, and before that he'd done two tours in Iraq with the Marines. He'd seen his share of dead bodies, but there was something about seeing his friend lying half in, half out of the tub, the gaping exit wound at the back of his head and the contents of his skull splattered over the backsplash, that he couldn't shake.

Fucking Vega. Killed him like a dog.

Turning Ford onto Vega and that piece of shit Jefferson Gray had been a mistake. He knew that now, but at the time it made sense. The DEA had been working in Colombia since Pablo Escobar and had done a hell of a job throttling the Medellín cartel.

At first, they went after the fields and the processing plants where the processors would dry the coca leaves, chopping them up with a string trimmer before using gasoline and battery acid to extract the freebase. It was a losing battle; for every plant they shut down, three more would pop up.

Due to the flammable nature of the compounds involved, and the fact that the cartels started hiring FARC—the oldest and largest of Colombia's left-wing rebel groups—to guard the processing plants, the DEA decided to switch gears. That was when Boggs first met Nick Ford.

The DEA was great at following the money, planning raids on drug houses and stash spots in the city. But out in the countryside it was a different story. The bush was FARC's territory, and the paramilitary group had the DEA outnumbered and outgunned.

It was Boggs's idea to hire contractors. Former Special Ops and Special Forces soldiers who knew how to operate in the jungle and could take the fight to the enemy. One of the first men he found was Nick Ford.

Ford was an outstanding leader. In six months his team hit more airfields, fuel depots, and hangars than the rest of the teams combined. After that, it didn't matter how much coke they produced; if the narcos couldn't get it out of the country, they were losing money.

Then President Díaz came to power in Venezuela and the whole dynamic changed.

"They are right across the border," Ford said. "Just give me the green light."

"You understand the only reason we are allowed to work here is because of the host nation, right? Colombia and the U.S. are allies."

"So?"

"Have you watched the news?" Boggs asked. "We aren't exactly welcome over there."

But Ford wouldn't let it go, and Boggs agreed to run it up the chain.

He was expecting to get shot down right away and was surprised when headquarters told him to write up an operations order.

"I need actionable intelligence," he told Ford the next time he saw him. "Names, places, pictures, and grids for the airfields. This has to be done *by the book*."

"Won't let you down."

Boggs didn't know how he managed to pull it off,

but a week later Ford was back in Bogotá with a full workup.

"That place is the Wild West," he said when they met again, pointing to the region on the map. "The cartel is bringing this stuff across the river and loading the dope into planes."

"Who owns the runways?"

"That's just it, this area is all flat scrubland. Someone makes a call and a dude in a pickup shows up. They have these weighted barrels that they drag behind the truck, flattens the grass down, and boom, you have a landing strip."

"Who's running the show?"

"Colonel Carlos Vega."

"Of the SEBIN?"

"I'm telling you, it is a different world over there. Instead of a bunch of cartels fighting with each other and the government, over there, the government *is* the cartel. They call it the Cártel de los Soles and it's made up of officers from the Bolivarian National Guard."

The Cartel of the Suns.

Boggs had heard the rumors, everyone at the DEA had, but to actually have proof that the Bolivarian National Guard, Venezuela's Army, was a state-funded cartel was crazy.

Two week later, Boggs got Ford the authorization he needed, and Operation Mongoose was a go.

Now Ford is dead. Did I do this?

32

AUBURN, WASHINGTON

President Diego Mateo was a name Hayes hadn't thought of since 2009. Not since he left Treadstone and buried all the memories deep into the catacombs of his mind.

The way Shaw worked the name into the conversation threw him for a loop. It almost seemed like an afterthought.

Or was it bait? Another test.

"Where are we going?" Waters asked, breaking his train of thought.

"First stop is Chicago. We've got to pick up a few friends," Hayes answered from the right seat of the Gulfstream GV.

"Chicago? This isn't an Uber," Waters said.

Hayes tugged the pistol from his holster and looked at Waters over the top of his sunglasses. "You remember when you volunteered for this and I told you that I had a pilot's license?"

"Yes. So?"

"Well, I don't need another pilot, so you can either stop asking questions or you can get the fuck out of my plane."

Waters turned his attention to the instrument panel and punched some numbers into the GPS. "Flight time to Chicago is two hours," he said, wiping the sweat from his brow.

"That's more like it." Hayes smiled, getting to his feet and walking back to the main cabin and the open laptop on a table.

Hayes logged in to Skype and typed a number from memory and waited for the connection to be established. When the screen blinked to life, it showed a blond-haired man with green eyes sitting inside a swank corner office.

"Hey, hey, if it isn't my old pal Hayes," the man said.

"JT, how are you, man?"

"Just grinding it out in corporate hell, living amongst the lettuce eaters, you know how it is."

"You up for a little action?" Hayes asked.

"Hold on a second," JT said, getting up from his chair and disappearing from view.

Hayes heard the sound of the man's shoes over the

carpet and the click of the door being eased shut, and a moment later JT was back in the frame, with an apostrophe of a smile at the edge of his lips.

"What do you have in mind?" he asked, leaning closer to the camera.

"I've got an op in Venezuela, need a guy who is handy with the steel and knows how to find people who don't want to be found."

"Sounds like my kind of gig. What's the timeline?"

"Chicago Executive in, uh"—Hayes glanced down at his watch—"two hours." He shrugged.

"Hell yeah, anything else?"

"Just bring your hunting gear," Hayes said, moving the cursor over the end call button.

They caught the jet stream on the way to Illinois and landed in Chicago ten minutes ahead of schedule. Waters taxied over toward the cluster of hangars on the east side of the field.

"There he is," Hayes said, pointing to the man with the black ball cap, a black Pelican case at his feet.

Hayes and JT met in Iraq when Hayes was working with Task Force 121 and JT was providing intel. JT had never hesitated to jump into action then, and clearly some things had never changed.

"So what do we have?" he asked, after climbing aboard.

"I need you to find a guy—well, two guys, actually," Hayes said, bringing JT up to speed.

"Just tell me who's first," he said, pulling his computer from the hard case.

"First we find Cole Boggs," Hayes said.

"And how do we do that?"

"Are you serious?" Hayes frowned at him.

"Yeah? Why?"

"If I knew how to find him, I wouldn't have flown three hours out of my way to pick up a self-proclaimed intel weenie."

Every target that Hayes had ever tracked down had a center point. It was just the way people were made. Everyone from the thug on the street to the most hardened terrorist had someplace or someone that was the center of their universe.

For Hayes it was his family, and that gave him an idea.

"JT, you have kids, right?" Hayes asked.

The shift in the man's eyes was like a wall going up. His lips tightened and his fingers curled into a fist. A defensive posture. Nonverbal clues that were designed to tell the right eyes that they were getting close to a line.

It was the reaction he'd been hoping for.

JT finally spoke. "What the hell does that have to do with anything?"

It was a polite question, one he'd asked hundreds of times since Jack was born. Ask a civilian out on the street and you got a straight answer. A yes or a no. But ask a cop or a soldier, men who had seen behind the shiny veneer draped over the so-called civilized world, and you got a totally different answer.

"Could you go two years without talking to them?" Hayes asked.

"Hell, no."

"Didn't think so. Boggs has a daughter," he said, pulling the file he'd gotten from Shaw out of the bag and turning to the beneficiary page. "Cassidy Boggs, sixteen, a senior at Highland Park High School."

"That's a good in," JT said.

"Do you want her Social?" Hayes asked.

"Dude, she's sixteen, what good is her Social Security number going to do? You have her digits?" JT asked.

"What are you thinking?" he asked, after reading off the phone number listed in the file.

"Kids these days live on their phones, man. See, look at all these texts," JT said, pointing at the screen.

But a quick scroll-through failed to identify any numbers outside of the Highland Park 469 area code. *Nothing.*

"Just because he isn't using a cell doesn't mean he isn't talking to her," JT said. "You ever heard of Instagram?"

"What is that, like Echelon or something?" Hayes asked, referring to the NSA's signal intelligence collection and analysis program that had come to light in 2013 after Edward Snowden leaked highly classified information to the world.

"No, man, it is a social media app," he said, rolling his eyes. "You are aware that we have something called the Internet, right?"

"Funny."

"Kids don't talk on the phone anymore. They text and then they become teenagers and all of a sudden it's like they work for the CIA. Crazy opsec. Let me show you my daughter's page," he said, logging in to Instagram and typing in @kielyBunny02. The page changed to selfies of a cute blond girl playing with a puppy.

"Ah, that nice."

"That's what I said, little Kiely out there playing with the dog, all wholesome and shit. I would have never thought anything about it, but then Kiely turns fifteen and all these dudes are all over her shit . . ."

"You okay?" Hayes asked, seeing the man's face turning red.

"These punks, man. Once boys start showing up, everything changes. So my wife tells her that we need to have access to her account."

"Seems fair," Hayes said.

"You'd have thought we were asking to put her diary on CNN, man, she totally flipped out. So we block her from the computer, and she is jonesing like a junkie at a methadone clinic. Comes back to the old lady and says, 'Here's all my passwords.'"

"That's good, right?"

"I think so, but my wife smells a rat, starts poking around and finds this." He clicked on a picture that showed a New Mexico State hooded sweatshirt: @ NMhoodieFinsta.

"What the hell is this crap?"

"This is my daughter's Finstagram account. Her fake account . . ."

"You think Cassidy has one?"

"Let's see." He typed Cassidy Boggs into the search bar.

"That's her," Hayes said.

"You sure?"

"Yeah," Hayes said, holding up the picture of Boggs he'd taken from the file. "Same nose and chin as her old man."

"Just going to drop this logic bomb right here," JT said to himself, his fingers clattering over the keyboard like a machine gun on full auto.

Beside him, Hayes watched the lines of numbers that represented the code appear on the screen. "Now I break through this little firewall and . . . boom, here we go," he said, indicating a name on the screen. "@ CowboyCounty1," JT said, pointing at the list of direct messages that started with "Daddy, when are you coming home from Colombia?"

Got him.

33

CÚCUTA, COLOMBIA

When Cole Boggs woke up, the girl was gone, but the hangover had just arrived. He sat up in bed, mouth tasting like a three-day-old ashtray, and waited for the room to stop spinning before grunting to his feet.

"Fucker." He cursed the empty bottle of Wild Turkey on the nightstand.

Boggs staggered to the bathroom, the acid churn in his guts directing him to the toilet, where he vomited until he tasted bile.

"Mother of God," he said and groaned, wiping his mouth with the back of his hand.

"Proud of yourself?" a female voice asked.

Boggs flushed the toilet and cast bloodshot eyes at the woman standing in the doorway.

Physically, Isabel Vargas was typical of the women he'd met in Colombia: strikingly beautiful in a gray tank top and faded jeans, with cream-white skin and black hair. But a glance at the almond eyes, judging him over the rim of her coffee cup, was enough to tell Boggs that if he was looking for sympathy, he'd come to the wrong place.

"Do me a favor," he croaked, standing up and moving to the sink.

"What?" she asked.

"Pull out your pistol," he answered, nodding to the Glock 19 holstered next to the badge that identified her as a police officer, "and shoot me in the head."

"Let's start with a shower," she said. "I'll make breakfast."

Boggs stepped into the shower and turned the hot water all the way up, adjusted the nozzle so it sprayed against the wall, and sat on the wooden bench in the corner. He lowered his head into his hands and let the steam roll over his body.

Boggs hadn't been looking for a woman when he came to Cúcuta six months ago. In fact, he wasn't looking for *anything* in Colombia. Everything he wanted was on the east side of the Río Táchira in Venezuela's Apure region, and the Puente Internacional Francisco de Paula Santander was the only bridge in the area that spanned the river.

His first order of business was to find a safe house.

Boggs needed a place that gave him a clear line of sight on the bridge—a place where he could monitor the narcos crossing into Colombia.

The condominiums at Prados del Este provided everything he needed. They were located a rifle shot from the bridge, and from the balcony of his third-floor condo, he could see both the bridge and Ureña on the other side.

Meeting Detective Isabel Vargas was a bonus, but Boggs wasn't sure how much longer she'd put up with his drinking.

After the shower he took a handful of aspirin, dressed, and went downstairs.

In the kitchen, Isabel was already at the table, an extra plate of bacon and eggs beside her. "I'm sorry," Boggs said in Spanish.

"Um-hmm," she hummed through a mouthful of eggs.

Boggs crossed to the coffeepot, poured a cup, and watched her. Any thought that he knew women because he'd been married before went out the window when he met Izzy. Being married to an American had not prepared him for what he would find in Colombia. South American women, much like their European counterparts, had pouting down to a science, and since they'd moved in together, he learned the difference between an angry pout, a playful pout, and the current disgusted pout.

Isabel finished chewing, took a sip of coffee, and swallowed.

"You were dreaming about Ford again," Isabella said. "You shouted his name."

Boggs watched as her hand slipped to the sterling silver locket that hung from her neck and knew where this was going. The locket was her prized possession, and Boggs knew that inside was the last picture of her family, before Colonel Vega murdered them.

"He . . ." she began, eyes filling with tears. "He would be alive if . . . if it wasn't for me," she said.

"Izzy, stop," Boggs said, reaching for her hand. "Ford's death, it had nothing to do with you," he lied.

Boggs hadn't always been a liar. In fact, the first week of ethics training at the DEA Training Academy in Quantico centered on *truthfulness*. Boggs remembered the instructor's words: "The moment you graduate and become a special agent, there is only one thing that matters. Does anyone know what that is?"

"Good casework," a woman in the first row said.

"No," the instructor said and nodded.

"Proper evidence handling," a man in the second row answered.

"No, c'mon, people, this is day-one stuff."

"The truth," Boggs answered.

"That's right." She smiled. "The truth. No matter how good your case is or what kind of evidence you have, a lie will destroy a case faster than a bullet to the heart."

It was a lesson that lined up with what he'd learned in the Corps—a place where honor and loyalty were everything. But being undercover was an entirely different animal. In Boggs's world, the truth would kill, and he'd been under so long that the lies came easily. He wanted to give up undercover work, but then his daughter, Cassidy, went on the college tour down to Florida State and decided she had to be a Seminole. One problem: There was no way to swing the out-of-state tuition, even with overtime.

CET changed that. Not only did he get travel- and hazard-duty pay when the team deployed overseas, but since he wasn't in the U.S. it was all tax-free.

"I feel responsible," she said, "and I want to make it right. I want to help."

"You are helping," Boggs said, eager to change the subject. He gave her hand a reassuring squeeze and nodded to the file open in front of her. "What are you working on?"

"The narcos killed one of our officers at the border yesterday. My boss wants me to look into it."

Just as with Boggs, it was the bridge that brought Detective Isabel Vargas to Cúcuta. Her command in the Metropolitan Police, a regional arm of the Policía Nacional de Colombia, had one primary responsibility:

keeping the violence on the Venezuelan side of the river from spreading into Colombia.

"I am doing everything I can," Boggs said.

"I know you are going over there today," she said, nodding to the east. "Let me go with you."

"No, Izzy," he said, cutting her off.

"Why? Why can't I go?"

"First and foremost, it's out of your jurisdiction. Second, it's dangerous, and third, and most important, if Colonel Vega finds you in Venezuela, he will kill you," Boggs replied.

"Fine," she said, snatching his plate from the table and carrying it to the sink.

Boggs watched her back, knowing that she was angry again. Nothing he could say or do, besides giving her what she wanted, would change that.

"Guess I'm finished," he said, getting to his feet.

He went upstairs for his pistol and was stuffing it into its holster when he heard the door slam downstairs. Boggs grabbed his bag and went to the closet. *Women,* he thought, grabbing one of the snakeskin boots from the shelf and taking out the fresh bottle of Jack Daniel's. He cracked the bottle and took a long pull before stuffing the booze into his bag and heading downstairs. Boggs locked the door and climbed behind the wheel of the old Jeep and drove east toward the river.

Besides the ever-growing tent city on the edge of

town, Cúcuta had remained relatively unscathed by the violence. But across the bridge, the Venezuelan city of Ureña was not as lucky.

Ureña had been a working-class town with clean streets and good sanitation as well as police who provided law and order.

While it was never a part of Venezuela that made it into the travel magazines, it had been a safe place to raise a family.

But that changed with President Diego Mateo's assassination in 2017.

Now Ureña was a city under siege. Occupied not by a foreign army but by its own countrymen. Men in T-shirts and cutoff shorts stood on every street corner, AK-47s slung over their shoulders. Above them, men with binoculars and cellphones stood on rooftops and watched, ready to place a call to the narco militia waiting on the outskirts of town.

Vehicles choked both sides of the road, along which trash blew like tumbleweeds. The street reminded him of Iraq. Graffiti-covered shops stood empty and riddled with bullet holes. There were scorch marks on some of the cars. And he recognized the blast patterns of RPGs.

But instead of fear, the scene offered a grotesque comfort. *Almost like home.*

The fact that Boggs didn't dispute the thought gave him the sick feeling that maybe he had been under for *too* long.

Maybe it's time to get out, he thought. *Live a normal life.*

A line of stopped cars at the end of the road signaled a checkpoint, and Boggs was reaching into the center console for one of the yellow envelopes full of cash he kept on hand for this very reason when a thump followed by a sharp inhalation of breath drew his attention to the back seat.

Someone's back there, he thought, eyes flicking to the rear-view mirror.

His hand moved to the pistol at his waist and Boggs sat up straight in his seat, trying to get high enough to see into the back seat. He couldn't see anything, but knew what he'd heard and cut the wheel to the right, aiming for the backside of a boarded-up garage.

Boggs kept his foot on the gas and bounced the Jeep over the curb. It hopped into the air, and when the tires slammed back to the ground, there was no mistaking the grunt of pain from the back seat. He stayed on the gas until he was safely behind the garage, then shifted into neutral and stomped on the brakes.

The tires locked up with a scream of rubber and came to a sliding halt. Boggs was out of the Jeep in a flash, moving around the side, the Glock leading the way when he looked over the side. There was a blanket on the floorboard.

How the hell did you miss that? he wondered. The answer came just as quick as the question: *Because I'm still fucking drunk.*

"You have three seconds to show me your hands or I will shoot," he ordered in Spanish, the Glock shaking in his hand.

The command wasn't out of his mouth before a hand tugged the blanket away and a face appeared.

"Jesus Christ, Izzy," he said, his shoulders sagging with relief.

"I'm sorry," she lied.

"What if I had shot you?" Boggs asked, shoving the Glock into its holster and reaching for her hand. "Do you have any idea what would have happened if the narcos had found you at the checkpoint?"

"But they didn't," Izzy said.

"Just get in the Jeep," he said, climbing behind the wheel, "I'm taking you back."

"No," Izzy said, crossing her arms.

Boggs was about to reply when an electronic chime drew his attention to the floorboard. He looked down, and when he saw his phone, he realized that it must have fallen out of his pocket when he jumped from the Jeep. Boggs bent and scooped it up; he was about to tell Izzy that yes, she was going back, when he saw the red 1 indicating an Instagram message.

"Just get in," Boggs said, his face softening at the thought of his daughter. He opened the app, a faint smile at the corner of his mouth. A smile that vanished the moment he read the message.

We need to meet.

"What is it?" Izzy asked, seeing the change in his expression.

"It's from my daughter, but—"

Before he finished his thought the phone dinged again, followed by an aerial shot of his Jeep sitting behind the boarded-up garage.

34

PENDARE, VENEZUELA

The storm built in the Atlantic, a churning black mass that rolled lazily across the ocean. Growing in size and strength until it ran headfirst into the trade winds that sent it screaming west. Three hours later it made landfall over Guyana, but instead of dumping its moisture, the storm kept moving, over the Pacaraima Mountains in eastern Venezuela, and across the Guiana Highlands, before finally losing steam over the Amazons and dumping its rain in a torrent over Pendare.

Colonel Carlos Vega stood at the opening of the hangar, chomping on the cigar clutched at the corner of his mouth. His dark eyes drifted over the muted outline of the yellow earthmovers huddled beneath the camouflage netting, and the rain pounded away at the dirt airstrip his men had just regraded.

The clattering whine of the machine in the corner of the room spooling down and the angry snap of voices drew his attention to the interior of the hangar, and Vega turned to see his aide, Captain Ramón Javier, arguing with a worker.

"What is the meaning of this?" Rosa, a man in ink-spattered coveralls, demanded angrily from the modular office at the back of the hangar. "We are behind schedule, who told you to turn that off?"

"Colonel's orders," Javier answered curtly.

"This is intolerable," Rosa complained. "We are behind schedule. I demand to speak to the colonel right now!"

"You have something to say?" Vega hissed, stepping into view, smiling at the fear that spread across the Peruvian forgers.

The gift of fear.

It was a lesson, oddly enough, that he'd learned from Gray's government. One that allowed him to take over the SEBIN.

When Vega first joined the military, President Rafael Caldera was on his second term, and the U.S. and Venezuela had a close working relationship. He had just started working for the SEBIN, the intelligence service that answered directly to the president, and was among a handful of promising young officers chosen to attend the School of the Americas.

Located in Fort Benning, Georgia, the School of the Americas, or SOA, was established in 1946. The primary goal of the SOA was to strengthen ties between the U.S. and her Latin American allies by educating promising young officers in the virtues of democratic civilian control over the armed forces.

By the time Vega was chosen to attend, the Latin American world knew the SOA by a different name: Escuela de Asesinos. The School of Assassins. The sinister moniker came from the violent acts perpetrated by the graduates when they returned home and used what they had learned from the CIA and Special Forces cadre to set up death squads, implement torture programs, and overthrow governments. It was from this same cadre that Vega was first introduced to the finer points of psychological warfare and kidnapping.

"N-no disrespect, Colonel, but you said that you wanted the work completed in three days, but now you tell us to stop."

"That is correct," Vega replied, coming to a halt in front of the man.

"The rain had already put us behind schedule, and when we were about to catch up, you tell us to stop. Why?"

"The American is on his way—" Vega began.

"The American?" Rosa snapped, his face red with anger. "Are you seriously—"

But before he could finish his sentence, Vega's right arm flashed from his side, the sound of his hand hitting Rosa's face echoing through the silent hangar with the snap of a bullwhip. The blow sent the Peruvian stumbling, and before he could regain his balance, Vega had him by the throat.

"You might be the best forger in the world, but if you ever interrupt me again, I will tear your tongue out with a pair of pliers," Vega warned. "Do you fucking hear me?"

"Y-yes," Rosa choked.

"Now go, make sure the machine is ready," he ordered, shoving him toward his office.

"Colonel, if I may," Captain Javier said, once Rosa was out of earshot.

"What is it, Captain?" Vega answered, immediately at ease.

"I . . . I mean no disrespect," he began, looking down at the ground.

"You may speak freely," Vega said, returning to his spot at the hangar doors.

"It's the American, sir. The man has no honor. He has betrayed his country, his friends—how do you know that he will come?"

The answer came not from Vega but from the distant hum of an approaching turboprop echoing through the rain, and moments later a dark blue de Havilland DHC-3 dropped out of the clouds. The pilot circled the field and lined up for approach.

"Fear is a powerful motivator." Vega watched the pilot fight the crosswind before planting the de Havilland's oversized tires on the runway with a splatter of mud.

Moments later the single-engine turboprop taxied to a halt outside the hangar, and after the pilot cut the engine, Jefferson Gray climbed down into the mud, a metal attaché case handcuffed to his arm.

"Hell of a day for a flight, Colonel," he said.

"There were some who doubted you would make it," Vega said, walking toward the row of tables next to the machine.

"Well, I imagine those people didn't see Senator Mendez on Fox News last night." Gray unlocked the cuff on his wrist and set the case next to one of the stacks of freshly printed twenty-dollar bills.

The mention of the interview sent Vega's mind drifting back to the late-night call from President Díaz.

"Turn on the Fox News," his boss ordered.

Vega rolled out of bed and turned on the satellite with a touch of the remote. The screen blinked to life, and he found himself staring at Senator Patrick Mendez.

"*I see the Díaz administration as a bunch of rabid dogs. It is a corrupt regime with known ties to Iran, Cuba, and the cartels. I think it is high time the United States did something to show President Díaz that we will not tolerate his actions.*"

"*Like what, Senator?*" *the reporter asked.*

"*Let me put it this way,*" *Mendez said, turning to the camera.* "*President Eduardo Díaz, the Security Council meets in three days,*" *he said, holding up his fingers,* "*and if I don't hear a response from your government before then, well, things are going to get mighty uncomfortable for you and your cronies there in Venezuela.*"

"*Is this man out of his mind?*" *Díaz shouted.* "*Who does he think I am, a dog to be threatened on national television? We had a deal. A deal, Carlos, and now this hijo de puta* wants more money? *Where am I going to get that kind of cash?*"

"Captain," Vega said, nodding to his aide, "go and see if Rosa is finished sulking." He waited until the man was out of earshot before turning his attention to Gray, who had picked up one of the twenties and was holding it up to the light.

"Look at me," Vega hissed.

"Problem, Carlos?"

"When were you going to tell me that Hayes was

still alive?" Vega demanded, looking for fear in the American's eyes but finding nothing but cold determination.

"You let me worry about Hayes," Gray said. "What I need to know is if Díaz is going to pay Mendez."

"He doesn't have it," Vega said.

"That's what I thought," Gray said.

"But that doesn't change our arrangement," Vega said, nodding to the open five-by-nine-foot shipping container in the corner. "There is enough paper in there to print five million dollars."

"Let me ask you something, Carlos. what is it that you want?"

"What do you mean?" Vega asked, temporarily caught off guard.

"Like you said, there is enough paper there to print five million dollars. That added to the five we've already loaded up is ten million. Last month that was all I wanted, but things have changed."

"Are you trying to get out of our arrangement?" Vega demanded, his hand slipping to the pistol at his hip.

"No, Carlos, what I'm saying is that a month ago this was a clean operation and five million was all I needed," Gray said, moving to the case. "But in thirty-six hours, Mendez is going to realize that I'm not coming back, and when that happens, it is going to take a hell of a lot more than five million to stay alive."

"Go on," Vega said.

"So my question is, do you want to keep working for the president of Venezuela?" Gray asked, thumbing his combination into the case and opening the lid. "Or do you want to be the president of Venezuela?"

35

PUERTO RICO

I still can't believe you sold the Gulfstream," Waters complained.

"Stop living in the past."

"Why don't we fly straight to Venezuela?"

Hayes shook his head, a hint of a smile hooking the edge of his lips. "Flying into a covert operation on a CIA-contracted aircraft is not my idea of tradecraft."

"This is why Air Potomac exists," Waters protested.

"You've been hanging around Levi a little too long," Hayes said, shouldering his assault pack and walking down the stairs. He pointed up at the tail. "JT, what do you see?"

"Looks like nobody's bothered to replace those numbers in at least a few years."

"Exactly, I think we'll be better off with our own ride."

The CASA C-212 cruised at 15,000 feet, a silver spark that glinted in the pale blue expanse of the sky. In the cabin, Hayes turned away from the window and fixed his attention on JT.

"You remember that time in Iraq?" he asked.

"We were there for six months, you think you might be able to narrow it down a bit?" JT said without taking his eyes from the screen.

"I was thinking of one specific time. we were in Mosul and you had the great idea—"

"Let me stop you right there," JT said, holding up his hand. "If you want me to do something illegal, all you have to do is ask. There is no need to go back to Mosul."

Hayes grinned, but before he could reply, Waters's voice came over the intercom.

"What happened in Mosul?" he asked.

"Hey, stick monkey, the grown-ups are talking," JT said, getting to his feet. "You just worry about getting us where we're going."

"Asshole," Waters grumbled before JT punched the privacy button with his index finger.

"Does he ever stop with the questions?" JT asked.

"Not so far." Hayes smiled. "But seriously, you owe me, and I'm calling in a marker."

JT's eyebrows shot up in surprise. "If you are calling in Mosul, this must be big. Tell me more."

"The guy I waxed in Washington mentioned a guy named Jefferson Gray."

"Let me guess, no Social?"

"This one might be a little more complicated."

"Challenge accepted," JT said.

"Gray works for the CIA." Hayes winced.

"No problem, I've got a back door already set up to get into their mainframe."

"Wait, seriously?"

"Yeah, check this out," JT said, turning the Toughbook so Hayes could see the screen.

Hayes watched him type `Applied Technical Concepts` into the address bar, and a moment later the company's webpage popped up on the screen. The landing page showed a glass-fronted building in Tysons Corner, Virginia, followed by the logos of the Fortune 500 companies that had contracts with the company.

"These dudes are big-time," JT said, pointing at the logos at the bottom. "They are making a killing in the private sector, made six billion last year, and they are still running this piece-of-shit page."

"And how does this help us find Gray?" Hayes asked.

"Think of it this way: if you were going to rob a bank, would you walk in the front door?"

"Not unless I wanted to go to jail."

"Same thing applies on the net. You don't just walk into the CIA's mainframe with a ski mask and a Tech 9 and start asking for secure documents."

"So how do you strong-arm the CIA?" Hayes asked.

"You use the service entrance, which brings us back to ATC, which provides all the data packaging for the CIA's mainframes. I just drop this little bit of code right here, and voilà."

```
>>>>CIA Remote Portal
_Access Granted
>>>>Connection Established_
Status: Online
Query: Gray, Jefferson
Access Denied.
```

"Well, that was anticlimactic," Hayes said, patting JT on the shoulder before leaning back in the chair. "I think I'm going to grab some shut-eye. You want to give me a shout when you actually have something?"

Instead of answering, JT was muttering to himself, fingers flying over the keyboard. "That doesn't make any sense, why would it be denied unless . . ."

Hayes had almost drifted off to sleep when JT slapped the table with the flat of his hand and shouted, "Hayes, you dirty motherfucker!"

"Hey, man, I was almost asleep," Hayes said, sitting up and doing his best to appear confused.

"Bullshit," JT said, "I'm calling bullshit, you played me."

"Played you? What the hell are you talking about?"

"What am I talking about? Is that how you want to play it? Fine with me," JT said, turning the computer so Hayes could see the screen. "You see that?" he asked, pointing at it. "You know what that is? It's ten years in a federal fucking pen."

Hayes leaned forward and read the words on the screen.

```
SAP/Directory/Operations—Gray, Jefferson
Critical Actions Program
Operations:
Silver-Lake. Emerald-Serpent.
   Syphon-Filter.
Treadstone 71
```

"I'm not going to jail, not for you or anyone," JT added.

But Hayes wasn't listening; all of his attention was taken up by the information on the screen. He'd never heard of the operations listed under Gray's name, but he knew enough about the DoD's code-name-generator database to know they were randomly created and had no attachment to actual places or events.

"You have any idea why the CIA is running a special-access program in Venezuela?" he asked aloud.

A special-access program was the security protocol the government used to protect its darkest secrets. Typically they were reserved for black projects, programs like Treadstone that would keep most Americans up at night if they knew they existed.

"No idea, and I'm pretty sure I don't want to know," JT answered. "Like I said, I'm not going to jail."

"You're not going to prison. Now shut up and see what you can find out about the Critical Actions Program."

JT huffed but did as Hayes asked, and after a few additional keystrokes, a second window opened up. "Looks like the Critical Actions Program is some kind of joint CIA/DoD special-mission unit. Your Jefferson Gray is at the top of the pyramid and his direct supervisor is Senator Patrick Mendez of—"

"The Senate Actions Committee," Hayes finished for him.

"You know him?" JT asked.

"Not personally, but I know his reputation," he answered, turning his attention back to the window.

The Senate Actions Committee was set up after the War on Terror expanded into Iraq. Around the time the CIA started using drones to knock off terrorists in places like Yemen, Pakistan, and Sudan. The Agency referred to these strikes as "targeted killings," but to the rest of the world, they were assassinations.

Oddly enough, the CIA made no attempt to hide

what it was doing, and soon the drone feeds started to show up in the daily military briefings at the White House. It wasn't until the media brought up Executive Order 12333 and began discussing the legality of the targeted killings that the president started to worry about the ramifications.

Known to officers in the intelligence community as "twelve-triple-three," the document signed by President Reagan laid out the legal framework of the national intelligence effort. It was Paragraph 2.11 that had the president's legal counsel worried, specifically the language that read "No person employed by or acting on behalf of the United States Government shall engage in, or conspire to engage in, political assassination."

To distance the White House from potential legal and political fallout, the president formed the Senate Actions Committee to oversee all of the Agency's black programs. Senator Patrick Mendez was chosen to head the committee, and with a scratch of the president's pen, he became the overseer of all the Agency's black programs—programs like Treadstone.

In an instant Hayes realized that he'd found the answers to the questions that had been haunting him since the attack back in La Conner. *So that's how they found me,* he thought.

This is not a coincidence, the voice warned.

36

The first sign that Waters had *not* checked the weather report became evident when the CASA descended to 15,000 feet. One moment Hayes was sleeping peacefully on the nylon bench and in the next instant he was flying across the cargo hold.

"Waaaaters," he yelled, bouncing off the bulkhead, "what the fuuuuck?"

"Just a touch of turbulence," Waters answered from the cockpit.

Hayes climbed to his feet and grabbed ahold of the anchor line cable. He managed to steady himself long enough to look out the port-side window, catch a quick glimpse of the jet black and the yellow fingers of lightning cracking across the horizon before a cross wind slapped the plane across the sky.

"On second thought, you might want to hook up," Waters said, his voice devoid of its usually cockiness. "Like, right *now*."

Dear God, please let me live long enough to kill him, Hayes prayed, stumbling to the back of the plane, where he snapped his static line into the cable and palmed the red button mounted to the strut.

"I'm punching through," Waters yelled as the ramp cracked open. He shoved the controls forward, sending the CASA into a screaming dive.

The clouds rolled into the cargo hold, the air heavy with the smell of rain and wet earth. Hayes was blind and being tossed around like a pea in a rattle can, too busy trying to stay on his feet to curse the pilot.

And then they were through, and the sky was clear and smooth as glass.

Below the plane the triple-canopy jungle shimmered in the haze of the twin turboprops. An endless sea of green, broken by sporadic scars of the black and coffee brown of the Arauca River as it coiled southeast toward Colombia.

"One minute out!" Waters yelled.

Hayes nudged the drop bag containing his gear closer to the edge of the ramp and snapped its static line next to his. Then he tightened his chin strap, eyes glued to the amber light mounted to the strut next to the ramp.

Since he was jumping off the ramp, Hayes couldn't see the drop zone, which put him at the mercy of Waters. Not only was the man responsible for keeping the plane steady and maintaining a safe jump speed, Hayes was also trusting him to tell him when to jump.

Too early and he would fall short of the drop zone. Too late and he would overfly it. Hayes was about to steal a glance into the cockpit, just to make sure Waters was paying attention, when the light flashed from red to green and Hayes kicked the drop bag off the ramp, waited for the static line to jerk taut, and then took a powerful step off the back of the ramp.

He shoved his chin tight into his chest, locked his feet and knees together for a moment before the prop blast hit him in the face. The exhaust was hot, and the acrid taste of the aviation fuel scalded his skin, sucking the air from his lungs.

The slipstream grabbed his legs and slapped them over his head, and Hayes fought to keep his body tight while falling at thirty-two feet per second. He kept track of his descent by counting in his head.

One thousand, two thousand . . .

A moment later the static line reached the end of its travel and yanked the chute from the pack tray. But instead of the violent jerk of the canopy opening up and gathering air, Hayes kept falling.

Looking up, he immediately diagnosed the problem: The risers that connected his harness to the chute were tangled and keeping the canopy from expanding. Hayes kicked his legs, trying to get the risers to unwind, knowing that he was falling too fast.

Pull your reserve.

His hands dropped to his chest and he was about to pull the rip cord when the chute caught air and the risers snapped tight, burning his neck and breaking his chin strap.

Usually Hayes spent the remainder of a descent in quiet reflection, enjoying the breeze against his skin and the warmth of the sun on his face, thanking the airborne gods that he was still alive and not a bundle of broken bones and skin on the ground, but as he steered the chute into the wind and got his first look at the drop zone, Hayes realized he had a second problem.

From the satellite imagery the clearing looked massive, but from a hundred feet in the air, the drop zone looked like a dot of brown in a sea of green. But it wasn't the size of the DZ that had him worried, it was the chute of the drop bundle below heading toward the trees.

The sudden cross-breeze grabbed his chute and shoved it hard to the right. Hayes reached up and grabbed the left riser with both hands. He tugged it into his chest, trying to steer the chute clear of the tree line.

Not happening.

Hayes let go of the riser, brought both hands to the

top of his head, interlaced his fingers so he could use his forearms to shield his face, and then he was in the trees.

Without any air to hold it open, the canopy collapsed, and Hayes was falling through the trees like a lawn dart. He saw the flash of the limbs and leaves through the space between his forearms, flashes of brown and green. Branches raked the exposed skin of his wrist and neck. He looked down and saw the jungle floor rushing up and he prepared himself for a broken leg or back, when the chute finally caught on a branch and pendulumed him into the trunk of a cacao tree.

The blow knocked the breath from his lungs and filled his mouth with the coppery taste of his own blood. Hayes shook his head and blinked the tears from his eyes. The first thing he saw was a pair of howler monkeys grinning at him from an adjoining limb.

"What the hell are you looking at?" he demanded.

The monkeys chittered away, leaving Hayes to take stock of his situation. He estimated that he was twenty feet above the jungle floor. *Too far to drop.* His only option was to deploy his reserve and use the chute to climb down.

Hayes pulled the metal rip cord handle free, releasing the pins that secured the front panels of the reserve. The moment the tension was released, the spring-assisted chute tumbled out of the pack tray and fell toward the ground.

Careful to keep his weight balanced, Hayes unhooked

his chest and leg straps. He reached out for the reserve, knowing that one wrong move would send him falling to the ground. Hayes managed to wrap his right hand around the silk and then coil it between his legs. Slowly he shifted his weight out of the harness, and after transferring all of his weight to the chute, he swung free. Unlike rope, the silk was too thin to get a firm grip, and he slid toward the ground like a fireman down a greased pole.

He landed with an *ummmmph* and a muffled curse.

That sucked.

Hayes rolled over to see if anything was broken and was about to sit up when a bearded man dressed in a faded brown campesino shirt, filthy jeans, and a dingy straw hat stepped out of the shadows.

"Cole Boggs," the man said, lifting a bottle of Wild Turkey to his lips and taking a long pull. "Welcome to hell."

37

LA ESTACADA, VENEZUELA

Hayes wasn't sure what to make of the man standing over him. According to Shaw, the man was considered *eccentric*. But as Hayes took in his clothes, the AK-47 strapped over his chest, and the bandolier of shotgun shells around his waist, *eccentric* was not the first word that popped into his mind.

This dude has gone completely around the bend.

"Adam Hayes," he said, getting to his feet and brushing the bark and dirt off the front of his clothes.

"I was *gonna* give you a nine," Boggs answered, resting his free hand on the machete hanging from his belt and pointing the bottle at the chute hanging from the tree. "But then you went and fucked up the landing."

"Cute," Hayes said, pressing the earpiece connected to his radio into his ear. "I must have missed the memo. Didn't know we were playing dress-up."

"My *ropas*?" Boggs asked, looking down at his chest. "What's wrong with 'em?"

"You look like a mix between Pancho Villa and Sancho Panza."

"Well, after all the fucking noise you made coming through those trees, we are going to need a posse to get out of here alive."

I like this dude.

"You let me worry about that, Sancho," Hayes said, turning on the radio and pressing the talk button. "Covey to Grinder."

"Do I get a call sign?" Boggs asked.

Waters's voice came over the radio. "Go for Covey."

"On the ground and linked up with code name Sancho," he said and grinned.

"Uh, roger that, Grinder. Be advised, looks like you have company coming in from your west. Two trucks coming from a camp by the river."

"Roger that."

"That's Vega's territory. we better *vámonos*," Boggs said.

"You mind if I . . . ?" Hayes said, reaching out for the bottle.

"Knock yourself out," Boggs said.

"I know you have your own way of doing things,"

Hayes said, taking the bottle. "And I want you to know that I respect that."

"Well, that's good, because to be honest I was kinda worried— Hey, what the fuck?" Boggs asked as Hayes turned the bottle over and dumped the contents on the ground.

"Let's get something straight, Sancho. I didn't jump out of a perfectly good airplane because I wanted to go day-drinking. This isn't a fucking picnic. You do what I tell you when I tell you, *comprende*?"

"Listen here, padna," Boggs interjected, the anger bringing his Cajun accent out. "I didn't come out here to pass a good time. Ford—he *was* workin' for me when they took him down."

"And now he's dead."

"You got somethin' you wanna say?" Boggs challenged, taking a step forward. "I loved that man like a brother."

"Easy, Sancho, I'm just telling it like it is. The way I see it, there are two ways this thing plays out," Hayes said.

"Enlighten me, boss man."

"You can fuck off—go find you a new bottle and a nice deep hole to hide in," he said, tossing the bottle into the undergrowth.

"Or?"

"Or you can come with me and get some payback," Hayes answered, before turning in the direction he'd last seen the gear bundle.

"They weren't lyin' when they said you was an asshole!" Boggs yelled at his back.

You have no idea, buddy.

Hayes hadn't understood the importance of standards until after he was assigned to the 82nd Airborne. He'd been with his new platoon for less than a month when they went to the range and Hayes noticed one of his squad leaders providing "corrective training"—the politically correct way of saying he was trying to smoke the soul out of the offending soldier.

Sergeant Mills had this kid doing push-ups, flutter kicks, and sprints until Hayes thought the boy was going to die. Wanting to be a good leader who was respected and liked by his men, green-as-grass First Lieutenant Hayes stepped in and suggested that Sergeant Mills had made his point.

Hayes never forgot the look of disgust on the sergeant's face.

The next day during physical training Sergeant First Class Jones joined Hayes for a run.

"Sir, Sergeant Mills told me what happened at the range."

As Hayes was a new lieutenant, every day at the unit was like drinking from a fire hose, and he had since forgotten all about the incident.

"Going to have to help me out here, Sarge."

"Sergeant Mills said that he was disciplining Private Andrews and you told him to stop."

"Yeah, I said that he'd made his point."

The look on his platoon sergeant's face was the same expression that he'd seen on Sergeant Mills, and he knew instinctively that he'd made a significant mistake.

"I fucked something up, didn't I?"

"Sir, a platoon is like a family. As the lieutenant, you are the benevolent father. You bring us the things we need, like bullets and food, and you keep the brass off our ass, and we love you for that."

"Okay."

"The noncommissioned officers, the sergeants," he said, pointing to himself and then over at the squad leaders, "we are the collective mother of this family."

"I think so."

"The privates, or 'joes,' as we call them, are the children. Are you tracking, sir?"

"I'm with you."

"Now, as parents we have worked hard all our lives, scrimped and saved so we could put a roof over the kids' heads. That roof and all the nice things under it are the standards that we live by. Still with me, sir?"

"Mom, Dad, and standards."

Sergeant First Class Jones nodded his agreement.

"So what's the problem?"

"The kids, sir."

"Kids?"

"*The privates, sir, the joes—they are our kids and they are evil, destructive motherfuckers.*"

"*Jesus, Sergeant,*" Hayes said, surprised by the conviction in the man's voice.

"*That's right, sir, they need Jesus, because if left to their own devices, our fucking kids will burn down our house with Mom and Dad in the fucking bed.*"

"*That's . . . that's some heavy stuff, Sergeant.*"

"*Heavy is the crown, sir. Just remember to always lead from the front and keep the standards; everything else will take care of itself.*"

It was a lesson Hayes had never forgotten, and why he wasn't surprised when he heard Boggs following him through the undergrowth.

"Your gear is this way," he said, jogging up beside him. "But we seriously need to get the hell out of here."

Twenty yards ahead Hayes could see the break in the trees that signaled the clearing, and by the time they cleared the tree line, sweat was pouring down his back. *Damn humidity.*

The jungle was a far cry from the thin, dry air that he'd become accustomed to in Washington. Beneath the trees it was thick enough that Hayes felt he could take a bite out of it. He was wondering how in the hell Boggs could stomach liquor in this heat when he saw the drop bag on the edge of the clearing.

"There it is," he said, breaking into a jog. "You got a vehicle?"

"Yeah, it's right over— Oh, fuck," Boggs said.

Hayes slowed and turned his head. He was about to ask what the problem was when he saw a jacked-up green pickup, the bed packed with fighters, burst from the far tree line.

"Who the hell are these clowns?" he demanded.

"Narcos," Boggs said, hands closing around the AK. "We've got to go."

38

LA ESTACADA, VENEZUELA

The wind had picked up, pushing graphite clouds across the saltwater-blue sky, when Hayes reached the gear bag. He pulled his knife from the sheath and hacked at the parachute harness, trying to get the bag free.

"Grinder, this is Covey," Waters's voice said in his ear.

Hayes didn't have time to talk, so he double-clicked the transmit button instead of answering. The technique was called breaking squelch, and he knew that in the plane Waters would hear the long blast of static and understand what was going on.

"Grinder, I am five kilometers to your east, and there is some nasty weather coming in. Visibility is dropping to zero. I'm going to have to pull out."

"Shit," Hayes said, throwing his arm through the carry loop and shouldering the bag. He knew that the CASA was unarmed, so it couldn't help in a fight, but knowing it was there made him feel like he had options.

"What?" Boggs said.

"We're on our own. Where is your truck?"

"Straight ahead, on the trail," Boggs answered, moving past him. "I've got a partner waiting for us."

Hayes did his best to keep up, but the weight of the bag and the humid air dragged him down.

A second pickup pulled abreast of the first. Hayes could hear the engines roar as the drivers hit the gas and steered toward the fleeing figures.

"C'mon, c'mon," Boggs said from the top of the hill.

Oh, you mean I should hurry up? Hayes thought, legs burning from the slight incline. At the top of the hill he paused to catch his breath. "Don't worry about me," he said, panting, "I'll catch up," and he watched Boggs scamper to the mud-spattered Jeep parked near the trees. There was a woman sitting in the passenger seat.

This humidity is kicking my ass, he thought, dropping his hands to his knees and looking back at the trucks racing to intercept him. He guessed they were a hundred yards away and closing. Close enough for him to see the muzzle flashes every time one of the narcos took a potshot at him, but still out of range of their AKs.

"*Hey!*" Boggs yelled, slapping the flat of his hand

against the side of the Jeep. "Are you *seriously* taking a *break* right now?"

Hayes stood up straight, wiped the sweat off his forehead, and turned to glare at the DEA agent safely ensconced behind the wheel. A bullet cracked over his head.

He dropped the bag and unhooked the clasps that held the Kevlar-reinforced cover. Ignoring the shouts from the pair of pickups bearing down on him, Hayes pulled out what looked like a green poster tube from the bag.

"What the hell are you doing?" Boggs shouted.

"Be right there, Sancho," Hayes said, yanking the retaining pin from the M72 LAW and pulling the telescoping body backward until it snapped into place.

First built for the Army in 1963, the LAW, or Light Anti-Tank Weapon, fired a 66-millimeter rocket that was considered underpowered by today's standards. But Hayes loved the rocket because it was small and light and had plenty of ass to get the job done.

"Let's see if we can get a tune out of this trombone," he said, slapping the front and rear sights free before shouldering the launcher.

One of the pickups had surged ahead, and Hayes was lining the sights on the truck when one of the narcos in the back laid his AK over the roll bar and fired off a burst.

"Not even close, asshole," he said to himself.

A second shooter opened up and the bullets kicked a line of dirt on their way up the hill.

"Good night, ladies," Hayes said.

He snapped the trigger down and the rocket screamed from the launcher. Traveling at 475 feet per second, the rocket's time of flight from the launcher to the front of the truck was almost instantaneous.

The warhead punched through the grill, slammed into the engine block, and detonated on impact. The overpressure shoved the nose of the truck down into the dirt, ripped the engine from the mount, and shoved it through the dash.

A wall of flame rushed toward the bed, scorching the men in the back on its way to the fuel tank. And then it was all over.

"Boom goes the dynamite," Hayes said, stripping an H&K 416 from the bag before closing the cover. He yanked a magazine from his belt, shoved it into the rifle, and racked the charging handle to the rear.

The driver of the second vehicle, seeing the lead truck disappear in a ball of flame, toed the brakes and slowed long enough for Hayes to tuck the buttstock into his shoulder, drop to a knee, and center his eye behind the Trijicon 4x32 ACOG mounted to the rifle.

He settled the red chevron on the tip of the driver's chin, thumbed the safety to fire, and fired two quick shots. The suppressor spat twice, *thwap, thwap*, and Hayes stayed in the glass long enough to see the back of the driver's head explode before getting calmly to his feet, scooping up the bag, and heading down the hill.

"What about him?" Boggs asked, pointing at the narco running across the field.

"The little fish, I throw away." Hayes smiled and hoisted the gear bag.

39

LA ESTACADA, VENEZUELA

The horizon was a sullen gray, like static on a busted TV, when the Jeep pulled out of the trees and bumped onto the hardpan of the road. In the distance, lightning forked over the green hills, Hayes observed from the passenger seat of the mud-spattered Jeep.

"I can't believe you let him get away," Boggs said. "That dude is on his way to Vega right now."

"Vega's small potatoes."

"Small potatoes? Are you serious? Colonel Vega is a psycho—well, shit, I don't need to tell you that, you guys trained him."

"What do you mean, 'you guys'?"

"Spooks, spies, agents, whatever you CIA cats are calling yourselves these days."

"I'm not a spy."

"C'mon, man, I was born at night, but it wasn't last night," Boggs said. "You've got the moves, and the look, and need I remind you that I just watched you jump out of an airplane."

"What are you talking about?" Izzy asked in Spanish as she leaned in from the back seat.

"He thinks I'm a spy," Hayes said, turning his attention toward the woman.

He'd seen the badge on her belt and the gun on her waist and knew that she was a cop. But on closer inspection, he saw the shield bore the Colombian flag, not the Venezuelan, and Hayes found himself wondering why she was here.

"Knows foreign languages." Boggs shrugged before pulling a pack of soggy Camels from his shirt pocket. "Trust me, baby, he's a spy."

"A spy, is that true?" Izzy asked.

"No, I'm . . ."

"You're what?"

"It's complicated."

"Are you married?" she asked.

"What is this," Hayes asked Boggs, "twenty questions?"

"Just making conversation," the man said, and shrugged.

"Well, in that case, I've got a few of my own, like why you thought it was a good idea to bring a civilian along," Hayes asked.

"It's complicated," Boggs said, flashing him a look that told Hayes he would fill him in later.

"Fine." Hayes nodded. "Then how about you tell me where we are going."

"Little town west of here called El Nula."

"Why the hell are we going west?" Hayes demanded. "You said the safe house was in La Macanilla, which is east of here."

"I need to drop off a stowaway," Boggs answered, nodding toward the woman in the back.

"No, we are *not*," Izzy interjected.

"*Yes*, we are," Boggs said.

"Hey, can we—" Hayes interjected, trying to steer the conversation back to why they were heading west instead of east, but they ignored him and continued bickering like an old married couple.

"*No*, we are *not!*" Izzy shouted.

When he tried and failed to get their attention a second time, Hayes decided he was done being nice. *The hell with this,* he thought, grabbing the wheel.

"Hey, what the—?" Boggs began, but before he could finish the question, Hayes jerked the wheel hard to the right.

The Jeep swerved off the road, tires bouncing over the mounded dirt that acted as a curb, and into a field.

Boggs tried to regain control, but Hayes held on tight, forcing the DEA agent to slam on the brakes.

"What in the—?" Boggs began when the Jeep slid to a halt.

"Shut the fuck up," Hayes snarled, reaching over and turning the key to the off position.

The engine died and silence fell over the interior, and once Hayes was sure it was going to hold, he turned in his seat so he was addressing both Izzy and Boggs.

"This Jerry Springer bullshit stops *now*, you understand me?" he said, waiting for both of them to nod before continuing. "Okay, let's try this again. I just damn near broke my neck jumping out of an airplane. You know why that happened?"

Boggs tried to look away, but Hayes wasn't having it.

"Look at me, asshole," he said, grabbing Boggs by the front of his shirt. "I jumped out of the plane because you said the safe house was in La Macanilla. Now you are telling me that it's in El Nula, which means instead of almost breaking my neck and getting shot up by narcos, I could have just driven my happy ass across a bridge. So how about you cut the bullshit and tell me what in the hell is going on?"

Boggs tore himself from Hayes's grip and took an angry drag from the cigarette. "Man, haven't you figured it out yet?" he demanded, blowing out a cloud of smoke.

"Figured what out?"

"That the CIA has a leak."

Hayes rolled his eyes. "If I had a nickel for every time I've heard that shit, I'd be a rich man."

"I know you look at me and think that I'm some whacked-out undercover dude who's been under so long he doesn't know which way is up."

"Well, you *do* look the part," Hayes said.

"Funny. Back when the DEA stood up this whole cartel exploitation gig, there were four of us working Colombia. We ran everything by the book, sent in our target packages, intel reports, locations of safe houses, everything, and never had a problem. Then we come across the border and now it's just me by my lonesome."

"Great story," Hayes said. "But it doesn't prove the CIA is leaking information."

"Suit yourself, broham," Boggs said, starting the engine and shifting into gear. "All I know is that the DEA sure as fuck didn't leak Ford's grid to whoever wiped his team out."

"How can you be so sure?" Hayes asked as Boggs bumped the Jeep back onto the road.

"Because I never sent it to them."

"Wait, back up," Hayes said.

Boggs flashed him a conspiratorial smile. "That got your attention, didn't it?"

"Yeah, and now you are going to need to explain."

"Easy, the DEA didn't have the location of Ford's

team, because I don't send shit back to the States. No reports, no memos, no birthday cards, nothing. Zero."

There is no way. Is there?

"Let's say I buy your little theory. Why does the CIA care about what you have going on?"

"Because I went after Vega," Boggs said.

At the mention of the man's name, the woman in the back began cursing under her breath with such vehemence that Hayes turned to see if they had picked up a sailor.

"I take it she isn't a fan, either," he said.

"Her father was the minister of justice under Mateo. He tried to indict Vega and—"

"And that piece of shit executed my family!" Izzy shouted.

Great, a drunk and a chick with a vendetta. This day just keeps getting better and better, Hayes thought, settling back to enjoy the rest of the ride.

He was still mulling over the situation and what Boggs had told him about the leak at the CIA when the Jeep crested a small hill, and far to the right, Hayes saw the white stucco gleam of a town.

40

CARACAS, VENEZUELA

Nestled in the verdant green foothills of El Ávila, Hacienda Bella Vista was a world unto itself. The sprawling estate, like many others in the area, had once belonged to a member of Hugo Chávez's inner circle—Juan Carlos Osuna, the dictator's finance minister. The man charged with curtailing the rampant unemployment and homelessness that plagued Venezuela in the late nineties.

But while his countrymen starved in the streets, Juan Carlos was busy skimming millions of dollars in state funds, using the money to import the Venetian glass that lined the bottom of his Olympic swimming pool and build the training pen where Colonel Vega stood,

watching his daughter work the chestnut Selle Français
gelding he'd bought for her quinceañera.

"Eyes up, Catalina," he admonished her as she
brought the horse around the turn and lined up on
the first series of hop-over poles. "Yes, good, excellent
position," he said, and clapped.

"Thank you, Papa," she said.

"I told you she would love it, María," he said,
grinning at his wife.

"You spoil her, Carlos," she said. "You give a little
girl everything she asks for and she will grow up to be
a little bitch."

"María." Vega feigned shock. "That is your daughter
you are speaking about."

"It's true and you know it."

"Perhaps." He shrugged. "But there are worse things
a father can do." He turned to the stone wall on the
south side of the sprawling estate.

It was a view he and his wife enjoyed, but for different
reasons. For his wife, the view was a reminder of how
far they had come from the small apartment on the east
side of the city. But for Vega, it was a constant warning
of where he was heading if this plan failed.

His eyes drifted over the city of his birth, ending at
the skeletal core of the Centro Financiero Confinanzas.

When construction began in 1990, Venezuela was in
the midst of a banking boom and the forty-five-story
skyscraper was to serve as the glittering headquarters of

the Confinanzas group. But when the lead investor died suddenly at fifty-five, construction was halted, and with the economic crash that followed, the building became known as Torre de David—the Tower of David— Venezuela's vertical slum.

It was here that Carlos Vega grew up, on the bottom floor of the tallest slum in the capital. Dreaming of the day when he would look down on the city that had tried to crush them into the gutter.

The appearance of the two olive-drab Tiunas climbing up the steep incline leading to the front gate of the hacienda signaled the end of his musings and the return to the business at hand. He followed the flagstone path to the front of the house, passing the stone fountain with the statue of Simón Bolívar, with his famous sword raised toward the heavens, on his way to the guesthouse.

Inside, he walked to the sideboard and chose a Cohiba Robusto from the humidor on the desk and snipped the end of the Cuban with a gold cigar cutter.

Where in the fuck is Gray? he wondered, striking a match against the bottom of the desk and holding the flame to the end of the cigar.

"Colonel," his aide said, knocking on the door.

"Bring him in," Vega ordered, extinguishing the match with a wave of his hand.

A pair of burly sergeants appeared at the door, dragging a wet rat of a man between them. His face bruised and purple, one eye swollen shut, the other wide with fear at the sight of the metal chair sitting in the center of a rectangle of cut plastic.

"No . . . no . . . no," the man begged.

"Quiet," one of the sergeants snapped, slamming him roughly into the chair and taking up a position behind him.

Vega took a long pull from the cigar and blew the smoke toward the man.

"Can I offer you something to drink?" he asked, moving to the sideboard. "Whiskey, perhaps?"

He didn't wait for an answer; instead, Vega pulled the stopper on a glass decanter and poured two fingers of Johnnie Walker Black into a glass.

"What is your name?" he asked, carrying the liquor to the man and handing it over.

"Alejandro, *señor*," the man answered, before downing half of the glass in one swallow.

"Do you know who I am, Alejandro?"

"Y-yes, *señor*," he said and nodded.

"Very good," he said, moving around the front of the desk. "I understand you work for us in Apure."

Alejandro gave a vigorous nod that told Vega he was eager to please.

"And what is it that you do?"

"I work with the sergeant," he began, turning toward one of his guards.

"Eyes front," the man ordered, cuffing him across the back of his head. "Answer the colonel's question, pig."

"I guard the airstrip."

"Now tell me what happened."

"I heard a plane flying in low over the trees. It sounded like it was going to land, but there are no shipments today, so I tried to call the boss on the radio."

"By 'boss' you mean . . . "

"Sergeant Gustavo," he said, nodding to the man who had hit him.

"And did Sergeant Gustavo answer?"

"No, *señor*, he was . . ." Alejandro began, but thought better of it at the last moment. "He was b-busy."

"Busy . . . hmm." Vega nodded, his eyes flashing to Sergeant Gustavo. *Busy doing what, Sergeant?* he wondered, but decided to save the question for later.

"Then what happened?" Vega asked.

"A man jumped out of the plane—he had a *paracaídas*, a . . ." The man paused, struggling for the word.

"A parachute," Vega said.

"*Sí, sí*, a parachute."

"And then?"

"There were ten of us and only two of them, so . . ." The man shrugged, and Vega assumed he was saying the math spoke for itself. "But . . . but . . ."

"Spit it out," the sergeant demanded.

"This man wasn't normal, he didn't run away like the others."

"There were others?" Vega asked.

"A man and a woman."

"This other man, the one who ran away, did you see his face?"

Alejandro gulped the rest of the liquor and hesitated before offering a nod.

Vega went to his desk, pulled open the center drawer, and took out a photo. He set the cigar in the marble ashtray and crossed back to Alejandro.

"Is this the man?" he asked, holding up a picture of Cole Boggs.

"*Sí*, Colonel, it is not a face I will ever forget."

"Do you know him?"

Instead of answering, Alejandro broke eye contact, paused to look down at the toe of his filthy shoes.

Vega dropped the picture at the man's feet, his right hand sliding behind his back, fingers coiling around the butt of the gold-plated .45. At the sight of the pistol the two sergeants stepped to the side, making sure they were out of the line of fire.

"This man is an American federal agent—a *sapo*," Vega said, pressing the barrel against the top of Alejandro's forehead and pushing the man's head back. Bringing his eyes up from his shoes. "Are you working with the gringos, Alejandro, is that why they let you live?"

"N-no—Colonel, on my life, no."

"Do you have a confession to make?" Vega leaned in. "You can tell me, whisper it soft into my ear, like you would in church."

For a moment the only sound in the room was the low hiss of the words tumbling out of the man's mouth. So soft and faint that despite being an inch from the man's mouth, Vega had to strain to hear him.

"Very good, Alejandro, very good." He nodded approvingly while he picked up the picture.

He carried it back to the desk, dropped it in the drawer, and pulled out a stack of banded hundred-dollar bills.

Vega tossed the cash into Alejandro's lap and turned to his aide. "They went to El Nula."

"Yes, sir."

"Help him up." He took the cigar out of the ashtray and pressed it to his lips.

"Yes, Colonel." The sergeants nodded.

"Fifty thousand dollars to the man who kills the gringo, do you hear me, Sergeant Gustavo? We reward those who are loyal," he said, blowing a cloud of smoke toward the two sergeants.

"Y-yes, sir." He coughed, closing his eyes against the cloud of smoke that rolled over his face.

"And we *punish* those who are not." Vega stepped through the smoke and pressed the 1911 to Gustavo's head and pulled the trigger.

EL NULA, VENEZUELA

El Nula was typical of the Central American towns Hayes had visited, with low-slung buildings painted in vibrant whites and pinks. The town was built around a square with a stately white cathedral and an open grass-lined plaza.

Boggs turned off the main road and Hayes watched as the welcoming pastels slowly shifted to the recognizable grays and weathered browns of the industrial district. He slowed in front of a two-story pillbox of a building.

"Here we are," Boggs said, parking the Jeep on the road.

Hayes's first thought when he saw the building was that Boggs couldn't have picked a worse spot for a safe house if he'd tried. Tactically, the fact that it was on the second floor of the building should have given them the advantage of the high ground. But all it took was a quick look up at the surrounding structures to realize the safe house was the runt of the block.

Boggs led the way, leaving Hayes to muscle the drop bag up the stairs by himself. *At least he left the door open*, Hayes thought, as he lugged the bag inside the apartment, past the kitchen to his right and into the living/dining room.

"I will make us something to eat," Izzy said, heading to the kitchen.

Hayes dumped the bag next to the balcony door and pulled out his cleaning kit. The Glock was filthy from the jump, and Hayes wanted to get the mud off before it dried. He carried the cleaning kit to the threadbare couch and set it on the table.

He pulled an oil-soaked cloth from the bag and spread it out on the table before dropping the mag and ejecting the round from the chamber. After breaking the Glock down, Hayes took a brush from the bag and scrubbed away the dirt.

"What's her story?" Hayes asked without looking up from the pistol.

"Her father was the minister of justice under President Mateo and one of the last honest men in the country."

"From what you said in the Jeep, it doesn't sound like that worked out too well for him. What happened?"

"While the rest of Mateo's cabinet was robbing

the country blind, Izzy's father was working to curb the corruption. He started with the military, tried to dislodge the generals who were letting the Colombian narcos bring drugs across the border. The generals went to Vega and paid him to handle the situation and—"

"And Vega killed him," Hayes said.

"Not just him, he killed Izzy's entire family," Boggs hissed. "She was the only one who made it out alive and, get this, now the fucker lives in their house."

"You're shitting me?"

"Nope," Boggs said. "Blood wasn't even dry on the floor before he started moving in. Guess he figured it would send a message."

Hayes turned his attention back to the Glock. He blew the last of the dirt from the slide before looking up.

"She can't stay here, you know that, right?"

"Yeah." Boggs nodded before glancing at his watch. "It's too late to try and cross the border now, but . . ."

"In the morning then," Hayes said, picking up a bottle of Rem Oil and using the needle tip to distribute the contents onto the slide rails.

"Fine."

Hayes set the bottle on the table and turned his attention to the balcony, leaving his hands free to reassemble the pistol. He felt Boggs's eyes on him and turned to see the man staring at him.

"Are you like the Rain Man of guns?"

"What?" Hayes said, slamming the magazine into the Glock and racking the slide to the rear.

"You're creeping me out."

"Relax, I just want to be ready if anything jumps off."

Boggs nodded thoughtfully. "Fair enough. So, speaking of jumping off, do you have a plan or something?"

"Where was Ford when he got hit?" Hayes asked.

"Somewhere south of the Orinoco, I think," Boggs replied.

"You think? He was *your* asset, which makes him your fucking responsibility, Boggs."

"Listen, I am about tired of your shit," Boggs spat. "You come down here with all of your spy shit, thinking you know how this works, but you don't."

Easy, the voice warned. *This guy might be a fuckup, but you still need what he knows, and you aren't going to get anywhere rubbing his face in it.*

"Look, it's been a long day," Hayes said, "and I appreciate your help. So why don't you fill me in on how this works?"

Boggs nodded and seemed to calm down. "I don't know how much undercover work you have done, but I can tell you that it is hard to get anything done when you have a leash around your neck. I spent most of my career undercover, so believe me when I tell you that there isn't a pause button you can hit when it's 'report time.' Ford and I operated under big-boy rules. I knew that he was out there doing his thing and would report in when he had the time."

"Fair enough." Hayes nodded. "When was the last time he made contact?"

"Two days before he was killed. Ford called in, said that he'd heard from one of his informants that there was a big load coming in from the south."

"How big?" Hayes asked.

"Big enough that they needed an Antonov An-12 to carry it all."

"Plane that size would be hard to hide," Hayes said.

"Well, that depends."

"On what?" Hayes asked.

"On who the plane belonged to." Boggs winked.

"Well, we know it *couldn't* have belonged to Vega," Hayes said, "because according to the official memo in your file, you were ordered to leave him alone."

"That dude is dirty as hell and nobody wanted to help me because he's in bed with the CIA."

"Here we go again with this."

"I'm serious, man." Boggs went to his bag and pulled out a camera. He thumbed the power on and brought it over to Hayes. "Check this out. This dude right here," he said, pointing at one of the pictures, "is as American as apple pie and he is all over the place."

Hayes reached into his assault pack and pulled out the ashen remains of the pictures Deano had printed out for him back in the States. He compared the two photos. It was the same man.

He remembered the conversation he'd had on the plane with Shaw.

"The last photo, the two men in the hangar."

"Vega," Shaw said, pointing to the man in uniform.

"And the other guy?"

"Never seen him before," Shaw said.

"Levi, look again," Hayes said, pointing at the photo. "You've never seen this guy before. You're sure?"

"Yes, Adam," Shaw replied, "I'm sure."

There was only one way to find out. Hayes grabbed a cylindrical case made of black nylon from his assault pack and carried it to the balcony. He unzipped the top section and carefully extracted the contents, snapping them together until he was holding what looked like an umbrella frame in his hand.

"Not a spy, huh?" Boggs said as Izzy walked in with coffee and two plates of food.

"What is that?" she asked in Spanish.

"It's a high-gain satellite antenna," Hayes said. "The only secure way to communicate out here."

He lowered himself into a crouch and adjusted the antenna so it had a clear view of the sky.

When he was satisfied, Hayes attached a coaxial cable to the base of the antenna. Back inside, he pulled out the Toughbook JT had given him and plugged the data cord into the port.

Hayes waited for the computer to boot up, and once a secure connection was established, he logged in to his email account and accessed the photos Deano had decrypted.

"These are the photos Ford sent me," he said, right-clicking on the image that showed Vega and the mystery man inside the hangar. "These coordinates are the geotagged location where the pictures were taken."

"I'm following."

"Good." Hayes stripped the lat/long from the geotag, opened a web browser, accessed Google Earth, and pasted the coordinates into the search bar.

"Pendare," Boggs said, nodding.

"You know it?"

"Yeah, I know it, but what was Ford doing there?"

"Well, I was kinda hoping you'd tell *me* that," Hayes said.

"Are you sure you put in the right coordinates?" Boggs asked, scratching his head.

"You saw me cut and paste them," Hayes said, clicking back to the photos and repeating the same steps as before. "See, same place."

"Well, that doesn't make a hell of a lot of sense."

"Why not?"

"First off, there isn't any narco traffic in the area."

"You sure?" Hayes asked.

"Fuck yes I'm *sure*, I'm a *drug* Enforcement Agent. Pendare is a big-ass jungle—there's nothing there but some mud huts and maybe some monkeys and shit."

Hayes slapped the computer shut with a curse, got to his feet, and walked to the window. He looked out at the sleepy town and felt the frustration welling up inside him. *Always have a backup.* Yet another lesson from Treadstone. He'd spent so much time and effort just to get down here and find the man, Hayes had never even considered what he would do if the man didn't have the answers he was looking for.

"You want a beer?" Boggs asked from the kitchen.

"Shit, might as well," Hayes said, rubbing his hand over his face and walking back to the couch.

Boggs came back into the room with two bottles of La Polar and handed one to Hayes before settling down in the chair across from him.

Hayes took a drink and looked around the room. Something about the place was off, but he couldn't place it.

"I know you spies always have contingency plans, so what was plan B?"

"No offense, Boggs, but I don't think you are ready for plan B."

"You don't think I can handle myself? I was a Marine before I joined the DEA, did two tours in Iraq."

"Well, semper fi, motherfucker," Hayes said, raising his bottle in a toast.

"Damn straight," he said, taking a pull from his beer. "You know, Ford told me about you. Said you served together in Afghanistan."

"We were in Special Forces together," Hayes said with a nod. "Nicky was a hell of a soldier. A pain in the ass when we were in garrison, but overseas, he was fearless."

"Sounds like him," Boggs said. "I used to tell him that he was the toughest son of a bitch that I'd ever met. You know what he'd say?"

"What's that?"

"He'd tell me that I only thought that because I'd never met *you*."

"I don't know about all that," Hayes said.

"Ford did, and here's the deal—he was my friend, too. Man, we had some good times in this place." He paused to take a drink. "So whatever crazy idea you got bouncing around in that head of yours, I'm in."

"I think it only fair that I begin with a little disclaimer," Hayes said. "You know that Rolling Stones song about time being on your side?"

"Yeah?"

"Well, that song wasn't written about this particular op. We have a very small window to make this happen."

"How small?" Boggs asked.

"About thirty-two hours," Hayes said, glancing at his watch.

"Are you serious?"

"As a heart attack. So before you sign up, I want to warn you that there is nothing surgical about plan B."

"Fair enough, but I'm still in." The man grinned. "So, lay it on me."

"Tomorrow I am going to take your Jeep and I'm going to pack it with as much ammo as it will carry," Hayes began, watching the smile on Boggs's face start to crumble. "And then I'm going to drive up to Pendare, grab a few of these *cholos*, and beat the shit out of them until they tell me what we want to know."

"By *ourselves*?" Boggs asked.

"Just you and me, padna."

"These guys do *not* play around, Hayes."

"What happened to all the rah-rah shit you were just spouting?" Hayes demanded.

"I thought you had a *plan*, like a real plan."

"I've got something better than a plan."

"What's that?"

"I've got a bagful of guns."

42

EL NULA, VENEZUELA

It was ten p.m., and Hayes was trying to plot their route to Pendare when Boggs walked in from the bedroom.

"She is *not* happy with *you*," the DEA agent said on his way to the kitchen, "but I told her she can't come."

Hayes heard the *psst* that came from Boggs popping the top on a fresh beer and bit down on his annoyance.

"It's for her own good," Hayes replied.

Boggs came back into the room, took a long pull from the fresh beer, and lowered himself to the couch.

"Did I ever tell you about the time Ford and I—"

"Look, man," Hayes said, cutting him off before he could launch into another story. "I'm not your mom, but oh four hundred is going to come pretty early," he said, looking up from the map spread out on the coffee table.

"Yeah, so?" Boggs said.

"How can I put this in language that you might understand?" Hayes asked, looking up at the ceiling. "Okay, let's try this. Has La Polar revolutionized the beer industry by adding a secret ingredient that magically improves a man's tactical proficiency?"

"Not that I know of," Boggs said, frowning at the bottle in his hand.

"So you trying to finish a case of beer by yourself instead of going to bed isn't going to help keep me alive."

"Uhhhh—"

"Since I don't want to die tomorrow, how about you take your ass to bed."

"Okay, okay, I get it, just let me—"

"*Now!*" Hayes snapped.

The silence that followed Boggs's departure rolled across the room like a cool breeze in the desert. "That's better," Hayes said and sighed, setting the pencil on the map and getting to his feet.

Hayes imagined that he had another hour or two of planning before he'd be able to rack out, but before he got back to work he needed to make sure the safe house was secured. He went to the drop bag, and, after a few seconds of rummaging through the guns and ordnance inside, pulled out a can of CS gas, a white-phosphorus grenade, and a length of galvanized wire.

After stuffing the wire and two grenades into his assault pack, he went into the kitchen. Hayes swiped the Jeep keys from the drainboard, grabbed a dish towel from the sink, and glanced through the off-center peephole to make sure the landing was clear before stepping outside.

Hayes closed the door behind him and licked his fingers before draping the dish towel over his hand. Even with the protection of the towel, the lightbulb was hot against his fingertips, but he managed to spin it free without burning his hand.

He wrapped the bulb in the towel and left it on the ground next to the door before easing down the stairs and climbing behind the wheel of the Jeep.

The size and disposition of the safe house, plus the fact that Boggs had been stone sober when he decided to leave the Jeep in front of it, had been nagging at Hayes since his arrival.

Which was why he was outside, squaring things away, instead of working on tomorrow's assault plan.

Hayes threw the Jeep into gear and, leaving the lights off, drove to the end of the block. He took a right and eased down the street, straining to find the alley he'd seen from the balcony in the darkness. When he finally spotted it, Hayes cut the wheel to the left, shifted into reverse, and backed the Jeep down the alley, angling the back seat so that it was directly below the balcony. He engaged the parking brake, centered up the wheels, and cut the engine.

With the Jeep in position, Hayes set to work making sure that it remained unmolested while he was upstairs.

Unlike the round M67 fragmentation grenade, which was designed to be thrown, the canister-like white-phosphorus and CS grenades were meant to be emplaced. White phosphorus, or Willie Pete, was the OxiClean of military munitions, and in Hayes's opinion, its versatility was limited only by a man's imagination.

Not only did it burn skin, clothes, metal, fuel, and ammunition, it was also great for starting brushfires and in a pinch could be used for an impromptu smoke screen. But Hayes's love affair with Willie Pete came from how well it complemented other munitions.

Hayes had come across positions in Iraq and Afghanistan manned by seriously dedicated insurgents. Men who'd stay in a firing position no matter what you shot at them. But no matter how dedicated they were to the cause, he'd never seen anyone stick around after calling in a shake-and-bake mission. A couple of rounds of high explosives intermixed with a liberal amount of white phosphorus and most insurgents were ready to call it a day.

However, since Hayes didn't want to blow up the Jeep, he decided on CS, the military's version of tear gas. He carried the canisters five feet past the Jeep and secured them to the metal fence by running a zip tie beneath the spoons. Once he was sure they would not come loose, Hayes tied the galvanized wire through the metal rings, pulled the wire across the alleyway, and headed back upstairs.

The entire process had taken five minutes, and by the time he got back up the stairs, the bulb was cool enough to handle. He left the bulb inside the towel, carried it to the edge of the steps, and crushed it beneath his feet. Careful not to cut his fingers with the slivers of glass inside the towel, Hayes walked back toward the door, sprinkling the shattered glass across the concrete.

"That should do it," he said, stepping inside.

Hayes threw the lock and went back to the coffee table. He woke the Toughbook with a swipe of the trackpad, and when the screen blinked to life he double-clicked the FalconView icon. Hayes waited for the program to load and turned his attention back to the map.

Hayes had always been fascinated by maps. It started in the fifth grade, during a visit to the Museum of Natural History. The exhibit was The Age of Exploration, and the proctor had stopped the class next to the eighteenth-century map of Africa.

"Why is it blank in the middle?" he'd asked.

"Back then, there were parts of the world that were still unexplored. Since no one had been there, the mapmakers left it blank."

Unexplored. For a ten-year-old boy stuck in a one-stoplight town, the idea of uncharted worlds—dark, shadow-draped forests that no one had ever seen—aroused an unquenchable curiosity. A curiosity that sent him to the local library for hours on end, flipping through atlases or reading back issues of *National Geographic*.

It was the same feeling Hayes had now, reading the black embossed letters that identified the hunter-green sea in southern Venezuela.

The Amazon was the last of the earth's great mysteries, and three hundred miles southwest of Hayes's current location, buried deep in the eighteen million hectares, a penciled *X* marked Pendare.

But the map didn't have the level of detail he needed to plan the op, and once the imagery loaded, he turned his attention to the Toughbook.

Hayes typed the grid coordinates copied from Ford's pictures into the search bar, and the satellite imagery of the area popped up on the screen. For the average user, there was no way to differentiate FalconView from a program like Google Earth. Both systems provided the same satellite-based imagery of a map. But where FalconView had a clear advantage was in the Combat Weapons Delivery overlay.

The first time he used the CWD's topographical overlay was in Afghanistan, when his team was planning a combat operation in the Tora Bora mountains.

Usually, they would have sent in a recon team, but to get a team on the ground required helicopter support, which would have alerted his quarry. FalconView's 3-D interface was the next best thing, and allowed his team to get a feel of the area without having to physically put eyes on it.

Once again, Hayes was going into unknown enemy terrain, and he hoped that Falcon View would help him find an advantage. But the moment he zoomed in on Ford's last-known grid coordinates objective, Hayes knew there wasn't any technology in the world that would help him see what was beneath the thick triple-canopy jungle.

The only thing Hayes knew for sure was that whatever the enemy was doing in Pendare, they didn't want anyone to see it.

He spent another ten minutes looking at the area from every angle possible, before giving up.

That shit is thicker than seventies shag carpet, he thought, closing the Toughbook and stuffing it back in his assault pack. *Might as well try and get some sleep.*

He set the assault pack next to the balcony door and then went to the drop bag, knowing that if anyone came, he was going to need more than the Glock 19 on his waist. Hayes pulled out a London Bridge low-visibility plate carrier and stuffed two extra pistol magazines into the mag holders. From the pouch on the front, he pulled out the pair of AN/PSQ-36 Fusion Goggles Enhanced.

Besides the forty-thousand-dollar price difference between the FGE's and a regular set of night-vision goggles, the most noticeable delineating feature was the presence of a third lens centered above the dual night-vision tubes.

The extra lens gave Hayes the ability to toggle between the traditional Heineken-green view of night vision or shift to thermal with a twist of a knob. When he was sure they were functioning, Hayes returned the goggles to the case and set the plate carrier beside the couch.

For a long gun, he deliberated over a short-barreled Knights Armament PDW, but in the end, he went with a Benelli M4 automatic shotgun, knowing that if the shit hit the fan, he wanted whoever was coming after him to stay down.

Hayes shoved the tube full of 12-gauge buckshot, stuffed an extra box of shells into the plate carrier, and secured the drop bag. Once he was sure everything was packed up and he could roll out at a moment's notice, Hayes turned off the light and lay down on the couch.

He was exhausted, but instead of falling asleep, he found himself staring at the ceiling. Something was hovering at the edge of his mind—that did-I-remember-to-turn-off-the-stove feeling that kept his mind from powering down.

He ran through the mental checklist of everything he'd done, trying to see if he had forgotten something.

Set up security, did the mission prep, packed up my shit. That's everything.

Once he was sure that he'd taken care of everything, he closed his eyes, blocked everything out, and finally drifted off to sleep.

The first few minutes of sleep were filled with a chaotic jumble of images and sounds that came from a mind trying to purge itself of the adrenaline-filled day. There was a snapshot of Hayes in the back of the CASA, followed by the hot-air rush of the prop blast on his face when he jumped from the door. Then he was falling, fighting the chute and the tug of the canopy filling with air.

Eventually, the chemicals in his brain leveled off, and Hayes settled into REM sleep, the choppy images drifting into the more linear dream state, and he found himself sitting in the safe house, listening to Boggs talk about Ford.

"I used to tell him that he was the toughest son of a bitch that I'd ever met. You know what he'd say?"

"What's that?" Hayes asked.

"He'd tell me that I only thought that because I'd never met you."

"I don't know about all that," Hayes said.

"Ford did, and here's the deal—he was my friend, too. Man, we had some good times in this place."

Hayes's eyes flashed open, and he was immediately awake, the tail end of the dream echoing in his head.

"*We had some good times in this place.*" If they'd used this apartment before, the location could be blown.

He sat up and glanced at his watch. It was midnight, or the witching hour, as they called it in Iraq. The best time to hit a target house.

They are coming, the voice in his head warned.

Hayes lifted the plate carrier over his head and snugged the straps tight around his waist. He pulled on the FGEs and grabbed the Glock and the holster from the coffee table and stuffed it into his waistband and was reaching for the Benelli when he heard the gentle crack of glass crushed against a boot.

They're here.

Hayes eased to the front door and glanced out the peephole. There were three of them in sterile BDUs, carrying suppressed AK-47s, eyes glowing green from the night-vision goggles.

A kill team.

The point man was already up on the landing, his left arm up, fist closed. The universal sign for halt. He was looking down at the ground, trying to figure out what he'd stepped on, while the second man in the stack had his rifle trained on the door.

These boys have skills, Hayes thought, thumbing the safety to fire. Then he remembered Boggs. *Damn it.*

Hayes eased himself away from the door and into the bedroom.

"Boggs, Izzy, wake up," he hissed.

Izzy sat up immediately, her hand snaking under the pillow and emerging with a pistol.

"What is it?" she asked in Spanish.

"We have to go, *now*," Hayes said, grabbing Boggs by the shoulder and giving it a shake. "Boggs, wake the fuck up."

"F-five more min . . ." the man mumbled, his breath heavy with booze.

What the hell?

Hayes bumped the light mounted to the end of the shotgun, a quick flash that illuminated the room and the three-quarters-full bottle of Wild Turkey that sat on the nightstand. Any question about whether the bottle was new or old was answered when Hayes saw the shine of the shrink-wrap seal on the floor.

Izzy was already on her feet, pulling on her pants. When she saw the bottle illuminated by Hayes's light, she cursed, leaned over the bed, and slapped Boggs on the back of the head. "Wake up, you drunk shit," she snapped.

Leave him, the voice ordered.

Hayes was tempted, but then he saw the thin foam-filled mattress Boggs was lying on and had a better idea.

"I'll handle him, you go watch the door," he said, walking out of the room.

He went to the balcony, slung the Benelli, and unzipped the assault pack.

"If he thinks I'm carrying his drunk ass out of here,"

he muttered, tugging a length of black rappel rope and a metal carabiner from the bag, "then he has another thought coming."

Back in the room, Hayes uncoiled the rope and stuck the free end in his mouth. He reached across Boggs, grabbed the far edge of the mattress, and folded it over, tacoing the passed-out DEA agent in the middle.

You need to hurry up.

"Yeah, you think?" Hayes said, leaning across the bundle.

Using his weight to hold the mattress closed, he looped the rope around the center four times, and when Hayes was sure there was no way for Boggs to fall out, he tied it off.

It's a pig in a blanket. He grinned, tying the carabiner into the rope with an overhand knot on his way back to the balcony. Hayes snapped the D ring into the assault pack's carrying handle, leaned over the low wall, and dropped it into the back of the Jeep.

"Look," Izzy said, pointing down the alley.

Hayes followed her gaze and saw the spray of headlights across the alleyway. "Get down," he ordered, dragging her into a crouch behind the wall. A moment later a white panel van pulled into view and the sliding door cracked open, revealing a second team.

Shit.

"Izzy, I need you to listen to me," Hayes said, looking over the edge of the balcony, knowing that he was running out of time. He grabbed the rope and pulled Izzy close. "Can you climb down?"

"Yes, but—"

She was scared. He could see the fear in her eyes, hear the quiver in her voice.

"Listen to me," he said, pulling her to her feet. "I am going to lower you down to the Jeep. You need to run toward the road—I will take care of Boggs. We will meet up at the square, do you understand?"

Izzy's hands shook on the rope, but she nodded that she understood.

Hayes helped her over the edge, and lowered her down to the Jeep. "Go," he hissed, pointing to the road.

Hayes waited until she was out of sight before turning his attention back to the alley. The arrival of the van explained why the kill team hadn't crashed the door yet. But more important than that, it made Hayes realize he needed a bigger hammer.

He opened the drop bag, grabbed an M79 grenade launcher and a 40-millimeter HE grenade. "Nothing says 'I love you' quite like high explosives," he said, cracking the breach.

43

EL NULA, VENEZUELA

Hayes ducked out of the Benelli's sling and leaned the shotgun against the wall. He held the M79 grenade launcher in his right hand and the 40-millimeter M381 in his left.

The M381 was an area weapon, with a killing radius of sixteen feet. It was designed to be used in the open, against troops in hardened positions—not fired at a door ten feet from the shooter's position.

Back home they called this a "hold-my-beer moment," and in Hayes's experience any action that began with that ominous phrase usually ended up with a trip to the emergency room.

Fuck it, he thought, shoving the grenade into the breach and snapping it shut.

The only thing left to do was close his eyes and wait.

Hayes pressed his back against the wall, took a deep breath, and cleared his mind of everything but the moment at hand. The self-imposed darkness forced the rest of his senses into overdrive and sent them straining to compensate for the sudden loss of sight. When Hayes heard the men crunch over the broken lightbulb he'd scattered in front of the door, he knew the entry team had resumed its approach on the breach point.

His eyes snapped open and locked on the dim band of light at the bottom of the door. A normal person wouldn't have noticed the flitter of the shadow across the threshold, and if they had seen it, they would have quickly dismissed it as a casual nothing.

But not Hayes.

He studied the threshold in the same manner that an ancient mariner studied the sea before a storm. Divining meaning from every subtle shift in his environment, realizing that every change in sight, smell, or sound offered a tiny preview of the violence building on the other side of the door.

The shadow across the threshold told him that instead of stacking up on the door and hitting the room with the Israeli rush—a tactic perfected by the Israeli Defense Forces, which relied on getting as many shooters into the room as quickly as possible—the team leader had sent a man to the other side. Setting them up for either a buttonhook or a crisscross.

Splitting the team meant no explosives. They were going to come in quietly, using a pick or a bump key on the lock.

A breath of a breeze carried a hiss of muted static up from the alley below, followed by a voice whispering in Spanish, "We're set. It is on you."

Hayes watched the knob jiggle and heard the scrape of a bump key followed by the *snick* of the deadbolt being defeated. He leveled the M79 at the door, the *thump . . . thump . ... thump* of his heart in his chest deafening in the dark room.

He thought he saw the knob turn, but couldn't be sure, and realized his finger had slipped to the trigger.

Wait for it . . . Wait for it.

The seconds stretched into what seemed like hours, until time felt as if it had stopped, and then the door swung inward, the creak of the rusted hinges as loud as a howitzer in the confines of the room.

Hayes lifted the grenade launcher and leveled the muzzle at the center of the open door. *Steady, now. Wait for it.* He watched the dark black outline of a muzzle break the threshold, followed by the green glow of the night-vision reflection off skin. Hayes closed his left eye, the launcher rock-steady in his right hand.

He waited for the first shooter to step through the door, and the moment he squared his front plate on the room, Hayes pulled the trigger.

The distinctive *thooomp* of the M79 caught the

assaulter off guard, and like a deer caught in headlights, he froze in the fatal funnel. Behind him, the number-two man was already moving, and he collided with his teammates just as the grenade slammed into the man's front plate.

BOOOM!

The 40-millimeter grenade detonated on impact, the explosion blowing the men out of the door and off the landing. Before their bodies hit the ground, the Benelli was pressed to Hayes's shoulder, the sights locked on the right side of the doorframe. His finger danced over the trigger and he fired three shots in the blink of an eye. *Boom . . . Boom . . . Boom.* Each shell of double-aught buckshot leaving a fist-sized hole in the wall.

The dry thump of a body thudding against the concrete told him that one of his shots had been on target. Down in the alley he heard a shout followed by boots slapping on concrete.

That's my cue.

Hayes stuffed the launcher into the bag, snapped the buckles, and tossed it over the balcony. He slung the shotgun over his shoulder, grabbed the rope hanging over the edge, and swung his leg over the wall.

"Hey, Boggs, it's time to go," he yelled, grabbing the rope and scooting off the edge.

Hayes guessed it was about a ten-foot fall from the balcony to the Jeep—not high enough to kill you, but tall enough to leave a mark. Thankfully, Boggs's deadweight slamming against the wall saved Hayes from any serious misgivings.

He tied the rope off to the roll bar, jumped behind the wheel, and started the Jeep. Hayes had hoped to be able to ease Boggs off the balcony, but at the sound of the rifle fire cracking off in the alley and the snap of the overhead, Hayes thought it best not to stick around.

The Jeep roared to life with a twist of the key, and Hayes kicked the FGEs onto his forehead and flipped on the lights. A rattle of small arms from his six was all the urging he needed to get the hell out of there, and he shoved the Jeep into gear, forgetting any thoughts he'd been harboring about easing Boggs off the balcony.

Hayes was under fire and it was time to go.

Sorry, buddy, but if you play stupid games, he thought, slamming the Jeep into gear and stomping on the gas, *you win stupid prizes.*

The Jeep surged forward, snapping the rappel rope taut. Hayes shifted into second and hit the mouth of the alley at twenty miles per hour. He bounced out into the street, cut the wheel hard to the right, and glanced up at the rearview. The mattress slingshotted into view, bouncing and skipping off the street, bits of foam stuffing flying through the air.

He glanced at the side mirror. A bobble of muzzle flashes told him that the shooters were running after him.

"Keep on coming, dumbasses," he said, nearing the end of the alley.

The Jeep bounced onto the street and Hayes made a hard right turn just as one of the shooters found his going-away present and the Willie Pete grenade exploded with a blinding flash.

Hayes didn't need to see the outcome to know that he'd just ruined their day. All he cared about was finding Izzy and getting the hell out of town, but as he scanned the street, there was no sign of her.

Half a mile down the road, Hayes cut the wheel to the left, downshifting into the turn. The mattress swung wide, hopped the curb, and bowled over a pair of trash cans, like ninepins. Hayes saw the shower of trash in the rearview and smiled, but knew he needed to retrieve Boggs before there was nothing left of the man.

He toed the clutch, shifted into neutral, and stomped on the brakes. The tires locked up with the stench of burnt rubber and Hayes engaged the emergency brake before hopping out.

By the time he reached the rear bumper, the mattress had skidded to a halt at his feet. It had taken a beating—the once-white cover was now jet black and shredded, but Hayes didn't see any blood when he picked it up and dumped it into the back.

"You alive, buddy?" he asked, jumping behind the wheel.

"Where's Izzy?" came Boggs's muffled reply.

"She's safe," Hayes lied, bending to cut the DEA agent free when two Ducati motorcycles appeared at the end of the street. He looked up just in time to see one of the riders point toward the Jeep.

"Looks like you are going to have to suck it up just a little while longer," Hayes said, jerking the mattress off the ground and tossing it into the back of the Jeep.

44

EL NULA, VENEZUELA

Who the hell are *these* guys?" Hayes asked, disengaging the emergency brake and shifting into gear. He pushed the accelerator to the floor and the Jeep surged forward, the engine spooling up as he shifted through the gears.

By the time the sport bikes turned to pursue, Hayes was a quarter-mile down the road. It was a sizable lead, but any daydream that he had about outrunning his pursuers in a twenty-year-old Jeep evaporated when they hit the straightaway and the riders opened up the throttle.

Use what you've got.

Hayes cut the wheel hard to the right, hoping the tight turn would gain him some distance. But the Jeep wasn't built for speed or maneuverability. It was an all-terrain vehicle and took the turn like a barge with a stuck rudder.

He downshifted using the centripetal force of the turn to try to drift the Jeep around the corner. The heavy tires chirped over the asphalt and the springs squealed in protest. Hayes felt the back end come loose and the Jeep started to slide, but he fought the wheel and managed to center the Jeep on the straightaway.

Hayes shifted into second and stomped the accelerator to the floor, but compared to the nimble motorcycles, the Jeep accelerated like a fat kid in a relay race. The needle was just clearing thirty miles per hour when one of the leather-clad riders lifted a Škorpion machine pistol from the bag strapped across his front and opened up on the Jeep.

Brraaap, braaaaaap.

The burst of yellow flame was followed by the thunk of bullets slapping into the rear quarter-panel of the Jeep.

This is not going to work.

Hayes spun the wheel to the right and bounced the Jeep over the curb and crashed through the chain-link fence surrounding an abandoned lot. The tires burrowed into the soft ground, tearing up clods of dirt and flinging them against the wheel wells.

The sound gave Hayes an idea. He took his foot off the gas, cut the lights, and tugged the FGEs over his eyes. He worked the wheel back and forth in his hands. Short, choppy strokes that dug the knobby claws lining the outer edge of the tires into the earth. Hayes let the Jeep's weight push it deeper into the dirt, and when he felt it starting to bog down, he got back on the gas.

The sudden acceleration sent the tires burrowing into the ground, and the back end fishtailed, spraying a rooster tail of earth and grass cascading over the riders. He let the RPMs climb, refusing to let the tires get traction, and cut a long, jagged rut across the field before finally hitting a patch of gravel.

Unable to see the Jeep through the makeshift smoke screen, a rider sprayed the area with a wild burst of automatic fire. But Hayes had already whipped the Jeep into a sweeping right-hand turn, rammed through the back side of the fence, and clattered down to the street.

Hayes blasted through the intersection and was looking for a way to cut north, toward the square, when he heard the crack of a pistol echo from that direction.

Izzy, he thought.

Behind him the bikes turned onto the street, their lights flashing off his side mirror.

A quick glance over his shoulder revealed one of the bikes peeling off, the rider heading west, while his partner raced after the Jeep like a hellhound on a hot trail.

Hayes had two options. He could take the turn east, follow the road to the end of the block, and then work his way back to the highway, or he could try to squeeze the Jeep through the tight alley on the far side of the road. The crack of two more pistol shots followed by a female scream made the decision for him and Hayes centered the hood on the alley.

He worked through the gears and was two feet from the opening when he realized that he might have misjudged the width of the alley, but by then he was already committed, and the only option was to keep rolling.

The bumper hit the edge of one wall and tore out a section of brick, the impact sending his head bouncing off the steering wheel, punching the FGEs into the bridge of his partially healed nose.

"Shit," he swore, tasting the blood on his lip, trying to keep the wheel as straight as possible.

The passenger-side mirror was the first to go, and when Hayes edged the wheel to the left, a sprinkle of glass from the driver's-side mirror pelted his face.

He could see the end of the alley up ahead and knew that in ten feet he'd be out in the open, but then Hayes realized why the other rider had turned west. They were going to try to flank him—cut him off from the highway.

Unless . . .

He took his foot off the gas, shifted into neutral, and the Jeep rolled to a halt with the scrape of the metal bumper against the wall. Hayes got to his feet and checked his positioning.

The Jeep was ten feet inside the alley, well outside the throw from the Ducati's headlight. Hayes twisted the FGEs from night vision to thermal and yanked the Benelli from the seat. He twisted around and laid it across the roll bar at the rear of the Jeep. All that was left to do was wait and listen to the growing hum of the approaching Ducati.

Hayes had to give it to the rider, the man was cautious. Instead of entering the alley at full speed, he cut the bike wide, let off the throttle, and spied the corner. He squeezed in the clutch, put his feet down to steady the bike, and scanned the dark alley.

Hayes held his breath, the front sight centered on the man's chest. His target was within range and he knew that he could make the shot. But what Hayes *didn't* know was if the rider was wearing a vest. He had to kill the man, make sure he went down and stayed down, and to do that he needed the rider to commit.

C'mon . . . c'mon, bite, you son of a bitch.

Finally the rider goosed the throttle, leaned forward across the handlebars, and entered the alley.

Just as Hayes had guessed, the bike's single headlight didn't have the strength to illuminate the length of the alley, and that, combined with the frosted visor protecting the rider's eyes, gave him the false impression that the alley was empty.

By the time he realized his error and saw his headlights reflected off the Jeep's glass, it was too late.

"Smile for the camera, motherfucker," Hayes said.

BOOM.

The shotgun roared to life, sending a spray of nine steel pellets, each the size of a .38-caliber bullet, toward the rider. The impact shredded the man's chest, bowling him off the bike.

Before the ejected hull hit the ground, Hayes climbed out of the Jeep and made the short walk over to the man.

"Nothing personal," he said, pressing the barrel against the frosted visor and pulling the trigger.

Hayes thumbed two more shells into the shotgun, jumped behind the wheel, and shoved the Jeep into gear. He scraped the Jeep through the alley, and when he reached the square, Hayes found it empty and dark.

Where is she? he thought, scanning the shadows that hung over the two-lane thoroughfare.

Unlike the surrounding blocks, there were no alleys on this stretch of road. No place for a vehicle to turn around. On the east side he saw a shattered shop window, and the Jeep's headlights picked up the glint of brass on the ground.

Hayes stopped the Jeep next to the shop and jumped out. "Izzy!" he yelled, thinking that he heard the thump of a car door closing. *Fuck*, he thought, scooping up one of the expended casings and flipping it over to look at the headstamp. It was a 9-millimeter, the same caliber as Izzy's Glock.

Doesn't mean it was her, he thought. *Lots of people shoot 9-millimeters.*

But any confusion about who the bullets belonged to ended when Hayes saw the silver locket lying on the curb. He picked it up and saw that the chain had been snapped and knew she was gone.

There is still a shooter out there, the voice warned—reminding him that the second Ducati was still unaccounted for.

He climbed back into the Jeep, his eyes locked on the faint black outline of the highway four hundred yards to his front. *There it is. Our way out.*

Hayes was tempted to make a break for it, let the second rider try his best to stop him. But he'd come too far and lost too much to do something stupid like leave an enemy at his rear.

No, Hayes thought. *We do this the right way. I'm getting the hell out of this place and the only thing I'm leaving behind are bodies.*

But first he had to find the second rider. There was no doubt that the man was out there, lying in wait. "But where the hell is he?" Hayes asked aloud.

Then he saw the faint orange that signaled the heat of the Ducati's engine speeding in from the west. It was the rider, and Hayes knew instinctively that he was heading for the massive stone fountain in the center of the roundabout.

That's where I'd go.

He swung the Jeep into the oncoming lane, using the fountain to shield his approach. Hayes stopped short of the traffic circle and buried the Jeep in the shadow of the fountain. "What is taking this guy so long?" he wondered aloud, craning to see around the fountain.

Finally the bike sped into view, the rider ducked low against the rush of air. Hayes wasn't sure which side of the circle he was going to take and waited until the rider leaned into the turn before shoving the transmission into gear and stomping the accelerator to the floor.

The Jeep chugged forward, Hayes working through the gears, waiting until the last moment before turning on the lights and engaging the high beams. The rider had time only to raise his left hand to his face, to try to shade his eyes against the sudden barrage of light, and then it was over.

It was a violent and one-sided collision.

The Jeep's front slammed into the front of the Ducati, its steel bumper crushing the front tire, crumpling the front suspension. On impact the rider was catapulted skyward, and Hayes watched him arc over the top of the Jeep.

He heard the plastic smack of the man's helmet over the screech of the tires and tugged the shifter into reverse, dragging the mangled bike along the street as he backed over the rider. Hayes was about to shift into gear when he heard a pained groan from the back seat.

"Wh . . . whaz . . . goin' on?" Boggs moaned.

"Ssshhhh," he whispered, engaging the clutch and shifting into first. "You're just having a bad dream." Hayes cut the wheel to the right.

He steered free of the wreckage, got back on the road, and thirty seconds later turned onto the highway, heading for Pendare.

PENDARE, VENEZUELA

Hayes drove through the night, following the monochromatic gray of the highway as it snaked east beneath the headlights. With Boggs passed out in the back, it was a silent drive, and Hayes's only companions were the monotonous whine of the tires and the mud scent that signaled the coffee-brown waters of the Río Arauca off to his south.

He drove until the horizon turned pink and the shadows began to recede, and then ten miles outside of Pica Pico, Hayes pulled off the road. He guided the Jeep into a gully, the dry dirt cracking under the tires, kicking up a cloud of fine dust that settled over the windshield when he came to a halt.

Hayes climbed out of the Jeep, stripped off the plate

carrier, and set it on the seat. He stretched his shoulders against the tightness that had built up in his back, closed his eyes, and savored the feel of the air against his sweat-soaked shirt.

God, that feels good, he thought.

For a moment there was nothing but the gentle breeze against his skin, and he realized there was a part of him that wished he could stay in the moment forever. Forget about what was waiting for him in Pendare. Forget about Treadstone, Gray, and Vega, just leave it all right here and disappear.

You tried that, remember? the voice said, bringing him back to reality.

"Yeah, I remember," Hayes said, his mind slipping back to the reason he was here and not at home with Jack and Annabelle.

If you want this to stop, you know what you have to do.

Before Hayes could answer, he heard Boggs's muffled yells drifting from the back of the truck. He'd forgotten about the man wrapped in the mattress, but at the sound of his voice, Hayes felt the heat that signaled the rage building up inside of him.

"This motherfucker," he snapped.

Hayes moved to the rear of the Jeep, his anger growing with each step, and by the time he bent over the edge and grabbed ahold of the rope, his vision had turned red.

Bracing himself against the side of the Jeep, Hayes bent his knees and ripped the mattress out of the back seat and flung it free. It slammed to the ground, kicking up a cloud of dust and a muffled curse.

"Hey, what the hell is wrong with you?"

Boggs might have stood a chance if he'd kept his mouth shut, but now Hayes would never know. He tore the knife from the sheath at his lower back, dropped his knee on the squirming bundle, and savagely hacked at the rope. The moment the blade cut through the last strand, Boggs came tumbling free, his filthy face bathed in anger.

"What the fuck is the—" he began.

But before he could finish, Hayes had him by the throat and was lifting him to his feet.

Kill him and get it over with.

"Notice anyone missing, you drunk fuck?" Hayes growled.

"Wh-what?" Boggs managed, his bulging eyes turning from the knife to the Jeep. "Izzy, where is—?"

"Gone, because you'd rather get drunk than worry about your girlfriend," Hayes hissed. "So give me one reason why I shouldn't drop your selfish ass right here."

"Because . . . it . . . isn't you," Boggs choked.

"That's where you are wrong," Hayes said. "This *is* the real me. It's who they made me."

"I-I—" Boggs stammered.

"You're what?" Hayes demanded. "Are you going to tell me that you're sorry?"

"I . . . was . . . sc-scared," Boggs choked.

Hayes watched the man's face turn purple, his eyes start to roll back in his head.

Get it over with and get moving, the voice ordered.

"No," Hayes said, releasing his grip and letting Boggs crumple to the ground. *I might be a killer, but I'm not a murderer.*

He stuffed the blade back into its sheath and forced himself into a jog, bounding past the Jeep and up the side of the gully. Knowing how close he'd come to killing Boggs. Afraid that the anger would come back and he'd lose control.

"H-Hayes," he croaked. "I-I'm s-sorry."

Hayes was panting when he reached the high ground, his heart racing in his chest, hands balled into ghost-white fists.

You're soft, and it is going to get both of you killed, the voice warned.

"Leave me *alone!*" Hayes yelled, dropping to his knees, pounding the earth with his fist until his anger was spent and his head slumped to his chest.

He was still there when he heard Boggs's tentative footsteps behind him.

"H-Hayes, I'm—"

"You're what—a burnout, a drunk? Someone who

is going to get me killed?" Hayes demanded without turning his head.

"Yeah," Boggs said, squatting down beside him. "I am a drunk and a burnout. I'm also a shitty dad and a bad husband, but I'm not a coward."

"Did you know that Ford's dad was a full-blooded Cherokee Indian?" Hayes asked, the sudden change of subject sending a confused frown over Boggs's face.

"No, I, uh, didn't know that."

"Yeah, he was Force Recon in Nam, did three tours. The first night we got home, Ford's mom threw this big party, lots of people inside the house. We were having a good time, but I guess I drank too much or something, because all of a sudden the walls started closing in and I couldn't breathe." Hayes paused. "I don't even know why I'm telling you this shit."

"Keep going, man. What happened next?"

"I didn't know if I was having a heart attack or what, but I knew I had to get out of there, so I ran out to the backyard, and kinda fell down in the middle of the yard, and the next thing I know, Ford's dad is kneeling down beside me."

"What did he say?"

"He said the same shit happened to him when he got back from Nam and how everyone told him it was normal and that it would go away on its own. He said that was a bunch of bullshit."

"Bullshit?"

"Yeah," Hayes said, turning his head and looking at Boggs. "He said that inside each of us there is a battle between two wolves. One wolf is good and wants to do good things. But the other, all he wants to do is destroy everything, tear you down, and keep you there until one day you can't take it and you eat a bullet." Hayes went silent and looked out over the flat scrubland, remembering the moment like it had happened yesterday.

"Then what happened?" Boggs asked.

"I asked him which wolf won," Hayes said, getting to his feet and brushing the dirt off his knees.

"And what did he say?"

Hayes looked down at the man, his eyes playing over the red finger marks on his neck and the shame in his eyes. *Like looking in a mirror,* he thought, offering his hand.

"He said the wolf that wins is the one you feed," Hayes answered, pulling the man to his feet.

"I fucked up and I'm sorry," Boggs said.

Hayes was about to reply when he heard the distant thrum of turboprops. "Quiet," he ordered, holding up his hand.

"What is it?" Boggs asked.

"Sounded like a plane. Something heavy," he said scanning the sky.

"I don't—"

Pointing to the four-engine cargo plane skimming east across the sky, Hayes said, "It's an Antonov 12, same model that Ford was tracking, and what do you want to bet it's heading to Pendare?"

PENDARE, VENEZUELA

It was 1300 when they finally pulled into Pendare. Hayes hadn't been sure what to expect from an Amazon mining town. His expectations were based on what he'd seen in the movies—a generalized picture of a muddy shanty town, lacking even the most basic of necessities.

Pendare did not disappoint. The town looked like it had been built from materials found during a scavenger hunt. The only permanent structure was a wilted brick building with AMAZONIA MINING LTD painted across the side in flaking letters.

"Now, I've seen some shitholes in my time, but this place . . ." Hayes whistled.

"Where do you want to start?"

"Let's go to the building not made of trash," Hayes said, parking the Jeep in front of Amazonia Mining.

"So how do you want to play this?" Boggs asked, stepping out of the Jeep.

Instead of answering, Hayes tugged the Glock off his hip and reached for the gun bag.

"Don't tell me you are going in there without a gun."

"Boggs, I don't go to the bathroom without a gun," Hayes said, trading the Glock for a large leather holster with an equally large revolver inside.

"That's not a gun, it's a fucking cannon."

"You just let me do all the talking," Hayes said, and clipped the pistol to his belt. He was almost to the door when he saw the strip of paper with a handwritten note advising that the proprietor was having a siesta.

"Now what?" Boggs asked.

"That place looks open," Hayes said, pointing to the red structure with a gravel lot full of mud-spattered trucks and a sign that showed a pig drinking a beer.

Hayes read the sign. "Cochiloco."

"Crazy Pig? What the hell is that?" Boggs asked.

"I figured you of all people would be able to pick out a bar," Hayes said, pointing to the stack of rusted kegs sitting on the side.

The bar was native ingenuity at its finest. The exterior was a façade made out of wood taken from shipping crates and stained red.

It didn't matter where Hayes was going, he

approached every room the same way. He grabbed the door handle with his left hand, his right closing around the butt of the .357, and then tugged the door open.

He'd cleared 80 percent of the interior before crossing the threshold. During his time at Fort Bragg, Hayes had been to his share of dives, but it wasn't until he joined Treadstone and started hunting men across the globe that he gained a true appreciation for the meaning behind *shithole*.

But Cochiloco put them all to shame.

To call it a shithole was an insult to the word. The inside was two aluminum shipping containers with a floor made of plywood. A rectangular section of split timber made up the bar, and the four tables were empty cable spools. He saw that the left side of the room was empty and jerked his head in that direction, signaling for Boggs to take the corner and hold it.

The right side was a different story—there were two men: a native passed out on the floor and a thick-necked man with the air of someone who knew how to take care of himself, sitting with his back against the wall.

"Keep your eyes on that one," Hayes said, noticing the man's right hand duck beneath the table.

"Got it," Boggs said and nodded.

"This place open early or just never close?" he said, crossing to the bar.

The barman wore the weary, wrung-out look of a

man who has spent his life listening to other people's problems. The scars on his fist attested to what happened when he got tired of hearing them.

Hayes knew from the look in his eye that the man had been in the business long enough to recognize trouble, and when the barman saw the pistol at his waist, he reached for something below the bar.

"*Tranquilo*, easy," Hayes said, holding up his hands, palms out. "We don't want any trouble. I just have some questions to ask and then we will be on our way."

That was when he noticed the third man sitting in the shadows. Unlike the rest, this man didn't look like shit. His clothes were clean, and his arms and face were tanned—the skin around his eyes wrinkled from squinting at the sun.

The pilot.

"You fly that Antonov in?" Hayes asked, walking over to the man.

"What's it to you?" he asked.

"I apologize. Where are my manners? Can I buy you a drink?"

"Already got one," the man said, nodding to the mostly full mug of beer on the table.

"Well, you sure do," he said, grabbing the glass and pouring the contents on the floor. "Problem solved." He shrugged. "Now, how about that drink, and while we're at it, how about the coordinates to that airfield you just landed at."

"Haaayes," Boggs alerted him.

"I see him," he said, already alerted that Muscles was on the move by the ponderous scrape of the chair against the plywood.

"Someone pull your chain, son?" Hayes asked, without taking his eyes off the pilot.

"We don't serve Americans here."

"What about him?"

"I said, *fuck off*."

"Now you're just being rude. Do you know this guy?" he asked the pilot.

"Y-yes, Mr. Vega hired him to—"

"That's enough," the man said, "and you need to get the fuck out of here before I lose my temper."

"Do I know you from somewhere?" Hayes asked, turning to face the man, who towered over him.

"I said, get the hell out of here."

"It was someplace shitty. You were working a security detail, and someone got lost. C'mon, help me out. Damn, it's right there on the tip of my tongue."

Then he remembered.

"You worked for that asshole Kaplan in Belgrade," Hayes said, snapping his fingers. "You had a dog's name, like Rex, or Champ, or—"

"I've never seen you before."

"Ace, that's it," Hayes said with a triumphant snap of his fingers. "I'm right, aren't I?" Hayes asked, turning to the pilot and receiving a nod of affirmation. "You don't remember me? The night on that convoy and you got lost and—"

"This is the last time I'm going to tell you," Ace said, his hand dropping to his pistol.

"You pull that pistol," Hayes said, his voice turning to ice, "you better be ready to kill me."

Every man had a tell, something he did when he got nervous or was about to lie. The entire time Hayes was badgering Ace, he was watching his face, cataloging his reactions, which is how he knew before the taller man had made any overt move that he was going for his pistol.

Ace was fast, but not fast enough.

Hayes was moving before the pistol cleared the holster. He grabbed the man's wrist with his left hand before the muzzle of the battered Sig could rise past his kneecap. He stepped in and drove his right elbow, smashing across the man's face, and felt blood spurt onto his arm.

Using his left hand, he swept the man's arm out of the way, his right hand closing around the hilt of the blade strapped at the small of his back. Hayes was a gunfighter by trade, but had been raised around knives and fists, and while he preferred the bullet, he trusted the blade.

The blow knocked the man off-balance, and Hayes took advantage, tugging on his right arm, pulling him toward the ground.

Ace fired two shots. The bullets hit the floor, spraying the two men with fragments of wood.

The blade came out with the gentle hiss of steel on leather, and Hayes was bringing the blade around when he saw the barman reaching for whatever he kept beneath the bar.

You're out of position, the voice warned.

Hayes tried to turn Ace in front of him, use the man's body as a shield, but when he drove the blade between Ace's ribs and saw the barman come up with the FAL, Hayes knew he was about to die.

Boom, boom, boom, boom.

He flinched, waiting to feel the burning pain of the bullets, and then he saw the spread of crimson across the barman's chest and smoke trailing from the muzzle of Boggs's Glock.

"Owe you one," he said, yanking the blade from Ace's side and waiting for the Sig to clatter to the ground before he let the man fall.

"Anytime," Boggs said, holstering the pistol.

Hayes reached down and wiped the blade across the man's shirt before returning it to the sheath.

"You really know that guy?" Boggs asked.

"Small world, huh," Hayes said, turning to the pilot. "Now, I know that nobody is going to miss that piece of shit, but you seem like a nice guy, so what's it going to be?"

PENDARE, VENEZUELA

According to the pilot, there were only two ways to reach the airfield. The first was by air, the second was through the main gate.

"So this is the airfield," Hayes said, marking the position on the map with an X. "Now, where is the road?"

"Here," the pilot said, tracing the route from the X to the town of Pendare. "But unless you brought an army, I wouldn't even think about it."

"You let me worry about that," Hayes said.

Twenty minutes later, Hayes eased the Jeep into a dry streambed two miles short of the road the pilot had marked on the map. Hayes cut the engine and scanned the tangle of vines and stocky rubber trees that formed an impenetrable curtain around them.

"End of the line," he said, cutting the engine and hopping out.

"You don't want to try and get any closer?" Boggs asked, looking down at the map.

"Can't risk it, especially if they have Izzy," Hayes answered, taking an olive-drab compact from his pack. He popped the lid, revealing four colored squares of oil-based paint.

Hayes started with the green, using the color as a base to cover the white of his face and neck. For contrast and shadows, he used jagged bands of gray and brown— ignoring the black since it wasn't a color found naturally in the wild. When he was finished, Hayes returned the compact to his pack and doused himself with DEET before tugging on a pair of gloves.

"How do you think Ford got in?" Boggs asked.

It was the same question he'd been asking himself since the pilot gave them the coordinates to the airfield. There was only one possible answer.

"Same way I am. He walked."

"Through that?" Boggs demanded.

You always were a stubborn bastard, Hayes thought, reaching for the map.

"You do much land navigation in the Corps?"

"At Parris Island, but not too much after that. Mainly used GPS over there."

"It's a dying art," Hayes said. "And fighting in the desert sure hasn't helped. Over there you never have a problem getting a signal." Hayes pulled the GPS from his pocket and held it up to the sky. "But out here, under this shit, it's a totally different ball game."

Nothing, he thought, looking at the blank screen.

"Looks like we are going to have to do it the old-fashioned way," he said, spreading the map out on the hood. "We are here," he said, pointing at the X he'd penned on the map. "According to the pilot, this mysterious airfield is two miles north of us."

"Right where Ford took those pictures," Boggs said.

"Yep, and if we want to get to the bottom of this story, there is only one thing to do."

Hayes folded the map and stuffed it inside the plastic bag he'd brought with him and walked to the rear of the Jeep. He opened the drop bag and tugged a rectangular hard case free.

"More spy shit?" Boggs grinned.

"Nope, we are going primal," he said, snapping the lid open and pulling out a compound bow.

"Are you serious right now?" Boggs asked.

"The jungle is like the desert; sounds and smells carry a lot farther than you think. I'll use the gun if I have to, but this gives me the opportunity to operate with stealth."

"But c'mon, a bow?" he asked, pulling one of the arrows from the quiver. "I mean, this doesn't even *look* like an arrowhead," he said, pointing at the inverted Y of the broadhead.

"I wouldn't do that if I were you," Hayes warned, a second before Boggs's finger touched the metal ring at the tip.

"You didn't poison it, did you?"

"No, dumbass," Hayes said, taking the 125-grain carbon-fiber arrow from his hand. "It's a mechanical broadhead—a Rage Hypodermic—and I just saved you a finger."

He tugged the Spyderco folding knife from his pocket and flicked the blade open. "This is the lock ring, which holds these two nasty beasts in place," Hayes said, pointing to the ten-inch serrated blades on either side of the point. "And when the arrow hits the target . . ." He pressed down with the tip of the knife and snapped his hand out of the way before the blades deployed with the *snick* of a switchblade, forming a twenty-inch cutting surface.

"There is something *wrong* with you," Boggs said.

"Maybe so, but right now I'm all you got, so you stick to the plan and we might get out of here."

"Roger that, I will keep my ass here," Boggs said, imitating Hayes's voice, "and keep the radio on and my eyes open."

"And?" Hayes asked.

"And if you are compromised, I get the hell out of here."

"I'm serious about that, Boggs. No cowboy shit."

"Hayes, I'm not going to let you down."

"I know," he said, shouldering his assault pack and stepping through the green curtain.

Having spent most of his life in the South, Hayes thought he knew about humidity, but he'd never experienced anything like what he found as soon as he moved off the trail.

It was as hot and muggy as a greenhouse on steroids beneath the dark green of the triple-canopy jungle, and by the time he'd gone a quarter of a mile he was sweating profusely and the camo face paint he'd applied was starting to run.

The terrain was a nightmare, an uphill slog over roots and around tree trunks the size of Buicks. Out of everything, Hayes hated the "wait-a-minute vines" the most. The thorny plants got their name from the fact that because of the jagged thorns, the only way to get untangled was to stop and pry them from your skin. Trying to rip free only resulted in jagged tears of flesh that soon left a man covered in blood.

But no matter how careful Hayes was to avoid the vines, it didn't take long to draw first blood.

Shit. I should have brought a machete.

He wiped his face with the back of his glove, the caustic scent of DEET stinging his nostrils.

Hayes pressed forward, moving slowly but steadily, stopping every twenty yards to look and listen for anything that didn't fit in the landscape. He kept a pace count in his head, noting every time his left foot touched the ground, knowing from his time in the army that every sixty-three paces equaled a hundred meters.

Overhead, a troop of howler monkeys barked in protest of the gentle breeze blowing in from the east. He looked past the monkeys, his blue eyes seeking a hole in the trees. What he saw confirmed his greatest fear: Angry gray clouds had crept silently over the crystal-blue sky like a roll of lead sheeting.

Hayes was a mile in when he dropped to a knee, checked his map, and pressed the talk button on the radio. "I'm at waypoint one," he gasped.

"Copy, waypoint one. You don't sound like you are having fun."

"The heat," Hayes admitted. "It's no joke."

"There's a storm coming in," Boggs warned over the radio. "It looks pretty rough."

Hayes had come too far to turn back now. He looked at the map and saw that the airfield was a little less than a mile away. He was in Indian country, close to where Ford's team had been hit, and he wasn't turning back.

"I'm going to keep moving. Let me know if things get bad."

"Roger that."

He got to his feet and started cutting for sign—checking the undergrowth for broken branches, bent stems, and leaves and soft soil for any tracks. Despite its name, a rain forest was actually not as wet as a jungle. In fact, because of the thick canopy, most of the rain never made it to the ground, which made it hard to find a track.

To combat this, Hayes stayed on the lookout for a "track pit"—a puddle of water or patch of mud that would trap the prints of anyone or anything that passed through.

He found one beneath a ragged hole in the canopy, near the base of a tree. The pool of water was small and covered with monkey tracks, but near the edge, Hayes found a faint heel print. He dropped to his stomach and, staying as low to the ground as possible, scanned the area, looking for the next track.

The second track was just a scuff, a faint transfer of mud over bark. He pulled off his glove and pinched off a piece of the dirt, squeezing it between his fingers to test the moisture content. The fact that it didn't crumble told him that it was fresh.

He replaced his glove and took a tentative step forward.

Tracking in these conditions was an art—painfully slow and full of stop-and-start moments. Hayes knew that while he was pressed for time, if he lost the track, he'd have to start all over.

It took five minutes of searching the ground before he found the next print on the far side of a log. He examined the moss on top of the wood, saw that it was pressed down, and then turned his attention to the other side, looking for the toe print that he knew was there.

He found it, a forward sloping gash in the ground, but without a full boot print—one well-defined print—there was no way of knowing *who* he was tracking. It was the first rule in tracking: Find a print that is distinguishable from all the rest. Trying to follow multiple prints was like trying to herd kittens—a waste of time and energy. Hayes had been taught the easiest way to cut sign was to find one print and stick with it.

Then he saw it, a print that stuck out. Hayes got the entire print—the logo stamped clean in the middle of the tread: VIBRAM.

Ford's sole of choice. It's his boot.

Hayes moved forward, ignoring the clap of thunder rolling through the trees. A cool breeze rustled the canopy and brought the scent of rain.

He was literally walking in Ford's footsteps, and as he pressed on, Hayes tried to imagine what his friend had been thinking. Was he tired, angry? Did he know he was being hunted?

A wedge was the preferred method of travel because it spread out the team, put men on both flanks. But the terrain was too tight for that, and with all the growth, it would have been easy for the men to get separated.

He would have used a file, Hayes thought, *one man*

in front of the other, with the point man a hundred yards ahead of the column in case they ran into trouble.

Hayes crept forward, eyes alert for any change in color, anything that would tell him the men had come this way. One print led to the next, and soon Hayes had identified the entire team and knew they'd been in a file, just as he'd guessed.

He could tell they had come in from the east. He didn't need to pull out the map to understand. Hayes had spent enough time studying it to know every dominant terrain feature in the area.

Ford used the river. That's how he got in.

The light was failing, and he knew that the storm was overhead, the clouds blocking what little sunlight might have made it through the trees. But he kept moving, knowing that he was close.

The first drops splattered through the trees. Then the clouds opened up and the rain fell hard and driving against the top of the canopy, like a hammer banging atop an anvil. The moisture drifted down through the canopy, creating a wet fog that cast the jungle floor in shadows of black and blue.

Turn back, his inner voice warned.

"Fuck no," Hayes swore, ducking his head against the rain, the bow slick in his hands.

Then he heard the buzzing sound emanating from the black shimmering cloud. *Flies.* As he crept closer, the rotting stench of decaying flesh rose through the wet scent of mud. On the ground he saw a glint of brass, leaves covered in dried blood, and blackened divots that marked where grenades had detonated.

But, ultimately, it was a spot of white flesh protruding from the freshly turned soil that marked the final resting place of Ford's men.

Hayes ducked his head in respect and, swearing to avenge the men, soldiered through the rain, crossing the last hundred yards to the slight rise of his overwatch position. He lowered himself to his stomach and, being careful not to expose any part of himself, crawled to the edge. He pulled the spotting scope from his bag and draped the olive-drab netting over the objective lens so *if* the sun came out, it wouldn't glint off the glass, and then he pressed his eye to the lens.

48

PENDARE, VENEZUELA

In the darkening gloom of the storm, the airstrip and its accompanying defenses lay before Hayes like a partially excavated skeleton. Someone had hacked back the jungle, clearing away a brown postage stamp of what appeared to be a long-forgotten firebase.

The perimeter defenses were a joke—knee-high grass had grown over the rusted wire, and thick jungle vines that could grow to three hundred feet in length had coiled their way up the legs of the closest guard tower. On the far edge, a fire flickered in an oil barrel. Hissing against the rain, it illuminated a knot of buildings hunched like refugees beneath the weight of tattered sandbags.

Other than the fire, the whole place looked like it

could be abandoned, but on closer inspection, Hayes saw signs of fresh work, and the longer he studied the area, the more he understood the ingenuity of the place.

At first glance the runway appeared too short and tight to accommodate a cargo plane. The surface had been recently graded. Someone had taken all of the debris and carried it to the far end, where it was packed down, forming a ramp.

The east side was littered with hulks of planes that had overshot the runway, but it was the Antonov An-12—parked beneath the massive camo net that hung before the dilapidated hangar—that proved it *was* possible to bring a large plane in.

Hayes had no idea how the pilot had managed to squeeze the big turboprop plane into that tiny field, but there it was, backed up to the hangar. And the presence of the men straining to carry pallets covered in cellophane up the ramp told him it wouldn't be here long.

What do they have on the pallets? Is it dope? Hayes wondered.

He patiently worked the focus knob back and forth with his thumb, making tiny corrections until the image cleared, and he saw that the fat squares loaded atop the pallets weren't full of dope, they were full of cash. Stacks and stacks of brand-new hundred-dollar bills.

Suddenly everything made sense, and Hayes knew the reason they had killed Ford and sent a kill team after him had nothing to do with drugs and everything to do with money.

The rage built inside him, burning hot despite the driving rain. He swung the spotting scope over the perimeter, taking in the defenses and the men on guard, and knew that he could end it right here.

Hayes backed away from the edge and pressed the talk button with his thumb.

"Boggs," he said over the radio.

There was nothing but static.

"Boggs, can you hear me?"

Damn it, c'mon, answer.

He tried again, but with the same result.

Hayes knew the radio worked by line of sight and wasn't sure if his transmission was being blocked by the trees or the thick cloud bank that had moved in overhead—either way he knew that he needed to move to high ground if he wanted to contact Boggs.

He glanced to his left, remembering the little finger of land he'd seen on the map, knowing it was close. If he could get there, he could call Boggs to him and they could end this right now.

Hayes packed up his spotting scope, shouldered his bag, and grabbed the bow. He nocked an arrow in the string, knowing the chances of being discovered grew the longer he stuck around. Then he slipped back the way he'd come.

Thankfully, the egress route was mostly downhill and

much easier than the way in. He was moving toward the spur he'd seen from his hide sight when he heard voices to his front.

Just let them pass.

It was the right decision, but the narcos had almost passed by when the radio hissed to life.

"Hayes, there is a . . ." Boggs's voice squawked over the radio.

Shit.

Hayes threw himself to the ground, his finger finding the knob, turning it until it clicked off, but knowing it was too late.

"Did you hear that?" a voice asked in Spanish.

Hayes hazarded a quick glance, lifting his head to get a clear view of the men. There were four of them.

Fuck.

"The colonel is on his way, forget it," one of the men said.

"No, there is something there," the man said.

Hayes heard a twig snap and knew the man was stepping closer.

If he gets a shot off, you are done. Kill him now and go.

Hayes took a breath, spread his feet shoulder width apart, and turned to the side. He flexed and tugged the bow to full draw in one smooth motion. Cloaked in the shadows, Hayes centered the sight on the man's chest, took a breath, and loosed the arrow.

The arrow flew soundlessly from the bow and slammed into the target's chest at three hundred and seventy feet per second. On impact, the mechanical broadhead snapped open and the razor-sharp twenty-inch cutting head sliced cleanly through the man's heart before punching out the other side.

Hayes was already moving before the man tumbled to the ground, knowing he had to kill them all—and fast.

"Ramón, hey, Ramón, what are you doing?" one of the men asked, taking a step forward.

Hayes shifted to the left, a second arrow already nocked, the bow coming up on target. It was a side shot, and he aimed for the armpit. He'd seen four-hundred-pound elk taken down with a bow and knew it had the power to punch through the man's arm and still have enough ass to hit his heart.

He fired and moved to the right, eyes searching the shadows for the rest of the men. Besides identifying his targets, Hayes also had to make sure he had a clean firing lane. Unlike a bullet, the arrow wasn't moving fast enough to punch through the undergrowth, and the smallest twig could knock it off course.

Which is exactly what happened on the third shot.

The last two men were five paces away from their dead comrades and moving in the opposite direction. Hayes knew that if they kept moving he could get them all, and was looking for the perfect shot when his foot found a dry twig.

Snap.

The break of the dry wood echoed like a rifle shot. The man on Hayes's left snapped his eyes toward the sound and caught Hayes out in the open.

"Hey!" the man yelled at the same moment Hayes released the arrow.

He knew it was off target as soon as he released it. He could hear the arrow crashing through the trees as he dumped the bow. His hand fell to the revolver on his right hip and he yanked it free.

BOOM.

The .357 echoed like a hand grenade, a jet of fire leaping from the muzzle. Unlike the arrow, the big bullet had no problems with the trees and snapped through the limbs before blowing the man off his feet.

"Contact," the remaining soldier yelled, opening up on full auto.

Hayes fired two shots at the muzzle blast before the hail of fire pinned him down. His left hand found the radio and twisted the knob.

"Boggs, I'm blown! Get the hell out of there," he yelled.

Not waiting for a response, Hayes stuffed the revolver back into its holster and fumbled the Benelli from his shoulder. He flicked the safety to fire, his breathing short and fast. *Calm down, you've been here before.*

He knew from the way the shooter was firing blind that he didn't have a target, and Hayes waited for the man to sweep his fire to the left before he circled back to the right. The moment he saw camo, Hayes fired, staying on the trigger until the man went down.

But the damage had been done. Hayes heard the wail of a siren from the airstrip and the sound of men and dogs crashing through the trees.

"Over there, he's over there!"

A narco appeared through the trees, his Kalashnikov blinking from his hip. The rounds snapped high through the brush, giving Hayes time to rip a frag from his pouch, tear the pin free, and sidearm it toward the man.

And then he was running for his life.

49

PENDARE, VENEZUELA

He's here!" a voice shouted over the radio, followed by the chatter of automatic fire.

"Damn you, Gray," Colonel Vega snapped, grabbing Izzy by the hair and shoving her toward a sergeant before pointing toward his aide. "Javier, you are in charge—get the dogs, push him south."

"What about the prisoner?" the sergeant demanded.

"Put her on the plane!" he yelled, pointing toward the Antonov.

He spun on his heel and sprinted to a Huey gunship on the airstrip. He shielded his face against the spray of stones and dirt kicked up by the downdraft and ducked his head beneath the blades. The heat from the turbines scalded his neck.

Fucking Gray, he snarled, climbing past the gunner manning the .50-caliber machine gun and grabbing the headset off the rack.

"*Vámanos,*" he snapped into the radio.

The pilot juiced the throttle, lifting the aged bird over the trees. In the back of the cabin, Vega worked the radio. He twisted the dial to air-to-ground and depressed the talk button.

"Javier, I am in the air, where is he?" Vega demanded, leaning forward so he could see out the Huey's bug-spattered canopy.

"We are pushing him south," the man answered, his voice low over the scream of RPGs.

Vega lifted a pair of scarred binoculars to his eyes. He panned across the green canopy of the treetops, but it was too dense to penetrate.

"Dogs, we need dogs!" he yelled over the radio.

"We have two K9 teams on the ground; one more is on the way," Javier answered.

"There!" the pilot yelled, pointing at a spark of orange from an exploding RPG. "Targets, two o'clock."

"I see them," Vega said. "Bring us around."

The pilot turned north, away from the attackers, and pulled a grease pencil from the arm of his flight suit. He waited until he was out of sight before dipping the nose, and then he pushed the red button on the stick.

There was a flash of fire from the pylon attached to

the side of the Huey and the 70-millimeter rocket lit off, racing toward the ground.

The pilot made a mental note of his point of aim, and when the rocket exploded, he made the necessary corrections and drew a rough circle on the glass with the grease pencil.

"Going up," the pilot said.

Vega grabbed the lanyard bolted to the roof and held on.

The pilot pulled the Huey into the sun and its rays blinded Vega, turned his vision white, robbing him of his sight. The rest of his senses went into overdrive. He felt the helo shudder, knew it was losing airspeed. Through the headphones he could hear the *beep, beep, beep* from the cockpit, the sensor warning the pilot that he was about to stall.

For a moment they were weightless, the sun hot on Vega's face.

He felt it shift to his cheek and then it was gone. They were turning, the Huey accelerating.

Vega opened his eyes and blinked the stars from his vision. He saw the ground through the canopy and his men pushing Hayes toward the south.

In the cockpit the pilot switched the mode of fire from single-shot to ripple fire and centered the grease-pencil circle on the target below.

The pilot depressed the trigger and the rocket pod came to life, unleashing twelve 2.75-inch rockets in the blink of an eye at point-blank range. Before the rockets even hit the ground, the pilot pulled the helo out of the dive.

Vega twisted toward the open troop door on the left and saw the ground erupt in flame and dirt. The pilot kicked the rudder to the right and banked into a tight turn, the g-force pushing Vega into his seat.

The pilot twisted the helo around and the door gunner opened up with the .50.

Ddddddduuuu . . . ddddddduuuu . . . ddddddduuuu.

50

PENDARE, VENEZUELA

Hayes sprinted through the jungle, the bullets snapping overhead as he ducked around trees and vines. He leapt over the fallen log that lay at an angle across his path and threw the shotgun's barrel over the top.

His backtrail was alive with men in camo BDUs. They weren't bothering with tactics, choosing instead to form up into a skirmish line and spray the area ahead of them with rifle and machine-gun fire.

There was no time to aim, and with so many targets—no need. Hayes simply fired, his finger working the trigger until he'd run the Benelli dry. Then he was up and running.

He tugged the radio free, and just in case Boggs

couldn't hear the running firefight crawling toward him, Hayes thumbed the talk button.

"I'm compromised!" he yelled over the growing rate of fire. "Get out," he ordered, zigging to the left.

Hayes thumbed the last of his shells into the shotgun on the run and was about to turn and fire when he heard the helo thumping over the trees. He glanced skyward and saw the Huey through a break in the canopy diving toward him, flames flashing from the pylons.

"Oh, shit," he yelled, a moment before the first rocket exploded high in the trees.

The second rocket hit the ground to his rear. The explosion lifted Hayes off his feet and shot-putted him through a tangle of vines and down a ravine. Something snagged the Benelli, ripping it from his hand as he tumbled down the hill.

Hayes landed face-first in the brackish water, ears ringing, sweat and blood dripping down his face.

Overhead the Huey had set into a tight orbit, and the bullets from the door gun were shredding through the canopy. The bullets splintered limbs and eviscerated leaves before slamming into the ground in great geysers of earth.

Keep fucking moving! the voice screamed.

Hayes scrambled to his feet and followed the cut to his right. He tore the compass from his pocket, got a quick heading angled up the opposite slope. The vines and branches tore at his face, slapping tears into his eyes.

But there was no time to think about pain, only surviving. He tugged his last grenade free, ripped the pin, and threw it over his shoulder. Up ahead he saw a break in the trees at the top of an embankment. His legs burned and his breathing was ragged, his pursuers closing in fast behind him.

He was halfway up the hill when the Jeep burst into view and slid to a halt. Hayes felt a flash of hope, the realization that he had a chance if he could only make it up the incline.

"*Cole!*" Hayes yelled, digging deep, ignoring the burning in his chest and the darkness at the edge of his vision.

The grenade exploded behind him, drowning out the screams of the men caught in the explosion.

Hayes could see the Jeep clearly now, and Boggs standing up behind the wheel, neck craning toward the sound of gunfire chattering behind him.

"*The saw . . . throw . . . me . . . the . . . SAW,*" he gasped, ducking his head against the bullets snapping through the limbs behind him. "Throw it," he choked, bursting out of the trees.

"It's locked and loaded!" Boggs yelled.

The M249 Squad Automatic Weapon weighed seventeen pounds, but with all the adrenaline flowing through Hayes's veins, it felt light as a feather when he plucked it out of the air, dug his feet into the ground, and slid to a halt.

He spun, snapped the stock to his shoulder, and pressed the safety to fire just as the men appeared through the trees. According to the manual, the SAW's max rate of fire was one hundred rounds a minute before the barrel started to melt. Hayes had never been in a situation to test it, but as he slammed the trigger to the rear, he hoped someone had.

The SAW chattered to life, the recoil vibrating through his body, forcing Hayes to lean all of his weight into the machine gun to keep it under control. He held the trigger down, working the muzzle back and forth like a fire hose.

He could feel the heat coming off the barrel through the handguard, but he stayed on the trigger, even when smoke obscured his vision and he could no longer see his targets. He slung lead until he ran through the hundred rounds inside the cloth drum.

When the SAW finally fell silent, the barrel was bright red and starting to droop, and Hayes let it fall and jumped into the back of the Jeep.

"*Go, go, go!*"

"What the hell happened to stealthy?" Boggs demanded.

"Just fucking drive." Hayes tugged the substantially lighter bag of guns toward him and refilled his magazine and grenade pouch.

The only rifle left was a battered AK-47. Hayes racked a round into the chamber and climbed into the front passenger seat.

"What did you see?" Boggs shouted over the wind rolling through the open Jeep.

"Money, a fucking warehouse full of hundred-dollar bills," Hayes said, twisting open a Nalgene bottle full of water and pouring the contents down his throat.

"Are you serious?" Boggs asked, slowing as they approached the dogleg in the road.

"I'm—" he started to reply, but then they came around the corner and saw the pair of mud-spattered pickups pulled across the road, the PKM machine guns mounted to the back pointed at the front of the Jeep.

Hayes didn't have time to do anything but get the AK-47 up to his chest and his finger on the trigger when the gunners opened fire and the windshield exploded inward.

The DEA agent yelled out in pain and his hand shot to his chest, blood splattering over the side of Hayes's face.

"Boggs!" he yelled, catching the man slumping face-first into the wheel out of the corner of his eye. He expected the Jeep to slow, but instead it surged forward. Hayes realized Boggs's foot was pinning the accelerator to the floor.

Hayes dropped the AK and reached over for the wheel, knowing that since they couldn't stop, his only option was to try to run the roadblock. He managed to center the Jeep on course and had resigned himself to trying to smash through the trucks when a fighter in a baggy T-shirt stepped out into the road five feet in front of the speeding Jeep, a black handkerchief tied over his mouth and a dark green orb in his right hand.

At first Hayes didn't understand what he was seeing. The fighter was too small to be a man, and for a moment, he thought that he was about to be killed by a midget. But then his mind cleared, and he realized what was really going on.

It's a kid.

But there was nothing childlike about the frag in his hand.

The Jeep was less than two feet away, close enough for him to read the yellow stenciled writing on the olive-drab body: GRENADE, FRAG, DELAY, M67.

Hit him.

At that moment Hayes was so desperate to survive that he would have hit a priest if he was standing in the road with a fragmentation grenade. But he couldn't kill a kid, no matter what it cost him, and he pushed the wheel hard over at the same moment the boy fastballed the grenade at the Jeep.

51

PENDARE, VENEZUELA

The frag hit the hood of the Jeep with a solid thump. It rolled up to the windshield wipers and stopped. Hayes's adrenaline took over, and he violently shoved the wheel to the left, hoping to fling it free.

The Jeep shot off the road, its brush guard tearing a hole through the undergrowth. The front end cleared the edge and the nose dipped down. Outside the Jeep, the trees blurred past the window, and even with the brake pedal pushed to the floor, the Jeep continued to pick up speed.

A glance at the speedometer showed the needle creeping past forty miles per hour.

By the time Hayes looked up and saw the massive

rubber tree in his path, the only thing he could do was step on the gas and yank the wheel hard over.

The passenger side of the bumper clipped the tree hard and sent the Jeep spinning. Hayes fought to regain control, tried to hold on, but the wheel was ripped from his hands.

His head slammed into the frame, a sharp blow that sparked his vision.

The back end banged into a second tree, shattering more glass, but Hayes ignored it. He grabbed the wheel with his left hand, forced his tingling right to comply to his will, and then he had both hands on the wheel. Hayes turned into the spin, putting everything he had into it.

The Jeep was slow to respond, but he felt the tires get traction, which allowed him to get some forward momentum, and finally he managed to straighten it out when he looked up and saw the edge of a cliff.

Hayes was reaching for the emergency brake when the vegetation cleared. He yanked the lever upward, the metal hitting the stop and tearing free from his hand. The tires locked up and the back end fishtailed, but the SUV was too fast and way too heavy.

He watched the ground coming, knowing there was nothing he could do.

The front wheels bounced over the edge and the front end pitched forward. Hayes was weightless, and then he was falling.

"Hold on," he yelled at Boggs.

The Jeep slammed into the ground with enough force to fold the brush guard backward into the engine compartment. The radiator exploded. Hayes's head rebounded off the wheel and stars sparked in his vision. He tasted blood in his mouth, and slowly his vision faded to black.

Hayes's eyes blinked open, his vision hazy from the blood running down his face. The view from the shattered windshield was wrong, but his mind reeled to place the problem. The smell of gas, burning oil, and plastic scorched his nose, and when he tried to move his arm, Hayes realized that he was upside down. Trapped inside the burning vehicle.

He forced his head to the left, looking for his friend. Shards of safety glass dug into his scalp. Slumped against the wheel, Boggs looked dead.

"Hey, buddy, you still with me?" he said and groaned.

"Fuck," the DEA agent mumbled. "I can't . . . I can't feel my legs."

The voices were getting closer.

"Here, he's here!" a voice yelled.

"Alive, the colonel wants them alive," a second voice shouted.

That ain't happening.

Hayes could smell fuel and knew he had to get out

of the Jeep. He kicked at the folded windshield and managed to create a hole large enough to fit through.

Beside him, Boggs moaned.

Hayes turned to him. "We got to roll, man. I'll climb through, then I'll pull you out."

He ducked through the opening where the windshield had been. Hayes felt his flesh catch on something, but ripped free and scrambled from the wreck, and forced himself to his feet. Hayes was trying to get his balance when he saw the top of a head pop up at the back of the truck that had followed them.

The narco rushed around the truck, a sawed-off shotgun in his right hand.

They were face-to-face, close enough for Hayes to see the man's eyes widen in surprise over the bandana tied around his mouth. The narco froze.

Hayes didn't.

With the pills finally out of his system, the conduit that connected Hayes to the training he'd received at Treadstone was wide open, and he reacted without hesitation, emotion, or thought. He was a machine, programmed for one purpose: to kill.

Hayes fired a left-handed jab to the man's sternum. It was a solid blow that landed square and knocked the narco back on his heels. Before his knuckles found flesh, he'd stripped the Glock from the holster with his right hand. The moment the barrel cleared leather, Hayes double-pumped the trigger.

Boom . . . boom.

"You want some of this?" he yelled in Spanish, the Glock coming up into a two-handed grip.

Rifle fire erupted from the other side of the SUV. The hollow cracks followed the bullet pinging off the Jeep. Hayes grabbed Boggs, making sure to keep his neck steady in case the man had a spinal injury, and slowly pulled him free of the wreck.

Hayes was spent, his arms useless, legs barely keeping him up, but he managed to drag Boggs around the back of the Jeep and set him against a tree.

"Here, take this," he said, tugging Boggs's Glock from its holster before ripping his shirt open.

"J-just go," he wheezed.

One look at the wound and the uneven movement that came with the pained inhalation told Hayes that Boggs had a sucking chest wound. He needed to relieve the pressure or the man was going to die.

The trauma kit in the Jeep.

"Hold tight."

"G-go," Boggs whispered.

"You hold on, buddy, I'm going to get you out of here," Hayes said, crawling inside the Jeep, his head throbbing like someone was beating on his skull with a chisel. He flattened himself out, crawled under the roll bar, and snatched the kit off the back of the driver's seat.

Hayes winced when a round punched through the

passenger seat, leaving a jagged hole in its wake, and ripped the kit free. He banged his shin on the way out. Another stab of pain, but he was working off pure adrenaline now and pushed it away.

"Burn him out!" someone yelled in Spanish.

Hayes threw the kit to the rear of the Jeep and drew the revolver.

"Where is he?" one of the men asked in Spanish. "Did you get him?"

"I'm here," Hayes said, stepping into the open, then centered the revolver on the closest target, a stocky man with black hair sticking straight up.

"No, no, no!" the second shooter yelled, trying to throw his AK to the ground, but it was too late.

Boom.

The Smith & Wesson roared, bowling the fighter over, and Hayes turned to the second man and dropped him with two quick shots. But more were coming, and Hayes knew that he was out of time. He ran the pistol dry, shoved it into the holster, and was turning back to Boggs when a narco came around the corner, his AK up and ready. Hayes lowered his head and speared him.

He felt the man's breath rush from his body as he drove him into the ground. Hayes brought his elbow down across the man's face and felt blood spurt onto his arm. Achieving the mount, Hayes ripped the AK from the fighter's grip, breaking a few fingers in the process. Every second counted. He knew that he needed to end the fight quickly.

He launched a blade-hand strike at the man's throat, fracturing his larynx and crushing his windpipe. The narco desperately gasped for air, but was soon still.

Hayes swayed when he got to his feet. His vision was blurry, and rounds tore at the ground around him. He scrambled back to Boggs and dumped the kit's contents on the ground. The gunfire was getting closer and Hayes could hear voices when the firing died down. Boot falls pounded the dirt on the other side.

Hayes's hands shook when he ripped open the pack of gauze. He managed to stuff it into the bullet hole and secure an ACE bandage around Boggs's torso.

The narcos were gathering for another attack, but this time the rifle fire started slowly. The hits sounded like rocks being thrown against a tin shed, and the misses whizzed overhead like angry hornets.

Hayes ignored it, focused everything on trying to save Boggs's life and knowing that he was fighting a losing battle. He remembered the Iridium satphone in his assault pack and crawled to the rear of the vehicle, but it wasn't there.

Realizing that it must have fallen out during the rollover, Hayes shot a glance up the hill, where a gun crew was trying to set up a PKM machine gun.

Hayes knew he had two options: He could go now, before the machine gun was up and functioning, or sit back and watch Boggs die. It was a no-brainer. He didn't even hesitate.

He simply rushed the hill, snagging a fallen AK from a dead fighter, and emptied the magazine on the run. He was lucky one of the rounds hit the fighter before he could get the PKM into action. Hayes scooped up the man's weapon, and the men on the road turned and fled.

Ducking into the sling, Hayes snatched a frag from the dead man's belt. He ripped the pin out, took two steps, and let the spoon fly free.

Counting in his head, he forced his battered body up onto the road.

Hayes set his feet, heaved the frag at the men.

The grenade detonated right above their heads. It bowled the fighters over in a cloud of blood and flesh, peppering Hayes with bits of metal.

And then it was still.

Hayes ditched the empty rifle and stumbled back to his pack. He reached inside, yanked out the satphone, and ran back to the Jeep, where he found Cole already dead.

There was no time to mourn, only time to sling the assault pack, snag a radio from one of the dead fighters and a pistol from the other, and then he was running back toward the trees, seeking shelter in the jungle.

52

PENDARE, VENEZUELA

Run, you idiot.

Hayes sprinted toward the tree line, ignoring the leaden weight in his legs.

A gunman's excited voice boomed over the radio in Hayes's hand. "Pedro, he is here. Bring the dogs."

"Air One, I've got a runner."

Hayes ducked his head and crashed through the brush, the stinging slap of a tree branch hot across his face. He wanted to head east, but it had been years since anyone had thinned the woods, and the forest floor was choked with wait-a-minute vines, briars, and knee-high saplings.

The obstacles made it impossible for Hayes to travel in a straight line, and he was forced to constantly change directions. He'd been on the wrong side of a tracking team before and knew his only chance of staying alive was to split up the K9-handler team.

The most effective way to achieve this was for Hayes to kill the handler. But all he had was the pistol, and he wasn't waiting around to take a shot. He knew that distance and speed were the only things that were going to save him, but he was exhausted and wasn't sure how much gas he had left in the tank.

Just run.

If there was a way to actually fool the Malinois's nose, Hayes hadn't heard of it. He knew the cartels had tried everything. Coffee, brake cleaner, oil. It didn't matter what they used to mask the scent of their coke, a dog's nose was just too sensitive.

The way he'd heard it explained was that a human could smell a hamburger, but a good scent dog could smell the flour the bun was made from, the plastic from the bottle of ketchup, and even the soap the cook had used to clean his hands.

He knew from experience that both the handler and the dog would be amped up. The dog would find his fresh trail, scent the blood-and-sweat mixture, and pull hard on the lead. The handler would know that his dog had a lock, and if Hayes was lucky, he would let him run.

Hayes was hoping that the handler wouldn't be too keyed up to keep his dog calm and let it overexert itself.

Fooling the dog was out of the question. But the handler was a different story.

In the Army they had called it counter tracking, and at its core the tactic was meant to make the handler think the dog had lost the scent.

This terrain wasn't the best place to try to pull it off, but right now, Hayes was grasping at straws.

He cut north, using a running pace count to tell him when he'd traveled fifty meters. When he reached that distance, he dropped and rolled on the ground. Once he was sure that his scent had been firmly deposited on the matted jungle floor, Hayes jumped to his feet and took a zigzagging sprint back to his start point.

Facing west, he ran a series of tight circles before arcing south and repeating the process all over again.

He repeated the process three times, and when he was done, he was covered in dirt and exhausted. His body ached to stop, but he pushed himself, knowing that he needed to make up the time lost.

The terrain rose beneath his feet, and the effort of running uphill caused a lactic burn in his legs. As he climbed higher, the air grew colder until he felt like he was breathing fire. The vegetation started to thin, the space between the trees growing more pronounced.

Hayes went internal, shutting off his brain. Converting the pain into fuel.

Bent almost double, he clawed his way toward the summit, over the thinning grass and the slabs of granite.

But there was only so much his body could take, and he finally came to a halt beside a gnarled rubber tree.

He tried to hold himself up, but his shaking muscles refused to support his weight. When his arm gave out, Hayes stumbled into the tree. His legs gave out, and then he was on the ground, clothes soaked in sweat, every inch of exposed skin raw and red from the slap and scrape of the branches.

Hayes looked up at the sky. The past ten years of his life had been spent building a wall around the man he used to be. Doing everything he could to stay free of Treadstone. He'd thought that he'd never need those skills again. Believed that his enemies would just forget the man he'd once been.

He'd lied to himself. Allowed himself to get soft. Weak.

There was movement on his backtrail. A shimmer of black among the green of the woods. The snap of breaking branches and the baying of the tracking dogs, and for the first time in his life Hayes was afraid.

Hayes somehow managed to get to his feet. He was about to push himself away from the tree—

Stop.

What is it? he asked himself.

Listen.

He didn't hear anything. Not the trackers, or the dogs, or the helicopter. Just the hammering of his heart in his ears.

The first shot snapped over his head, followed by the *crack* of a high-powered rifle. Hayes kept low and scrambled for the summit.

A second shot rang out and the bullet sparked off a boulder, bits of granite tearing across his skin. The gunfire came from all directions, the bullets snapping and hissing all around him.

What, did you think they were going to bring you in?

He saw a clearing off to his left and ran for it, the sound of the blood in his ears slowly replaced by the thunder of rushing water.

"He's trapped!" a voice yelled in Spanish.

Hayes flashed out of the trees, his boots skidding across the wet granite that had replaced the bare earth. He threw his arms out and felt himself tipping forward over a ledge. Suddenly he was in freefall, tumbling toward the river thundering against its banks twenty feet below him. It was swollen and angry, the water foaming over the jagged rocks that jutted from the surface.

Every instinct telling him to reach out for something. To stay out of the river.

Don't fight it.

Hayes hit the water, the impact knocking the breath from his lungs. Then the river had him. It pulled him under, flipped him end over end like he was in Satan's washing machine. He ducked out of his jacket, kicked off his boots, and clawed his way to the surface.

His head broke the water and he caught a quick breath before the current dragged him under. It was an ancient and one-sided fight. Man against the elements. A truly humbling experience. Hayes wasn't ready to die, and the fact that he was standing on death's door gave him superhuman strength. He fought free of the current's icy grip, somehow got his head above water a second time.

But it was a losing battle.

The river carried him downstream, bouncing him off rocks and submerged roots. His hand slapped against a boulder. He scrambled to get a grip, but the rock was slick with moss.

As he slipped under the water, he felt someone grab a fistful of his hair. A painful yank and his head broke the surface.

"Got your ass," a gravelly voice exclaimed.

The sun was shining full in Hayes's eyes and he couldn't see the face of the man standing in front of him. The man grabbed Hayes's belt and used it to pull him to his feet.

Hayes was already running on fumes and had no energy left to dodge a brutal punch to his stomach. The blow to the gut emptied his tank. His knees buckled, and when the man let go of his hair, Hayes dropped to the ground. A boot to the ribs sprawled him on his back.

The man loomed over him, his body eclipsing the sun.

Hayes blinked the stars from his eyes, and when his vision cleared, he was staring down the barrel of a .45.

"You fucking move," the man said, pressing the pistol to the center of his forehead, "and I will empty your fucking skull."

Hayes had lost count of how many guns had been held to his head. But it wasn't the kiss of steel to his skin that made his blood run cold, it was the face of the man staring at him from over the sights.

Gray.

He heard the snap of branches and the scramble of feet behind him and turned in time to see a muzzle crashing down on his head, and then the world went black.

53

PENDARE, VENEZUELA

Hayes blinked when they took the hood off.

It smelled of bleach and standing water. And reminded him of a gym locker room. The cinder-block walls were painted an off-white. In the center was a white card table and two folding chairs.

The guards wore sterile BDUs, and Hayes could tell they weren't soldiers.

"Strip," the older guard ordered in Spanish. He threw an orange jumpsuit on the table.

Hayes took a seat and checked the room.

The younger guard stood by the door, holding a shotgun. The other stood a few feet behind the table. He had his hand resting on the butt of his pistol.

"I'm not putting that shit on."

The guard shrugged.

Hayes wasn't in any position to make a move. And since he wasn't sure where they were taking him, he decided not to go naked.

He tugged the jumpsuit on.

"Sit," the man said in Spanish.

One of the men brought a plastic bin over and dropped it on the table.

"What do you want me to do with that?"

"Put your shit in the bin and keep your mouth shut," the other guard commanded.

Hayes unbuckled his watch. He was pretty sure he would never see it again, but dutifully put it in the bin.

The door opened and a thin man in a lab coat approached the table tentatively. He took a penlight from his pocket. Hayes guessed he was in his late twenties. He had a wisp of a mustache on his upper lip, and he was sweating. The penlight shook in his hands.

It made Hayes wonder what they had told the men about him.

The light hurt his eyes. His head was killing him. It felt like a tiny jackhammer was doing roadwork on his brain.

"I think he has a concussion."

"He's fine," the older guard said.

The younger guard nodded and snapped a pair of handcuffs around Hayes's wrists. "This way," he said, pushing Hayes out the door and using the muzzle of the rifle to prod him along the hall.

It was a short walk, but it left Hayes dizzy. He felt goose bumps on his arms. Followed by a wave of nausea.

Hayes didn't plan on sticking around and did his best to memorize the route, taking note of what looked like an arms room before the older guard shoved his pistol into his back.

"Inside," the man commanded.

He shoved Hayes into a chair and shackled his handcuffs to a chain attached to an eyebolt drilled into the concrete floor. Before he walked out of the room, the guard took the opportunity to slap Hayes on the back of the head.

Hayes tried to get to his feet but quickly learned that while there was enough play in the chain to allow him to move his arms from left to right, there was no way he could stand up. He worked his arms back and forth, testing the bolt for play, but it was firmly anchored in the concrete, and the harder he pulled against the bolt, the deeper the metal cuffs dug into his wrists.

Finally he gave up and instead studied the room.

Like the chain, the chair was bolted to the floor above a copper drain with dried blood around the edges.

On the wall to his right was a typical backyard spigot. A green hose was coiled neatly below it.

Hayes knew the hose wasn't for drinking. It was for spraying blood down the drain, but it made him thirsty.

"Sure am thirsty," he said.

Straight ahead was a mirror. His reflection wasn't looking so good.

"Hey!" he yelled. "Can I have some water, maybe some aspirin, you know, for the concussion?"

Nothing.

This is not how I saw this day going.

Hayes knew that everything depended on who walked through that door.

As if on cue, the door swung open.

Well . . . fuck.

Gray entered the room with a folder, a pair of black gloves, and a disappointed look on his face.

"You just won't die, will you?" he asked.

"Sorry to disappoint," Hayes said.

"Before we get started, I have to tell you something. To be honest, I didn't have much hope for this day. Honestly, I thought you were too smart to fall into Vega's little trap. But then it worked and . . ." He paused dramatically, arms spread wide. "Well, it was like Christmas morning."

"Didn't have the balls to pull the trigger, though."

"Well, I would have shot you, but . . ."

"But what?"

"Well, I still need you, at least for a few more minutes."

"Just so you know," Hayes said, "I'm going to kill you."

"I doubt it." Gray smiled.

"That's what Black said."

"Yeah, well, Black was a blunt instrument, a tool to be used and thrown away."

"Can we just get this shit over with?" Hayes asked. "I mean, either kill me or torture me or whatever the hell you are going to do, but please, shut the fuck up."

Gray smiled, but his eyes grew hard and angry.

He was faster than Hayes gave him credit for, and Hayes barely had time to tense up. Gray's fist came in like a sledgehammer, cracking Hayes's rib.

"You want to get to the point, well, here it is," Gray said, slapping a manila folder on the table with the CIA seal on the front. He opened it, pulled a paper clip off the documents, and laid them side by side.

"You know what this is?"

"I hope it's a menu. 'Cause I'm starving."

Gray's face flexed upward for a moment. It was like his muscles were trying to remember how to smile, and then, without blinking an eye, he backhanded Hayes across the face.

All Hayes could do was flinch before Gray's knuckles cracked across his nose.

"What the fuck is it with you people and my nose?" Hayes demanded, blinking away the tears as Gray grabbed a handful of his hair and slammed his face down hard on the table.

"Stop being a smartass, then, and listen up. No, this

is *not* a menu. It's a confession," Gray snarled, letting go of his hair.

"Well, I'm kinda hungry," Hayes admitted.

"Tell you what, sign on the line. And I'll give you something to eat. Deal?"

Hayes reached across the table; the chains rattled as he pulled the papers close, but before looking at the paper, he glanced up at Gray.

"How the hell did an asshole like you make it into the CIA? I mean, don't they have standards?"

"Because I am smarter than everyone else."

"Then how'd you end up in this dump instead of doing something useful, like fighting the War on Terror?"

"Useful? The War on Terror, are you serious right now?"

"Hey, man, I'm just asking, because fighting a war seems a lot better than whatever the hell you and Colonel Psychopath have going on out there. I mean, what are you going to do with all that money, anyways—buy some friends?" he continued.

"Tell you what," Gray said, glancing at his watch. "I'll give you sixty seconds to decide if you want to sign the paper or run your mouth."

"What exactly am I confessing to?" Hayes asked.

"For killing all the people you killed. Ford, Black . . ."

"Is that all?"

"And for being an asshole."

"An asshole? Really?"

"Thirty seconds," Gray said, looking at his watch.

"So that's how we're going to play it."

"Yep. Twenty seconds."

"I forgot my glasses," Hayes said, shoving the papers off the table while palming the paper clip.

"Fine with me," Gray said, bending down to scoop the papers off the ground before crumpling them into a tiny ball and placing it on the table. "I am really going to enjoy this." He smiled, taking the gloves from the table and tugging them over his hands.

"Good for you," Hayes said, and sneered.

"Still have five seconds," Gray said, walking around the table. "Is there anything you want to add?"

"Yeah, why don't you go—"

"Time's up," Gray said, driving his fist into Hayes's mouth.

It was a meaty, wet collision that rocked him back in the chair.

His ears rang from the blow. Gray knew exactly where to hit a man. Hayes's eyes immediately teared up. He could taste the blood. See it spatter on the table.

Gray hit like an ox. The next shot was to his solar plexus. It doubled Hayes up like a cheap folding chair.

He retched. The air rushed from his lungs in a crimson mist and speckled the front of his jumpsuit.

The only reason the chair was still standing was because it was bolted to the floor. Hayes almost fell off.

But Gray grabbed his jumpsuit with his right hand. His left came crashing down in an open-handed slap.

Pop.

"*Woooooo!*" Gray yelled, turning to face the mirror. He raised his arms above his head, like a boxer working an invisible crowd. "I tell you *what*—it feels gooood to be back."

Gray rolled his head around on his shoulders and launched into a quick shadow-boxing routine before the mirror. He was back in his element and totally enjoying himself.

Hayes, on the other hand, was in agony.

His heart was hammering like a machine gun on full auto, and his lungs burned from lack of oxygen. When he went to take a breath, he choked on the blood filling his mouth. The edges of his vision began to spot, and he knew he was about to hyperventilate.

His mind was overwhelmed by the sudden amount of damage. It panicked and allowed the primal side to take over. The result was similar to a DVD skipping halfway through a movie.

"Hey!" Gray yelled, bringing him back. "That was just round one. Don't tell me you've already had enough."

"Fuck it," Hayes croaked.

"What was that? Speak up, Alice, I didn't hear you."

Hayes knew what he had to do.

He leaned forward in the chair and pursed his

shattered lips. A rivulet of crimson spit poured from his mouth. It hit the floor with a wet smack.

"I'll make you a deal," Hayes said, his voice low and defeated.

Gray cracked his knuckles and took a triumphant step closer.

"You wanna deal? I'm listening."

Hayes lolled in the chair. His breathing was short and choppy against the pain that came with each inhalation.

Through hooded eyes he looked at the mirror. There was no fight left in his eyes.

"I'll give you a chance to leave."

"*Leave?* Shit, I must have hit you harder than I thought," Gray said.

He was less than a foot away, and there was victory in his eyes.

"Where the hell am I goin'?"

"I don't . . . want to . . ." Hayes panted.

He had to economize his words. It hurt too bad to breathe.

"Don't want to what?"

"To . . . kill . . . you."

"You're going to kill me? Mighty hard to do with those cuffs around your wrist and that chain holding you to the floor." Gray smiled.

Hayes mumbled something unintelligible.

"What?" Gray leaned in. "Don't pass out on me, boy."

"Not . . ." Hayes muttered.

"Not what?"

Gray reached forward to slap him in the face, and Hayes suddenly looked up, his eyes clear.

"Not handcuffed," Hayes spat.

He dropped the act so fast that it froze Gray in his tracks. Hayes drove his left hand into Gray's groin. He grabbed his balls and twisted. Gray bellowed like an ox beneath the ax.

He doubled over, mouth wide open. Hayes shot to his feet. He kept his head down, aiming at Gray's chin.

The impact was brutal. There was a snapping sound. Gray's teeth exploded inside his mouth. His jawbone quickly followed. Hayes's hands encircled the man's head. He felt his fingers touch. Rising up to his full height, Hayes paused.

His ribs screamed in protest. The pain was a white-hot lance. Hayes flexed his muscles and yanked down with all his might.

Gray's head hit the table so hard it left a dent in the metal. Hayes let go. The man hit the floor like a bag of trash. Blood poured from the jagged gash on his forehead.

Hayes walked over to Gray and tugged the man's Glock from the holster at the small of his back.

"Should have taken the deal," he said, lining up the sights on the man's forehead and pulling the trigger.

54

PENDARE, VENEZUELA

The interrogation room was soundproof, which gave Hayes one advantage—whoever was outside would have no idea that he'd just killed Gray. He cracked the door and yelled out in Spanish, "Give me a hand with this guy."

He quickly stepped aside.

The door opened, revealing the guard who had taken his clothes. "That was quick," the man said, stepping into the room and freezing in place when he saw Gray's body on the floor.

Before he could recover, Hayes pressed the Glock to the back of the man's head and fired.

He stuffed the pain back into its box and climbed out of the orange jumpsuit. The guard's clothes were small, but he made it work, and after cramming his feet into the man's boots, Hayes stepped out into the hall. Every breath came with a stab of pain. His legs shook, and blood ran into his eyes.

But he kept moving, knowing that he was on the clock.

Hayes leaned against the wall, keeping himself upright by sheer force of will, leaving behind a smear of blood. Up ahead he saw the arms room. He peeked through the door, ready to kill the soldier who'd been inside. But the man was gone, and the steel cage door locked.

"Now what?"

Keep moving.

Hayes had almost reached the hangar when he saw a door he'd missed on the left. He was planning on bypassing it when a guard stepped out holding a steaming mug of coffee.

"Who are—"

Hayes shot him twice in the chest and shoved him through the door. On the other side, Hayes found a small kitchenette with a rusted sink, an ancient stove, and a filthy microwave.

He stuffed the pistol into his pants before tugging the oven away from the wall. He stomped down on the gas line, breaking it. Hayes held his breath against the rush of natural gas, ejected a round from the Glock, and set the bullet in the filthy microwave. He twisted the knob to the left and closed the door, guessing that he had sixty seconds before the makeshift bomb exploded.

He was nearing the end of his strength when he finally stumbled into the hangar. The Antonov was idling just outside the hangar door, but he had to cross at least a hundred feet to reach the plane. Hayes scanned the area around him, looking for anything he could use to get to it. But there was nothing but a set of old tools and a drip pan full of oil.

Hayes was about to give up when he saw the clipboard on top of the tool chest.

No one ever questions a man with a clipboard, he thought.

He stuffed the Glock in his waistband, grabbed the clipboard, and, summoning the last of his strength, forced himself upright. He squared his shoulders, wiped the blood from his nose with the sleeve of his camo shirt, and stepped out of the shadows.

Just act like you belong, he thought, before boldly walking across the hangar.

The short walk from the door to the Antonov seemed to take forever, and Hayes fought the urge to break into a run, knowing that it would only draw attention to him.

He'd just made it to the bottom of the ramp when a crew member appeared at the top of the cargo hold.

"We're leaving!" the man shouted.

"Paperwork," Hayes yelled back, "for the cargo."

The man cursed and shook his head.

"Well, hurry up, then," the man said.

Hayes forced himself to jog up the ramp, keeping his head low to hide the pain twisting across his face. By the time he reached the top, his vision was swimming and he felt himself close to passing out.

"Are you okay?" the crewman asked.

Hayes nodded, not trusting himself to speak as he handed the clipboard to the man.

"This is a service record," the man shouted over the roar of the engine. "I thought you said you had the bill of lading."

"My mistake," Hayes gasped, jerking the Glock from his waistband and managing to pull the trigger before falling against the pallet of cash in the cargo hold.

The gunshot echoed inside the plane, and when it receded, he thought he heard someone calling his name.

"Hayes!" the voice shouted again.

"Izzy?" he asked, looking up to see the woman rushing toward him.

"Oh, my God, your face. What happened?"

"No time for that, close the ramp," he said.

"I don't—"

"The red button to the right, just push it," he said, pulling himself to his feet and hearing the whine of the hydraulics as the ramp began to close. "Now help me to the cockpit."

Izzy ducked under his arm and half dragged, half carried him through the cargo hold.

You are almost there.

Hayes grabbed the knob, twisted the door open, and stumbled into the cockpit. Alerted by the movement behind him, the pilot from the bar turned to look over his shoulder, and when he saw the Glock pointed at his head, the blood drained from his face.

"Me again." Hayes winced, dropping into the empty copilot seat.

"W-what do you want?"

"I want you to get this bitch in the air."

IN FLIGHT

Izzy called her boss from the air, and by the time the An-12 crossed the border, the Colombian Air Force had scrambled a pair of A-37 Dragonflys to escort the transport to Bogotá.

In the cockpit Hayes watched the light attack jets ease into position off of both wings. "Nice and easy," he warned the pilot. "Just follow their lead and this will be over before you know it."

Hayes's mind went back to the first radio call they'd made after the pilot lifted the transport into the air.

"Gray is dead, but Vega is still alive," he'd said. "I need a team to go after him."

"No," Shaw had replied. "You're done."

"Done? What do you mean, done? You told me that

they were shutting Treadstone down at the end of the month," he said, looking at his watch. "That means I have twelve hours."

"There has been a change in plans," Shaw replied.

"Not for me," Hayes said, locking eyes with Izzy. "Do you have any idea what Vega was going to use that money for? He and Gray were going to use it to subsidize a coup, including bribing Senator Mendez to keep the U.S. from siding against him."

The weariness in Shaw's voice carried through the phone. "Adam, even if you could prove that, my hands are . . ."

There was silence on the other end of the line, and Hayes knew Levi was mulling it over. Weighing the options, seeing which one put him back on top.

"I'm pulling you out. It's time for you to come home, see your family."

"And what, Vega gets a pass?"

"No!" Izzy hissed, her fingers digging into Hayes's shoulders.

"Adam, this isn't negotiable. You are done. Pack your stuff, I'm sending a plane."

"I can't do that," Hayes replied, cutting the connection.

"Does this mean Cole died for nothing?" Izzy asked, her eyes red rimmed from the tears shed for the DEA agent.

"No," he said, looking at the pallets of cash strapped

in the cargo hold, "but we are going to do this *my* way, which means I have to contact JT and you have to stay in Bogotá. Do you understand?"

She nodded and wiped away the tear rolling down her cheek.

Near Paraguachón, Colombia, Hayes was traveling sterile, his only weapon the Walther PPK tucked at the small of his back, when he limped into the train station and bought a ticket to Caracas.

The passenger train was old and well past its serviceability date. Despite the lack of air-conditioning and creature comforts such as a working restroom, the train was usually packed. But instead of the hordes of camera-laden tourists and unwashed migrants, today there were only a handful of passengers.

Hayes didn't care what it cost him, Mendez wasn't getting a pass, and if Shaw wouldn't help, Hayes would find someone who would.

Izzy.

By the time the train squealed to a halt in the capital, he'd been traveling for eight hours and his sweat-soaked shirt clung to his muscled torso like Saran Wrap. The brakes squealed and the train decelerated in preparation for its arrival. Hayes could see the platform through his window; it was a jostling mass of families pulling into the station.

He got to his feet, snatched his carry-on from the floor, and ducked off the train, wading through the throng of families pressing forward. Around the edges, police in riot gear and soldiers armed with automatic rifles presided over the crowd. Hayes could see them scanning the scene, but all he could do was pray they weren't looking for him.

Outside the station, Hayes powered on the prepaid phone and texted the number Izzy had given him.

Here.

The reply came a moment later.

Hotel Classico. Good Luck, followed by a picture of a Mitsubishi SUV in a parking stall.

Hayes flagged a taxi and gave the driver the name of the hotel.

The man eyed him for a moment, and Hayes saw a hint of concern flash across his face.

"Are you sure? There are much better hotels than the Classico."

Hayes knew what the man was thinking. He assumed he was another Western journalist here to cover the rioters clashing with President Díaz's troops in the streets of Caracas.

Grief and suffering were always big business, and he was sure the cabbie got a healthy tip for every customer with a fat expense account that he brought to a hotel.

"The Classico is fine," Hayes said, and smiled.

If Hayes had been staying at the Classico, he might have taken the cabbie up on the offer to take him somewhere else the moment he pulled up at the door.

"I tried to tell you, sir," the man said, and shrugged.

"I'm sure it's fine," Hayes said.

"Suit yourself."

Hayes slung his go bag and walked through the front door.

Any worry about having to sneak past the desk clerk was alleviated by the sound of the man's raucous snoring. With that problem out of the way, Hayes focused on the task at hand. He snatched a newspaper from the dented coffee table in the center of the lobby and followed the sign to the rear stairwell.

He stopped before the door that led to the parking garage and folded the paper into a tight square. After checking for an alarm, Hayes opened the door, stepped outside, and wedged the paper between the lock and jamb. He eased the door shut, and when he was confident that it wouldn't lock behind him, he ducked into the shadows to wait for his eyes to adjust to the gloom.

If anyone knew he was coming, this is where they would hit him. While he was unarmed and away from prying eyes. From his position he saw the Mitsubishi SUV backed into its parking corral.

Everything Hayes needed to kill Vega and whoever

was dumb enough to try to stand in his way was in the back of the SUV. He was exhausted and still in pain from the beating he'd taken at Pendare, but he forced himself to remain cautious—to wait, watch, and listen until he was *sure* that he was alone—and then he angled around the back of the SUV. Hayes snatched the keys off the rear tire, unlocked the door, and crawled behind the wheel.

The Classico might be a dump, but it still had cameras, which made it too dangerous to risk checking his cargo.

You've waited this long. You can wait until you get to the safe house.

In the garage, he started the engine and followed the ramp up to the street.

He drove toward José Félix Ribas, the barrio on the eastern hillside of Caracas. Hayes had seen poverty before, but never like this. He guessed the entire neighborhood was two hundred acres max, but according to Izzy, it was home to more than 120,000 people.

The house was in the barrio. The structure looked more like a brightly painted storage shed than a home, but it had a garage and running water, which was all Hayes had asked for. He pulled inside and, after locking the metal door, opened the back hatch of the SUV and dug his finger beneath the sheet of upholstered plywood that covered the spare tire well. He pushed down and felt a metallic click. Inside the hidden compartment was a low-profile ballistic vest, a satphone, GPS, a Glock 19, a plate carrier stuffed with magazines and grenades and a suppressed H&K UMP45, and a Barrett .50-cal.

But it was the suppressed Mark IV pistol in the Pelican case that sent a grim smile across his face.

Just like old times.

Inside, he took a shower, placed the phone on the side table, and lay down on the bed.

He didn't know how long it would be until it rang. An hour, a day, a week? The only thing he knew for sure was that soon after he received the call, Vega would be dead.

The call came three hours later.

He checked his watch, silently counting the rings. On the third ring the phone fell silent.

His eyes flashed to the canvas go bag that sat packed next to the door. Everything he owned was packed inside the bag.

Hayes tugged a pair of latex gloves over his scarred knuckles and took a container of Clorox wipes from the bag. It took him five minutes to sanitize the room. When he was done, Hayes strapped the vest against his skin, slammed a fresh magazine into the Glock, and racked a round into the chamber. He shoved the pistol in the holster. He pulled a loose jacket over the top and then, after checking the room one last time, lifted the canvas go bag onto his shoulder and stepped outside.

56

CARACAS, VENEZUELA

Hayes left the barrio and took the coastal road through the hills, windows down, so he could smell the salt air breezing in from the Caribbean. There was something about Third World countries, the beauty of the landscape, that made him wonder if God knew the suffering the people would face and at least wanted them to have a good view.

He glanced south down into the Caracas Valley, saw the shimmer and glint of the buildings in the fading sun, and knew that in more capable hands the people might have had a chance.

But left to men like Vega, all they would ever know is suffering.

Well, I'm going to do my part, Hayes thought,

pulling the SUV off the road, the headlights playing over a primer-gray Nissan pickup with JT sitting on the tailgate.

Hayes cut the engine and climbed out, the squeal of the rusted hinges echoing through the night.

"You sure know how to pick them." JT smiled, his teeth white behind the black face paint. "Vega has that place locked up tighter than a drum."

"If it was easy, everyone would do it," Hayes said, opening the hatch and pulling out his gear.

"You sure about this?" JT asked, handing over the latest satellite imagery of the target area.

"Don't see how I have much of a choice," Hayes said and shrugged, strapping the plate carrier over his chest, and shoving a new set of batteries into the FGEs. "Unless you know a way to get him to come out to us."

"You take care of yourself," JT said, shouldering the Barrett and disappearing into the shadows.

Hayes was under no illusions about what lay ahead, and knew the odds of making it out alive were low. But if today was his day to die, Hayes was sure of one thing: He wasn't going alone.

Before stepping off, Hayes pulled out the black balaclava Izzy had given him and studied the subdued gray skull painted over the face. He tugged it over his head and adjusted the earpiece before conducting a radio check with JT.

"Got you five by five," JT replied. "Ready when you are."

Here goes nothing, he thought

Besides the balaclava, Izzy had provided a map she'd sketched from memory, but even with her insider knowledge, Hayes and JT knew the hardest part of getting inside the compound was negotiating the seven-foot walls without getting flayed by the shards of glass embedded in the top.

Luckily, Izzy had an answer for that, too. "There is a tunnel," she'd said, pointing at the map. "Well, it seemed like a tunnel back then. Actually, it's more of a drainage culvert where the runoff from the hacienda flows down to the valley."

Hayes followed Izzy's map down the hillside until he came to the culvert with the missing bottom grate. He lowered himself to his knees, but instead of lying flat and wriggling through the gap, Hayes took a breath, closed his eyes, and let the world fall away for a moment.

In an instant he was back on the beach, Jack running through the surf, his laughter rising with the tide, and Annabelle standing next to him. Her blond hair blowing in the breeze, soft brown hands wrapped tight around his. Hayes held on to the moment, seeing the world not as it *was* but the way it *could* have been, and then it was gone.

I'm sorry, buddy, he thought, letting the pain and loss roll over him, kick-start the rage in his heart until the river of fire was churning through his veins, and then he was through the gap, following the drainage tunnel under the wall. When he came up on the other side, Hayes was inside the compound.

He activated the FGEs, brought the H&K UMP45 up to his shoulder, and moved along the wall, staying in the shadows as he made his approach.

Hayes had been in Caracas for less than six hours, long enough to see the suffering down in the valley. The families on the streets, the lines outside the empty grocery stores, and the starving dogs on the street. Nothing like what he saw before him. While the rest of the city didn't have running water or sanitation, the immaculate grounds on the far edge of the compound had built-in irrigation, and in the spray of the halogen security lights, the grass and gardens were a vibrant green.

But as Hayes edged closer to his target, it became obvious that Vega had been preparing for this meeting. Radiating out from the house was a fifty-yard dead zone where every blade of grass, tree, and shrub had been stripped from the ground, leaving a barren wasteland.

The scrape of a match followed by a flash of fire drew his attention to a guard leaning against a bulldozer five feet to his left. The man touched the match to the tip of the cigarette and blew a cloud of smoke into the air.

Looks like I found my ride, Hayes thought, pressing the push-to-talk on the front of his vest.

"You ready to punch this time card?" he asked over the radio.

"I'm sitting on G, waiting for O," JT replied.

"Roger that, give me a ten-count, then go loud."

"Ten . . . nine . . . eight," JT began, his voice as even as a metronome over the radio.

Hayes tugged the KA-BAR from the sheath at the small of his back, the blade hissing free with the whisper of steel on leather. He crept forward, leading with the ball of his foot before rolling his weight into the step.

"Seven . . . six . . . five . . . four . . ."

Hayes moved behind the guard, clamped his hand over the man's mouth, and twisted his head to the left. In one solid stroke, he drove the blade deep into his throat, the arterial spray hot across the fabric of the balaclava.

The man's body started to shake, a violent tremble that came with the realization that he was dying. Hayes held him close, waited for his knees to give out, and let him fall like a marionette with cut strings.

Hayes was just climbing onto the 'dozer when he heard the *boom* of the 50-caliber roll down the mountain.

He knew from the briefing that JT had loaded the Barrett with ten rounds of MK 211 high-explosive incendiary/armor-piercing ammo, or HEIAP. Inside each round was a layer of explosive zirconium powder and Composition A packed tight around a tungsten core, and when the bullet hit the junction box on the north side of the house at 2,800 feet per second, it exploded, tearing a ragged hole in the wall.

The halogen searchlights flickered, and darkness fell over the ground as Hayes jumped behind the controls and twisted the key. The bulldozer roared to life in a cloud of diesel. Hayes lifted the blade and shoved the stick forward, sending the earthmover clattering across the yard.

But the security floods didn't stay off long, and Hayes was halfway across the lawn, trying to tie off the stick, when the lights blazed to life, illuminating a platoon of soldiers filing from the pool house.

"JT, he's got a generator," Hayes said, securing the control stick into the forward position. "Hey, man, the lights are back on."

"No shit!" JT shouted. "Just give me a second."

But Hayes didn't have a second, because standing in front of him was a soldier with an RPG-7 on his shoulder.

Oh, shit, he thought, watching the soldier's finger close over the trigger, but before he had a chance to shoot, the Barrett barked from the hill and the soldier's torso evaporated in a pink mist.

"Owe you one," Hayes said, diving free from the bulldozer.

He ducked his head, rolled over his shoulder, and came up in a crouch, the UMP45 chattering in his hand.

Hayes stitched a burst across the closest target, scooped the blood-spattered RPG from the ground, and circled around the side of the house.

The thunderous boom of the Barrett rolled down the hill a final time, and just before the bulldozer plowed through the north wall of the house, the generator exploded.

"I'm moving to the exfil site," JT said. "Clock is ticking."

"Roger that," Hayes said, his eyes drawn to a bay window with Colonel Vega standing in the den, surrounded by a scrum of soldiers trying to pull him into the next room.

Hayes snapped the RPG to his shoulder, ignoring the rattle of gunfire from his left, and mashed the trigger. The rocket screamed from the launcher and hurtled toward its target, but before it slammed through the glass, Hayes saw the soldiers shoving Vega through a door and into another room.

One of the men stopped and pointed toward the window, and then the RPG detonated, dousing the room in flame and black smoke.

Hayes sprinted to the left, the distant *thump thump thump* of an approaching helo telling him that Vega was heading toward the roof.

Hayes shucked the empty mag from the submachine gun and shoved a fresh one home on his way to the door, knowing that he was running out of time.

Just get to the roof.

He booted the door and found himself in the back corridor Izzy had drawn on the map. Hayes had two options: He could hook left toward the dining room and the grand staircase or brave the gauntlet of open doors lining the hall to his front and take the service stairs.

Go with what you know, he thought, activating the infrared laser mounted to the top of the submachine gun, flipping the selector to full auto, and creeping forward.

A muzzle inched from the open door to his right. Knowing there was no time to acquire the target, Hayes swung the laser to the right of the frame, over the spot where he imagined the shooter's body would be, and yanked the trigger. *Thwaaaap, thwaaaaap,* the submachine gun chattered on full auto.

Hayes hooked into the room, saw a target to his left, and stitched a burst into the man's body before snapping right and dropping the wounded man with his second shot.

"The hall, he's in the hall," a voice yelled as Hayes moved to the door and yanked a frag from his kit. He tugged the pin free and let the spoon fly. *One, two, three,* he counted in his head, eyes locked on the door across the hall.

Hayes heard the men coming closer but knew there was no time to wait. He hooked the frag out the door and dashed across the hall.

"There!" But before the narco had a chance to fire, the grenade detonated in the hall with an echoing *whooomp.*

Go now.

Hayes was already moving back into the hall, through the cloud of smoke and the jumble of bodies writhing on the floor. He saw the stairs to his left and raced to the top, taking them two at a time.

He heard the helo coming in, the pitch of the deep chop of the blades cutting through the air, telling him the pilot was settling into a hover. *Almost there,* he thought, blasting the guard at the top of the landing on the run and then turning to his right, racing up the final set of stairs that led to the roof.

Hayes forced himself into a sprint, lowered his shoulder, and bull-rushed the door. The impact ripped the hinges free, sent the door skidding across the roof, with Hayes a half-step behind.

He launched himself through the doorway, ducked his head, and tucked into a roll.

Off to his right, the helo hovered over the roof, its skids a few feet short of touching down. Vega and his two soldiers knelt at the edge of the roof.

Hayes came up on one knee and held the laser steady over the cockpit. He knew the .45 ACP didn't have the velocity to punch all the way through the thick glass, but he was sure they had enough ass to crack it, and that was all he needed.

Not today, he thought, mashing the trigger to the rear.

Thwaaaaaap.

The bullets smacked into the glass across the pilot's face, and the moment he saw the canopy spiderweb, the man yanked the stick to the left and banked the helo clear of the house.

"Kill him!" Vega screamed in Spanish to the soldiers.

Hayes dumped the empty UMP and tugged the Ruger MK IV from the small of his back. The integrally suppressed pistol was an assassin's weapon, virtually silent compared to the throaty chatter of soldiers' AKs, and the recoil felt impossibly puny in Hayes's hand.

But he'd been in the game long enough to know that in a gunfight it wasn't the caliber that mattered, but the placement of the round. Which is why Hayes took his time.

He lined up his shots, ignoring the 7.62 slapping the roof around him, and with a smooth pull of the trigger sent a .22 crashing through the right eye of each of the shooters.

The men crumpled to the ground, and Hayes got to his feet as silence returned to the roof.

"Just you and me now," he said, centering the pistol on Vega's chest.

"Whatever they are paying you, I will double it . . . *triple* it," the colonel begged, holding his hands in the air.

"Not everything is for sale," Hayes replied, stopping three paces in front of Vega.

"Then take me in, let the courts decide what to do with me."

"You still haven't figured out how this works," Hayes said, lining up the front sight on the man's forehead.

"You would shoot an unarmed—?" Vega began, but the *thwap* of the Ruger in Hayes's hand ended the question on his lips.

The bullet hit Vega in the center of the forehead and snapped his head back. The colonel took an involuntary step backward, his foot finding nothing but air, and then he was tumbling over the edge.

Hayes holstered the smoking pistol and stepped to the edge of the roof in time to hear Vega's head bounce off the stone drive with the wet splatter of a ripe melon. He looked down on the man's lifeless body and the pool of crimson spreading across the stone.

"You're damn right I would," he said, before turning back the way he'd come.

Hayes walked through the silent house and out the front door.

"On my way out," he said over the radio.

"Roger that."

Hayes eased down the steps and was about to pass Vega's body when the chirp of a cellphone from the man's pocket stopped him in his tracks. Hayes knelt beside the man, tugged the phone from his pocket, and flipped it open.

"What's the status?" a man with a Texas accent demanded.

"Who is this?" Hayes demanded.

"This is Senator Patrick Mendez, who the hell is *this?*"

"Your worst nightmare."

"Hayes?" the man hissed. "Is it safe to assume they are dead?"

"Not *all* of them," Hayes answered, "but I'll be seeing you soon."

"Hayes, wait—"

But he'd already hung up.

57

CARACAS, VENEZUELA

Hayes squeezed through the rusted grate and moved toward the yellow glow of the IR chemlight that JT had left to mark the trail. From the culvert, Hayes moved laterally across the rock face, clearing the first hundred yards without any trouble. But twenty yards shy of the apex he was forced to bend double and claw his way over the loose shale and boulders that lined the terrain.

Hayes took his time, knowing that one misstep would send him tumbling down the hillside, and by the time he made it to the top, his shirt was wet beneath his plate carrier. He paused to catch his breath and savor the breeze that rolled over his body, sending chills up his bare arms. The cool salt air drew his attention north, toward the inky black shadow of the Caribbean Sea.

He was making his way to the flat finger where JT had set up the landing zone when the distant hammer of automatic rifle fire rolled up the incline. Hayes turned, expecting to see a line of army vehicles curling up the drive that led to Bella Vista, but the compound was still and quiet as a grave.

"Things are getting bad down there," JT said, emerging from the shadows, a pair of night-vision binoculars in his hand.

Hayes flipped up the FGEs and pressed the binos to his eyes.

Down in the valley a large mob was gathered outside a burning building, and figures clutching machine guns and RPGs were firing at a target on the far side of the street.

"Is that the armory?" he asked, a sick feeling welling up in his guts.

"Yeah," JT said as a flurry of tracers zipped across the street into the mass of soldiers blocking the road.

Fucking Vega, he thought.

"Hey, we did our part," JT said, clapping him on the shoulder.

Hayes wasn't so sure, but the approaching buzz of the helo told him there was no time to dwell on the matter.

Waters brought the Mi-17 into a hover and Hayes

ducked his head against the downdraft, waiting for the dust and dirt to settle before hustling to the helicopter. He followed JT inside, and by the time Hayes had closed the door and lowered himself into the troop bench, the Russian-built helicopter was airborne.

Waters pivoted the helo north and Hayes waited until they were over the Caribbean Sea before leaning his head against the skin of the helo. The adrenaline of the operation had long since worn off and Hayes was bone tired—worn thin like a pat of butter spread over too much toast.

He closed his eyes, the helo's vibrations lulling him into the meditative state that came after every mission. For a moment, his mind was as calm and still as the endless black sea that seemed to stretch out forever.

So much death. Deano, Martha, Ford, Cole. And for what?

A tap to the leg tugged Hayes from his thoughts. He opened his eyes to find JT leaning in, the helicopter's radio headset in his right hand.

"Shaw," he mouthed.

Great, Hayes thought stuffing the Bose headset over his ears and clicking the transmit button.

"Yeah?"

"You want to tell me why I'm getting shit from Senator Mendez at zero two hundred?" Shaw demanded, his voice still ragged from sleep.

"I think you dialed the wrong number," Hayes said. "Callers looking for the psychic hotline should hang up and dial 1-800-I-Don't-Give-a-Fuck."

"Do you have any idea the penalty that comes with threatening a U.S. senator?" Shaw growled.

"You worried about your job, Levi?"

There was silence on the other end of the line, but when Shaw finally spoke, his voice was ice cold. "Fine, have it your way. Waters is under orders to fly you to Antigua, where an Agency plane is waiting to bring you back to the States."

"You had your chance to play the boss back in Caracas," Hayes said. "If memory serves, you took the coward's way out."

"Adam, I am warning you, if you are not on that plane—"

Shaw's threat fell on deaf ears because Hayes had already ripped the headphones from the wall jack and tossed them across the helo.

"What was that all about?" JT asked.

"You trust me, right?" Hayes asked.

"Wouldn't be here if I didn't."

Hayes nodded and got to his feet. "Just want you to know that I'm sorry."

"Sorry?" JT frowned. "What are you sorry fo—"

Before he could finish his question, Hayes had tugged the MK IV from his waistband and cracked JT across the side of the head with the suppressor.

"For that," he said as he grabbed his unconscious friend by the shirt to keep him from falling out of his chair. Hayes buckled him in and then headed for the cockpit.

By the time Waters realized who was standing beside him, it was too late.

"What's our position?" Hayes asked, noting the nervous look in the man's eyes when he glanced up at him.

"Here," Waters said, pointing at a spot on the map.

"I'm going to need you to make a detour," Hayes said.

"You talked to the boss," Waters said, "so you know I can't—"

"I'll make it easy for you," Hayes said, bringing the pistol up and aiming at the radio.

He pulled the trigger, the MK IV silent beneath the whine of the turbine. The only sign that Hayes had fired was the smell of gun smoke in the air and the smoke coiling from the hole in the radio.

"You're fucking crazy," Waters yelped.

"That's not nice," Hayes said, looking out over the canopy and seeing lights off to the east.

"Now, I'm guessing those lights off to the east are Curaçao," he said, tapping the map strapped to the pilot's thigh with the suppressor. "All I need you to do is get me close."

"Fuck it," Waters said, banking the helo east.

"You're a good man, Charlie Brown." Hayes stuffed the pistol back into his waistband.

He walked back to the cargo door and tugged it open.

"Low and slow," he yelled.

Waters flipped him the bird but inched back on the throttle and dropped the Russian helicopter down until all he could see was the dark black of the water.

"Catch you on the flip side," Hayes yelled. Then he jumped.

According to the U.S. government, it should have been impossible for Hayes to travel from Curaçao to the United States without a valid passport. But Treadstone had trained him well, and ten hours after slogging onto shore, Hayes was back in the States.

It was almost noon when he used the last of Vega's cash to rent a Cadillac CTS in Destin. Might as well drive in style, he thought, taking the keys from the man behind the desk.

"Will there be anything else, sir?" the man asked.

"I think that will do it," Hayes said, shoving the paperwork into his back pocket.

He crossed the lobby to the door on the west side of the building. Like all windows this close to the Gulf of Mexico, it was tinted and gave the impression of a premature dusk. But Hayes wasn't fooled. He'd spent enough time in the Florida Panhandle to know what was waiting for him on the other side. He paused to slip the dark aviators over his eyes before opening the door.

The noonday sun pounced like a golden jaguar, and even with the shades, Hayes found himself squinting against its glare. Across the lot the midnight blue Cadillac shimmered in the heat. By the time Hayes made it to the door, his back was wet with sweat.

The Caddy had been sitting out in the sun all day and the interior was hot as an oven. Hayes left the door open and started the engine, noting that the previous occupant had left the A/C cranked to full. The fan kicked on with a rush of hot air that smelled of stale cigarette smoke and suntan oil, and Hayes waited for it to run cold before closing the door.

He buckled the seat belt over his chest and pulled the iPhone he'd picked up in Tallahassee from his pocket. Hayes held his thumb over the sensor, and after unlocking the phone, accessed the phone-tracking app JT had sent him. He typed Annabelle's number into the search bar, and a moment later a blue dot appeared on the map.

He pulled out of the lot and turned east on Harbor Boulevard, following the road past the T-shirt shops, bars, and high-rise condos that lined the strip. With summer in full swing, the road was packed with out-of-towners in minivans and large SUVs on a yearly pilgrimage to the Gulf Coast.

Forty minutes later Hayes passed a white sign with

navy blue letters welcoming him to Seaside, Florida. He let off the gas, watched the speedometer fall to the posted thirty miles per hour, and followed the GPS dot to a beach access on the south side of the road.

He parked the Cadillac under a silver palm and got out, his heart pounding at the sight of the pewter Honda Pilot parked at the front of the lot. It was Annabelle's car, the one he'd bought to replace her Accord a month before Jack was born.

This is a bad idea, the voice said.

But Hayes wasn't listening. He had made up his mind, and for better or worse, he was going to see it through.

He followed the wooden ramp through a break in the sand dunes, past the ochre sway of the sea oats and salt grasses swaying in the breeze. The ramp doglegged at a set of stainless-steel showerheads, where a group of children were cleaning the sand off their feet. The sight inspired him to kick off his own shoes.

Hayes flashed a smile to one of the kids and carried his shoes the final five yards through the dunes onto the cocaine-white beach. He stood there for a moment, savoring the warm sand beneath his feet, the gentle crash of the turquoise breakers rolling in through the surf zone, before he pulled the phone from his pocket.

He turned to the left, lining up the dot with his current position and then checking the distance to target readout. *Twenty yards. Here goes nothing.*

Hayes started across the beach, his eyes darting back

and forth behind the dark sunglasses, scanning the mass of sun-kissed bodies lining the beach.

Then he saw them. Annabelle sitting on a beach chair, her blond hair tied up in a bun on the top of her head. Jack sat next to her on the ground, his hair white as cotton in the sunlight. Hayes moved behind the white lifeguard tower, wanting nothing more than to run down the beach, kiss Annabelle's lips, and lift his son high in the air.

You know what that would do, the voice warned. *In fact, just you being here puts them at risk.*

Hayes looked down at the phone, wanting more than anything to call Annabelle. Tell her how much he loved them both. But watching their smiling faces, Hayes couldn't bring himself to ruin their moment.

It's time to go, the voice ordered.

"See you guys soon," Hayes said, his voice barely a whisper. Then he turned and headed back the way he'd come, a contented smile spreading across his face.

EPILOGUE

WASHINGTON, D.C.

The black Lincoln Town Car turned onto Embassy Row, the tires swishing over the fresh rain that left the asphalt wet and glinting in the streetlights. In the back, Levi Shaw adjusted his tie and looked at the single sheet of typed paper in his hand that contained his resignation.

It's finally over.

The driver slowed in front of a white stone mansion with a manicured lawn and eased up the circular drive. Built in 1901, the Townsend House, with its acre garden, was the last of America's gilded mansions and the current home to the Cosmos Club.

The Cosmos Club was the pinnacle of status in Washington, D.C., and membership was restricted to the über-elite. Among its most notable members were three former presidents, two vice presidents, a dozen Supreme Court justices, and Senator Patrick Mendez.

Which is the reason Shaw found himself outside.

"This won't take long, George," Shaw said, climbing out of the car and adjusting his tie before stepping through the door.

Everything about it, from the monochromatic marble tile of the lobby to the gilded chandeliers whose warm glow accentuated the man behind the desk's disdain at the sight of his approach, was meant to remind men like Levi that they didn't belong.

"May I help you, sir?" he asked.

"Levi Shaw. I'm here to meet Senator Mendez."

"He is in the library. This way, sir."

Shaw found Mendez pacing back and forth in front of a window, his cellphone pressed to his ear.

"I understand that, sir, and I can promise you that I am addressing the situation. No, sir, I was *not* aware of Jefferson Gray's actions and will do my . . ." Mendez held up his index finger and motioned for Shaw to take a seat in the oversized leather club chair to his right.

He shook his head and calmly addressed the senator. "I won't be here long enough for that."

Mendez's eyes ticked to his face, then down at the paper in his hand.

"Mr. Speaker, I'm going to have to call you back," he said, hanging up on the phone. "You know who that was?"

"No."

"The speaker of the House. Now, if I can tell the third most powerful man in the world that I need to call him back, I can tell *you* to take a seat."

"Like I said," Shaw replied, handing over his resignation, "I'm not sticking around."

Mendez looked at the paper. "How long have you been with the CIA?" he asked.

"Almost thirty years."

"Thirty years," Mendez said, his eyes switching from the paper to Shaw's face. "I can't imagine how much shit you've been force-fed in thirty years. I can use a man like you," Mendez added, balling up the paper.

"Senator—"

"Just hear me out. This thing in Venezuela was bad business, but you handled it. Cleaned it up. Took care of Hayes when no one else could. Now you have a chip in the game. You come work for me, and I'll make sure Treadstone has permanent funding."

"I'm done," Shaw said.

"I don't think you understand the way this works. I'm not *asking* you," Mendez said, getting to his feet and stuffing the crumpled ball of paper into Shaw's handkerchief pocket. "I'm *telling* you. Now get the fuck out of my face."

Two blocks away, Adam Hayes made his way to the rear of an abandoned three-story row house. He shrugged out of the coyote-brown Eberlestock Switchblade pack and set it on the ground at his feet. Hayes knelt beside the bag, unzipped the side flap, and pulled out a twenty-inch Kodiak Bear Claw tool before turning to the window.

With a pry bar on one end and a fork on the other, the Bear Claw looked like a miniaturized version of the Halligan tool fire departments around the world used to force entry into burning houses, and despite its diminutive size, it worked as advertised.

Hayes jammed the lip beneath the rotted wood of the window, grabbed the handle, and tugged on it until the lock popped free. With the window open, he returned the Bear Claw to the pocket, tossed the bag inside the room, and climbed up after it.

The bottom floor was a mess. Most of the windows on the west side had been broken out and were now replaced with sheets of plywood to keep out the elements. In the den, someone had spray-painted gang signs and profanity across the brick fireplace.

Hayes scooped up the pack, found the stairs, and followed them up to the third floor. He found a room on the north side of the house where someone had painted a target on the wall with black spray paint.

Used syringes were stuck like darts all around the bull's-eye. The room stank of stale urine and burnt flour, and it was so bad that Hayes almost gagged when he came in.

The only piece of usable furniture was a sagging old table, which he dragged into the middle of the room, centering it in front of the window. Once he had the table where he wanted it, Hayes laid the bag on the surface and unzipped the flap.

Hayes was a professional and had learned long ago that when it came to weapons and tools, it was better to "buy once, cry once." Which is why when he decided to have a custom hunting rifle built, he went to Brandon Ward of Mountain Top Gunworks. Everything about the rifle, from the eight-hundred-dollar folding Manners stock to the thousand-dollar Proof composite barrel, was built to Hayes's specifications and designed to be light, accurate, and deadly.

He lifted the rifle with his right hand, pulled a suppressor from the sleeve inside the bag, and screwed it over the threads at the end of the barrel. Hayes had spent months looking for the lightest suppressor on the market before stumbling across the Texas Silencer Company. While most manufacturers were still using steel-bodied suppressors, Texas Silencer's Outrider was made from titanium, and at twelve ounces, it weighed half as much as its closest competitor.

With the suppressor secure, Hayes lifted the rifle and

a small sandbag from the pack and climbed onto the table. He made sure the table would hold his weight before removing the protective caps that covered the spiked tips at the end of the bipod and then extended the legs and set the rifle on the table.

Hayes positioned the sandbag under the buttstock and made a few adjustments. When he was sure that the rifle was level, he settled his cheek to the stock and looked through the Nightforce NXS 8-32x56 scope mounted to the rail.

He adjusted his body, shifting the rifle's scope onto the second-story window two blocks away.

The view through the scope blurred when Hayes twisted the magnification ring to thirty-two power, but he patiently refined the parallax knob, making tiny adjustments until he had a crystal-clear view of the two men talking inside the Cosmos Club.

Mendez was holding a sheet of paper in his hand and Hayes squeezed on the bag under the stock. The compression of the sand nudged the buttstock toward the ceiling, and the muzzle dipped, allowing Hayes to read what was typed on the paper.

A resignation notice? What game are you playing, Levi? he asked himself.

He watched as Mendez crumpled the paper into a little ball. At any other time Hayes would have laughed at the shocked look on his former boss's face.

But not now.

Hayes realized that despite all of Shaw's bluster, the man had no idea how to handle men like Mendez.

But I do, he thought.

Sitting behind the gun, Hayes was in control. It was his time to impose his will on those who wanted to kill him, and no one was going to get in his way. Hayes began an all-too-comforting ritual. He shoved the magazine into the rifle and leaned forward, pressing his weight into the buttstock.

The bipod began to slide, before it finally dug into the table. Hayes placed his cheek softly on the buttstock and worked the magnification knob until the reticle cleared. *Range, two hundred meters, no wind.*

When he was satisfied that he had everything the way he needed it to be, Hayes pressed the Bluetooth into his ear and waited for the cloned cellphone to ring.

A moment later the earpiece chirped in his ear.

"That was quick," he said, slipping into a Boston accent.

Mendez's voice oozed through the Bluetooth. "Mr. Speaker, I sure am sorry about that."

"Not at all." Hayes smiled as the senator stepped in front of the window, his cellphone to his ear. "You are a busy man."

"Just trying to do the Lord's work," Mendez answered.

Hayes made a final adjustment to the scope before his right hand found the bolt.

The Defiance bolt action shoved the bullet silently into the chamber, and Hayes dropped his eye off target. He took a deep breath, forcing his heart rate to slow, and then he looked up.

"You really thought you were going to get away with it, didn't you?" Hayes asked, dropping the accent.

There was silence on the other end. The only sign that Mendez had heard the question was the look on his face through the scope.

"Hayes—no, listen, we can—make a deal," Mendez stammered.

"You can make a deal with Vega when you see him," Hayes said before pulling the trigger.